Rider of the Crown

Melissa McShane

Night Harbor Publishing
Salt Lake City, UT

Copyright © 2015 Melissa McShane
ISBN-13: 978-0692534632
ISBN-10: 0692534636
Published by Night Harbor Publishing
All rights reserved

No part of this book may be used or reproduced in any way whatsoever without written permission except in the case of brief quotations embodied in critical articles and reviews.

This book is a work of fiction. Names, characters, businesses, organizations, places, events, and incidents either are the product of the author's imagination or are used fictitiously. Any resemblance to actual persons living or dead, events, or locales is entirely coincidental.

Night Harbor Publishing
340 S. Lemon Avenue #9773
Walnut, CA 91789
www.nightharborpublishing.com

Cover design by Yocla Designs
North sign and shield designed by Erin Dinnell Bjorn

First Printing
10 9 8 7 6 5 4 3 2 1

Northern Wastes
Ranstjad
The Eidestal
Ruskald
Wasteland
Snow River
Daxtry
Marandis
Highton
Steepridge
Avory
Tremontane
Aurilien
Olontor
Silverfield
Kepa River
Cullinan
Veribold
Waxwold
Kingsport
Harroden
Huddersfield
Haizea
Ravensholm
Eskandel
Umberan
Tremontane and Environs

For Jana
PiC and Tremontane's number one fan

This book takes place 25 years
after the events of *Servant of the Crown.*

A glossary and pronunciation guide is provided
at the back of this book.

Part One: Ruskald

Chapter One

Imogen shielded her eyes and looked out across the plains. The dry grass, tall and burned yellow by the summer sun, bowed before the warm, gusting wind that whipped strands of Victory's mane into her face. "That's a Ruskalder warband out there," she said. "A raiding party, I think."

Dorenna followed her gaze. "They don't look like they're going anywhere. I think they see us, too."

"We're not exactly hiding. Still, I think we should move in that direction. See what they have in mind."

Revalan, on Imogen's left, reined his excitable mount in. "I suppose it might come to blows."

"Which I would deplore, naturally," Imogen replied, her eyes still fixed on the distant group of men. They were Ruskalder; they would all be men.

"Naturally," Dorenna said with a grin.

Imogen looked around at the men and women of her *tiermatha*. "Let's just wander in their direction. They'll probably cut and run if we force the issue. Hrovald wants to at least look like he's upholding the truce."

The riders nudged their horses into a trot—a nonchalant trot, Imogen hoped—in the direction of the intruders. She wasn't really certain they *were* intruders, here on the uneasy, ill-defined border between Ruskald and the Eidestal, but by the furtive way the Ruskald warband was moving, *they* certainly believed they were. Victory strained at the reins, wanting to run free across the grassy plain, and Imogen thought about giving her her head, letting her trample the unmounted Ruskalder under her huge hooves, but it was a whim she would never indulge. Someday, Imogen would be Warleader of the Kirkellan, and she didn't need a reputation for rashness. She'd leave that to her little sister, who wasn't destined to be anything in particular. Imogen had never envied her.

The Ruskalder raiding party, seven men in leather armor and armed with both short and long swords, stood their ground as the *tiermatha* approached. "You're in Kirkellan territory, friends," Imogen called to them in Ruskeldin. "Hrovald's truce binds you to return to your own lands."

The men looked at each other, then at her. They all wore the same expression, and although Imogen had rarely met a warrior of Ruskald she wasn't trying to kill, and didn't have much experience reading their expressions, she knew what they were thinking: *who let a woman lead this troop?* One of the men, his blond hair falling halfway down his back, said, "It's you who are trespassing."

"Prove it," Imogen said. Her mother insisted the Ruskalder preferred aggressive interaction, that their warlike natures were as much because of their love of conflict as Hrovald's spurring them to battle, and this was the best way to interact with them. She hoped the *matrian* was right.

The man grinned, white teeth shining in his short blond beard. "Don't need to. Who's to see, all the way out here?"

"I will. And we outnumber you. *And* we're mounted. That's three marks in my favor."

"We're just a hunting party," the man shrugged. "Your boss lady never said we couldn't hunt the border. If we cross, well, no harm done."

"I'm sure whatever you're hunting will appreciate your use of military weaponry."

The rasp of metal on leather sounded from the back of the group. Without looking around, the speaker said, "Stand down." He bared his teeth at Imogen.

"Your King and my m—my *matrian* are negotiating a treaty between our people," Imogen said. "You don't want to step on that before the ink's even dry, do you?" If he attacked, they'd fight, and though she wasn't afraid of this lot, she *was* afraid of her mother's reaction if Imogen were responsible for setting Ruskalder at Kirkellan throats once more.

The man locked eyes with her for a moment longer, then gestured at his men to retreat. The one who'd loosened his sword began to protest, and the speaker casually punched him in the stomach. "Pity our people will no longer go to war together," he said as the man doubled up over his fist. "The Kirkellan are formidable, even if half of them are girls."

Imogen wanted to point out that half the Ruskalder were girls too, but she took his meaning; the Ruskalder only respected warriors, and as far as they were concerned the Kirkellan warriors *were* the Kirkellan people. She and her warriors watched the Ruskalder retreat, if you could call it that; they strolled across the plains as casually as if they were the only ones under the sun, their long hair flying like pennants in the brisk wind. When they'd dwindled to mere specks, Imogen gestured, and the *tiermatha* turned and rode back in the direction of the war camp.

Even though her group was the last to return from riding the borders, the *matrian*'s flag still didn't fly over the great tent with its many-peaked roof, so the negotiations at the midway camp were going on far longer than the *matrian* had anticipated. Imogen rode to the enclosure where Victory was stabled, inhaled the sour-musk smell of dozens of horses sweating in the summer heat, and dismounted. The tall mare twisted her head around and butted Imogen in the forehead. "Impatient?" Imogen said, laughing, and stroked her horse's nose. "Let's get you settled."

Victory having been groomed, fed, and petted, Imogen left her in the company of several other horses and walked back through the camp. The truce had come none too soon. So many gaps among the tents marking the dead by their absence, so many stones waiting to be transported to the *tinda* to be added to the memorial. Even the usual noise of the camp was subdued, with little of the good cheer the Kirkellan usually exhibited whether they were celebrating or arguing or just having a conversation about the weather. The Kirkellan were fierce, but they'd always been small by comparison to the Ruskalder, who under Hrovald's leadership had pressed the kinship hard, and for what? A few more square miles of grassy, treeless Eidestal that meant nothing to them and everything to the Kirkellan? When she was Warleader, she'd regain those lost miles.

She let the noise of the camp calm her spirits, called out greetings to the men and women she passed, and rolled her shoulders to release the tension of the encounter with the Ruskalder. She passed the *matrian's* vast brown tent made of dozens of reindeer hides stitched together and ducked into a smaller one adjacent to it, the hides dyed imperfectly in dozens of shades of black that gave it a patchwork appearance, like a piebald gelding if its colors were black on black. "Afternoon, Father," she said, and bent to give the man sitting cross-legged on the ground a kiss on the cheek.

Father laid tack and round punch down and returned the greeting. "Anything exciting happen on your ride?" he asked.

"Nothing special. Scared off a Ruskalder raiding party." Imogen flung herself onto a pile of multicolored down cushions. "Did Gannen go to the negotiations with mother?"

Father shook his head. "Just Caele. The boys are out riding and Neve is…actually, I don't know where Neve is." He picked up his work and continued mending the worn leather. "I'm surprised to see you back so early."

"I wanted to tell Mother about the raiding party. Not that it matters, if we work out the treaty. I wish I'd gone with her. It has to be more exciting than riding in endless circles and arguing with Kallum about which of several mutually boring directions we should go next." She lay back on the pillows, eiderdown cased in jewel-toned silks, and stared at the tent roof. Wooden ribs radiated from the central pole like a cartwheel, holding the skins taut. "It's hot in here. Should I raise the walls?"

"If you like. I find it comfortable." He fastened the last strap and shook out the harness. "I think I may test this out, if you wouldn't mind giving me a hand up."

Imogen stood and helped her father to his feet. Father got his weak right leg steady under himself and thanked her. "Do you need an arm?" she said. "You look as if you've been sitting on the ground for far too long. Why didn't you use your stool?"

"Stop nagging, daughter, you sound like Caele," Father remarked amiably. "I just need to stretch it out a bit. This warm weather eases the old wound somewhat."

"Well, when you fall over, remember I offered." Imogen stepped back and watched him stretch. Even leaning to one side, he was a tall man; fully upright, he was a few inches taller than Imogen, who was herself nearly six feet tall, though he was thin where she was plump. His gyrations made her need to stretch as well, so she did. "There's nothing to do. Thundering heaven, but I'm bored."

"You could go for a ride. You could tidy up the tent. You could read a book."

Imogen groaned. "Boring. I mean the last two. And if I get back on Victory I'm going to ride all the way to the midway camp and burst in on the proceedings. Mother specifically said I wasn't to do that."

"Well, you can't say I didn't give you options." He grinned at her and limped in the direction of the horse lines. Imogen flung herself back on the cushions and grumbled.

The Kirkellan had been losing, everyone knew that, but the Ruskalder had suffered heavy losses as well. A peace treaty was a good idea for everyone involved. Heaven knew she wasn't hungry for war, or the bloodshed that followed its banners. But a Warleader in peacetime had nothing to do, which meant Imogen, Warleader in training, had nothing to do either. As much as she loved Victory, there was only so much riding a person could do, even if that person was Kirkellan. She wasn't bookish and, like every sensible person, hated chores. She remembered the Ruskald warrior, and despite herself agreed with him: it was a pity their people wouldn't go to war against each other anymore. Why couldn't someone come up with some form of conflict that didn't entail bodily harm?

She rolled off the cushions and stood. She could take Victory out to the track and run a few courses. It might bleed off some of her energy and keep her from bursting in on the peace negotiations, and if she could convince Kallum to join her she could prove Victory was a much better jumper than his Darkstrider. She decided to look for him, wondered where the rest of her *tiermatha* had got to, and walked out of the tent directly into one of the *matrian*'s bodyguards. She apologized to the woman, who grunted, but stepped aside. So Mother was back. Imogen changed her mind about the track, ducked inside the great tent, and crossed its expanse to where her mother stood.

Imogen's mother Mairen, *matrian* of the Kirkellan, was a short, round woman with dark hair and expressive blue eyes the color of a winter sky. She ignored Imogen and said to the younger woman next to her, "I think we can trust Hrovald's greed to keep him honest. He wants our horses."

"And I say we've given him far too many concessions as it is," Imogen's sister Caele said. Caele resembled a shorter, paler version of Father, and right now her lovely mouth was scowling. "I want a peace treaty as much as anyone, but not at the cost of our sovereignty. And before you repeat, again, that we aren't subordinating ourselves to him, I have to remind you, *again*, that as long as he thinks we are, he's going to behave like our liege lord."

"And what do you suggest we do, Caele? Take a stand that gives him the opportunity to walk away entirely? Sit down, Imogen. We can let him do a little chest-pounding if it keeps his warriors off our flank." Mother took a hearty swallow from a flask at her left hand.

"What about the other matter?" Caele said, looking at Imogen. "I say it's slavery."

"And I say you exaggerate." Mother looked at Imogen as well. Imogen, who'd taken a seat on a convenient camp chair, looked from one to the other, eyebrows raised. Caele still looked like she'd eaten something bitter. Mother had the calculating expression she wore when she was working out the best way to convey unpleasant news. Imogen's eyes settled on Mother as the more dangerous of the two. Mother's expression made her uncomfortable.

"Caele," she said, "let me have some time alone with Imogen, please." Caele's bitter expression turned into exasperation, and she threw up her arms and left the tent.

"Are you trying to make me nervous? Because it's working," Imogen said.

Mother dragged another camp chair next to Imogen's and sat, not speaking. The silence stretched out. Imogen, trying to fill it, said, "You promised the King of Ruskald something I'm not going to like, didn't you?" A pit opened in her stomach. "You didn't give him *Victory*, did you? Mother, she's not yours to give! Even if she was, that would be so unfair when we have all those horses—"

"It's not Victory, love," Mother said. She cleared her throat. "You know what a *banrach* is, don't you?"

"Of course. But I—" She suddenly felt as if she'd been punched by that Ruskalder warrior. "*No,*" she breathed. "Oh, no. You did *not* sell me into slavery—"

"The *banrach* is not slavery and you know it," Mother said coldly. "It's a limited-term marriage of convenience. The Ruskalder feel very strongly about kinship ties. The King insisted our two, as he put it, 'houses' be joined in some kind of family relationship. I argued him down to the *banrach*. He *wanted* to marry Neve."

Imogen's heart revolted at the idea. "She's only fifteen, barely an adult. How could he think that was an acceptable match?"

"Precisely."

"And you're comfortable sending *me* off to live in this man's house for five years?"

"You're older, you're stronger, you're a better fighter, and you won't let Hrovald intimidate you. Think, Imogen. It can't be Caele, it can't be Neve, and he would only take Gannen or Torin by adoption, which would be permanent. And he refuses to even consider anyone of another family."

"But, Mother—this gives him so much power over us! You know whatever we say, I'll be going as a hostage for your good behavior!"

Mother looked tired. "I didn't make any promises. If we do this, it will be your choice."

"Thank you for not pressuring me at all," Imogen said mulishly.

"I'm serious. If you say no, we'll find another way."

"You said there were no other ways."

"*I will find another way.*" Mother took Imogen's hand and squeezed it. "Think about it, but don't think too long. We're meeting in the morning and I'll have to give him an answer then."

Imogen didn't squeeze back. "I have to go," she said, rising. "I—I'll think about it."

"Thank you." Mother released her. "Have a good ride."

Imogen crossed the camp, ignoring anyone who hailed her, and saddled Victory in silence, barely acknowledging her horse's greetings. It was true, she did her best thinking on horseback, but right now she needed a distraction more than she needed to think. So she headed for the track.

The third thing the Kirkellan always did when they made a new camp, after settling their horses and pitching tents, was to build a racing track that was part obstacle course, part speed track, and one hundred percent training course for the renowned Kirkellan war horses. Someone had put a lot of effort into this one. Bales of hay marked out the curving loops of the obstacles; some of those turns were surprisingly sharp. The straightaway was longer than Imogen was used to, and there were four hurdles instead of three. She recognized Saevonna of her own *tiermatha* coming around the last bend, her horse Lodestone taking it wide and fast. Other riders milled around the starting point, waiting their turns.

Imogen sidled up to the group, glad she didn't know any of them well, because she didn't feel much like talking. It was too hard not to remember the dead when you were standing where they'd used to laughingly challenge you. Einya and Darah of her own *tiermatha*, killed in the last great battle two weeks ago; Einya had been her friend since before either of them were warriors. The thought of more fighting sickened her.

The afternoon sun wasn't quite low enough to interfere with her vision, but she closed her eyes and let the sunlight pour over her before the wind whisked it away. The *banrach* was ancient, outdated, so old it came from the days when both men and women could lead the Kirkellan and people still believed in gods rather than an ungoverned, impartial heaven. Mother must want this alliance badly to be willing to entertain the idea at all—but she was right; however distasteful it was, it was a lot less binding than the alternative. Even so, it was five years out of her life, and if Imogen didn't have to share the King's bed she still had to share his house, and who knew what challenges *that* might mean.

She'd promised she'd think about it, but she couldn't face it right now. How could she train to be her sister's Warleader from deep inside Ruskald? How could she train to be *anything* in a country where women barely had rights, let alone permission to be warriors? And she'd be away from her family for five years. Much as she groused about how annoying they were, she loved her siblings and she would miss them. Torin and Neve might both be married by the time she came back.

"Imogen. It's your turn," someone said, nudging her, and she opened her eyes and walked Victory onto the track. A timed run would give her a real workout, but she wasn't in the mood to push Victory hard through the curves. As they passed the starting line, she shouted to Victory, who went from a walk to a gallop in the space of five breaths.

This was what life was really all about, she reflected, the horse under you, the wind in your hair, the ground racing past. She leaned into the first turn, felt Victory go wide, and corrected for the next turn. On the final turn, she leaned out, snatched up a waiting javelin in her left hand, and hurled it toward the target; it glanced off the frame, and she cursed. Time for more throwing practice.

Her horse was one of the finest bred by the Kirkellan, and Imogen shouted for joy as Victory quivered, bunched up her muscles and flew—there really was no other word for it—over the first stile. Imogen loved that moment when they left the ground behind almost as much as she loved the moment when Victory landed and a jolt went through Imogen's body, the earth reasserting its grasp on them both.

She took the final straightaway at speed and let Victory slowly come to a halt rather than reining her in hard, even though that meant leaving the straightaway for the last fifty feet. She heard cheering behind her and turned Victory in a tight circle to see the riders waiting at the track's head shouting and waving their arms. When she trotted back to meet them, the man at the head of the line said, "That's the fastest anyone's taken the straightaway all day. Victory, right? I'd say I'm jealous if it wouldn't hurt Dawn's feelings."

Imogen was still flushed from her ride. "She's the best, that's certain," she said, and stroked her horse's mane. "I wouldn't trade her for anything."

"You want to make a timed run?" said one of the others waiting in line. "You look like you could use it."

Was it so obvious, the turmoil in her heart? "Thanks," she said, "but I'm ready for a slower pace now." She nudged Victory, and they rode away from the track, away from the camp, off westward where she wouldn't encounter anyone, Kirkellan or Ruskalder.

The long, slow ride was as much to give Imogen time to think as to let Victory cool off. *I know what the drawbacks are,* she told herself. *The benefits? I get to serve my country.* She made a face. Why couldn't she serve her country as Warleader? *I keep Neve safe. I…what else? I get first-hand diplomatic experience. Mother's been saying she thinks I could stand to learn something other than fighting and riding. I get to experience a wonderful new culture…no, I can't keep a straight face just thinking that to myself.* She shook her head. *I can bring peace to two countries.*

She brought Victory back to the paddock just as the sun was setting, cared for her needs, then trudged through the camp to the *matrian*'s tent. Inside, she found her mother writing in her journal under the flickering light of a lantern that cast the *matrian*'s shadow, huge and deformed, against the far wall. She put the book aside when Imogen entered and sat looking at her in silence.

Imogen took a deep breath. "I'll do it, on two conditions," she said. "Victory comes with me. And so does my *tiermatha*."

Chapter Two

Imogen paced the confines of the midway tent, waiting for her betrothed husband to arrive. It was half the size of her family tent and as creamy white as that tent was black, supported by two poles as thick as her wrist. Father sat on a camp stool, watching her pace, restlessly moving his bad leg as if he wanted to join her. Mother sat at the negotiation table, four folding legs topped by a rare and precious sheet of planed ash, pretending to read the documents outlining the terms of the treaty. The Ruskalder and the Kirkellan languages were close enough to be mutually intelligible, but there was no sense in not being careful with something as important as this. Caele stood in the tent doorway, watching for Hrovald's party. None of Imogen's other siblings were there, but then this wasn't the kind of marriage you wanted a lot of witnesses for.

Having made her decision, Imogen was ready for the whole thing to be over with. Or, more accurately, for the whole thing to begin. She'd explained her decision to her *tiermatha* the previous night, nervous about their reaction—she had, after all, sealed their fate as surely as she'd sealed her own. They might decide five years in Ranstjad surrounded by Ruskalder warriors was too much for their oath's sake, let alone for the demands of friendship. And they had been angry, but not at her.

"It's a barbaric custom," Saevonna had said.

"As if we'd let you go alone," Kionnal had said.

"I'm surprised you thought you needed to ask," Areli had said.

All twelve were in agreement, though Imogen thought their agreement might have been helped by the knowledge that they wouldn't have to leave their horses behind. Their unqualified support relieved Imogen's mind, though only temporarily. Now, waiting in the midway tent, she was angry and nervous and uncertain all at once. She'd never met Hrovald, even in battle, but she knew him to be ruthless, hard, and a ferocious fighter who led from the front. Mother said he was cunning as well, that their negotiations had been fierce, requiring all the *matrian*'s skill to keep the terms of the peace fair.

"Stop pacing," Mother said, not looking up from her documents.

"It's either this or I run out of here screaming."

"Stop exaggerating, Imogen," her sister said. "It's not the end of your life." But her lips were white, and Imogen knew she didn't believe a word of it.

Father grabbed her hand as she passed him, arresting her in mid-pace. "There will be runners back and forth between Hrovald and us," he said. "We'll write often, and you'll write to us. Assuming you know how to write, that is."

Imogen rolled her eyes at him. "Thank you for your confidence in me." She squeezed her father's hand, and he released her. She went to the tent's back door and looked out at her *tiermatha*. They looked back expectantly. "Is he here yet?" Dorenna asked. Imogen shook her head. They went back to talking quietly to each other and to their horses. Imogen envied them their calm.

"Hrovald will think you belong to him," she said. "He won't believe a woman could be in command of a troop, even a small one."

"Let him think that," Dorenna said. "It might be useful to us, later on. And it's not like you really command us. We just let you believe it so you'll feel good about yourself."

"Funny, Dor. I just think you should be prepared for him to order you around."

Saevonna stopped stroking Lodestone's neck. "You don't suppose he'd order us to bed him, do you?" she asked, horrified. "He's not going to believe any of us women are real warriors."

Imogen was equally horrified. The thought had never occurred to her. She ducked back inside the tent. "Mother, what if—"

"They're here," Caele said, turning away from the front door and going to stand next to her mother, who remained seated. Imogen bit her knuckle. Her stomach was leaping about as if she and Victory were taking jump after jump across the track. She went to stand behind her mother, trying to look serious and forbidding, though she was afraid she only looked ill. Mother continued to study her paperwork as if her daughter's life wasn't about to change forever.

Two Ruskalder warriors in full gear, leather armor reinforced with steel plates, and armed with the short and long swords they traditionally carried into battle, entered the tent and scanned its interior. Satisfied, they held the flap open and a small group of men ducked through it. Imogen's eye immediately went to the man in the center. He was shorter than she was—all right, many men were shorter than she was—and his eyes were cold and his lined face forbidding. He carried himself with the kind of confidence that only came from having won many victories in personal combat. She guessed he was in his mid-fifties. He wore battered, stained leather armor, and his long, greasy, graying hair was tied back with a leather string. He surveyed the tent, his eyes passing over Imogen as if she meant nothing, and for a moment she agreed with him. Then common sense reasserted itself and she shifted into a fighting stance, daring him to meet her eyes again. She would not let him frighten her.

Hrovald stared down at Mother, who still hadn't risen. He said nothing. Mother shuffled the documents into a neat pile and tapped the edges on the table. She finally stood and met Hrovald's eye. "A fine day to make peace," she said. She spoke Kirkellish, a show of defiance just this side of a challenge.

Hrovald snorted. "That remains to be seen. Is that her?" He nodded at Imogen, a swift jerk of the head. "She's fat. Got hips made for bearing children." He spoke his own language, but harshly, as if it were a foreign tongue even for him.

Imogen sucked in her breath, ready with a stinging retort about the likelihood of her letting him touch her, let alone bearing his children, but her mother overrode her. "The *banrach* does not include bedroom privileges, as I'm sure you remember," she said coldly. "It will simply make our families kin, as if you and I were brother and sister. If she returns to us with a child in tow, we will trample your army under our hooves."

"Brave words," Hrovald said, and smiled the way a predator might. "I accept your offer of kinship. Have we agreement on the treaty?"

Mother handed him half the pages in her sheaf. "Cease hostilities along the border. Favored trading status. A gift of fifty horses to you to show our goodwill. And the hand of Imogen of the Kirkellan in the oath of the *banrach* for a period of five years, to bind us in kinship."

Hrovald didn't even pretend to read the documents. He slapped them down on the table and took the pen lying there, and signed at the bottom with a flourish, then signed Mother's set as well. Mother scrawled her name on both copies, shook them to dry the ink, and handed one back to Hrovald. He passed it to one of his men. "And the marriage, this thing of yours with the unpronounceable name, we do it now?"

Mother glanced over her shoulder at Father, who got heavily to his feet. "Sit on opposite sides of the table," he said, and Imogen sat in the seat her mother had vacated. One of Hrovald's men, a skinny youth with unkempt hair and bad skin, brought another stool which he set down awkwardly in front of Hrovald. Hrovald cuffed the young man around the ear, more of a token than an actual blow, but the youth staggered backward as if he'd been punched. Hrovald sat down and looked at Imogen as if she were the least interesting thing he'd looked at all day. Imogen tried to keep her countenance blank. Those empty, hard eyes frightened her a little, and showing fear to this man would probably prove fatal.

"Clasp right hands," Father said, and Hrovald put his elbow on the table and offered his hand as if he wanted to arm-wrestle her. Imogen took his hand. It was dry and as hard as his eyes. She could smell stale sweat and rancid oil coming off him in nose-clenching whiffs that made her skin feel greasy and itchy; she scratched her arm with her free hand and resisted the desire to pinch her nostrils shut.

Father took a strip of pale red cloth from inside his jerkin and wrapped it loosely around their joined hands. "The *banrach* binds two people in a marriage of the spirit rather than the body. Each participant makes oath before the other, and the terms of the oaths are binding upon the participants and their families. If one of the oaths is broken, the *banrach* is dissolved and the oathbreaker must make reparations to his or her spouse's family. If a participant chooses to end the *banrach* before its term is concluded, that person must make reparations as well. Do each of you understand what you are about to undertake?"

Imogen nodded. Hrovald looked at Father and grunted. Father laid both his hands over their clasped ones and bowed his head for a moment. Then he looked at Hrovald.

"Hrovald, King of Ruskald," he said, "will you accept Imogen of the Kirkellan as your wife in spirit under the terms of the *banrach*, giving her all rights and privileges accorded to a wife of the flesh, except those forbidden by the *banrach*?"

"Yes," Hrovald said. Imogen felt him grasp her hand more tightly and wondered what he was thinking.

"Will you support her materially and sustain her spiritually?"

"...Yes," he said, and Imogen guessed he was taken aback by "sustain." She was leery of it herself. She barely wanted contact with the man and she certainly didn't want him sustaining her in any way.

"Will you join her family as son and brother, and receive all due rights therefrom?"

"Yes."

"Will you treat with her family in honor, keeping all the oaths you have sworn in this treaty between our peoples?"

"Yes."

"Imogen of the Kirkellan, will you accept Hrovald, King of Ruskald, as your husband in spirit under the terms of the *banrach*, giving him all rights and privileges accorded to a husband of the flesh except those forbidden by the *banrach*?"

"Yes," Imogen said. Out of the corner of her eye she saw Hrovald turn his attention on her. It was unsettling.

"Will you accept his material support and sustain him spiritually?"

"Yes." There was no way Hrovald would accept material support from a woman.

"Will you join his family as daughter and sister, and receive all due rights within?"

"Yes."

"Will you represent the Kirkellan in honoring the oaths sworn in this treaty between our peoples?"

"Yes."

"I bear witness to watchful heaven that—"

"We don't worship your heretic faith," Hrovald growled. Father looked surprised at the interruption.

"Is it acceptable if I ask for the approval of both?" he asked. Hrovald nodded.

"Then I bear witness to the gods of the Ruskalder and watchful heaven that the oaths made by Hrovald of Ruskald and Imogen of the Kirkellan are made without duress and are binding upon both. You should each of you treat the *banrach* as seriously as any marriage ceremony, not to be dissolved lightly. You are now husband in spirit and wife in spirit." Father removed his hands and unwrapped the cloth. Hrovald released Imogen immediately. Imogen quelled the urge to wipe her hand on her trousers.

"Let's go," he said, and rose, knocking over his stool. Imogen stood up, startled.

"But...right now?" she protested.

"Nothing left to do here. Make your goodbyes."

Mother said, "Two hours, to fetch her things. After all, we came to this not knowing if you would accept."

Hrovald shrugged. "Two hours. We'll wait at the border." He gestured to his men and strode out, the lanky youth bringing up the rear, glancing once at Imogen as if frightened.

Imogen took a deep breath, trying to keep from crying, but then her father put his wiry, muscular arms around her and she couldn't help herself. She cried quietly, not wanting Hrovald to hear her weakness. "There, *lilia*, there, it's not forever," he said, and she clutched at him desperately. She heard Caele curse and fling open the tent flap and storm outside.

Mother said, "Connor, we don't have much time."

"Show some compassion for once in your life, Mairen," he said in a low, cutting voice.

Imogen lifted her head from her father's shoulder to look at her mother. She looked as if she'd been slapped. "Father," she said, and stepped away from him.

He closed his eyes briefly, shuddered, and turned toward his wife. "That was uncalled for," he said, "and I didn't mean it."

"You think I don't know what this means?" she whispered. "I just sacrificed my own daughter for the sake of peace. If that doesn't make me a stone cold bitch of a woman, then I don't know what would." She held out her hand to Imogen, who took it and let herself be drawn into her mother's embrace. "I'm sorry," Mother said. "I did the best I could."

"I know," Imogen said. "It's only five years. I can bear it for five years. Then I'll come home and you can throw me a celebration that lasts five nights."

Mother released her daughter and smiled at her. "You're strong and smart. The time will fly by like nothing. And I'm comforted to know you'll have friends with you."

"Me too." Imogen wiped her eyes. "We'll have to ride fast if we want to get to the rendezvous in two hours."

"Go. And take our love with you."

The *tiermatha* set off for the border in the orderly formation they were still perfecting since their newest members had joined them just two months before, two warriors watching the rear, the rest in ranks spaced evenly around Imogen, who rode point. They passed an unusual number of patrols, and Imogen realized the Kirkellan had turned out to bid her farewell, which almost made her cry again.

The Ruskalder King's camp was nearly dismantled by the time they reached it, half an hour after Hrovald's deadline, but Imogen reasoned they wouldn't leave without the King's bride. The Ruskalder had settled on a rise near the border, or at least what Imogen assumed was the border. The plains here, carpeted with tall green grass and speckled with tiny three-lobed white flowers, looked no different than they did anywhere else. It made the idea of border negotiations seem absurd, like fighting over an invisible line in a dark tent when both combatants were blindfolded. For a moment, Imogen felt angry, as if she were being sacrificed for something that didn't exist. Then she remembered that however invisible the border might be, it was real enough that people had fought and died over it for the last five years. Real enough to make her sacrifice necessary.

As they neared the former camp, two sentries in the ubiquitous Ruskalder leather armor blocked their way. "You don't need an escort from here," one said. The other eyed the *tiermatha,* particularly the women, as if assessing his chances against them if it came to blows and not liking his conclusions.

"The honor guard is coming with me to Ranstjad," Imogen said, daring the sentry to make an issue of it. "A wedding gift to the King."

The first sentry looked at her with narrowed eyes. Imogen stared back with the arrogance of royalty, which she realized she now was. *Queen of the Ruskalder. What an unnerving thought. Maybe they don't have queens, like in Tremontane where the ruler's spouse is just a Consort.* Finally, the sentry stepped aside. "Keep your hands off your weapons 'less you want the camp to turn on you. Don't look like any wedding gift I ever saw."

Imogen nodded to the man and prodded Victory into motion. Every man they passed did, in fact, look at them as if violence was on his mind. Riding casually into the middle of a Ruskalder war camp, even one mostly dismantled, frightened Imogen, which made her angry; she stiffened her face so as not to give either of those feelings away. She would have to watch herself constantly to avoid showing signs of weakness. It was going to be a very long five years.

Hrovald waited beside the remnants of his tent, mounted on a slim gray gelding beside which Victory looked enormous. He glanced at her horse, glanced at the *tiermatha,* and said, "You insult me by bringing a bodyguard into my house?"

"It's a wedding gift," Imogen repeated. "A gesture of respect."

Hrovald grunted. "Generous gift indeed." He removed his helmet, scratched his greasy head, and put the helmet back on. "They'll take orders from me?"

"They always take orders from their leader," Imogen said, hoping the warriors behind her could keep straight faces and not draw attention to the fact that she hadn't said who their leader was. Dorenna was right; if Hrovald believed the *tiermatha* was his, they might be able to turn that to their advantage.

"And to think I didn't bring you anything," Hrovald said drily. "Let's go." He kicked his horse in the ribs and moved out at a trot. Imogen and the *tiermatha* fell in behind him. He shouted a command, and the warriors formed up around them. There were at least two hundred men, Imogen estimated, in the King's warband, and this was only a fraction of his army. Even counting their horses, who fought as well as any warrior, the Kirkellan were seriously outnumbered. Peace was the best option. Imogen comforted herself with that thought as she rode into enemy territory, surrounded by enemy warriors, behind an enemy King to whom she was oathbound for the next five years. She straightened her spine. She was a warrior of the Kirkellan and she would show these people no fear.

Chapter Three

Imogen had never seen so many trees in one place before. They had quickly left the plains behind and now rode through a forest of evergreens, their dark green needles shading and cooling the path beneath them. Imogen and her *tiermatha* had to duck, frequently, as their horses were much taller than those the Ruskalder—the few who were mounted—rode. Imogen reached up to push a branch out of the way and wondered what this forest would look like in winter. Behind her, Revalan protested as the branch she'd deflected sprang back to skim across the top of his head.

She wanted to ask how far it was to Ranstjad, the capital of Ruskald, but was reluctant to draw Hrovald's attention to her in any way. After they'd left the camp, he'd mostly ignored her and communicated with her in grunts and gestures when he didn't. She couldn't tell if he was dismissive of her because she was a woman or because she was a foreigner; it might have been both. In any case, he exuded menace, as if he were always just two breaths away from exploding into violence, and she wasn't convinced the terms of the *banrach* would keep him from turning that violence on her. Then she'd have to fight to defend herself, and though she was a good fighter, younger than Hrovald, and possibly heavier, she wasn't certain the fight would end well, especially if she wasn't mounted. Even so, a part of her wished to test herself against the belligerent King. Let him dismiss women fighters when he was spitting teeth.

They came out of the forest and made camp on the flat ground surrounding a low hill, bulbous and rocky under its patchy growth of shrubs and grass. In the distance, Imogen saw a wide, slow-moving river and colored specks that might be boats headed downstream. She thought about climbing the hill to get a better look, but the idea of leaving Victory behind made her anxious. She contented herself with riding through the camp, ignoring the stares, until Hrovald shouted at her to come back in a peremptory tone that embarrassed and angered her.

The *tiermatha* was outfitted as if for a long-range patrol, carrying one tent for every three people and plenty of rations, but these turned out to be unnecessary. Hrovald gave up his own tent to his bride and provided another for "his" *tiermatha*, and they ate what the warriors had killed in the way of their march. The rabbit was tough and gamy, but Imogen was hungry enough not to care. After sunset, she retired to Hrovald's tent and lay sleepless, fully clothed, wondering if despite her mother's warning he would come to her that night. There was nothing to stop him but his oath, and suppose he didn't mean to keep it? She fingered the knife at her side and twitched at every sudden sound, every flicker of movement across the tent's canvas. Eventually she drifted off into an undisturbed sleep.

They reached Ranstjad late the following afternoon, their path gradually converging on the river's until they were marching beside it, listening to its chattering voice. They and the river emerged from the crowded green forest abruptly into a broad, flat lowland so perfectly circular it had to be artificial. The city lay several miles away across the grassy plain, dominating its surroundings and defying the forest to overwhelm it. Imogen had never seen a permanent city before and gaped at it in wonder. As their company approached the city, she was even more astonished at its size and, surprisingly, its beauty. A stone wall some thirty feet high surrounded Ranstjad, its stones rough-hewn granite that sparkled when the sun's rays struck them at the right angle. The gray-green river passed the city on the right, where docks supported by enormous gray logs thrust upright into the deep river bed emerged from the walls. Brightly painted boats of all sizes lined up to receive cargo and, Imogen assumed, passengers. She had seen no boats traveling upstream and wondered how any of the shipmasters returned home from their journeys downriver.

To the left of the city lay tents and picket lines and corrals so familiar a lump rose in Imogen's throat. She controlled it by reminding herself this was no doubt the Ruskalder warriors' camp, and only superficially similar to her home, but it was hard not to look for the great tent and her mother's flag flying over it. A shouted command, and the warriors peeled off from the formation and marched in loose columns toward the camp. Imogen had to admire their discipline even though, treaty or no, she still thought of them as the enemy. The men in those marching columns had harried her people for too long for her to forget the conflict easily.

Hrovald, his advisers, Imogen, the *tiermatha* and about thirty warriors continued across the plain toward the city gate. She wondered why there wasn't a road leading to the city. She knew permanent settlements built roads for quicker travel, so why wasn't the capital of Ruskald so provided? It was obvious where travelers had passed by the places the grass was bent and broken at the roots, but that was all. Imogen gave a mental shrug. She was only going to be here for five years; who cared how the Ruskalder got from place to place?

The double gate was made of thick, tall gray logs bound upright by pitted metal bands the width of Imogen's two palms. At the gate, two guards in leather armor saluted the King with much less formality than Imogen thought Hrovald would demand. Unseen hands sent the gates swinging slowly open, and Hrovald's party passed through.

Imogen gawked openly at the city beyond, knowing she looked foolish but not caring. She was an outsider, a foreigner, and there was no point trying to conceal that fact. The road beyond the gate was made of packed earth and was wide enough for four horses (three, if they were Kirkellan mounts) to ride abreast. Tall wooden buildings with steeply slanted roofs covered with shingles stained dark brown lined the road, all painted in what would have been bright colors had they not been so weather-beaten and chipped. Fresh paint would have been cheerful; this was depressing and a little ominous.

The buildings leaned toward the road like vultures, as if waiting for a predetermined signal upon which they would fall on whoever was foolish enough to stop beneath them. They made Imogen, born and bred on the treeless Eidestal, feel as if a weight were pressing down on her. All bore small windows lined with thin paper or in some cases paned with glass, something Imogen had rarely seen because it didn't bear up well under the strain of the Kirkellan's constant traveling, and all the windows had heavy shutters that would keep the buildings warm during the heaviest snows. The doors were also painted, though with fresh, undamaged coats of paint, and all bore symbols of the Ruskalder gods just above the latch, a circle with a diagonal line through it, or a U balanced on a horizontal line, and rarely the rough shape of an eye, two curving arcs and a pinpoint dot at the center. Imogen knew nothing of the Ruskalder religion except they still believed gods ruled in heaven. No doubt she'd have plenty of opportunities to learn more.

The street was thronged with more people than Imogen had ever seen packed into one place, talking and laughing and arguing. Women stood outside their doors and swept, or called out to neighbor women across the way. Children ran across the street, not noticing the oncoming procession, and were pulled out of the way as one by one the Ruskalder registered first that horses were coming down the street, and second, that their King was among the riders. Men bowed, women swept the street with their curtseys instead of their brooms, and children stared openly at the Kirkellan horses and the men and women who rode them. The Ruskalder raised their heads after their King passed and stared at Imogen. She looked down at angry, awed, frightened faces and had to look away. Here, she was the enemy.

They traveled down the streets and drew silence in their wake. Hrovald seemed not to notice his subjects' reaction, or maybe he simply took this respectful, or possibly fearful, silence for granted. He led his little group to another wall, shorter than the first but made of the same glittering granite and equally imposing. The guards at this gate seemed more fearful of their King than the ones at the city gate; they opened it quickly and stood at rigid attention as Hrovald's party passed through.

Beyond lay three large wooden buildings painted an unscathed green and yellow, surrounding a hard-packed earth courtyard on three sides. The buildings to either side of the courtyard looked like boxes, unadorned wooden boxes dropped into Hrovald's courtyard by a whimsical heaven, or possibly by one of the Ruskalder gods. Each was two stories tall, built of planed wood and dotted with glass windows in two rows. There was a single door in each building that opened on to the courtyard, both of them standing open at the moment. The two buildings were tucked under the eaves of the larger central house as if they'd been an afterthought, which, as Imogen considered the main house, was probably true.

The central house was built not of lumber but of yellow-brown logs stacked atop one another to create a building that looked more solid, more real, than anything Imogen had ever seen. The black-shingled roof sloped shallowly to either side until it fetched up against the boxes, whose steeper roofs of gray-brown shingles continued the unbroken line all the way to the ground. It had no windows, nothing to break its forbidding uniformity except a couple of chimneys made of brick rather than the metal Imogen was used to and a wide door made of the same yellow-brown logs and iron bands. The house glowered at the front gate and at anyone who dared to pass through it. Imogen glared back at it. She didn't intend to let Hrovald intimidate her and she certainly wasn't going to let his house do it.

The courtyard was nearly empty, with a few women crossing between the box-buildings and a handful of warriors standing near the central house's door who came to attention when the King rode in. Imogen relaxed, aware of how tense the hostile crowds had made her that she was able to relax in the presence of Ruskalder warriors. Hrovald dismounted, and Imogen and the *tiermatha* followed suit. He handed off his horse's reins to an approaching groom, who led the animal away around to the rear of the right-hand box. Imogen made as if to follow the groom and was startled when a man stepped into her path and held out his hand. "What?" she said, too weary to be polite.

"I'll take your horse, madam," he said. Imogen sucked in a horrified breath.

"Take my horse? I've cared for Victory since she was a foal!"

"You're my wife now. It's beneath you," Hrovald said. He was halfway to the door and sounded impatient.

"The horses of the Kirkellan are like family," she spat at him. "Seeing to Victory's needs is no less beneath me than…than a woman caring for her child. I will not give her over to a stranger, however you may trust him." She nodded at the groom; after all, this wasn't his fault.

Hrovald glowered at Imogen. She stood her ground, fingers gripping Victory's reins as if to keep her from slipping away. "You think you're in a position to make demands, wife?" An evil light glittered in his eye.

Sick fear began roiling in her stomach. She could feel the *tiermatha* drawing close around her, prepared to defend her, and she had a terrible vision of how this might end: her friends, herself, bloody and dying on the hard earth of Hrovald's courtyard. There was no one to force him to honor the treaty here, nothing to spare her but his own whim. But to give Victory to another's care, to show weakness to him…she drew herself up to her full height and glared back at him.

He pursed his lips in thought and examined her coldly. "Savages," he said, turning away. "Do as you wish. Attend me when you're finished, wife." He went into the building. Imogen relaxed. She looked at the members of her *tiermatha,* who followed her around the side of the courtyard to the stables.

The stables were a pair of long buildings with sagging roofs like the wrinkled faces of a couple of men who'd once been warriors and were now just old. Imogen wrinkled her nose at the faint smell of ammonia rising from the ground. They were also nearly empty, which was fortunate because the stable master was struck dumb when he saw thirteen Kirkellan horses file into his domain. "I hope we have room," he said when he'd gotten over his fit of astonishment. "They're well behaved, I assume?"

Every member of the *tiermatha* gave him the same disdainful look at once. "Better than your animals, probably," said Kionnal, patting Revelry's neck. Revelry showed his teeth as if he thought the question was stupid, too.

Each stall was equipped with a rusty bucket for water hanging on the wall and a long, narrow wooden manger for hay on the floor. Victory only barely fit into her stall, backing gracefully but with an expression Imogen knew meant she was plotting trouble if she had to stay cooped up for very long. Imogen traded glances with the others; something would have to be done about this if it was going to be long-term housing for their horses. Victory didn't seem any more enthusiastic about settling in than Imogen was at settling her there. Imogen spent more time than was necessary comforting her horse, brushing Victory's coat and checking her feet for stones until Victory protested. She began to shift nervously, picking up on Imogen's mood, and Imogen soothed them both until she felt able to face Hrovald for what was effectively the first time since they'd left the Eidestal, with its rolling plains, for this looming wooden city surrounded by pines.

Finally, she couldn't delay any longer. "I wish you could come with me," she said.

"Why can't we?" Revalan asked.

"He only told me to attend him, not you. I don't want him angry with you."

"With his personal *tiermatha*? You think that's likely?" Dorenna said.

"I don't know what to think. Just—tell me when you find out where you'll be billeted, all right?"

The *tiermatha* exchanged glances. "I don't like it," Dorenna said.

"She didn't ask us to like it," Kionnal said. "We'll see you soon, Imogen."

So Imogen left the stable and crossed the courtyard to the great house alone, pretending she had an army at her back. The door opened directly into a room bigger than any Imogen had seen in her life. She reflected there were a lot of things she'd never seen before embarking on this "adventure." The enormous yellow logs of the walls fitted neatly together at the corners and were swabbed with pitch to cover the cracks. A vast open hearth ran the length of the back wall, easily big enough to hold a whole tree, or three or four oxen. Two long trestle tables planed smooth stood perpendicular to the hearth, with benches pulled up on either side. A smaller table stood parallel to the fireplace, chairs lined up along one side with their backs facing the fire. Imogen thought it might be comfortable during the winter, then wondered if it mightn't scorch your back instead. The log walls rose to meet the ceiling high above, which was made of planks and stained dark with old smoke, suggesting the giant fireplace wasn't as efficient as it might appear. Imogen remembered a camp-stove that had been improperly cleaned one spring and how it had driven her family out of the tent, coughing, when it was first lit the next autumn, and thought despondently of how much more space there was for this fireplace to fill with smoke. There were no windows, and Imogen wondered how warm the room would be in winter. Then she remembered she'd be there to find out.

Hrovald sat at the small table, tearing into a roast chicken. "Sit," he said, using a drumstick to point at the seat beside him. Imogen sat. Her stomach rumbled loudly, and Hrovald laughed. "Food for my wife," he shouted. "Relax, you make me tired just looking at how alert you are all the time." Servants brought more roast chicken, piles of fist-sized boiled potatoes, and a mug of dark beer. She gobbled her food, not caring to impress Hrovald with her table manners.

"I like to see someone enjoy their food," he said, wiping his mouth on his sleeve. "Especially a well-fed woman like you. You didn't like me calling you fat, did you? It was meant as a compliment. I have no use for skinny wenches."

Imogen shrugged. "I like the way I am."

"You should do. Even if you are a fighter and an abomination." Hrovald said this last with no rancor. "You won't do any fighting while you're in this house, understand? I won't be made mock of by my men for having a wife who doesn't know her place."

A thousand possible responses rushed into Imogen's head. She opted for the diplomatic "I'm not Ruskalder, so I don't see how it would shame you for me to go on as I've always done."

Hrovald slammed the table, startling Imogen. "I won't have you arguing with me, woman. You'll do as I say or there'll be consequences."

"Are you threatening me?"

"That's a warning. You married me and you'll behave like a proper Ruskalder wife, or the alliance is null. Don't think I don't know you chose this to spare your people more bloodshed. I think you want this strange marriage of yours to work for their sakes and not your own. I've already given up my rights to your body, so don't think I'm going to give up any more."

Imogen swallowed hard and unclenched her fist. Screaming obscenities and launching herself at his throat would be stupid. He thought so little of her abilities he'd given her a sharp knife, not thinking of it as a weapon in her hands. And he was right. She was here for the sake of the Kirkellan. She raged and wailed inside at the thought of five years without fighting, without training, but what else was she to do? She still had Victory. He could hardly complain about her going for a ride every day or so. Wasn't that something women did, even Ruskalder women?

"I'll abide by your wishes…husband," she said, "but my—the women of the *tiermatha* have to train or they won't do you any good in combat."

"You expect us to go to war again?"

"I expect you're the kind of leader who plans for every contingency."

Hrovald gave her a narrow-eyed, suspicious glare. "None of my men will fight a woman."

"Then they can fight their companions. But they *will* fight."

Hrovald sucked chicken juice off his fingers. "Very well," he said. "They can bunk in with the warriors. Your quarters are across the courtyard from mine. And stop thinking I'm going to ravish you in your sleep. As if I'd want to bed a woman who thinks she's a warrior."

"Your warriors had better not try it with the *tiermatha*," Imogen said, "unless they want to lose their favorite body part."

Hrovald laughed. "Serve 'em right, but I think you'll find they don't want to be sullied by a female fighter any more than any sensible man would." He wiped his fingers on his sleeve and pushed back from the table. "I have business to deal with," he said. "One of these women will show you where to go. Next I see you, you'd better be properly dressed." He strode out of the room without looking back.

"Your Majesty?" said a voice near Imogen's shoulder, and it took her a moment to realize the woman was addressing her. "I'm supposed to show you to your room now." The woman sounded timid, and Imogen wondered if she was afraid of Imogen's potential recalcitrance reflecting badly on her. From what she knew of Hrovald, it might.

She followed the serving woman through a door leading off the great hall, down a hall and into a narrow, low-ceilinged passageway inside one of the adjoining box-buildings. They climbed to the second story—stairs, yet another thing Imogen had never seen before—and went down a hall to a door with posts and lintel carved with five-petaled flowers, the kind that grew across the plains every spring and perfumed the air with their scent. The servant opened the door for Imogen and bowed her inside.

The room was dimly lit by the setting sun, and Imogen looked around for a lantern, but was startled by a faint glow that grew into a bright, steady light that filled the room. Imogen turned and saw the light came from a sphere on the wall behind her. The servant was just removing her hand from a wooden knob below the sphere. It had a flower carved into it. Awestruck, Imogen touched the knob and felt it turn under her fingers; the light dimmed. She turned it back and the light brightened. "There's another one of these on the far wall," the servant said. Imogen crossed to look at it, then turned the knob herself and watched the sphere begin to glow. "Amazing," she breathed.

"You don't have Devices where you come from, your Majesty?" the servant said.

Imogen shook her head. "I've never seen anything like it before. How does it work?"

"I'm not really sure. I know it's the lines of power, the ones connecting us with the gods' heaven, that provide the energy to make them go. I could bring a Deviser here to explain it better, if you're interested."

"I'd like that. Thank you."

Now she looked at the room in the bright light. The bed pillows were huge and square and set on a wooden framework high above the ground. A polished wooden chest stained red sat at the foot of the bed. There was a table and a chair and a round mirror big enough for Imogen to see half her body at once, and a long mirror on the wall in which she could see her *whole* body at once. A big cabinet stood against one wall; she opened the door and found it empty. The chest contained blankets. She'd never had this much space to herself in her whole life. She felt hollow and excited at the same time. Suppose she got so used to this she couldn't go back to her comfortable tiny room in the family tent?

"What's your name?" she asked the servant abruptly.

"Anneke, your Majesty."

"Anneke, what do you do here in Hrovald's house?"

"I wait on the tables, your Majesty."

"Do you suppose Hrovald would mind if you helped me instead? I don't know anything about your culture and I don't want to make too many mistakes."

Anneke's face lit briefly, then fell. "I don't want to get above my station, your Majesty."

"Then who *can* I get to help me?"

Anneke hesitated. "There aren't any ladies in the house right now. You'll have to find someone used to helping a lady with…with dressing, and things."

"Then why not you?"

Anneke hesitated again. "I suppose…if you ask the chatelaine, she might give permission."

"Then I'll do that. And I suppose I need new clothes." Imogen made a face. Being Queen of the Ruskalder was going to take a lot of work.

Chapter Four

"I'm not wearing this," Imogen said flatly.

"But you have to wear a dress!" Anneke wailed. "And this is the biggest one I could find!"

Imogen turned and looked at her rear end over her shoulder. "I look like I've been poured into this thing like a sausage into a casing. I can't even raise my arms higher than my chest without the seams tearing. I'm not saying I won't wear a dress, I'm just saying I won't wear *this* dress." She turned to face the mirror again. The smooth fabric strained across her full breasts and outlined her round stomach. The dress was cut narrow through the upper thighs and flared out a few inches above the knee, which constrained her walk to a hobble. The neckline plunged to reveal her cleavage, which combined with the tightness of her bodice made her feel as if she were only one wrong move away from spilling out of the dress entirely. The only good things about it were that the fabric was wonderfully soft and it was a beautiful red color she thought made her skin look warm and glowing. It was just too bad it had been made for a woman two sizes smaller than Imogen.

She presented her back to Anneke and said, "Get it off me."

"But—"

"This can't possibly be what Hrovald had in mind when he said I had to wear a dress. We need someone to make one that fits me, that's all." She carefully removed her arms from the sleeves and let Anneke pull it off over her head. While Anneke hung it up inside the cupboard, Imogen pulled her shirt and breeches back on. "Can you find me a seamstress?"

"Yes, but—"

"I'm not wearing the dress. It's not my fault all the women here are short and skinny." Imogen knew that wasn't true, but at the moment she was irritable because she felt like a giant next to Anneke, who was barely five feet tall and might have weighed a hundred pounds fully dressed with big rocks in her pockets. After Anneke left, she decided to go for a ride rather than sit around waiting for her to return. She'd just have to weather Hrovald's anger if he saw her in her Kirkellish clothing.

Victory acted as excited to see her as if their separation had lasted a week rather than thirteen hours, most of them spent sleeping. Imogen laughed and rubbed her cheek against her horse's smooth nose. "Missed you," she whispered, and began to saddle her up. It was immediately obvious there wasn't enough room in the stall to maneuver around the big horse, so she led Victory out into the narrow passage between the two rows of stalls. The stable master came around the corner and took a step back as if surprised to see her.

"Your Majesty," he said, "you should let me do that for you."

"I can tell Victory to bite you if you try," Imogen said complacently. The man blanched.

"I think…his Majesty would prefer I not let his wife do this kind of labor," he said.

Imogen paused, headstall in hands. "I've already explained to *my husband*," she said, "that it is a Kirkellan custom to care for our horses ourselves. You won't be in any trouble for letting me do this. You might be in trouble if you don't."

The man stepped back, holding his hands in front of him like a warding gesture. "I mean no disrespect."

"Would you like to meet her?" The man looked confused. Imogen smiled and took his hand. "Victory, this is—sorry, what's your name?"

"Erek," the man said, his eyes wide. Imogen brought his hand to rest on Victory's nose.

"Victory, this is Erek, and he'll take care of you sometimes, so be nice to him, okay? No biting." She said the last just to needle the man; Victory had never bitten anyone in her life except the occasional Ruskalder warrior, but that had always been under provocation. Erek pulled his hand back quickly, and Imogen laughed. "I'm only teasing, Erek. She's very smart, so watch yourself around her or she'll think she can play tricks on you. Now, I think you and I need to have a chat."

Erek looked wary. Imogen had the feeling he was only worried about offending her because it might offend Hrovald. As long as they could come to an arrangement, she didn't care who he was worried about. "Erek," she said, "you can see, can't you, that this stall is far too small for Victory? She needs plenty of room to move around."

"I—your Majesty, I don't think there are any bigger stalls—"

"Then you'll have to make one, won't you? Someone should be able to just knock a wall out between two stalls. But she needs a bigger stall and, Erek, I suggest you get right on that, because I want it ready by the time I get back from my ride." She finished putting Victory's tack on and swung herself into the saddle. "And then we're going to have another chat about her care and feeding. That rusty bucket is completely unacceptable. You do realize Hrovald gained fifty Kirkellan horses as part of the peace treaty? I'm sure most of them will end up here. You might want to think about where you're going to put them."

Erek looked as if he'd forgotten how to breathe. Imogen leaned over and patted him on the back. "I'm glad to know I can trust you to watch out for Victory," she said. She noted, looking around, that her *tiermatha's* horses were gone. So they'd moved over to the warriors' camp. The empty stalls echoed the hollowness she felt at the idea. "I'm going to ride outside the walls, Erek, and I'll be back in a couple of hours." She nudged Victory into a trot before the man could protest.

She found her way to the gate without any trouble, only taking a wrong turn once. She tried not to look at the Ruskalder she rode past, not wanting to see their anger or disgust at her presence. Outside the city, she turned left and jogged along, paralleling the city wall. Once or twice around the city was what she had in mind, nothing more. Nothing Hrovald could turn into a weapon against her or the *tiermatha.* Just an easy circuit, and then back to trying to be a Ruskalder lady. She grimaced and urged Victory into a slightly faster gait.

It was a beautiful summer day, cloudless and blue, and if she ignored the wall of trees circling the city in the distance she could almost imagine herself back home on the plains. It felt good to be alone, just the two of them under heaven. Impulsively, she shouted a command, and Victory took off across the open plain, running as fast as she was able, which was for a Kirkellan horse very fast indeed.

Soon they came upon the river, probably icy from its source high in the Spine of the World, and Imogen had to rein her horse in or run straight into it. They stood and watched it for a while. In the spring it would flood its banks and be fast and frigid; now, in the heart of summer, it dawdled along, ruffling the tall grass along its bank. There didn't seem to be a bridge.

She turned and rode beside it toward the docks, where she stopped to watch the boats being loaded with more of the giant logs and piles of animal skins. The men and women—interesting, they were dressed in trousers just like the men and doing the same work—nearest her stopped what they were doing to watch her in turn. She waved. They didn't wave back. Eventually Imogen, feeling uncomfortably like a trespasser, turned and rode away. When she glanced back over her shoulder, she saw they'd resumed their work. It was no doubt the reaction she'd get from everyone she met, at least until they got used to her. If they ever did.

She turned and went back the way she'd come, passed the city gate and went on following the wall to the right. She soon came upon the military camp and decided to take a long detour around it rather than ride straight through. She didn't like the idea of being surrounded by Ruskalder warriors, even if she was nominally their Queen and they were bound not to interfere with her. But she soon found her detour wasn't wide enough. She heard the sound of wood clashing against wood, metal on metal, long before she saw the training grounds, which were set some distance from the camp and were clearly in use today. She thought about turning around, but then saw some familiar figures sparring to one side of the field, and trotted toward them, her heart lifting at the sight.

"Imogen! Come to practice with us?" Dorenna said.

"Promised Hrovald I wouldn't, remember? But I'd like to watch for a while." Surely Hrovald couldn't object to that. She dismounted and led Victory to where they'd both be out of the way of the fighting.

Kionnal and Areli faced off against each other, the red-headed Kionnal shifting right to left and back while Areli, tall and lanky, balanced on the balls of her feet and waited for him to attack. "If I'd wanted to dance I would've stayed with the camp," Areli said with a grin.

"You never want to dance with me," Kionnal complained.

"Because you're a terrible—dancer!" Areli lunged and caught his practice sword in the crossguard of hers, using her momentum to lift his arm out of her way and swiveling in to punch him in the side as if wielding an invisible short sword. "Dead," she said.

"Damn. I swore I wouldn't get caught by that again. You'll have to show me the block."

Areli released his arm and kissed her lover quickly, looking around to see if they'd been observed. "Happy to oblige," she said. "But I think it's all about speed."

"Find me a javelin, and we'll see who's faster."

"Get out of the way, you two, and let a real man show you how it's done," Revalan said. "Come on, Imogen, I can't get a good workout without you."

"You want to test that theory?" A hulking Ruskalder approached, twirling a wooden practice sword in his left hand. His long blond hair was familiar, and Imogen realized this was the leader of the raiding party they'd turned back from the border days before. "I could use a new sparring partner."

Revalan looked at Imogen, then at his other comrades. "I suppose so," he said. "What did you have in mind?"

"Straight across fight? Three points for the win?"

Revalan nodded. "And the judge?"

The man looked across at Imogen. "I think the Queen can be impartial, even if she is one of you." His eyes lingered on her breasts, and Imogen clenched her hand on Victory's reins. She couldn't attack him for looking, however unwanted his interest was.

"Agreed." Revalan began to limber up. The Ruskalder continued to twirl his sword, smiling in a way that made Imogen uneasy. She saw they'd begun to gather an audience of warriors smiling the same unpleasant smile. She wished Revalan hadn't accepted the challenge and hoped he'd be able to win, or at least hold his own.

The two men tapped their swords together to indicate the beginning of the bout, and Revalan immediately darted in past the Ruskalder's guard to tap him on the chest. "First point," Imogen said. Dorenna made a noise of encouragement, but otherwise the crowd remained silent. It was eerie. Imogen felt it was too soon to celebrate.

The men circled one another, clashed, separated, and circled again. The Ruskalder feinted to one side, Revalan took the bait, and his opponent hit him hard on the shoulder. Revalan winced and put his hand to the spot. "Watch it," he warned.

Imogen said, "First point to—?"

"Karel," the man said, grinning more broadly. He twirled his sword again. Imogen wished she could take it away from him and hit him hard across the buttocks. He certainly looked like he deserved a smacking.

Now the bout got serious. Karel claimed another point, though without the resounding strike he'd made before, then Revalan tagged the man's knee just hard enough to send him to the ground. A murmur went through the watching crowd, and they shifted in a way Imogen Imogen feared meant real violence. "You struck his shoulder, he struck your knee, it's even between the two of you," she said in a loud voice. Karel didn't seem angry about it. He continued to grin that nasty smile as he got to his feet. "Match point," Imogen said. Maybe it would remind them this was a workout and not a fight. *Hah. And maybe Hrovald will come out here and spar with me.*

The two had barely resumed their fighting stance when Karel, fast as a snake, lunged and struck Revalan across the ribs with a crack everyone heard. Revalan bent over, trying to catch his breath, as the crowd cheered and Karel smirked. He offered Revalan his hand, which the Kirkellan accepted, though he released it as soon as he was standing upright. The *tiermatha* muttered angrily among themselves, glaring at Karel. Imogen dismounted and went to her friend. "Are you all right?" she asked in a low voice. Revalan nodded, but his lips were white with pain. She glared at him, exasperated, wondering why he thought such a transparent lie would fool her. "The bout goes to Karel," she said, an unnecessary afterthought.

"Your impartiality is appreciated, your Majesty," Karel said, bending to pick up the sword Revalan had dropped. He contemplated it for a moment, then offered it to her, hilt first, as if it were a real sword. "I'd like to test my skills against yours."

Imogen almost took the wooden sword. Having watched his bout against Revalan, she was certain she could defeat Karel, and it would be sweet indeed to let him be bested by a woman. Oh, how she itched to pick up a blade again, even a wooden one. But she'd promised Hrovald, and she was just enough afraid of him, afraid for the *tiermatha's* sake as well as the treaty's, that she meant to keep her promise. She shook her head. "Sorry," she said, "but I don't think I should fight the men who are meant to protect me."

"Come now, just days ago we were simply two warriors facing one another across the border," Karel said. His smile had gone from taunting to disturbingly personal.

"Then you should have asked just days ago," Imogen said lightly. "But I'm sure any of the *tiermatha* would be happy to oblige you. Even the women."

A murmur went up from the crowd. Karel raised his hand, and the noise stopped. Imogen wondered if he was a warrior of rank, or if it was his personal charisma that controlled these men. "Another time," he said.

"I'd be happy to give you time to rest, if you're worried about an unequal fight," Dorenna said. Her face was placid, but her eyes were as hard and cold as Hrovald's ever dreamed of being. Imogen grabbed her by the arm and squeezed. Dorenna ignored her.

Karel raised his eyebrow. Dorenna didn't look like a warrior. She was the shortest of the *tiermatha* and had a delicate face with wide, innocent dark green eyes. She was also a master of the sword and a vicious, ruthless fighter who had an arsenal of dirty tricks up both her sleeves. Imogen closed her eyes. Dorenna was going to humiliate Karel, and then her life wouldn't be worth a snowdrift in the summer sun.

"I think we're done for the day. Thank you for the demonstration, Karel. *Tiermatha,* please escort me back to the King's house?" She squeezed Dorenna's arm until her fingers grated against the bone.

Dorenna stared Karel down for a moment longer, then walked back to where Rapier was tethered and mounted in silence. Imogen resumed her seat on Victory, who had observed the bout with the stolidity of an experienced war horse. Imogen wished she could have been as unaffected.

They rode back to the city in silence. Halfway there, Dorenna said, "Thanks for stopping me."

"Thanks for not turning your anger on me," Imogen said.

"I wouldn't do that."

"You were pretty angry. I wasn't sure how much self-control you had."

"She could have taken him easily," Areli said.

"And then the whole army would have been looking for ways to kill me and make it look like an accident," Dorenna pointed out.

"Oh. Right."

"Are you all right, Revalan? Honestly, this time."

"I think he cracked my rib," Revalan said, feeling his side and wincing.

Imogen closed her eyes and breathed deeply. It was either that or scream. "How's your billet? Any problems?"

"Other than the thinly veiled hostility and the need for us to go everywhere in packs?" Kionnal said wryly. "Everything's wonderful."

"Have they actually attacked you?"

"Not overtly. Not yet," Kallum said, serious for once. "They're trying to goad us into attacking first, and then they can claim self-defense when they kill us. And the women—"

"We can handle it," Areli said.

"You shouldn't have to."

"I'm sorry I brought you here," Imogen said.

"Well, we're not," said Saevonna. "Things will get better. They'll get used to us. And before you know it, five years will have passed and we'll be sad to say goodbye."

"That's not going to happen, Saevonna."

"I know, but it's such an optimistic thing to say, don't you think?"

Imogen stabled Victory—Erek's men hadn't finished the new stall, but she reassured him their progress was acceptable—and then the *tiermatha* walked Imogen to her new home and bade her farewell. She felt miserable watching them ride away. She needed to stop thinking about how long it would be before they could all go home. That would just make it feel longer.

A young man was seated at the high table when Imogen entered the hall. She recognized him as the spotty, lanky young man Hrovald had slapped at the *banrach*. "Hello," she said. The young man jumped up and wouldn't meet her eyes. "I've seen you before."

He nodded. "Hesketh," he said. "You're my stepmother."

This was Hrovald's son? She couldn't imagine two people less alike in the world. "Oh," she said lamely. "How old are you?"

"Seventeen."

Only two years younger than her. Stepmother. Imogen felt dizzy. "You'll call me Imogen and not Mother, all right? Because I don't think I'm ready to be the mother of someone as…as mature as you."

He shrugged. "It's up to Father." He stared at his foot, which began tracing circles on the floor of its own volition. "I've never seen a woman dress like you."

"All the women dress like me where I come from."

"I don't like it. Women should look like women."

Imogen rolled her eyes. "As soon as I get a dress that fits, I'll look like a woman."

"You're big for a woman, too."

"Can't do anything about that." Imogen began to understand how Hrovald could so casually abuse this boy. He practically begged to be slapped. She was on her way out the door when he said, "Are you going to give me a baby brother?"

"Of course not!" Imogen said, shocked. "Your father and I have a…diplomatic marriage. No babies. Not ever."

Hesketh looked relieved. "Good," he said. "I don't want a brother." He went back to staring at his foot. Imogen made a hasty exit.

Anneke was in her room when she returned. She looked as if she'd been there for a while. "I found a seamstress," she said, "if you want to come with me now."

"It's not as if I have anything else to do," Imogen sighed. Her *tiermatha* was being harassed and she had a limp rag for a stepson. Getting fitted for a dress would apparently be the highlight of her day.

CHAPTER FIVE

Over the next few weeks Imogen fell into a pattern that, if not exciting, at least kept her from being completely bored. In the morning she rose early and exercised as much as the confines of her room would allow. It wasn't the same as the workout she got from practicing swordplay, but it kept her from falling into despair at how her skills were slipping away from her. Then Anneke helped her dress in one of the four gowns she'd acquired from a seamstress in town, all of them in bright colors that contrasted wildly with the dun and cream and sable favored by the Kirkellan. She ate breakfast alone in the great hall, the room Hrovald referred to as the *skorstala*. Hrovald never joined her, though she wasn't sure whether this was because he rose very early or was still abed. She didn't much care, so long as she was spared his menacing presence.

After breakfast she spent a few hours failing to be a well-bred lady. Hrovald was serious about her behaving like a proper Ruskalder wife; he'd hired half a dozen companions for her, each of whom was skilled in some talent Hrovald expected Imogen to learn. Imogen resisted. She saw no point in learning skills that would be useless to her on the plains, warrior or no. But after the first few days of mulishly resenting her minders, Hrovald entered the room set aside for her training, looked at each of the women in turn, then casually struck one of them so hard she fell out of her chair and cried out in pain. Imogen shot out of her seat and ran up against Hrovald's icy stare. "You're not learning fast enough. Suppose now they'll try harder."

"It's not their fault!" Imogen shouted.

"It is if I say it is," Hrovald said. "Or maybe you're the one needs to try harder. Don't force me to come back in here, wife." He left the room without looking back. The other women gathered around their fallen companion, and Imogen strode to the window, blinking back tears of fury. He was going to make her comply by threatening those helpless women, was he? Damn him. It worked. Imogen couldn't let them come to harm no matter how much she resented and despised what they were trying to teach her. She turned back from the window and resumed her seat. "I'm sorry," she said. "Why don't we start with spinning?"

Spinning and weaving turned out to be beyond her, though she became skilled enough to satisfy Hrovald, who didn't seem to care how good she was at anything so long as she was doing it. She didn't like reading any more now than she had as a child, especially now she was expected to do it aloud, and with feeling. But to her surprise and faint horror she discovered she liked needlework. More than that, she had a talent for it. Her companions were all so delighted at her progress Imogen thought they might have begun to despair at ever turning their oversized barbarian charge into a lady. She liked watching flowers and trees and horses come to life with just a few stitches, and found half an hour spent working a tapestry soothed her the same way riding Victory did.

Riding Victory took up most of her afternoon. The battle over this with Hrovald had been as fierce as she'd expected. "Damned Kirkellan savage," he'd shouted. "I should never have let you keep it."

"Ruskalder women ride," Imogen said, trying not to lose her temper. If Hrovald decided to separate her from her horse…how far would she let Hrovald push her? Even for the sake of her people? "I'll wear a dress. I'll use one of those strange saddles. I won't do anything unwomanly. I just want to ride in the afternoons."

Hrovald swore again and turned away. "Do what you want, just don't bother me with it," he said, and Imogen had sent Anneke to obtain a saddle that would accommodate her Ruskalder gowns, then hid in her room and cried in embarrassment and anger. Her fear of what Hrovald might do to the people she loved was starting to wear on her. If only she could strike at him…but she couldn't, and all that was left to her was to obey his whims and try not to count the days left of her captivity.

She was preparing to ride out one afternoon when a flurry of activity in the courtyard turned into half a dozen Ruskalder horses being led into the stables. "Excuse me, your Majesty," Erek said, leaving Imogen to saddle Victory alone, not that this was a hardship. She soothed her horse, unnecessarily since Victory was placid among other horses unless she was in battle.

One of the men leading the horses approached her. "You're to go into the *skorstala*, your Majesty," he said. "The King commands it."

"Why does he want me?"

"He doesn't give reasons, just orders. Now, your Majesty."

Imogen released Victory into Erek's care, shoving aside the man he was speaking to. She tried not to be rude to Erek, who was quick to anticipate Victory's needs, but today Hrovald's peremptory summons irritated her. Probably it would turn out to be some trifling thing he'd come up with just to exercise power over her. Her palms itched for her saber, which she'd left behind with the Kirkellan, fearing Hrovald might think it, too, was a "wedding present." Let him dismiss her when she had him up against the wall of the *skorstala* with her blade to his throat.

The high table had been removed, and in its place were two ornately carved chairs, one larger than the other. Hrovald sat in the bigger one, wearing a clean jerkin and a sour expression. He jabbed his thumb at the smaller chair. "Sit," he said.

"What is it?" Imogen said.

"State business. You just sit there and look like a Queen. None of this will matter to you."

Imogen sat, feeling even more irritated. He could at least give her an explanation. It was more of his nonsense about what a Ruskalder lady was supposed to do. If this took too long, she might as well not bother with a ride. She tapped her toe impatiently, then stilled it when Hrovald glared at her.

The *skorstala* door opened, admitting a handful of men who approached Hrovald rapidly. They wore tunics bearing the emblem of Ruskald, a howling crag-wolf, that looked like they'd been hastily donned over dirty white shirts and trousers stained with the grime of many days' hard travel. Their leader was a white-haired man with rosy cheeks that would have made him look cheerful if his mouth hadn't been drawn down into a grim frown. "Your Majesty," he said, going to one knee before Hrovald and bowing his head briefly.

"What happened?" Hrovald said.

"Our embassy was expelled," the man said. "King Jeffrey North learned of our actions along the Snow River."

He held out a rolled sheet of parchment to Hrovald, who took it and scanned its contents, then crumpled it and threw it at the man, who didn't flinch as it bounced off his chest. "Damned puppy," Hrovald snarled. "He thinks he can make demands?"

"No more than King Anthony did," the man said.

"Are you making excuses for him, Jafvran?"

"Of course not. I'm saying there was never any chance the Tremontanans were going to turn tail just because Dyrak—"

"Do not say that name again!" Hrovald shouted, leaping to his feet and shoving his throne back a few inches. "Dyrak was a fool and a coward. He'd have given up our rights to the Snow for the sake of a few useless trading concessions. I'm not going to let that whelp Jeffrey dictate my actions."

"We're not in any position to declare war against Tremontane, Hrovald. Unless you're willing to consider importing gun Devices from Eskandel."

"They're an abomination against the gods. If we can't defeat our enemies using our wits and our swords, we don't deserve to win. Let the heathen Tremontanans blaspheme."

"Then we're still at too much of a disadvantage against them."

"I'm not planning to declare war. Yet. For now…." Hrovald sat again and put both his hands flat on his knees. "It's unfortunate those settlements along the river keep being attacked by Ruskalder raiders. I condemn the incidents, but I can't be expected to control everyone in the country. Nothing I can do."

Imogen made a noise in the back of her throat. Hrovald really was a bastard, if he could plot the deaths of innocents just for the sake of needling another country. "Did you have something to say, wife?" Hrovald said, irritably.

"Nothing," Imogen said. He'd been right; none of this mattered to her. She was Queen in name only.

"Jafvran, this is Imogen of the Kirkellan, my new wife," Hrovald said. "Jafvran is—was—ambassador to Tremontane. Guess we'll have to find something else for you to do, eh? Wife, fetch drink for us! Let's show our guest hospitality!"

Imogen left the room, more annoyed than ever. She'd lost her chance at a ride and had to play serving maid to a handful of despicable men, one of whom never let her forget her obedience was the price for her people's safety. She wished more than ever that she dared saddle Victory and just ride away from Ranstjad. Today she almost felt reckless enough to do it.

She had to dine with Hrovald and his officers in the evenings; there was no getting around that. She was the only woman at the high table and the only woman in the room who wasn't a server. It made her sick to think of how many of her people these men had killed, until she remembered her people had killed any number of Ruskalder too. Her new role had changed her perspective, and not, as far as she was concerned, for the better; she didn't *want* to see things from the Ruskalder point of view.

And yet…it probably should have occurred to her that Ruskald had its share of women and children and families, and most of them had lives they tried to live as war raged around them. Her minders were all kind and didn't treat her like an enemy, though they occasionally laughed at her mistakes—but then Imogen laughed at her mistakes, too. Anneke was gradually relaxing around her and might, Imogen thought, turn out to be a friend.

But Hrovald's officers, particularly Karel, made Imogen nervous. She knew she was the Queen of Ruskald in name only, that her marriage was a diplomatic fiction, but most of the Ruskalder treated her as if her rank was legitimate. Karel, on the other hand, looked at her as if he were thinking about what she looked like without her clothes on and what he might do to her if he ever encountered her in that condition. It was the dress, she thought, that made her feel so vulnerable. Dressed in her usual clothes, armed and armored, she had no doubt she would be able to give the big man a workout he wouldn't soon forget. But sitting gowned at the high table with his leering attention fixed on her, she almost wanted to duck under Hrovald's arm for what little protection that might afford.

"Shouldn't you tell Hrovald what's going on?" Kionnal said, brushing Revelry's mane while Imogen looked on.

"And say what? His most trusted, most experienced warrior keeps looking at me in a funny way? I think Karel would have to assault me in front of witnesses for Hrovald to care."

"He thinks of you as his possession. Maybe he'd be jealous."

"I'd rather not put myself in his power any more than I have to. Going to him to solve my problems would be…a debt I don't want to incur. Besides, I think Karel is trying to unsettle me more than actually threaten me. If I could just stop shuddering every time he looks at me, he might stop."

"Good luck with that," Kallum said. He and two of the *tiermatha* were just returning from a ride and had caught the tail end of the conversation. "Karel gives me the shivers and I'm not even his type."

"And I bet he's not your type, either," Imogen teased him.

"Not at all. I like 'em slim and dark." Kallum dismounted and led Darkstrider to his stall. "Not that I'm interested in any of the Ruskalder, slim or fat. I'd always be wondering if my lover was waiting his chance to stab me in the back." The other members of the *tiermatha* murmured agreement.

"Have things gotten easier, in the barracks?" Imogen asked.

The *tiermatha* exchanged looks. "A little," Kionnal said. "But we always knew it would take months for them to get used to us and possibly years for them to get used to the women."

"You'll notice we still travel in packs," Kallum said. "They may not be as hostile anymore, but there's no sense giving them a chance to jump a lone Kirkellan warrior."

Imogen laid her face along Victory's cheek and heard the horse breathe noisily out her mouth with a *harrumph* sound. "I wish we could—no, forget I said anything. I'm glad things are getting easier for you."

"What about you, Imogen? It must infuriate you that Hrovald won't let you practice. Aren't you worried—" Kionnal elbowed Kallum sharply in the ribs to shut him up, but Imogen could complete the sentence for herself.

"Yes, I'm worried. Riding Victory isn't enough for what I'm giving up in losing the daily practice. But it's not like I'm going to forget how to fight, and I'll still have plenty of good years as a warrior ahead of me." They all knew what she would never say—she was losing the prime years of her fighting career, she would have to work hard to make up the loss five years from now. Imogen hadn't realized, when she'd agreed to sacrifice herself, that this was the sacrifice she'd be expected to make. She tried not to think about it. *Think about Neve,* she told herself at night, alone in her bed at three o'clock in the morning when the homesickness was worst, *think about the Kirkellan overrun by Karel and his men.* It never worked.

"Hrovald only said you couldn't fight. He didn't say no practicing tactics," said Kallum.

"I thought of that, but—" Imogen lowered her voice—"I know they're not the enemy any more, but I'd rather not hand them our tactical maneuvers." Kallum's lips went tight with anger, but he nodded. Looking at her *tiermatha,* so eager to find a way to help her, made her want to cry. She wasn't alone in this horrible place.

Three months passed, and she told herself the softening of muscle she felt was imaginary. She wrote letters home and received letters in return, which she had to read in the privacy of her room because they made her cry until her throat hurt. She'd become friends with her ladies-in-waiting and with Anneke, who turned out to have a good sense of humor and no fear of Victory. Imogen would take Anneke up in front of her on the uncomfortable saddle and the two would have leisurely rides across the plains. Autumn was coming and the green grass had turned yellow and dry, which didn't stop Victory from lipping at it whenever they stopped. They followed the river to where it entered the forest, whose green shades stood out even more against the yellow grass and the cloudless blue skies and the gray-green swirling current of the river.

"Watching the river makes me miss my family," Anneke said.

"Aren't you from Ranstjad?"

Anneke shook her head. "My family lives in Hvartfast, south of here. I came to Ranstjad to earn money. That was before Hrovald came to power."

Anneke didn't look to be more than sixteen. "How long ago was that?"

"Three years. Don't you know the story?"

Imogen stretched out on the dead grass, felt moisture creep into her thin wool gown, and thought better of it. "I only know Hrovald defeated the old King," she said, sitting up.

Anneke plucked blades of grass and began plaiting them. "Hrovald built support for himself in the army," she said. "He attacked Ranstjad in the night and killed Dyrak and as many of his guard as he could find. The rest—there's an old tradition, says anyone who fights to defend the old King is guilty of treason against the new King. So some of them fled. And nobody wanted to challenge Hrovald."

"But did that really make any difference? We kept on fighting the Ruskalder—sorry—without noticing a change. It wasn't until my *matrian* made peace overtures that we even knew Dyrak was dead."

"Dyrak was a good King," Anneke said. "Hrovald…he changed a lot of things. We're not all as warlike as you think. Yes, I know, we wanted your territory and your horses, but Hrovald turned it into a sort of…male privilege ritual." She tossed her plaited mat of grass into the air and watched it drift to the ground. "We've never had women warriors, but Dyrak would have let you fight. I've heard he respected the Kirkellan warriors regardless of what sex they were."

Imogen hugged her knees. "I always thought Ruskalder fought because they love fighting."

"Well, I always thought Kirkellan slept with their horses and never bathed," Anneke shot back, grinning. Imogen laughed.

"I guess we both had some wrong assumptions," she said, standing and dusting off her rear end, which was damp." She offered her hand to Anneke and pulled her to her feet. "Shall we ride a little farther before we go back?"

The first snow fell that afternoon. Watching the snow through her window, Imogen felt the first genuine pleasure she'd had since coming to Ranstjad. Snow in the Eidestal was a cold, miserable thing that forced the Kirkellan to huddle inside their tents around camp-stoves and wait impatiently for clear weather, horse-riding weather. Now she stood in her bedroom, which was heated by another of those ingenious Devices, warm and cozy with a glass of wine in her hand, watching the puffy flakes fall over the courtyard, and thought, *This isn't so bad,* and felt guilty at thinking it. But not much.

The snow was less exciting the more there was of it. In the Eidestal, snow blew in from the roof of the world and passed straight through to Veribold, never drifting more than a few inches high. Here, so close to the Spine, the snow fell and fell and didn't go anywhere, piling high against the wooden houses of Ranstjad and heaping in the corners of the courtyard as the weeks passed. Anneke told Imogen the few passes south, which at the best of times were impassable to more than small groups of travelers, would soon be closed to all but the most foolhardy; even the river was too dangerous to travel at this time of year. Imogen couldn't see that it made any difference, since Ruskald and Tremontane were now only a heartbeat away from war and were unlikely to have a good trading relationship. Traffic between the Kirkellan and Ruskald continued unhindered, and as long as she still got letters from home, the condition of the passes meant little to her.

Victory loved the snow. Imogen forgot this every year, and every year she was surprised again at how eager her horse was to get out into it. With her shaggy winter coat, the cold bothered her not at all, and when after three days of no riding Imogen finally gave in to Victory's big pleading eyes, the horse romped through the shallow drifts like a three-month-old filly, bouncing Imogen until she had to pull her up sharply with a stern word. Eventually she dismounted and watched the silly creature trot around, throwing up her head like a girl tossing her hair in the wind. It was ten minutes before Victory tired of her game, at which time Imogen was trotting in place and blowing on her fingers to keep warm. She mounted, took the reins in her numb fingers, and decided it was time to go home.

There were two strange horses in the stables when she rubbed Victory down, but aside from noticing they weren't nearly the quality of her own horse, she didn't pay much attention to them. She kissed Victory's broad nose and strolled across the courtyard to the small door that led to the wing where her room was. There was more activity in the courtyard than usual, warriors rushing from the great hall out of the courtyard, horses being saddled up, but nobody paid her any attention.

Back in her room, Imogen quickly stripped out of her riding dress and struggled into a green dress that was, all right, maybe she'd gained a few pounds, but they looked good on her even if they did make her clothes a bit too tight. Where was Anneke? She reached her arms around to her back and concluded there was no way she was going to get it fastened up by herself. She sat on her bed and stewed. If *she* were in charge of clothing, all dresses would fasten up the front so a woman could put her own clothes on and not be dependent on someone to dress her, as if she were an infant.

She had almost decided to put her Kirkellan clothes on so she at least wouldn't be trapped in this room, and Hrovald be damned, when Anneke hurried in, flushed with excitement. "Sorry, sorry, sorry," she exclaimed, going to fasten Imogen's dress. "It's just that everything's a madhouse down there. Did you see her? They must have passed you, if you were out riding."

"See who?"

Anneke fastened the last button and spun Imogen around to face her. "The Princess of Tremontane," she said, her eyes wide. "Four of Hrovald's riders pulled her out of a carriage wreck and brought her back to Ranstjad. *Elspeth North* is in the great hall right now."

Chapter Six

Imogen ran down the stairs as quickly as she could, then stopped to catch her breath before entering the *skorstala.* A North in Ranstjad. What under heaven was she doing this far from home? Why hadn't the riders taken her south? Her presence in Ruskald, even if perfectly innocent, could be pretext for the King of Tremontane to march to war. Heaven only knew what Hrovald had in mind.

Having recovered her composure, Imogen swept through the door and into the *skorstala.* Hrovald and a slender blond girl seated at the high table looked up at her entrance. Hesketh, standing near the fireplace, kept his gaze on the floor as usual.

"Wife!" Hrovald shouted. "Come and meet our guest. Your Highness, this is my wife, Imogen of the Kirkellan. Wife, meet Elspeth North."

"I'm pleased to make your acquaintance," the blond girl said in perfect, unaccented Ruskeldin. She was short and slender and altogether the kind of girl who made Imogen feel like a giant, which irritated her. Elspeth looked young, no more than sixteen, and had delicate features like Dorenna, huge brown eyes like Kallum, and porcelain skin like no one Imogen had ever met. Her smile when she extended her hand to Imogen was shy, but her gaze was direct, and she showed no fear at being in the heart of an enemy stronghold.

"Her Highness was traveling from Veribold when the last storm came up and caused her carriage to go astray," Hrovald explained.

"My driver went for help," Elspeth said, "but I'm afraid she was lost in the snow."

"Terrible storms we get up here," Hrovald agreed. "It's fortunate for you my riders were patrolling the border. I hope you weren't too inconvenienced."

"No, they were very kind. I really am most grateful." Elspeth sipped her wine. "I just hope I can return home soon."

"Impossible," Hrovald said, looking downhearted, which told

Imogen he was faking. Downhearted was not an emotion Hrovald entertained. "The passes through the Spine of the World are dangerous even in good weather. With winter upon us, they're closed to all traffic until spring. The only people who get through, this time of year, are my runners, and they take their lives in their hands every time they go. I've sent one to your brother the King—wouldn't want him to worry—but I couldn't allow you to try that route, not after we've gone to all this trouble to save you." He laughed heartily.

Elspeth looked dismayed. "But I can't stay here all winter! I'm going—I mean, I have so many things I'm responsible for, back home!" She now looked as if she were trying very hard to hold back tears. Imogen's irritability increased. The girl's helplessness seemed exaggerated, her tearfulness a weapon to induce sympathy in everyone around her. *Wait until you're stuck here for five years, Princess.*

"Don't take it so hard, your Highness. We'll make you as comfortable as we can. Wife, see to our royal guest's needs. Two outlanders like you, you should get along well." Hrovald drained his cup and slammed it down on the table, making Elspeth jump. He shoved his chair back. "Until suppertime, then," he said, and strode out of the great hall to the courtyard.

Elspeth stared into the fireplace as if it were a window on her southern home. After a few moments of this, Imogen cleared her throat, and Elspeth jumped again and turned to look at her. "What am I to do, your Majesty?" she said in a quiet voice. Her brown eyes brimmed with tears.

"You can call me Imogen, for a start," Imogen said, "and we'll see about a room for you, your Highness." Far from garnering her sympathy, the girl's tears annoyed her. She might be a hostage against the King of Tremontane's good behavior, but eventually he'd give Hrovald what he wanted, and the girl would be back with her family. Hardly any time at all.

Elspeth nodded. Then her face crumpled and the tears spilled over her cheeks, and her shoulders shook as she tried to suppress her sobs. Despite herself, Imogen felt a pang of sympathy and knelt on the floor and grasped the girl's shoulders. "There's no need for tears," she said. "You'll be comfortable here and the time will pass quickly." It was a lie, but no sense making the oversensitive Princess cry harder.

"I know you're not stupid," the girl said, as quietly as she could between sobs. "The passes are closed, but farther west the way south is open all the way through the Riverlands. You know Hrovald won't let me go until Jeffrey gives him what he wants. That messenger sent his terms to my brother. I'm not a guest. I'm a hostage."

Her quiet words startled Imogen, who'd forgotten that however delicate the Princess might seem, she couldn't possibly be ignorant of the political realities of her situation. Based on what Jafvran had said, Tremontane was only inches from being at Ruskald's throat, and Hrovald was ruthless enough to take any advantage he could, even if it was in the person of a sixteen-year-old girl.

"What does Hrovald want?" she asked. Elspeth shook her head, but her sobs intensified, and Imogen had the feeling Elspeth knew very well what Hrovald wanted, and it was something that would be very hard for the King to give up, sister or no. Maybe Elspeth wasn't exaggerating her misery, after all.

She looked down on the shining blond hair and felt some of her resentment fade away. She stroked Elspeth's head and murmured, "Shh, shh, it will be all right. Hrovald won't dare hurt you, and I'll watch out for you, and the time will pass before you know it. And for all we know, your brother will think of a plan to get you back without paying ransom. So dry your eyes and let's see about finding you a place to stay. I think there is a room across from mine that's empty. They have Devices and everything."

They went up the stairs, where Elspeth looked at the room Imogen showed her with dismay. "It's...rather rustic, isn't it?" she said, picking at the gray wool blanket covering the bed as if hoping it might change into something else. Imogen could only imagine the luxury of the palace in Aurilien, if Elspeth could turn up her nose at two light Devices and a heater and even a Device that went inside the mattress to warm the bed at night. Imogen felt defensive of her adopted home, which surprised her, and prepared some responses for any disparaging comments the Princess might make. But the girl had good manners and didn't complain at all.

Imogen sent Anneke in search of some clothing Elspeth could change into, her own being wet and stained from her journey, and sat and talked to the girl while they waited. Imogen was surprised to learn Elspeth was actually eighteen and a student of languages—"I have a gift for it, it's why I speak Ruskeldin so well"—at the University of Kingsport. Imogen wasn't sure what a university was, but she gathered it was a great honor to attend it. Elspeth, for her part, was horrified by the *banrach* and only imperfectly concealed her horror. But she blushed when Imogen said, "I wish I was back home, but if I can prevent a war, then I think I can endure it for five years," and replied, "I feel silly, now, for protesting a wait of only a few months."

Anneke brought back armfuls of clothing, including undergarments and nightgowns. "No, please stay," Elspeth begged when Imogen would have left her to change, so Imogen sat facing the door to give the girl—young woman, really, but though she was only a year younger than Imogen, she seemed much younger—some privacy. Some of her irritation returned. The Princess was so *needy*. True, she was in the house of her enemy, but so was Imogen, and *she* didn't need company in her dressing chamber. Then she was ashamed of herself. Elspeth had been coddled and protected her whole life; she couldn't be expected to face challenges the way a warrior of the Kirkellan would. And she was bearing up well, all things considered. Perhaps she did cry a bit more than Imogen would have, but she remembered sobbing over her letters from home and the tears she shed in the privacy of her bedroom at three o'clock in the morning and felt like a hypocrite. She determined to be kind to the Princess and ruthlessly chased away her irritation.

"Will you help me button this?" Elspeth said. Imogen turned around and began fumbling with the tiny buttons.

"Maybe Anneke should do this," she said.

"No, please, I'd rather have you—unless it's beneath you. I'm sorry, I forgot you're the Queen." Elspeth sounded so dismayed that Imogen laughed.

"No, it's not beneath me. In fact, it might be beyond me." She finished with the last button and Elspeth started rooting around for a pair of shoes that would fit. It seemed most of them were too large. Imogen said, "So your brother Jeffrey, he's the King of Tremontane? I thought the King was named Anthony."

"That was our father. He died three years ago, very suddenly, just after our oldest brother Sylvester adopted out of the family and made Jeffrey the heir."

"I don't understand what 'adopted out' means."

Elspeth held up a pair of shoes, examined them critically, then tossed them aside. "In Tremontane, when you get married, you make oath to your spouse's family, or he makes oath to yours, and that's being adopted. Pass me that shoe, please? Sylvester's wife is Baroness of Silverfield, and she would have had to give that up to adopt into the North line, so Sylvester gave up his bond to our family instead. It was a surprise, really. Oh, these fit well, don't you think?"

"They look comfortable." Elspeth looked just like a life-sized doll, slender and short with those tiny feet. Imogen felt a pang of jealousy. She was comfortable with her body, liked how curvy and plump she was, but looking at Elspeth North made her wonder what it would be like to be small and dainty and helpless and have people clamoring to take care of her. Then she thought of how Elspeth acted younger than her years, and how fragile she seemed, and wondered if Elspeth behaved the way she did because she'd been treated like a doll all her life. Why would Imogen want other people to take care of her when she was clearly capable of taking care of herself? She thought of Victory, and her *tiermatha*, and the jealousy melted away.

"Who was that young man standing by the fireplace?" Elspeth asked, pulling on a soft-sided pair of boots.

"Hesketh. Hrovald's son by his second marriage." Imogen thought about commenting on the young man's personality, or lack thereof, but decided that would be catty. Time enough for Elspeth to figure it out herself.

"Are you his third wife, then?"

"Fourth. His first wife divorced him, which might account for his attitude toward all women. His second wife died giving birth to Hesketh. His third wife died of lung fever about four years ago. And now there's me."

"But you aren't...you don't...." Elspeth stammered to a halt. Imogen, puzzled, looked at her blushing face and figured it out.

"No, didn't I say? The *banrach* is a marriage...not exactly in name only, but a marriage of spirit and not of the flesh. I can't even imagine having sex with Hrovald." She shuddered. "I've never met his mistress, but I know he has one, so he enjoys sex, but I don't think he likes women except in their proper place, which is either in his bed or out of his sight."

Elspeth's blush had intensified. "So you've never...made love with him...."

"No. Not with anyone, actually. I've never found the right partner. And I'm a little superstitious about birth control—one mistake and say goodbye to your *tiermatha* for two years."

"You don't—I mean, the Kirkellan don't wait for marriage?"

"Not really. Though we don't have sex with anyone we wouldn't want to have children with, just in case. Why, is that a custom of your people?"

Elspeth nodded. She was so red Imogen started to worry about her. What a strange country Tremontane was, to make sex both a mystery and an embarrassment. Or maybe it was just girl-woman Elspeth's reaction. "It strengthens the marriage bond if you wait to make love until after it's formed," Elspeth said.

"I don't understand what a marriage bond is."

"It's when you swear oath to your husband or wife and the lines of power bind the oath. It's like an extension of the bonds that tie our families together."

"We don't have anything like that. Neither do the Ruskalder."

"There are more lines of power in Tremontane than anywhere else. It's like when you wrap yarn into a ball, right? The strands are closest together at the top and bottom and spread out wider everywhere else.

That's the example my history professor used, anyway. She said the more lines of power, the stronger the influence they have on earth, and the better able they are to bind people together. I don't know how to explain it better than that."

Imogen had never heard of anything like that. She knew what lines of power were, that they tied heaven to earth and, according to Anneke's Deviser, provided the magical energy that powered all Devices, but that they might affect the oaths people swore...? She had an image of the *banrach* bound not by her oath or Hrovald's, but by heaven's presence. Would that even be breakable? This was definitely not a conversation she'd pictured having with the Crown Princess of Tremontane, not that she'd pictured having *any* kind of conversation with the Crown Princess of Tremontane, ever.

"Take whichever clothes you want," she said, derailing the conversation so Elspeth's color could return to its usual pink-and-white, "and Anneke will dispose of the rest. Then I think you should come to meet Victory."

Victory liked Elspeth as much as she did Anneke, which either said something for the horse's perceptiveness or said Victory would like anyone who fed her raw vegetables between meals. "I've never seen a horse as big as her before," Elspeth breathed, her eyes shining. "I have a horse at home, but he's nothing special. I mostly ride him in the Park. Jeffrey doesn't really care for horses."

"I'll take you for a ride in a day or so, after the next storm blows over," Imogen said, rating the King of Tremontane down a few notches. "And—oh, Saevonna, come and meet Elspeth North."

Saevonna was leading Lodestone past the stables, followed by three others of the *tiermatha*, but turned aside to join Imogen. "Elspeth, this is Saevonna, a member of my—I mean, Hrovald's *tiermatha*. That's a Kirkellan warband, very highly trained and deadly in combat. And that's Jathan, Lorcun, and Maeva. There are eight others, wandering around—where *is* everyone, Saevonna?"

"Kalain, Revalan and Aden went into town looking for entertainment. And before you say anything, yes, Dorenna told them to behave themselves or you'd make 'em dance naked in the snow. The others are still at the practice yard. It was a good day, Imogen. Nobody tried to start a fight and we had some practice bouts with some of the Ruskalder. Things might be looking up."

"I'm not getting my hopes up too high, but that does sound promising."

"I'm not going to get excited until one of those men is willing to fight *me*. So we may have a year or so to go." Saevonna rolled her eyes. "I have to take care of Lodestone now. She hasn't been feeling well and I feel bad making her haul me around. A pleasure to meet you, miss."

"She didn't know who I am," Elspeth said in a low voice as they left the stables.

"You'll find a lot of people here don't know the North name," Imogen said. "I don't know how you feel about that."

Elspeth considered. "I think I'd like to be unknown for a while," she said finally. "It feels safer to be anonymous. To not be someone whose name makes her a pawn. I *hate* being a pawn."

Imogen privately thought Elspeth's surname was like a shield, but she couldn't argue with the girl's logic. "You can join me and my ladies in the morning, if you want," she said. "It's boring, but it's not as boring as staring south out your window wishing you could fly." Elspeth blushed again. No wonder she seemed younger than she was, if she blushed at absolutely everything. "And—" Imogen was struck with an idea. "I don't suppose you'd be willing to teach me your language? I'm probably not as quick a study as you are, but it would give us both something to do and I wouldn't mind having the skill."

Elspeth's blush faded, and she smiled. "I'd enjoy that," she said.

Elspeth turned out to be a charming companion. Imogen's ladies-in-waiting were nice but subservient, Anneke was a good friend but lacked the common experience that would make them truly close, and she hardly ever saw the women of the *tiermatha*. Elspeth, on the other hand, was, despite their cultural differences, of the same rank as Imogen, which gave them things in common Imogen had never had with anyone before.

Elspeth was endlessly patient with Imogen's struggles with Tremontanese; Imogen, for her part, found she could keep up with Elspeth's discussions of politics more easily than she'd believed. It seemed her mother's tutelage hadn't been wasted. Between her lessons with Elspeth, her needlework, and her rides on Victory, Imogen found the short winter days passed quickly.

"I am to make – no, *making* – *a scarf for I* – damn – *me,"* Imogen said, waving a length of knitting at Elspeth. "Only it's terrible and it looks more like a noose than a scarf," she added, reverting to Ruskeldin.

"Your Tremontanese is much better, though." Elspeth stuck her knitting needles into her ball of wool and stretched. "Agneta, is it time for a rest?"

Imogen's lady-in-waiting shook her head. "Your Highness should show more diligence. How will you care for your family's needs if you cannot master the wifely arts?"

"I'll pay someone to knit for me," Elspeth said grouchily.

"The Kirkellan don't knit," Imogen added. She laid down her knitting and sighed. *"I am tired of the knitting,"* she said in Tremontanese. *"I wish to do the* – what's the word for embroidery, Elspeth?"

"We say *needlework,"* Elspeth said. "And that bores me too. My mother tried to make me a needlewoman and I just couldn't sit still for it."

"I like the needlework," Imogen said, reverting to Elspeth's language. *"It is*…um…*peaceful. We listen* – no, *hear much with the hoop in the hand."*

"Now if you can just learn to drop your articles, you'll be most of the way to fluency."

"Then I will speak the three languages. Damn. *Three languages.* I don't suppose you'd teach me to swear in Tremontanese?"

"I don't know any swear words."

"I don't believe you."

"Well, I'm going to pretend I don't, anyway. Agneta, *please* tell me it's dinner time?"

CHAPTER SEVEN

One morning near the end of the year Imogen was startled to find Hrovald at the breakfast table before her. "Sit," he ordered, not looking up from his meal. Imogen sat, and told herself she'd been planning to do that anyway. "The Samnal starts in less than a week, so you'd better start readying the rooms for our guests."

Imogen felt the dizziness Hrovald's statements usually left her with. "What's a samnal?"

Now he did look at her, eyebrows furrowed. "Mean to say you're the daughter of a chief and you don't know anything about your enemies? The Samnal is when all the chiefs come to this house to talk business and pretend they don't want me to choke on a chicken bone and die. It's your job to play hostess. Start figuring out where you're going to put everyone and what you're going to feed them. They're here for five days. It should be five days that remind them of why I'm the King, understand?"

"I understand. I'll be ready."

"Good. Eat up. Don't bother with that swill, it's gone off. Call for a new cask." Hrovald shoved his mostly empty trencher aside and stood. "Find something for Hesketh to do. I don't want him moping in a corner. Makes the chiefs think I'm weak, with an heir like him. I don't suppose you'd be interested in bearing me another one?" He roared at his unfunny joke, and Imogen managed a smile that lasted until he left the room. Then she buried her face in her hands and sighed deeply. Host the Samnal. She had no idea what that meant. Fortunately, she knew who did.

She'd sought out Inger, the chatelaine of the King's house, the first week she was there. She didn't know what a chatelaine was, but from Anneke's explanation, she learned Inger was the one who ran the house and knew where everything was. That sounded like a good person to have on her side. Inger, for her part, had been standoffish until she realized the new Queen didn't want to interfere with her work, and it didn't take long after that for them to become friends.

"Already working on it," Inger told her later that morning. "The oxen are coming for the slaughter, we've broken open the stores of ale, and a team of men are out clearing the grounds for the camps. The chiefs all bring an honor guard," she explained when Imogen looked puzzled, "but they have to camp outside the walls because we don't have room for them, and since the chiefs all stay at the King's house they aren't much of a guard, see?" She snorted and waved away a man who wanted her attention. "Part of Hrovald's plan to remind everyone who's King around here, not like they'd be forgetting that with his army just around the corner."

Imogen nodded. Inger was a tall, heavyset woman with red hair pulled back tightly from her face. She wore a ring of keys jangling at her waist that she played with when she was at rest, as she was now. Her long fingers clinked the keys together, one at a time. "Does Hrovald really need to intimidate his…subordinates all the time?" Imogen asked.

Inger shrugged. *Clink.* "Came to power through treachery, probably fears he'll go the same way," she said in a lowered voice after looking around to see no one was close enough to hear. "Or maybe he just likes having power over people. I notice he never calls you by your name when he can say 'wife' instead, like he owns you."

Imogen had noticed this as well. "So what am I responsible for, during this Samnal?"

Clink clink clink. "Playing the hostess during meals and the entertainments. Making sure the chiefs' needs are met—you just bring their requests to me, if it's something you can't do. Handing out prizes for the competitions. I wish we still had these in summer. So much easier to host…we could have the entertainments in the courtyard instead of the *skorstala*, and the competitions are fiercer."

"Why isn't it held in summer?"

Inger scowled. "To show everyone if Hrovald wants a thing, they all have to jump to make it happen." She rattled her keys once more. "You should probably spend more time back here while we're preparing, give you an idea of what to expect. And I'd warn those Kirkellan warriors not to be drawn into the competitions. Bad enough losing without losing to a foreigner."

Imogen's days now became much busier, leaving her little time to ride and even less to visit with her friends, though she did pass Inger's advice along. She learned a great deal about how the King's house was run, enough that when the first runners came from the gate shouting that the chiefs had come, she felt confident she could give the impression she was Queen in fact as well as name.

She stood beside Hrovald on the steps to the main house, shivering in the cold breeze that swept eddies of snowflakes across the frozen ground. Hrovald didn't seem disturbed by the cold. He wore a finely stitched shirt and unstained leather jerkin, and his boots looked expensive and not of Ruskalder or Kirkellan make. In front of them the *tiermatha,* dressed in their finest Kirkellan armor, was drawn up in two rows, standing at attention like a colonnade of statues and looking fierce and foreign. Hrovald had tried to exclude the women from the formation, but the entire group had gone stony and Hrovald had backed down. Imogen thought he might have been intimidated and felt a moment's pride in her *tiermatha*. At least someone was allowed to stand up to him.

They watched the gate swing open and a double column of warriors march through, followed by a man on a Kirkellan horse of very high quality. So Hrovald had shared out his goodwill gift with his underlings. An excellent ploy for keeping them satisfied.

This man, however, didn't look satisfied. His full beard obscured most of his features, but his eyes were stern and his heavy eyebrows furrowed over a beaky nose. He wore thick furs over a rigid leather jerkin and his gloved hands held the reins as if he were prepared to pull his horse around at the least provocation. "Hrovald," he said neutrally, and saluted him.

"Ingivar," Hrovald said with a smile and a salute. "Welcome to my house."

"Your house is far more welcoming than it was last year," Ingivar said, bowing to Imogen. "We are all pleased to have a Queen again. I give you good morning, your Majesty."

"I give you good morning, Ingivar," Imogen replied. "Be welcome."

"See to the disposition of troops and return here," Hrovald said, "and we will tell great lies of battle." He smiled again. Ingivar didn't. He saluted his King again and wheeled his horse around. Imogen wondered how Hrovald dared order that man around, with his hard, stern eyes and commanding presence. Ingivar didn't look like the kind of man used to taking orders, and Imogen felt cold thinking of how ruthless Hrovald had to be to keep his chiefs in line.

They repeated the ceremony of greeting seven more times throughout the day. None of the other chiefs were as formidable as Ingivar. Knoten of Hvartfast did everything except lick Hrovald's boots; Olof of Sjoven was a huge man who didn't seem terribly bright; Jannik of Hjolden stared at the *tiermatha* as if he expected some treachery on their part. The *tiermatha* continued to fill their ceremonial duties without complaint, though when Imogen caught Saevonna's eye the woman wrinkled her nose in momentary contempt. They did not appreciate being treated as Hrovald's toys, his reminder to the chiefs that he was powerful enough to have a *tiermatha* of the Kirkellan at his command. They were even less happy when he ordered them to stand an honor guard in the *skorstala* at supper that evening, watching Hrovald and the chiefs and the officers eat without having been given food themselves. They were too well disciplined to show annoyance, but Imogen was angry on their behalf.

When the meal was finished, she watched them file out in the direction of the kitchen and longed to go after them and complain together, but Hrovald put his hand on her shoulder when she would have risen and forced her into her seat. "Not quite yet, wife," he said in a low voice, then stood and smiled a smug, possessive smile. The room went silent.

"Welcome to the Samnal! Welcome to my house! This is a time of celebration, a time to bid the old year goodbye and welcome in the new. Welcome to my wife, Imogen of the Kirkellan, and to our honored guest, Princess Elspeth North of Tremontane." A murmur went up at that, and to Imogen's right Elspeth tensed at being the focus of so much attention. "You'll show them the respect due their stations. Now! Tomorrow is for talking. Tonight is for drinking!"

He waved at the servants standing near the doors at the back of the *skorstala;* they dragged the heavy doors open and brightly-dressed women poured into the room, cartwheeling and walking on their hands and tossing balls through the air at one another. Musicians set up in one corner and began playing a lively melody with a strong thrumming beat. Male servants wheeled in a procession of kegs in cradles and brought dripping mugs to the chiefs and their men. Imogen stared in wonder at the beautiful display until Hrovald jabbed her in the side and said, "Out. Take the girl with you."

Imogen started to protest, then saw one of the officers pull a dancing girl into his lap and fondle her breasts as she kissed him. "Oh," she said, and grabbed Elspeth's hand and dragged her into the kitchens. *That* kind of entertainment. She'd heard Ruskalder celebrations could be wild, but she hadn't imagined what kind of wild they might be.

"Did you see that?" Elspeth demanded. "How could they do that to those women?"

"I'm pretty sure the women like it," Imogen said. They passed through halls thronged with servants into the kitchen, where they found the *tiermatha* lounging around eating from plates they held in their hands.

"Servants are having their meal too," Kallum said. "Nowhere for us to sit. Guess that tells us how we rate."

"Don't you know? Decorations don't eat," Dorenna said sourly. "I can't believe Hrovald thinks he can treat us like some kind of honor guard."

"Wish we could participate in these competitions of theirs," Kionnal groused. "I'd like to see his face when we trounced his best men."

"Inger's right. Nobody wants to be beaten by a foreigner. You want to ruin all the progress you've made toward being accepted?" Imogen stole an only slightly shriveled apple and bit into it. They all ate in silence for a while. Elspeth stood silent by the door, and Imogen considered her.

Had Hrovald used her to send his chiefs a message? Imogen had been watching Ingivar when Hrovald announced Elspeth's identity, and he'd looked furious for a moment before regaining control of himself. Whatever game Hrovald was playing, he'd drawn his chiefs in too, probably against their will. Imogen wondered how far Hrovald could push those men before they pushed back. They might, except for Ingivar, be lazy or stupid or afraid of Hrovald, but they commanded large parts of the Ruskalder army and were therefore a danger to Hrovald if he ever lost control. Not that he appeared to be in danger of that.

"You look farther away than usual," Kallum said, startling her out of her reverie. "Did you go somewhere nice? Somewhere not here?"

"Unfortunately, no," Imogen said. "I think I'm going to bed. I want to avoid having to fight off drunken Ruskalder, much as I would enjoy a good fight. Coming, Elspeth?"

They went the long way around, outside the King's house and across the courtyard, shivering in their thin wool dresses. "We're not in any danger, are we?" Elspeth said when they reached their wing and went upstairs. "You might be able to fight off a drunken Ruskalder, but I'm sure I can't."

"Hrovald's protection extends to both of us. Anyone who attacks us would be severely punished."

"That wouldn't be much comfort, since we'd already have been attacked."

"I was afraid you'd think of that." Imogen stopped outside their doors and took a closer look at Elspeth, whose hands were wound tightly into her skirt, and felt bad about being so quick to dismiss the girl's fears. Elspeth was right; she wouldn't be able to defend herself if one of those men decided the dancing girls weren't enough. "Look, why don't you stay with me tonight? I'm pretty sure those men have plenty of willing female company and don't need to go looking for the unwilling kind, but there's no sense taking any chances."

"I'm not a coward, Imogen."

"It's not cowardice to be sensible."

She waited for Elspeth to get her nightgown, then turned the key to lock them both in her bedroom. She lay awake after Elspeth fell asleep, thinking of Hrovald, of the Samnal, of what would happen in the days to come. Anneke said things had been different under Dyrak. Imogen wished she'd been here then. Then she laughed at herself. She *wished* she didn't have to be here at all.

CHAPTER EIGHT

The next morning Imogen was joined at the breakfast table by several visiting officers and a handful of chiefs. She made polite conversation and learned the warriors would spend the day sparring in preparation for the fights the following day, and the chiefs would sit down to discuss government and foreign policy. Imogen realized she was curious about those discussions. She'd never cared about government before, preferred to leave it to Caele and her mother, but that was before a government treaty stole her life. And she wanted to know what Hrovald's plans for Elspeth were. If he started a war with Tremontane, the Kirkellan as his allies would be pulled into it, and Imogen was sure Mother didn't want that.

She knew Hrovald wouldn't let her sit in on their discussion, but it proved remarkably easy for her to get inside, thanks to Inger. "The chiefs will see it as a mark of respect for you to serve them with your own hands," she said, "even if you are unskilled. If you flash some cleavage at them, they won't care if you drop a tankard in their laps."

Imogen rolled her eyes, but changed into her tightest, lowest-cut dress and received a lightning-fast course in serving drinks. Then she gathered a double handful of wooden mugs, pushed the door to the *skorstala* open with her rear end, and backed quietly into the room.

"—not sure trade won't suffer as a result, but it's worth trying," said one of the men whose name Imogen didn't remember.

"It's been working in Sjoven for the last year," Olof said. "Keep an open mind."

"Fair enough," Hrovald said. "What's next? What are you doing in here, wife?"

Imogen stayed calm in the face of his roar. "Is it too early for drink, then? I thought you wanted me to show respect for our guests." She leaned over to set two mugs down and heard the chief to her left suck in a breath. *Yes, I do have magnificent breasts, don't I? Too bad for you this is all you're ever going to see of them.*

Hrovald studied her with narrowed eyes. "Don't get in our way," he said, then, to the chiefs, "We need to discuss taxes. I'm not seeing the kind of revenue stream I need to maintain the army. Why have collections dropped?"

"We're recovering from five years of war," Ingivar said. It was hard to read his expression behind all that hair, but he sounded neutral, as if his King hadn't just implied his chiefs were holding back taxes. "The economy needs some time to regrow. If we didn't maintain a standing army—"

"Let's not go over that argument again," Knoten said. "The King is conscious of security. We don't want to leave ourselves open to invasion."

"By who? The Kirkellan are our allies. Veribold isn't interested in expanding its borders. Or do you know something about Tremontane we should be privy to?" Now Ingivar was becoming angry. "Something to do with that tiny blonde you exhibited at supper last night?"

"Yes, why *is* the Princess of Tremontane here?" Jannik said. "Jeffrey North won't go to war over the Riverlands, but he might go to war over her. She's a liability."

"Hrovald knows what he's doing," Knoten said.

"My reasons are my own," Hrovald said. "She's our guest until the passes clear. That's all."

"Nothing to do with your vendetta, then? I find that hard to believe." Ingivar made a gesture that silenced Knoten.

"You think I arranged to pull Elspeth North out of the snow? I'm not saying she doesn't provide us with an attractive bargaining chip, but I intend to deal honestly with Jeffrey. As long as he gives me what I want."

"Then it *is* about your vendetta."

Hrovald slammed his tankard down on the table and shouted, "Do not question my motives or my authority! I will use the girl to get us concessions from Tremontane that will make it difficult for them to go to war against us. If you think that's not enough, then challenge me and see if you can do better."

Ingivar stared back at Hrovald, expressionless in the face of the

King's wrath. "I don't want to quarrel with my King," he said. "You understand the situation better than I do."

Hrovald glared at him, then sat down at the table. "I believe we were talking about taxes," he said in a mild voice that had no trace of the anger he'd displayed so explosively seconds before. "The army must still eat. Any suggestions?"

Imogen stood, and served drinks, and collected empty mugs until her feet hurt. She learned a great deal about the trade goods Ruskald produced, and its relations with Veribold, and provisions for refurbishing a number of old churches. She listened to an argument about whether some of the troops should be mustered out, an argument that devolved into a shouting match between two of the chiefs, which Imogen the warrior found fascinating. The Kirkellan had no standing army, just warriors the *matrian* could call together in time of war. The idea of being told not to be a warrior anymore was strange. The chiefs said nothing about the Kirkellan and nothing more about Elspeth or Tremontane. By the time the meeting adjourned, Imogen only knew three things: the Tremontanan King and Hrovald had bad blood between them, her feet hurt, and she had inadvertently volunteered to serve drinks at every private meeting the chiefs had in the next four days.

She went back to her room, kicked off her shoes, and massaged her feet. *I wonder what the odds are of getting someone to do this for me. Not good, probably.* Someone knocked on her door, and Elspeth peered around it without waiting for an invitation. "Where did you go?" she asked peevishly.

"I was attending the Council meeting as a serving wench. Come all the way in and shut the door. You know I'm not here to entertain you. What have you been doing all morning?"

"Sitting around doing nothing. I was afraid to go anywhere without you."

"You could have asked one of the *tiermatha* to babysit you."

"I'm not a baby, Imogen."

"Then stop acting like one." Imogen closed her eyes and took a deep breath. "I'm sorry. I shouldn't have said it that way. What I meant was, you're a grown woman and you can take action for yourself. And if you stay in public places you can guarantee you'll be safe from being attacked."

Elspeth sat on the bed next to Imogen. "I'm sorry I'm not as brave as you."

"You're brave in different ways. You don't let Hrovald cow you, which is more than some of his chiefs can say."

"I guess that's true." Elspeth bit her lower lip and turned away. "What is it now?" Imogen said.

"Nothing. I just…wish I was home."

"I wish we were certain Hrovald's message reached your brother. It would be awful for him to go the whole winter believing you were lost, or dead."

"Oh, Jeffrey knows where I am," Elspeth said absently.

"What do you mean? Did Hrovald tell you the message went through?"

Elspeth's face went paler than usual."…Yes," she said.

"You are a terrible liar. How does the King know where you are?"

Elspeth went to the door, looked both ways down the hall, then shut it and returned to stand in front of Imogen. "You can't tell *anyone* what I'm about to tell you," she said in a voice barely above a whisper. "Not even the *tiermatha*. No one. Understand?"

"Not really, but I promise," Imogen said. Her friend's small face had never looked so serious.

"Do the Kirkellan have inherent magic?"

That was a direction Imogen hadn't imagined this conversation taking. "You mean the *cadhaen-rach*? Of course. It's not very common, though. I only know of three people in the kinship who have it."

"But you don't think there's anything wrong with it."

"Why should I? It's mostly harmless tricks, a few useful skills, but hardly wrong."

"In Tremontane people are afraid of it. Hundreds of years ago the country was practically ruled by people called Ascendants who used source—you know, the magic that builds where lines of power cross?

Anyway, they used source to dominate the kingdom, made people do what they wanted, until they were finally overthrown, but for a long time anyone who was even suspected of having inherent magic, even if they weren't Ascendants, might be killed. Even now, if you have inherent magic people might try to drive you out of business, or shun you, or refuse to sell to you. It doesn't matter what talent you have, unless it's something obviously useful like healing."

"And I take it you're working up to telling me your brother has some kind of inherent magic."

Elspeth nodded. "He always knows exactly where any member of his family is. So he knows I'm alive and he can work out I'm in Ranstjad. Simple, right? No threat to anyone. But the Ascendants were so closely tied to the Valants, the last royal family before the Norths, that part of what brought Willow North to power was the fact that she didn't have inherent magic. If people in Tremontane knew their own King was…tainted, it could mean the end of his rule. So you absolutely cannot tell anyone, please?"

She looked so serious Imogen wanted to smile, but suppressed the urge, knowing Elspeth would be insulted and hurt that Imogen didn't take her seriously. And if Tremontanans did have such a prejudice against the *cadhaen-rach*, her fears weren't really anything to laugh at.

"I swear by watchful heaven I won't tell anyone," she said. "It must have driven him nearly mad, knowing you were safe those first few days and not being able to tell anyone."

"I know," Elspeth said. "That's why I have to believe Hrovald's messenger made it there safely. I don't know if even Mother knows about his talent. I only know because I got impatient that he always won at hide-and-seek and I blackmailed him into telling me why."

"You're more ruthless than you look."

"I know. It's the only weapon I have. Can we go watch the contests? I heard today they work out who's going to compete in the challenges tomorrow. It sounds more interesting than knitting, anyway."

"All right. I just want to change my dress. Help me with the buttons." Imogen peeled off the dress, made a face at it, then found something less form-fitting. "Elspeth," she asked as the girl began buttoning the new gown, "why does Hrovald have a vendetta against your brother?"

The hands stilled against her back. "What vendetta?" Elspeth said, her voice shaky. She went back to fastening the buttons.

"I don't know, but it was something Ingivar thought might influence Hrovald's negotiations over…over you."

Elspeth fastened the last button. "He doesn't have a vendetta against my brother," she said. Imogen turned around to face her. Elspeth's face was red and she wouldn't meet Imogen's eyes. That was a strong reaction for a simple question. Imogen thought about pushing the issue, but decided against it. For now. Anything that affected Hrovald's relationship with Tremontane was something Imogen, and by extension Mother, wanted to know.

They watched the matches from an elaborate spectator stand Hrovald's men had erected the week before. It had a box near the top for Hrovald and his Queen with warming Devices embedded below the seats, so it was quite comfortable for Imogen and Elspeth. Too bad the matches were all boring. Knoten of Hvartfast had told her at breakfast the chiefs all brought their twenty best fighters, and they and Hrovald's twenty best fought elimination rounds today, wrestling and sword fighting and pole-climbing. That way only the best of the best fought in front of the King and Queen, and, incidentally, kept the King and Queen from being bored out of their skulls. Elspeth thought it was exciting. Imogen had to restrain her from cheering on her favorites, reasoning their opponents might see her favor as an unfair advantage. The fighters certainly became more energetic in her presence. Imogen felt another pang of jealousy. No one had ever brightened up like that when *she* walked into a room. All right, it was true she didn't actually want it to happen, but it would be nice if it happened *once.*

Imogen had to serve the chiefs again the next morning. Ingivar proposed a network of roads the other chiefs argued against. Imogen couldn't see why, unless it was that the money for roads would have to come out of the cost to maintain the army. Not for the first time, she wondered why Hrovald insisted on keeping those warriors ready to attack when there wasn't anyone for him to fight. Unless he really did want to invade Tremontane, but that would be stupid, particularly with the advantage Tremontane's gun Devices gave them. Maybe Hrovald's ego was invested in the army. That wasn't unlikely, but would he really waste money supporting an army that didn't have an enemy to fight?

That afternoon the *tiermatha* was once again pressed into service as an honor guard to—speaking of Hrovald's ego—escort the King and Queen and Elspeth North to the box. They ranged themselves around it on the spectator stand as if they expected someone to attack Hrovald. Imogen thought some of his chiefs might have wanted to, and if Ingivar was going to do it, he likely wouldn't care that the *tiermatha* was in his way, but the chiefs took their seats with barely a glance at Hrovald's pet *tiermatha*. To Imogen's right, Areli coughed and muffled it with her fist.

This day's contests were a lot more exciting than the previous one. Karel swept the sword fighting challenges, and even though Imogen detested him, she had to admire his skill and grace. A skinny boy from Knoten's troop won the pole-climbing contest, and she had to bite her knuckle to keep from laughing at how the mostly-naked men humped and heaved to get to the top. The wrestlers weren't nearly as good as Revalan, and Imogen darted a glance at him to see what he thought of their amateurish efforts, but he remained impassive. Areli coughed twice more during the wrestling matches, and Imogen was afraid Hrovald might get angry at her disruptions, but he remained focused on the contests, shouting out encouragement to anyone who did well, regardless of whose warrior he was.

Finally the competitions were over, and Imogen handed out prizes: an elegant Ruskalder longsword for Karel, who leered at her when she laid it in his hands as if she'd done something intimate; leather and brass belts for the wrestlers; a fur cape for the pole-climber, who looked very cold in his skimpy clothing. Imogen thought he would look better if he ate more. The *tiermatha* escorted them back to the *skorstala*, Areli coughing more frequently now. As soon as Hrovald left them for the privacy of his room (and, Imogen thought, his mistress), Imogen turned on Areli and said, "How long has that been going on?"

"Just this morning. It's just that my throat's so dry," Areli said, and coughed again. It sounded wet, not dry.

"You look like you're coming down with something. I think you should take a rest day tomorrow."

"Hrovald won't like it."

"He'll like even less having a member of his *tiermatha* coughing and wheezing and looking feverish." Areli's eyes were over-bright and her cheeks were flushed. She coughed again behind her fist.

"All right. Kionnal can keep me company."

"I said a rest day, not a screwing-each-other's-brains-out day."

"We *do* have self-control, Imogen. Besides, the way I feel, sex sounds like too much work."

"You really must be sick." Imogen swatted Areli's punch away.

Imogen thought there were fewer people at supper that night, but remembered the warriors were throwing a celebration for the winners at the camp. She wondered why Olof of Sjoven wasn't there; it wasn't like him to miss a meal. Then she accidentally caught Karel's eye, and he gave her a lascivious look. She glared back at him and forgot everything else. *I should be grateful he's not leering at Elspeth.*

The *skorstala* was, to Imogen's surprise, empty the next morning except for Hrovald, who was tearing into a steak so raw it was almost bloody. "Where is everyone?" she asked.

"Gone," Hrovald said. "You should have been up earlier. Going to take a lot of work, treating everyone."

Imogen was confused. "Where did they go?"

"Home. Don't want to stay where illness is, do they? Feel free to kick out anyone whose room you'll need for an infirmary."

"What—there's sickness? I don't understand." She felt as if she were missing half the conversation.

Hrovald shoved a chunk of meat into his mouth and chewed. "Not usually this slow, are you, wife?" he said around his mouthful. "Sickness. Here. In my house. Chiefs ran away like little girls so their men wouldn't catch it, though it's probably too late for that. It's your job to care for the sick. So get to it."

"But—what sickness?"

Hrovald swallowed and chased the steak with a mouthful of beer. "Lung fever."

Chapter Nine

Areli had lung fever. Two days later, so did Kallum, Lorcun and Dorenna. Imogen could only watch helplessly as her friends coughed and choked on the fluid filling their lungs. Hrovald's insistence aside, Imogen had no experience treating sick people and had never even heard of lung fever before coming to Ruskald. Once again she had to depend on Inger's competent, soothing presence. Imogen learned how to administer medicine to someone who was coughing so hard she could barely breathe. She learned how to change bedding and clean up those so delirious with fever they couldn't use a chamber pot. She learned how to support someone through a coughing fit, to make room in an already crowded chamber for one or two or six more beds, even to cook a thin gruel to sustain people whose appetites had disappeared with their good health.

Imogen remained healthy. She'd never been sick with anything more than a runny nose and hoped her robust good health would continue. She was even more grateful that Elspeth didn't seem affected either. The last thing she needed was the Tremontanan King's heir coming down with this potentially deadly illness. However, after the first frantic day, when new cases came in from the camp and the household every hour, things settled down. Imogen hoped that meant everyone who was going to catch it had already done so.

Three days later, they had their first fatality.

Imogen cried over the warrior, though she hadn't known him, and watched as two men—could they catch lung fever from a dead body?—carried the young man out wrapped in the sheet he'd lain on when he took his last rattling breath. Then she stripped the rest of the bedding, laid out fresh, and waited for someone else to need a dead man's bed. She knew it was morbid thinking, but after five days of fitful sleep and worry over Dorenna, who was much sicker than the rest of the stricken *tiermatha,* she couldn't help wonder how many more people would die before this thing ran its course. She refused to imagine Dorenna might be one of them.

Her life became a constant round of medicine, gruel, chamber pots, dirty bedding, clean bedding, and bodies. More bodies every day. She didn't have time to worry about Elspeth and was actually happy the girl was spending all her time in Hesketh's company. The boy was a sniveling waste of air, but if he kept Elspeth entertained—or was it the other way around?—he must not be so bad.

She'd put the *tiermatha* in a separate room, the first four now joined by Maeva and Revalan, and told the healthy ones to lock themselves in their barracks and stay away from anyone who was sick. They protested, and she shouted, "Shut up and listen! We don't know why some people get sick and others don't. We just know the sick ones all had contact with other people who had the illness. I will not watch any more of you end up in that room, do you hear me?"

Kionnal slammed his fist against the wall. "You can't keep me from her," he growled. Imogen stared him down until he turned his head away. She laid her fingers on his arm, and he jerked it away.

"I'm sorry," she said. "I really am. I promise if...if it gets bad, I'll come for you. I swear." Kionnal still wouldn't look at her, and no one said anything. She left the room so they wouldn't see her cry. Then she went back to the rest of her *tiermatha*.

Inger told her it wasn't as bad as it looked. Imogen thought it looked pretty damn bad. At least the febrifuges worked, and everyone except for Dorenna was conscious and clear-headed. They just coughed. It was a cough that sounded as if their lungs were being torn from their bodies, and from the looks on their faces it felt as agonizing as it sounded. Sometimes the coughs brought up mucus, and Inger said that was good too. The only thing she wouldn't reassure Imogen about was Dorenna's condition. Dorenna had been delirious for almost a day, and her brown hair was dark with sweat now the fever had broken. When she coughed, it was in a series of short, barking hacks that brought up no mucus and made her moan in pain when they stopped. Imogen sat beside her friend, taking her hand and squeezing it for some sign Dorenna knew she was there. No response. Her hand was dry and hot, which meant the fever was coming back, and Imogen wasn't sure she could get Dorenna to take another dose of febrifuge. She laid Dorenna's hand down gently on the blanket and stood up.

"Where's Kion—" Areli's question was interrupted by another bout of hacking.

"In the barracks with the others. I made him stay away so he wouldn't catch it. He wanted to come."

Areli nodded. "Glad you made him stay away," she said with a weak smile. "He's such a baby when he gets sick."

"Not tough like you."

"No, I—" She coughed again. "I'll be back on my feet soon. I feel better already."

Imogen felt her heart lift and had to suppress her unfounded hope. "You'll be fine soon."

"Is Dorenna…?"

Imogen looked back at that corner of the room. "No change." She didn't believe in lying to her *tiermatha*. Suppose she gave them false hope and Dorenna—she refused to complete that sentence. She patted Areli's hand and said, "I have to get back to the main room. Do you want some water?" She poured water for Areli and supported her head while she drank it, then returned to the other room to discover someone else had died while she was gone. She no longer cried for each death. There had been seventeen in eight days. Was that a lot? She didn't know. She wondered how bad it was in the rest of the city.

She didn't see Hrovald at all. He'd locked himself and his mistress in his quarters and ordered food left in the hallway and isolated himself in every other way. She kept track of Elspeth to reassure herself the girl was still well. She didn't need her wandering around the makeshift infirmary being useless and pretty. Imogen took a deep breath to dispel those cruel thoughts. It was possible Elspeth was good in a crisis, but Imogen needed her to stay away more than she needed another pair of hands, however competent they might be.

On the tenth day, Imogen entered the infirmary to see Inger sitting beside a young warrior, helping him eat some gruel. "You think your washing water is going to help a fellow get well?" he teased, making a face. His eyes lacked the feverish glitter, his skin wasn't flushed, and when he coughed, it was a normal sound, not the great hacking tearing noise she was used to. Inger looked at her, then eased the man back onto his pillow and drew her out of earshot.

"Yes, he's over the worst of it. Don't get your hopes up. It's more usual for people to stay sick with this for two weeks to a month, and the ones who get it worst don't fully recover for a month or so after that. You need to face reality so it won't kick you when you aren't looking."

"But that man *is* well?"

Inger sighed. "Seems like. We can thank the gods he pulled through. Or whatever you heathens worship." She smiled a crooked smile, and Imogen smiled back. It felt rusty, but she hadn't lost her smile entirely.

People still died, far too many people, but fewer than at first, and there were fewer still new patients. And others began to recover. Three weeks after she fell ill, Areli's cough disappeared, and one by one the *tiermatha* began to recover and rejoin their comrades. All except Dorenna, who continued dangerously ill. Imogen was grateful Kallum and Areli could take over watching her so Imogen could get some rest; she trusted Inger, but couldn't bear for Dorenna to be left alone with no one she loved watching out for her, especially if...the worst happened.

But the day came when there were so few beds filled Imogen could actually retreat to her bedroom and, fully clothed, sleep in her own bed for more than two hours at a time. When she woke, she felt rested the way she hadn't in a month. She stretched, reveling in the silence. It was shameful of her, resenting the noise the coughing patients made, but it *was* such a horrible noise, and it was so nice not to hear it—

Just as she thought that, she heard a cough outside her room. She sat up and groaned. Was some sick person wandering around up here, and why had Inger let that person get away? She got out of bed and went to the door. There was no one there. She looked at the door across from hers. A horrible dread struck her. She knocked on the door and entered without being asked.

Elspeth lay on her bed, curled up on her side and clutching her knees until her knuckles were white. Her eyes were closed, her face was flushed, and tears streaked her cheeks. As Imogen watched, she raised her head from her pillow just an inch or two and coughed a great, wet, hacking cough. She whimpered when she was done, but showed no awareness that Imogen was in the room.

Imogen swore. She rushed to Elspeth's side and picked the girl up, cradling her like a kitten. "No, no, no," she heard herself chanting as she went carefully down the stairs and into the infirmary. She couldn't put Elspeth in there. There were too many other sick people. She crossed the infirmary with her burden and went into the room where Dorenna still lay. The beds hadn't been made. "Sorry, sorry," she whispered, laying Elspeth down on a bare mattress, then rushed about finding linens and a clean pillow and making up a bed for her. *Nightgown, she needs a nightgown*, she thought wildly, and rushed back out and ran into Inger. "Get her a nightgown," she snapped, and Inger ran off without asking questions.

Imogen began undressing Elspeth, carefully, as each movement made the girl whimper again. Imogen knew the first stages of the illness were painful, but none of her other patients had reacted so vocally to being moved. She told herself it was just that Elspeth was so small, not that her illness was severe. Why hadn't she paid more attention to the girl? How long had Elspeth lain there untreated? She removed Elspeth's shoes and rolled her gingerly on her side to unbutton her dress. Inger returned with a nightgown and helped Imogen take Elspeth's dress off, then her undergarments, which were made of cotton rather than the silk Imogen was accustomed to. There were a few spots of blood on her pants—*didn't she finish her monthlies just a week ago?* Imogen thought, but didn't have time to worry about it now. They put the nightgown over her head and eased her into the bed. Elspeth opened her eyes and looked right at Imogen. "Don't let him touch me," she said, then closed her eyes as another coughing fit struck her. Imogen held her close to her chest as she weakly sobbed when it was over.

"It's all right, you're going to be all right," she said, and had an irrational but vivid picture of herself explaining to the Tremontanan King how she'd let his sister die. *That will not happen.*

Inger brought the febrifuge in a small cup. "No, you have to drink it all," she insisted gently, and Elspeth gulped it down and made a face. Imogen thought it must be good, if Elspeth was able to react like that, but then she had to hold the girl while she coughed and coughed until her lips went blue and Imogen had to strike her on the back to get her to take a breath. They propped her up on pillows and withdrew a few feet. As if in sympathy, the semi-conscious Dorenna hacked and coughed a few beds over.

"It's bad," Inger said in response to Imogen's unspoken question. "She's too little to have many reserves for fighting this. If we can't get her to eat, she might end up starving instead of coughing herself to death."

"I'll make her eat," Imogen said. "I refuse to let her die."

"That's in the gods' hands, not yours."

"Then I'll have to tell the gods they can't bloody well have her."

"Let's hope they don't listen to your blasphemy, heathen that you are."

Imogen left the care of the other patients to Inger and busied herself entirely with Elspeth and Dorenna. She made up one of the beds for herself and caught naps when she could, sleeping restlessly, jerked awake by her patients' coughing. She told herself coughing was good. Silence was…not good. She fed Dorenna once a day, most of it going down her front, but enough going into her that had it not been for her worsening cough, Imogen would have felt relief at her progress. But Dorenna continued delirious, and her coughs grew wetter but stopped producing mucus, and Inger's face when she looked at the woman was impassive, which meant nothing good.

Imogen fed Elspeth as often as the girl would let her, despairing of getting her to eat even the smallest bite of the gruel. Elspeth was periodically aware of her surroundings, but at those times she clung to Imogen as if terrified, and Imogen didn't have the heart to push her away. More often, she was delirious, and they couldn't get her fever to break. Her coughing shook her slight frame and seemed to hurt her terribly. Had Imogen not already cried out all her tears, she would have wept for the girl's pain.

A week passed. Dorenna was unconscious all the time now. Elspeth's face grew sharper as she lost weight despite Imogen's best efforts. Inger insisted they cut her hair off in the hope it would reduce her fever. The febrifuges started to work, but the fever returned as soon as the dose wore off. They tried taking her outside and packing her in snow, but it made her cry out in agony, so they brought her back to the bed and continued dosing her. She coughed, and coughed, and brought up wads of phlegm, and it didn't seem to make a difference.

Two weeks. Imogen sat by Elspeth's bedside, nodding off and waking every time the girl twitched. She hadn't slept for almost forty-eight hours, she thought, but exhaustion was the least of her worries. Dorenna was worse. She didn't cough as often, but remained unconscious, and the gruel Imogen spooned into her mouth just dribbled back out again. Elspeth's fever was currently in abeyance, though her monthly bleeding had started again, or maybe those first few drops had been an abnormality. Imogen was too exhausted to think about it further. She wiped sweat from Elspeth's forehead and tried to remember the last time she'd seen the sun. The windows were all covered because sunlight bothered the patients' eyes. Imogen wished she could go outside for even a minute, but if she was gone when Dorenna....

Elspeth coughed again, and Imogen wiped her mouth. More fluid. Inger said that was good, that if she could bring up whatever was choking her lungs, they wouldn't be so full of fluid that she couldn't breathe. She sat back and took a deep breath. The room was silent.

It was too silent.

Imogen felt her heart pound painfully, just once. She left Elspeth's side and went to Dorenna's bed. She looked far more peaceful than she did when she was awake, those delicate features looking as if they'd never heard of a sword, or a knife, or that trick she did where she dislocated her opponent's shoulder and...Imogen couldn't think anymore. She reached out to touch Dorenna's forehead, and shrieked when the woman's eyes opened and blinked at her. "Imo?" she said. "You scared me."

Imogen burst into tears and dropped to her knees beside the bed, gathering Dorenna in her arms and rocking her back and forth. "Imogen, you have to put me down, I—" She coughed, but not as painfully as before. "I hurt. And I feel so weak. How long have I been here?"

Imogen struggled to control herself. She gently laid Dorenna back on the pillow. "A long time," she said. "Six weeks."

"Damn," Dorenna said, staring at the ceiling. "I am so far off my training regimen I might as well start over."

Imogen laughed, a hoarse, disused sound. "We'll have you back in fighting shape in no time," she promised. "It's going to be a while before you can walk out of here, but...I'm so glad you're awake." She got heavily to her feet. "I'm going to give the *tiermatha* the good news. Everyone's been worried."

With Dorenna's recovery, the entire *tiermatha* recovered its spirits. Imogen wanted to rejoice with them, but there was still one patient under her care, and that one stubbornly refused to get well. Imogen's nightmares were now haunted by the King of Tremontane, who in her dreams was a blond giant with Hrovald's face who stalked her, crying out to avenge the blood of his sister. Elspeth's illness had passed into a new phase, one that none of the other patients had exhibited: delirious ravings about being attacked, pleas for help, babblings in languages none of them understood, though occasionally Imogen heard Tremontanese and was absurdly proud of being able to understand her. Her face was so thin her cheekbones stood out sharply and her wrists were so small Imogen could circle them with her hand and have her fingers nearly overlap her thumb. Imogen bathed her forehead, and fed her gruel and febrifuges, and prayed to heaven she would survive. And then she slept, and dreamed, and woke in a sweat.

She had just woken from one of these nightmares when Inger appeared beside her. "The King is looking for you," she said. Imogen thought for a wild moment that Elspeth's brother had come to Ranstjad to seek her out, then remembered there was another King closer to hand.

"Then he can come in here if he's so interested." Elspeth hadn't coughed for several minutes. Was that good, or bad?

"You know he won't come in here. He doesn't look happy."

"I don't give a damn about his happiness."

"You should, if you don't want him laying into some innocent person."

Imogen rubbed her eyes and groaned. "Would you give her her next dose? I'll be right back."

Hrovald waited for her in the *skorstala*. "Where have you been?"

"Taking care of your hostage. She's been ill."

"Stop wasting your time on her. You have duties."

"Hrovald, I don't think anything you want me to do is more important than making sure that young woman lives to be returned to her royal brother."

Hrovald slammed his fist down on the high table. "You will do as I command!"

Imogen stared him down. Her fear for Dorenna and for Elspeth had drained her ability to fear anything else. "Think again, husband," she said softly. "You have no right to force me. I am your wife because I choose to be. I follow your rules because I choose to do so. You may think of me as a Ruskalder wife, but I swore oath to a Kirkellan husband, and no Kirkellan husband has the right to insist I not follow my conscience when someone's life is at stake. So, *husband,* I intend to return to that room and continue caring for Elspeth North, and you should think very carefully about how far you're willing to go to stop me."

Hrovald glared furiously at her. His fingers curled into a fist, and briefly Imogen remembered the *banrach,* and the Kirkellan, and Ruskalder warriors slaughtering her people. If she didn't back down, what might he decide to do? *Enough,* she thought. *I'm not going to be a hostage anymore. If he breaks the treaty, it's on his head, and we Kirkellan will just have to endure. As we always do.* She straightened her spine. She wasn't some frail Ruskalder woman. She was a warrior of the Kirkellan, and she would show this man no fear.

Hrovald continued to glare, but his rage was fading. "Keep her alive," he finally said. "She's still a valuable...guest." He turned and left the *skorstala,* leaving Imogen feeling as weak as if they'd wrestled physically instead of verbally. Well, she'd have won either way.

When she went back to the sick room, Inger had Elspeth in her arms and looked at her with an expression Imogen didn't understand. She had just enough time to become afraid before Elspeth raised her head and looked at her with those enormous brown eyes. "Imogen," she said, her voice raspy as if her throat were raw, which it probably was, "I'm so hungry."

Chapter Ten

Elspeth ate like a starving person, which, Imogen thought, she probably was. Inger supervised her food carefully so Elspeth didn't vomit; Imogen, relieved beyond words that the girl was well, would have given her anything she wanted. They kept her in the room downstairs for a few weeks; she still had coughing fits and was prone to fever if she exerted herself more than to use the chamber pot. Imogen knew she was truly well when she started griping about being bored and was willing to accept knitting needles and yarn to alleviate the boredom.

"I'm tired of being in bed," Elspeth complained in Tremontanese when Imogen carried her up the stairs and settled her in her own bed. "There aren't any books in this place and I can't believe I agreed to the knitting."

"I cannot believe it either. Perhaps you are still—" Imogen didn't know the word for *delusional,* so she simply made a spiral motion with her finger near her temple. She helped Elspeth change out of the disgusting nightgown she'd worn for three weeks and put on a fresh one. Elspeth sighed with happiness."Amazing how much a clean nightgown can cheer you up," she said.

"Into bed," Imogen said, and settled her sitting upright with the blankets drawn to her waist. "I should to let you do what you want. Then I can say I tell you so when I carry you back after you fall down." Elspeth was still so thin it hurt to look at her.

"I'll stay put, but will you keep me company?"

"As much as I can. Hrovald is angry I am not there for him to yell. Or I get Hesketh. You are friends, to spend so much time together before you became ill."

Elspeth flinched and wouldn't meet Imogen's eyes. "Not Hesketh."

"Not being the friends—it is to say, you are not friends anymore?"

Elspeth shook her head. "I don't want to see him." Tears welled up in her eyes.

Imogen looked at her in concern. "What's wrong? Did Hesketh do something?"

"I don't want to talk about it. It's not important."

Imogen shrugged. "Then I will not talk. Do you want food?"

Elspeth shook her head again. "I want to sleep."

"You want to do things."

"I changed my mind. You were right, I feel tired. Will you come back in a few hours and I can eat then?"

"Yes. Now I will talk Tremontanese at people who do not understand and pretend not to understand the Ruskeldin." She'd hoped to make Elspeth laugh, but the girl just scooted down in her bed and rolled on her side to face away from Imogen. Imogen shrugged and shut the door behind her.

Elspeth was a terrible liar. Whatever had caused their falling out, Hesketh would know the truth. Unfortunately, Imogen couldn't find him anywhere. She concluded he was avoiding her, and decided she'd just have to wait for him to slip up and then—hah! she'd have him. She was slightly disturbed at how much glee she felt about tracking down the worthless little weasel, and decided she hadn't had enough exercise in the last two months. So she went to find Victory.

The horse was ecstatic to see her, though not as restive as she expected. Questioning Erek revealed the stable master himself had given Victory some exercise every day, even if it was just a couple of laps around the courtyard. Imogen thanked him so profusely he blushed, then she saddled her horse and went for a nice long ride on the plain. It was a beautiful day that matched her mood—clear, cloudless, sunny, and with a hint of spring in the air. The snowdrifts were smaller, blown away by the early spring wind, and yellow winter grass showed through in places. Victory turned up her nose at it. "I think Erek must have spoiled you, you great beast," Imogen said, patting her horse's neck. They trotted as far as the tree line and back again, then detoured to see how the *tiermatha* was doing. Aside from being too thin, Dorenna looked as if she'd never been ill. Imogen promised to come back the following day and then set off for the stables. She'd been gone much longer than she'd wanted to be, and Elspeth was probably waiting for her dinner.

Elspeth's door was open, and Imogen could hear her talking to someone, someone male. Hesketh. She crept up on them, but Hesketh's voice abruptly cut off. Accustomed as he was to avoiding his father's wrath, he seemed to have unnaturally acute hearing, or maybe he was just good at knowing when he was in trouble. He burst out of the room and shouldered past Imogen so quickly she couldn't stop him. "Hey!" she shouted, but he was down the stairs and gone.

"What was that?" Imogen said as she entered Elspeth's room, forgetting to speak Tremontanese.

"Nothing," Elspeth said, but she'd been crying again. "It was nothing."

"You don't cry over nothing."

"I don't want to talk about it."

"Elspeth, if something's wrong—"

"I said I don't want to talk about it!" she shouted, and flung her pillow at Imogen's chest. Imogen was so startled she didn't try to grab it.

"All right. We don't have to talk about it," she said. She picked up the pillow and handed it to Elspeth, who hugged it to her chest and tried so hard not to cry it was painful to watch. Imogen itched to sit on Elspeth until she gave up whatever secret she was clinging to, but that might break her, and Elspeth could be stubborn when she wanted. So instead she said, "What would you like to eat?"

Hesketh didn't try to talk to Elspeth again for the next few days. He went to ground so thoroughly Imogen knew she was never going to find him until he decided she'd stopped looking, so she did. Hrovald, on the other hand, was now underfoot all the time. He didn't mount the stairs to visit Elspeth, but he grilled Imogen on her condition, her appetite, and her recovery. He'd gone from being indifferent to Elspeth's survival to being very concerned about her health. It was unnerving. Imogen couldn't think what had made such a change in him, except he must be ready to exchange her for whatever it was he wanted the King of Tremontane to give him, and wanted to be sure his hostage was in perfect condition—or as perfect as she could be after nearly dying of lung fever. The man only cared about Elspeth, or any woman, for that matter, because of what she could do for him. Imogen's hands itched to wrap around his throat.

After a week, Elspeth had recovered enough to totter around under her own power and sit for a few hours in a comfortable chair. Despite her new independence, she pleaded with Imogen to stay with her at all times, and Imogen, remembering those mysterious tears, agreed. If Hesketh was bothering Elspeth somehow, and he was avoiding Imogen, then Imogen staying near Elspeth would keep Hesketh away from her. She watched Elspeth, her bright, shorn hair bent over her needlework in deep concentration, and remembered how she had looked lying flushed and feverish in her sickbed, and felt an unexpected love for her. She'd never had another person depend on her the way Elspeth did. Yes, her *tiermatha* looked out for her, and she looked out for them, but they didn't need her to take care of them. It felt good, knowing she could care for someone else like that. Elspeth was like a younger sister, only not one like her younger sister Neve, who roamed wild over the plains and had been known to bite unsuspecting people.

That evening, Elspeth came to the supper table for the first time since falling ill. Hrovald held her chair for her and complimented her appearance, and kept reaching across Imogen to offer her choice bites from his own plate. Elspeth was confused, Imogen suspicious. Hrovald had never been this solicitous of *her*. Of course, she hadn't fallen ill and nearly died, either, and she wasn't of strategic value...no, she was, actually, but she also wasn't tiny and delicate and needy-looking. Imogen thought the last without any rancor. Elspeth was what she was, and Imogen had discovered she liked caring for people far more than she enjoyed being cared for.

The meal was nearly over when the door crashed open and a messenger stood, panting, in the doorway. "He's coming," the man said.

Hrovald threw his knife down and climbed over the table, clipping the edge of Imogen's plate and making gravy drip over the side. "How soon?" he asked as he strode toward the messenger. They had a low-voiced conversation, then Hrovald shouted, "Clear the room! All of you, back to the barracks and await my command! And summon my *tiermatha*!"

Warriors fled. Hrovald shouted, "You, clear the table!" Servants snatched serving dishes and plates and mugs away, even though Imogen wasn't finished eating yet. "Faster! Damn you, stop dancing around like it's a celebration and get this out of here!" Imogen rose to leave the table, and he barked, "Sit down, wife! You'll want to be here for this." Then he looked at her, and at the table, and shouted, "The throne, the throne! Get this table out of my sight!"

Imogen and Elspeth backed away as servers took the high table to one side of the room and brought the ornate chair to set in its place. Imogen's smaller chair went beside it, and Hrovald gestured to Imogen to sit there. Elspeth looked confused and tired, and Hrovald shouted for someone to bring a chair for the Princess, which they put to Imogen's right. They all sat, and Hrovald looked around, then cursed and left the room, returning minutes later dragging Hesketh, whom he shoved in Elspeth's direction. "Stand over there," he said. Elspeth looked warily at Hesketh, but showed no sign of bursting into tears.

They waited. "Hrovald, what—" Imogen began, and Hrovald shushed her impatiently. Imogen subsided, irritable. The doors swung open again to admit the *tiermatha*, impeccably turned out and armed as usual. They took up their accustomed positions around the room. Imogen caught Areli's eye and raised her eyebrows in silent question. Areli gave the tiniest shrug and went back to being a statue.

They waited some more. Imogen was dying to know who was coming and why they were waiting in such state to receive him. Hrovald tapped his fingers on the arm of his chair, crossed one ankle across the other and fidgeted. She couldn't tell if he was anxious or excited. Elspeth looked as if she needed a rest. Hesketh hovered near her chair as if he wanted to touch it, but as usual kept his eyes fixed on his shoes.

The door opened. Hrovald straightened, uncrossed his ankles and put both his hands on the armrests of his chair so quickly it was as if the nervous Hrovald had never existed. The servant who opened the door stepped back to let another man enter the room. Imogen heard Elspeth make a tiny noise in her throat, but when she looked at the young woman, her face was expressionless.

The stranger was Ruskalder, tall and brown-haired, with an unmemorable face and broad shoulders. He wore a dark green cloak that brushed the floor, a leather jerkin and sturdy trousers and boots. He appeared to be unarmed. He crossed the floor in silence until he stood about ten feet in front of Hrovald, then took a parade rest position with his hands crossed behind his back. He stood there, silent, and stared at Hrovald with an expression that gave nothing away. Hrovald stared back. They remained that way for so long Imogen began to feel the urge to shout, jump up, anything to break the tension.

Finally, Hrovald said, "Well. Oujan. I didn't expect you to come yourself."

"Seemed like it would save time, all around," the man said. His voice was deep and smooth. "And I prefer Owen, now."

"Gave up your warrior's name, did you?"

"I gave up the name of a country that betrayed me."

"The country you deserted when you fought against its rightful King?"

"That's a conversation that will get us nowhere, Hrovald."

"*You will address me as your Majesty!*" Hrovald shouted, rising explosively to his feet. The man, Oujan or Owen or whatever his name was, seemed unimpressed by Hrovald's show of rage.

"As you wish, your Majesty, though we both know I'm no longer your subject."

"And yet you're here." Hrovald took his seat again. Now he was almost purring. Imogen heard Elspeth move beside her, looked at the girl and saw her face was so blank it had to be intentional. This man had to be what Hrovald wanted from the King of Tremontane. She wondered what was so special about him that Hrovald was willing to give up his considerable bargaining position with regard to Elspeth.

"You sent your terms. I'm here to fulfill them. I brought five riders to take the Princess back to Tremontane. They go. I stay."

Elspeth made another involuntary sound. Owen glanced her way, looked back at Hrovald, then jerked his head back to stare at Elspeth.

"What did you do to her?" he whispered as if he couldn't believe what he saw. Then he shouted, "You *dared* treat her so poorly!" and made a move in her direction. Lorcun and Kallum shifted position, and Owen looked at them as if noticing the *tiermatha* for the first time. He froze in place.

"Sir," Imogen said, standing so she would have his attention, "the Princess has been very ill. There was a lung fever epidemic, and she was struck particularly hard. She is only just recovered. I realize she looks ill, but I assure you I cared for her myself and have not allowed any harm to come to her."

"It's true," Elspeth said in a small voice. Owen's face was agonized, and Imogen thought, *Sweet heaven, he's in love with her. And I'll wager she's in love with him too.* No wonder the idea of being trapped away from her home all winter was so devastating. Imogen resumed her seat. There was nothing she could do. Poor Elspeth.

"You've heard my wife assure you she's well," Hrovald said. Imogen saw he was smiling, and her hatred for him increased. Did he know how Owen felt about Elspeth? Did it make his victory sweeter? "So, you've brought an escort for the Princess, and you'll stay in her place. I suppose you think that's an acceptable exchange. Dyrak's last warrior for the Princess of Tremontane."

"It's the exchange you asked for," Owen said, but he looked uncertain.

"Things have changed," Hrovald said. He pointed at Hesketh. "You see, the Princess is married to my son."

Imogen gasped and swiveled in her seat to look at Elspeth, who was crimson and again on the verge of tears. Was *this* what she'd been hiding, all this time? "But we haven't—isn't that something we should all have witnessed?"she said faintly. She couldn't bear to look at Owen. What must he think? This was some ruse of Hrovald's. There was no way Elspeth would consent to marry Hesketh, even if she'd been madly in love with him, and Imogen was certain that wasn't the case.

"You'll have to prove that," Owen said, his voice tense, and Imogen finally looked at him and saw barely contained anger. He didn't believe it either.

"Proof enough when her belly begins to swell with my grandson," Hrovath said.

Imogen felt faint. This could not be happening. Everyone was looking at Elspeth now, watching her sob into her hands. Imogen left her seat and went to kneel at Elspeth's feet, and took the girl in her arms. "Don't feel ashamed," she said in her ear. "It's not the end of the world. You don't have to marry him just because you had sex with him." Elspeth shook her head vigorously. "I know you have these…sweet, wonderful ideas about sex, and marriage, but it's all right if you made a mistake, I know it is."

Elspeth shook her head harder. "No," she cried, "no, it will never be all right ever again!"

Hrovald said, "Quiet your woman, Hesketh."

Imogen said, with a snarl, "Touch her and I swear I will rip your arm out of its socket and beat you to death with it." Hesketh, who hadn't moved at his father's command, took a few steps back.

"You know the tradition, Oujan," Hrovald said triumphantly. "Take the woman's virtue and you take the woman."

"A foul, outdated tradition only someone like you would want to resurrect," Owen said. "And not one King Jeffrey will see as binding."

"Then let him come against me in battle," Hrovald said. "By that time it will be too late. She will be bound to us by ties of birth and blood, and he will either have to repudiate her as heir or accept my son as her Consort-to-be. I wonder which way he'll jump?"

This was bad. Not only would Hrovald drag the Kirkellan into war with Tremontane, he would do it to make a play for that kingdom's Crown. All he had to do was make sure the King died in battle, and he'd hold the Crown in his hands. Hrovald in control of two countries…it didn't bear considering. And yet Imogen had to consider it, had to decide what to do, because she might not be *matrian* but she was the one on the spot. She took a breath, not sure what she was going to say, and Elspeth stood up out of her arms and dashed her tears away.

"I didn't want to," she said, her eyes fixed on Owen. "I thought he was my friend, and I felt sorry for him because his father is so awful to him—" she stopped speaking briefly to glare at Hrovald without a trace of fear—"and I thought, if he only had a friend, if he only saw he wasn't worthless, maybe he could stand up to him. I felt sorry for him, don't you understand?" She was pleading now, and Owen's face was expressionless. "I was so tired that day, I must have been sick already, and we were just talking, and—he kissed me. I didn't like it. He kissed me again, and then he pushed me, and he kept telling me not to cry, but it hurt so much and, and I'm sorry, Owen, I'm so sorry, but I couldn't make him stop...."

It took Imogen a moment to make sense of Elspeth's words. *Those spots of blood. I was so stupid.* Owen was quicker on the uptake. He roared and launched himself at Hesketh, who squealed, backed away, fell, and tried to scramble out of the way.

Hrovald shouted, "*Tiermatha*, stop that man!" and Imogen saw them break formation and lunge toward Owen, who'd managed to get his hands around Hesketh's neck and was squeezing until the boy's eyes bulged. In seconds they would be on him. Imogen stood, drew a deep breath, and screamed, "*Tiermatha*! *To me!*"

CHAPTER ELEVEN

The *tiermatha* stopped in mid-lunge and grouped themselves in a semi-circle near Imogen. Elspeth was sobbing again. Hrovald shook with rage. "*Kill him,*" he demanded.

"Sit down, Hrovald. Dorenna, make sure he does. Owen, let him go. I said *let him go,*" she repeated, as Owen either didn't hear her or didn't care to obey. She signaled to Kallum, who rapped Owen smartly on the head with the flat of his blade, then held the edge to his throat, but it was too late. There was a *snap*, and Owen released Hesketh, who fell to the floor, eyes staring, neck bent at an unnatural angle. Part of Imogen—all right, *most* of Imogen—rejoiced to see the little wart dead. But the sane part of her wished they'd stopped Owen, because she wanted to walk out of this room alive, and she judged Hrovald would be a lot more persistent about stopping them now Owen had murdered his heir in front of his face.

"*Traitors,*" Hrovald seethed. "So much for your vaunted obedience." He didn't even glance at his son's body.

"You weren't listening, Hrovald. I told you they'd obey their leader. I never said who that was." Hrovald opened his mouth to shout and Dorenna set the edge of her extremely sharp knife along the soft part of his throat. He shut his mouth again. Imogen looked around for inspiration. So. Hesketh dead. Hrovald furious but restrained for the moment. Owen embracing Elspeth as if he would never let her go—there was something good, anyway. The *tiermatha,* looking to her for instructions. Right. She was the leader. Time to lead.

"Owen, where is your escort? Owen. Pay attention. We still have to get her out of here safely."

Owen looked at her over the top of Elspeth's head. "Who are you?" he said.

"Queen of the Ruskalder, for a few minutes more." She took a few steps and faced Hrovald. "The *banrach* is annulled," she announced, speaking to the room at large but with her eyes fixed on Hrovald's. "You broke the oath of treaty between our peoples when you made a play for the Crown of Tremontane. And I personally refuse to stay married to a man who would let his son rape a woman and tell her that made her married to him. Keep an eye on him, Dorenna, I'd rather not kill him if we can help it." She turned to face Owen. "Where's the escort?"

"At the tree line, waiting for Elspeth to come out to them. You're really the Queen of the Ruskalder? Why are you helping us?"

Imogen rolled her eyes. "Let's focus on getting out of this city alive, and I'll tell you everything. And I'm not the Queen anymore. I'm Imogen of the Kirkellan, and this is my *tiermatha*."

She beckoned to the rest of her *tiermatha* and they gathered near the center of the room, leaving Dorenna to guard Hrovald. "You heard him," she said quietly. "We need to get out of the King's house, out of Ranstjad, past the camp and across the plain to the forest. Any suggestions?"

"The problem is to keep the alarm from being raised," Kionnal said. "We need to put Hrovald somewhere he can't make a stink for a while, and hide the corpse. An hour would be a good head start."

"True. What else?"

"Horses. We brought ours, but Victory's in the stable and I don't know what that man came in on. And Elspeth will need a ride," said Areli.

"Good. Owen, did you bring a horse? Yes? Good. There aren't any other mounts in the stable?"

"Nothing that will keep up with us. She'll have to double up with someone," Areli said. "Probably Kionnal, Revelry's the biggest."

"Fine. Lorcun, Maeva, Kallum, go get the horses saddled. If Erek asks questions, tell him I've decided to visit with you for the evening, but I doubt he'll say anything. I'm getting changed."

With no one to unbutton her dress, she tore at the seams until they shredded and she could step out of the remnants. She kicked them away sadly; she'd rather liked that dress. She donned her real clothes as fast as she could, regretted not having a weapon, and rushed back to the *skorstala*. The three she'd sent to ready the horses were still gone. Hesketh was still dead. And Hrovald was still furious. "Areli, go to the stable and get some rope. A lot of rope, not too thick. Don't let anyone see you do it." Areli grinned and slipped out the door.

Imogen walked over to Hrovald and relieved him of his belt knife, wishing it were a sword. Hrovald glared at her. "When I catch you, I will drink your blood," he snarled.

"Really? That sounds disgusting. It's a wonder your chiefs haven't risen up against you yet," Imogen said, absently, reviewing the layout of the great house and thinking about where she might stash Hrovald and Hesketh where they'd go undiscovered for an hour, or if they were lucky, two. "They're already plotting it, you know," she added.

"They're too afraid to plot against me," Hrovald said.

"You know, Hrovald, at some point too much fear overwhelms a person. They get to a state where they're so afraid they forget to be afraid. I'd be worried if I were you."

"Trying to get me to doubt my chiefs? Only a woman would think such a transparent ruse would work."

"No, I'm just talking to pass the time until Areli gets back. But it's too bad I'm never coming back here, or I'd wager with you about which ones are plotting to kill you."

Hrovald clenched his teeth and grated, "I should've forced you into my bed the first night I saw you, bitch, raped you until you lost that willfulness and behaved like—" Dorenna's blade pressed harder into his throat and he went still.

"You sure you want him alive?" she said. "I can make it look like an accident if you want."

"That's all right, Dor. I don't know what kind of conflict his death might create in Ruskald, and I don't want my mother mad at me if it spills over into the Eidestal. Hrovald, if you think that threat changes anything, you're even more sad and pathetic than I thought."

From behind her, Owen said plaintively, "No, really, who *are* you?"

Elspeth laughed, a sound that relieved Imogen's heart so much. "She is my dearest friend and she saved my life, and now she's going to save yours. Owen, what were you *thinking*, walking in here like this? Jeffrey can't possibly have agreed to it!"

"I didn't tell him. Did you think I'd let Hrovald keep you here, if I had the power to stop it?"

Areli returned bearing a large coil of rope. "They've almost got the horses ready," she said. "Kallum will knock when they're outside. I can't believe no one's come to see what's going on in here."

"Hrovald has everyone terrified of him. Too bad for him it means no one's going to come leaping to his aid." She took the rope and began cutting it into long sections. "Tie his hands and feet. Run a rope between the two, I want him hobbled. And I need a gag. You two, take care of the wet rag over there. We'll throw him in with Hrovald."

Hrovald struggled, but he was no match for three Kirkellan warriors. Imogen went into the hallway and checked to make sure it was empty before returning to beckon her *tiermatha* to carry their bound charge into a tiny storeroom Imogen knew wasn't used often. "Tie him to one of these shelves so he can't bang on the door," she added, then, when that was finished, leaned over to Hrovald and whispered, "I hope your gods drag you to whatever hell you believe in," and slammed the back of his head against the wall so hard he sagged in his bonds, unconscious.

Imogen led the way back to the *skorstala,* where Owen and Elspeth were continuing their reunion and the rest of the *tiermatha* looked restless. Imogen kept glancing over her shoulder, feeling as if Hrovald were going to burst through the door at any moment, followed by a hundred screaming Ruskalder warriors. It seemed like forever before Kallum knocked on the door, stuck his head inside, and said, "We're ready."

The horses stood in the courtyard, their hot breath faintly visible in the cool early spring night. A couple of kitchen maids crossed the courtyard and entered the King's house; Imogen focused on helping Elspeth mount. Those women wouldn't find Hrovald, they had no idea anything was wrong, it was only her imagination that they'd looked at her little party suspiciously. It was perfectly natural for the Queen to go riding with the hostage Princess after dark. In trousers. With the entire *tiermatha*. Imogen mounted Victory and gave the command to ride out in a voice that wasn't shaky at all.

They kept a leisurely pace even though Imogen's nerves were screaming at her to run, run through the dark streets and out the gate and across the plain to safety. At this time of evening, just after the supper hour, very few people were abroad, and those who were weren't inclined to stop and gawk at the procession of thirteen enormous horses filling the dark street. Imogen, at the head of the column, kept her eyes moving, looking for danger. A shout two streets away caused them all to jump, and Revalan had to rein Rohrnan in sharply when the excitable gelding shied at a cat that darted across the street in front of him. But nothing interfered with their progress through Ranstjad. Imogen began to breathe easier when the gate came into sight. One hurdle down.

The guards at the gate recognized Imogen and opened the gate without question. Two hurdles down. They might make it after all. They left the city and, feeling the eyes of the gate guards on her, Imogen signaled them to turn left as if they were going to the camp. It was risky, but she couldn't be sure the gate guards wouldn't be suspicious and raise the alarm. They walked along for a few minutes, then turned to cross the plain. Imogen signaled for everyone to continue and dropped back to talk to Owen. "Where did you leave your escort, exactly?"

Owen looked at the sky, which was clear and cloudless and sparkling, then at the horizon. "Over there," he pointed. "They have instructions to wait three days, then report to Jeffrey. So they'll be there."

Imogen nodded. "You must love her very much, to trade your life for hers," she said.

Owen smiled. "More than you can imagine. She saved my life, once. I couldn't do less for her."

The depth of emotion in his voice embarrassed her. "Why did Hrovald want you so much?" she asked. "Because you were one of Dyrak's guards?"

"The last of them. Hrovald hunted everyone else down and executed them. He was afraid one of us might turn out to be a rallying point for pro-Dyrak sympathy. I...sort of humiliated him, during my escape, and my death became personal, for him. But I didn't think he'd be so obsessed he'd agree to a straight-across exchange. He had to know

Jeffrey would give just about anything to get Elspeth back."

"Because she's his heir."

"No, because she's his sister. Though with him unmarried, her being his heir matters a lot. It's just the two of them now. Jeffrey needs to start producing heirs of his own." He laughed quietly. "Elspeth and I were supposed to be married at Wintersmeet. I—" His voice cut off abruptly, and she saw him turn his head to look at Kionnal, riding nearby. "We can talk more at the camp," he said. She wondered what else he'd been about to say, but just nodded and rode back to the head of the line.

They were almost far enough out that Imogen felt comfortable going faster when horns blasted from the camp, and shouts rang out across the plain. "That's it," Imogen said, "time to run," and she urged Victory into a trot. She risked a glance over her shoulder. *A mile from here to the camp,* she thought, *another five or six to the tree line, if we get enough of a head start, those warriors on foot won't know how to follow us.* She couldn't see if the pursuit had horses, but she assumed at least some of them would. *Nothing near our caliber of mounts,* she thought, *maybe a little faster because they're lighter, but they'll outrun their support and then we'll tear them apart if they catch us up.*

Imogen kept glancing back, every now and then, letting Victory guide them both. There were dark shapes coming up rapidly behind them—so Hrovald did have riders, and they were far quicker to respond than she'd hoped. She urged Victory on faster, and the horse obliged; it was dangerous to ride in this darkness, but far more dangerous if Hrovald's warriors caught up to them. They couldn't afford to let the Ruskalder riders catch them, slow them down enough for the bulk of the troops to arrive and overwhelm them.

There was a surrealism to the landscape, the pale dead grass emerging from the last snowdrifts of winter, the hard white stars above, the wall of black trees growing in front of them. Imogen felt as if she and Victory were flying, skimming across earth that flowed beneath them like water. She glanced back again. They were coming on far too quickly. Clearly Hrovald's men were more afraid of their King than they were of horses tripping and killing themselves or their riders.

No one was waiting when they reached the tree line. Imogen turned in her seat to look for Owen, but suddenly two people stood there as if they'd been trees until Imogen's presence had called them into human shape. Imogen was impressed.

"Rance, Cara, I have gotten her," Owen said in Tremontanese, sliding awkwardly off Revelry's broad back. His wasn't much better than hers. "But we are being chased."

"Who are these people?" Cara asked.

"Imogen of the Kirkellan and her *tiermatha*. Our rescuers." In Ruskeldin, Owen said to Imogen, "I owe you more than I can repay. Will you go back to the Kirkellan? Because we could use your help getting back to the border, if you're willing."

Imogen looked at her *tiermatha*. They each shrugged or nodded their consent. Kionnal added, "I'm not sure how they planned to get Elspeth home without horses, and I don't see or hear any nearby."

It turned out they did have horses, none that could match a Kirkellan steed, but which would outpace the *tiermatha* over the short distance. They all mounted up and rode, Owen in the lead this time, pointing their way. Imogen took up the rear position. She looked back over the plain one last time before they ducked into the forest. There were at least ten shapes now, no more than half a mile behind and gaining fast. Well, they'd have to maneuver through the trees just like everyone else. She dug her heels gently into Victory's side and followed the other riders.

Under the thick pine needles, it was almost black, and only Thistle's light gray rump kept Imogen from losing the group entirely. She was tired now, worn out from tension and worry, but still on edge listening for their followers. Their group made far too much noise for Imogen to hear anything else, like a warrior sneaking up on her. She wished desperately for a sword and even more desperately for her lost nine months of training. Years of battle experience couldn't be erased so quickly, she knew, but here in the darkness, with the enemy who knew where behind her, she felt soft and doughy instead of hard and strong. Victory, sensing her discouragement, flicked her ears and whickered at her. Imogen stroked her neck. "I promise we'll do real riding soon," she said.

She heard a shout and looked back to see a mounted warrior about a hundred feet away draw his sword and trot toward her between the lowering trees. Imogen shouted, "Move out!" and turned Victory around, not sure what she planned to do against an armed man, but no one else was in a position to take him on. She urged Victory into a trot, rode directly at the warrior hoping to intimidate him into making a mistake. Pine branches snagged her hair, making her duck to lie low along Victory's neck, and she felt her breath coming quick and shallow with the excitement of battle and made herself breathe slowly. Muscles ready but not tense, legs gripping Victory's sides firmly but not squeezing, hands holding the reins lightly but not loosely, everything in her crying out to attack.

As they converged on each other, the warrior raised his sword high in the air, readying a heavy strike. The branches rustled loudly, then the sword was gone, ripped from his hand from the entangling branches. He slowed, looking around for the blade, and Imogen punched the man in the jaw as she rode past, Victory's momentum adding to the force of the blow.

As she'd hoped, the man was as poor a horseman as he was a fighter; he lost his seat and landed hard on the ground beneath a knotty pine. Imogen brought Victory around, leaped down and picked up the man's fallen longsword. "Thanks," she said. She tested its balance; not a bad blade, though not the saber she was used to.

The warrior scrambled to his feet and drew his short blade. She saw his teeth gleam white in the darkness. "You'd better figure out how to use that real quick, girl," he said, approaching her with his sword at the ready. Imogen observed him, noted that he favored his left side and his grip on the sword was all wrong, shifted her own stance and met his first swing with a block that made her bones hum. She smiled. Oh, yes. She'd missed this. She let him swing at her a few more times, then went on the offensive, forcing him back with her superior weight and height. He wasn't smiling now, and his swings were getting wilder. Then he tripped on an exposed root, went down hard, and Imogen's sword took him in the throat. He didn't even have time to cry out.

Imogen stood over the body, breathing heavily. She looked around, listened, heard no evidence the man had companions. She had no idea which way to go. She cleaned the blade, retrieved the man's short sword and strapped it to Victory's side, just in case, then mounted and rubbed her shoulder. She was out of practice. It was lucky for her the man had been careless and cocky. She chose a direction at random and moved on.

After about a minute, another horse approached her in the dimness under the trees. She held her weapon in a guard position. "Where did you go?" Owen said.

"We were attacked from behind. I thought I warned everyone."

"You did. They took it as a sign they should move on, double-speed." Owen was close enough for her to see him clearly. "I'm—*watch out*!"

Imogen threw her weight to one side and Victory moved in that direction, enough that the sword blow aimed for Imogen's head connected with Victory's flank instead. The horse squealed and twisted. Imogen hung on and shouted at Victory. They turned to meet the next attack, which Imogen blocked with her sword. She shoved hard at her opponent, who laughed.

Karel. Of course.

He countered, and Imogen moved to block him again. His horse jogged nervously under him. Imogen called out another command, and Victory reared up and screamed at the other horse, which bucked and twisted. Karel lost his grip and fell, cursing. "You think that's a fair fight, woman? Why don't you get down off that monster and let's have a real test of skill," he shouted.

Imogen looked around. Where was Owen? It was just her and Karel in the middle of a very small clearing. The rest of his friends should be here soon. If Owen had gone to spur their party on, maybe she could buy them some time. Her arm already hurt from the unexpected exercise. She had no business challenging this man to any kind of fight. But she didn't have room here for Victory to get up any speed, and she was sure Karel wouldn't be as easy to kill as the first man. She closed her eyes, prayed, and dismounted.

Karel rushed her the second she landed. She ducked and rolled and ended up on her feet, ten feet away from him. "Drop the second sword, if you're so eager for a fair fight," she said. He smiled and drew out his short blade, showed it to her, then kicked it away to where the trees grew thicker. They circled one another until Imogen neared Victory; without looking away, she slapped her flank and gave her the command to withdraw. She could hear the silly animal move only a few feet out of the way. As long as she kept clear, Imogen was satisfied.

"Shall we just circle each other all night, or did you want to fight?" Karel said. "Or maybe you want to drop that sword and I'll give you what I know you've been aching for."

Imogen darted in, tapped the center of his chest, then pulled back for a real thrust he parried, but not easily. "Oh, I'm interested in a fight, but I thought you were offering yourself for target practice," she replied. He grinned that nasty grin at her and brought his sword around; she parried it and responded in kind. Their swords connected, and for a moment both pressed hard against the other's weapon, metal scraping against metal with a sharp *skree* until they both disengaged and began circling again.

Imogen started to sweat despite the chilly air. Her feet crunched against the thin layer of snow, slipping now and then—she'd have to watch her footing. All she could hear was the crunch of snow under her feet and his breathing and her own, hers a little heavier, a little faster. Damn, but she was out of shape. He darted in and her left shoulder flared pain. He grinned at her again and ran his tongue along his upper lip lasciviously. She bared her teeth at him. Wetness trickled down her arm, but the wound couldn't be too bad because she could still use it. She turned her body at an angle to prevent him doing that again, came in close and struck his sword arm hard. He dropped his sword and she moved in to press the edge of her blade against his throat. "Did you think our battle would end like this?" she asked.

Karel dropped to the ground, rolled, and came up wielding his sword in his left hand. "Did you think I would give up so easily?"

Now they went at it in earnest, blades clashing fast and loud, bodies circling, looking for an advantage. Her opponent got in a lucky strike that scored a thin line along her unprotected middle; it was unfair, she thought, that he was in armor and she wasn't, but then she remembered looking for fairness in a fight was a fast way to get killed. She wiped sweat from her eyes and brought her sword up to block yet another strike. He looked like he might be tiring, but not as much as she was. She had no business fighting this man, who might impale her with one breath and rape her bleeding body with another. The image sickened her and at the same time fortified her. She'd always planned to die in battle, but she wasn't going to fall at the hand of a man like him. She pretended to swing widely for his head, then thrust for his chest when he ducked the first swing. He barely got his sword in line in time, and she bared her teeth at him in a grin.

"You are a fearsome fighter," Karel said, sounding as if he really did admire her. "Even if you are a girl."

"You're a fearsome fighter, even if you are an ass," she countered, and his smile broadened. Then he struck, and her side felt suddenly hot and wet. She put her left hand there instinctively, and it came away bloody.

"Don't worry, I won't damage you *too* much," he said, lowering his sword. "I want us to have—"

"Spare me the details of how much fun you plan to have with me," Imogen said wearily. "If you win, you can say anything you like, but for now, shut up." The blood was flowing more freely now, and she felt herself weakening. *Stop thinking like Imogen and start thinking like Dorenna,* she told herself. *How would Dorenna win this battle? Well, she wouldn't have been drawn into it in the first place, stupid.*

She backed away from her opponent, buying herself some time. There, under the trees. She backed away some more, circling, looking from side to side to feign distress. Her foot tapped the hilt of Karel's discarded short blade. She nudged it around until she was certain how it lay, then pretended to stumble and fall, grasping the short sword's hilt in her left hand. Instantly he swept in for the kill, and Imogen launched herself at him, caught the crossguard of his sword with hers, and used her momentum to lift his sword out of the way and knock him off balance. She brought his short blade around and drove it deep through his belly, below his armor. "*Dead,*" she whispered, and his astonished eyes blinked at her. He slid off her sword onto the ground.

She leaned over, panting, then made certain he was dead before staggering over to lean against Victory. They were lost in the woods, she was bleeding from several wounds, and the rest of the Ruskalder army was hunting her, but at least she had her horse.

She did her best to bind her side and her shoulder, her whole body protesting that it wanted to lie down in the snow and rest, then examined the dead man's sword, his prize from the Samnal fights. It was beautifully designed and exquisitely balanced. It had her blood on it, so she figured she'd earned it. She strapped the other longsword to Victory's harness next to the other, cleaned off her new sword and worked his sword belt free of his body; she wasn't going to wander through the woods with a bare blade in her hand. Thus armed, she pulled herself atop Victory, which took her a few tries and hurt like hell, then hugged her horse's neck in pure exhaustion. How long had it been? If she could figure out which way to go, she might be able to catch up to the rest. She chose a random direction again and nudged Victory that way.

She'd only gone a few dozen steps when she heard Owen call to her. "You're going the wrong way," he said. There was blood trickling down the side of his face and his horse was limping.

"What happened to you?"

"There was another warrior. I had to let him chase me until I found a place where I could fight him." He touched his head and seemed surprised to find blood on his fingers. "It took me a while. I take it you were victorious?"

Victory whinnied, and Imogen laughed. "Yes, I was, but I think we should try to avoid fighting anymore and get Elspeth to safety as soon as possible," she said. She fell in behind Owen and watched for more attackers, but the forest was silent now except for their breathing and the harnesses' clinking. Imogen kept watch nonetheless until they reached the rest of their strange procession, which was waiting for them on the banks of the river.

"We should keep moving," Imogen said as she and Owen washed and bandaged their wounds as best they could. "Hrovald could still send more warriors after us."

"Just a day's ride, maybe two," Owen said, "then you can return home. Thank you."

"Thank me when we've reached the border," Imogen said, dried her hands on her filthy trousers, and mounted up again. She felt mostly certain they'd outrun their pursuit, but it took several miles of tense watching before Imogen felt confident enough to relax. Everything would go as planned. They would return Elspeth to her brother. They would ride home and tell Mother of Hrovald's treachery. And Imogen would finally stand before the King of Tremontane and tell him how she hadn't let his sister die.

Chapter Twelve

They reached the Tremontanan camp at sunset the following day, exhausted from the hard ride. "He's moved the front line," Owen said, giving the sentries a wave; they watched the procession pass, mouths gaping. Imogen would have disciplined them sharply for such behavior, if they'd been under her command, but she reminded herself she was a guest and Tremontanan military behavior was none of her business. "When I left, the camp was another seventy-five miles south of here. What the hell is he thinking?"

Owen and his scouts left their horses at the picket line, where they were claimed by men and women who led the animals away to be cared for. "Jeffrey will want to see you," he said to Imogen, "and I'm sure he'll want all of you to rest here overnight before returning to your people." Imogen stared at him, her mind dull from all the riding. "Please, Imogen, Elspeth wants to see her brother. And I need to ask him some questions, assuming he doesn't kill me outright."

"The Kirkellan don't let others care for their horses, Owen," Elspeth said. Imogen shook the cobwebs out of her brain and dismounted, wincing at the pain from the wound in her side, and laid her cheek against Victory's smooth one. She'd need to get the injury properly stitched soon.

"I'll take her," Dorenna said, "and you go see the King. Do you suppose any of these southerners speak our language? We'll have to mime asking for water and a currycomb."

Imogen nodded her thanks and followed Elspeth and Owen through the camp. It was more regimented and orderly than a Kirkellan camp, which tended to sprawl to reflect the mood of the individuals pitching their tents. The tents were made of heavy canvas, white or gray or tan, and when she caught glimpses of the tents' interiors through open flaps, they were as bland and neutral as the exteriors, unlike the brightly colored and textured Kirkellan tents. Men and women stared at her as she passed, which made her uncomfortable, so she squared up her chin and shoulders and pretended not to see them. Unlike the Ruskalder, their interest was curious; like the Ruskalder, they saw her as an outsider.

Owen led them to a large tent near the center of the camp, not as big as the *matrian's* but still very large, with peaks where multiple tent poles held up the roof. A flag bearing the triple-peak emblem of Tremontane flew from the highest pole, just above another flag in blue and silver whose emblem she didn't recognize. Fully armed men in helmets, chain shirts, and metal plates at shoulders and legs stood to either side of the flap. They moved to bar the door, but then recognized Owen and stepped away, startled. They didn't seem to notice Elspeth and paid no attention to Imogen. She'd have disciplined them for that, too. *A strange warrior approaches the King's tent and you don't have a plan to kill her? Poor discipline, fellows.*

Owen held the tent flap for Elspeth and Imogen, who had to duck her head to pass through, then ducked through himself. The inside of the tent was as stark and bare as the others Imogen had seen, with the addition of several rugs over the grass. Canvas partitions sectioned off part of the tent, though they were currently folded down so Imogen couldn't see what lay beyond. Camp chairs stood here and there, but all were unoccupied. A large square folding table stood to one side, surrounded by several men and women who were preoccupied with the objects lying on its surface.

"If we put a force here, we can—" one of the men was saying, but a woman glanced at the doorway, did a double take, and said, "Sweet holy heaven."

That drew the attention of the rest of them. An extremely handsome young man, tall and black-haired, recovered from his surprise first. "Owen," he began, angrily, "what the hell—"

Elspeth let out a sob and rushed forward with her arms outstretched. The man's fury turned to open-mouthed astonishment. "*Elspeth,*" he said, and folded her into his arms, bent his head to kiss her shining hair. "Dear heaven, what did they do to you?"

"She was very sick," Imogen said in her halting Tremontanese. "She is still not well completely. I promise I cared for her the best—as best as I could. We had to cut her hair because of the fever. I am sorry."

The man lifted his head and fixed her with an intense blue-eyed gaze that startled her. "Who are you?" he said.

"This is Imogen of the Kirkellan," Owen said. "It is because of her we escaped Hrovald's city alive."

The King of Tremontane tucked Elspeth under his arm and came around the table. "I owe you everything," he said. "Anything I can do for you—you brought me my sister and my best friend—anything at all, it's yours."

He stretched out his hand toward her, and reflexively she took it. "Um," Imogen said, overwhelmed by his words and the force of his presence and those blue eyes fixed on her. "I need nothing. I cared for Elspeth because she needed me. I must go to my mother soon. She will want to know how Hrovald wanted to take the Crown of Tremontane."

The King looked puzzled and released her hand. "The Crown?" he said. He looked at Owen. "What do you mean?"

Owen glanced around at the listening ears. "This should be private," he said.

The King nodded. "Leave us," he commanded, and the men and women filed out without a word of argument.

"Jeffrey, if you want me to stay," said the woman who'd first noticed their presence.

"Thank you, no," he said, his firm tone contrasting strongly with his polite words, and she left the tent without comment. Imogen was impressed. She judged the King to be in his early twenties, certainly no older than twenty-five, but his quiet air of authority commanded the loyalty and, from what she could see, the respect of his subordinates. She'd seen her mother behave exactly the same, but Mother had had years of practice. This young man had only had three.

Owen held out his hand for Elspeth to return to him. He drew the King closer to the center of the tent, away from inadvertent or intentional eavesdroppers. Imogen followed. She was a part of this too. "Swear to me you will not yell, or rage, or tear around throwing things until you hear all," he said.

The King made an exasperated face. "You went off against my express command and it's sheer luck you made it back alive, let alone with Elspeth," he said. "Don't think succeeding at your insane mission means I won't rip you a new one."

"That is not what I mean," Owen said. "Swear."

"Fine. I swear not to throw a fit. What is so dire?"

Owen lowered his voice. "Hrovald's son raped Elspeth."

The King looked briefly confused, as if he didn't understand the words. He glanced at Elspeth, and realization, then fury, swept across his features. He opened his mouth to roar, then saw Owen's warning expression and turned away to control himself. Elspeth's chin quivered, and Imogen told her in Ruskeldin, "Let your brother be angry on your behalf, Elspeth."

"I feel as if this will hang over me for the rest of my life," she whispered in the same language. "Everyone will look at me and know how I was shamed."

"If anyone should be ashamed, it's that turd Hesketh, and he's dead," Imogen said. "This is just a thing that happened, yes? And I can't tell you how to live with it or how to let it go or *if* you should let it go. I just know you are still the same person we all love, and you should remember that."

Elspeth smiled at her with watery eyes. "I wish I were more like you," she said.

"No, you don't. I'm grouchy in the morning and I sometimes smell like horse."

Elspeth laughed. The King looked down at her and the anguish in his eyes lessened. "What was his plan? How could that give Hrovald a hold on Tremontane?"

"He planned to say Hesketh's…physical relationship with Elspeth meant they are married, and wait for her to give birth to Hesketh's child, who will—would then be an heir to the Crown." Owen looked as if he wished he had his hands around Hesketh's throat again.

"It doesn't work like that."

"If he can to kill you in battle, it would."

The King glanced at Elspeth again. "What will we do if she...."

Elspeth buried her face in her hands. Owen's arms tightened around her. Imogen said, "She is not carrying a child."

They all looked at her as if they'd forgotten she was there. "How do you know?" Owen asked.

Imogen rolled her eyes. "She had her...." What was the word for *monthlies*? She switched to Ruskeldin. "You had your bleeding while you were sick," she told Elspeth. "It was long enough...didn't you have another while you were recovering?"

Elspeth gasped in relief. "No. I was afraid...."

"Well, sometimes when you're sick and lose weight you don't bleed."

"You could have said."

"I thought you knew. It's not exactly something that comes up in polite conversation."

Elspeth beamed. "I'm not pregnant," she said in Tremontanese, and hugged Owen tightly. The King sagged onto a camp chair and rubbed his face.

"I don't know if I can stand any more surprises," he said, and one of the guards stuck his head through the door and said, "Your Majesty, there's a fight going on near the horse lines."

Imogen swore and ran out of the tent back toward where she'd left the *tiermatha*. She arrived, breathless, to see a woman dangling from Victory's reins, screaming over the sound of Victory's terrified neighs, dragged here and there by the horse's restless, frantic movement. The horse kept backing away and coming up against a ring of the *tiermatha*, who were trying to soothe her, but no one wanted to get in the way of nearly a ton of frightened horse.

Imogen shouted, "Get your hands off Victory!" which was useless because in her panic she'd slipped into Kirkellish, and ran toward the screaming woman. She tore the reins from the woman's hands and shoved her out of the way of Victory's enormous hooves. The woman stumbled into Victory's neck and fell, making Victory scream again.

Imogen prayed the stupid woman had at least enough sense to crawl out of the way, then flung her arms around the horse's broad neck and whispered to her as if she were Elspeth in the middle of a weeping fit. Victory reared, lifting Imogen off the ground and making her side feel as if it were being ripped open again, but Imogen tugged on her mane and said, "None of that." Victory reared again, but less violently, and Imogen began to breathe more easily, aware of how stupid that stunt had been. Victory would never hurt her intentionally, but in a maddened state, who knew what she might have done?

"There are a lot of Kirkellan horses here," the King said. Imogen turned to see him standing in the crowd behind her, his guards close behind. Nobody seemed overawed that he was among them, though they did make room so no one was very close.

"This is my *tiermatha*," Imogen said. "They are also—were also ones who brought Elspeth home." She turned toward them and said in Kirkellish, "What in the *hell* is going on here?"

"I *told* the woman just to hold Victory's reins," Dorenna said, exasperated. "Well, I gestured it, anyway. I don't know if she just wanted to show politeness, or if I'm just not good at gesturing, but they have a…a *thing* that buzzes around. I have no idea what it's meant to do, but she put it on Victory and she went insane. I don't blame her. I'm really sorry, Imo. I shouldn't have let her go, but I needed both hands—"

"It's all right, Dor, it was an accident," Imogen said, trying not to think about the conversation they'd be having now if someone had been hurt or even killed. She stroked Victory's mane again and added, "That's the King over there. He's very grateful that we brought Elspeth and Owen back. I couldn't think of anything to ask him for, but if there's something you want, he's in a giving mood."

"Your horse is dangerous," someone said at Imogen's elbow. It was the woman she'd pulled off Victory, the one who'd tried to use some sort of awful Device on her. "She shouldn't be with the rest of the animals. Who knows what she might do? I want you to—"

"What is your name?" Imogen said, cutting her off.

"You have no right to make demands of me—"

"What did you put on my horse?"

"It was a simple grooming Device. What kind of creature overreacts like that?"

"The Kirkellan do not use the Devices," Imogen said, raising her voice and forgetting Elspeth's instructions about dropping articles. "The Kirkellan take care of the horses with the own hands as heaven intends it to be. You put a buzzy thing on my horse and scared her and you are now wanting to make it her fault she is scared? I will find this buzzy thing and I will make you eat it unless you apologize to Victory right now."

The woman was red with fury. "Apologize? Me, apologize?"

"Madam, for a stable mistress you seem remarkably ignorant about Kirkellan horses," the King said. Imogen glanced his way; he looked amused, and his rich baritone voice held suppressed mirth. "You should know better than to use a Device I happen to know is untested outside the military on a horse that doesn't belong to you. I suggest you do as the lady tells you and apologize to the horse."

The woman looked confused. "The horse?"

Imogen glared at her and jerked her head in Victory's direction. Victory nodded as if she understood the conversation.

The woman looked from Victory to Imogen and back again. "I'm sorry," she said in a stunned voice. "It won't happen again."

"Thank you," Imogen said, and led Victory to where her stable mates waited. Victory made a noise that might have been a chuckle and plunged her nose into a bucket of oats. Imogen patted her fondly. "You great beast," she said.

"So that's the King? Can't believe he's related to Elspeth," Kallum said. "He is *exactly* my type."

"Please don't seduce the King of Tremontane," Imogen said. "I need him to be friendly until tomorrow morning when we can all go home."

"Oh, if I seduce him, he'll be friendly for as long as you like." Kallum's eyes gleamed in the fading light. Imogen hit him on the shoulder.

Behind them, Owen cleared his throat and said, "It would be a very bad idea for you to try that."

"He's kidding," Imogen said, hoping it was true. "Owen, can you show us where we can get some food and bunk down for the night? I think everyone's ready for a real bed."

"I can take them to the mess tent, and you to the camp healer, but first Jeffrey wants you to eat with us."

Imogen sighed. "I'm not really in a condition to be polite."

"Yes, everyone who was down at the enclosure just now knows that. Elspeth wants you to get to know her brother. Jeffrey's interested in talking to a woman who can drag that beast of yours back to the ground. And I just enjoy your company. Please join us?"

She sighed again. "All right. I don't suppose you can find someone who speaks Kirkellish to translate for the *tiermatha*? I hate deserting them."

Owen was able to find a translator, and he and Imogen walked back to the King's tent in the gathering darkness. "He's not like Hrovald, you know," Owen said. "Not full of his own privilege or arrogant or anything like that. Just a little stiff around strangers."

"He seemed relaxed enough to me."

"Trust me, he's on edge. He's decided as long as Hrovald's going to attack us, he's going to try to keep the territory he's occupying right now. It's a long arm of Ruskald that extends between Veribold and Tremontane, and apparently it's a national security nightmare. Trying to keep it changes the nature of the war, but Anselm—he's the commanding general of the armies—thinks it's worth the effort."

"That's quite a lot to demand of an army."

"They're more loyal than you can imagine. No, you're Kirkellan; you probably understand perfectly well."

Jeffrey North didn't seem stiff at all when they entered the tent. A second folding table had been set up and four camp chairs were ranged around it. Elspeth had changed into sensible trousers and shirt, both too big for her, and soft boots, which made Imogen uncomfortably aware of her stained trousers, her dirty shirt borrowed from one of Owen's riders, since the first was torn and bloody from her fight, and how itchy her scalp was. The King didn't seem to notice. He pulled her chair away from the table and held it, and after a moment Imogen realized he was waiting for her to sit. She'd never had anyone do that before, and it was unsettling. *I can't call this man by his first name, I just can't,* she thought. She'd never respected Hrovald, Elspeth was like a sister, but the King of Tremontane's air of confident power made it impossible for her to think of him so informally.

The King sat at her right hand, Owen to her left, and Elspeth across from her. Elspeth gave her a bright smile and said, in Tremontanese, "Is everything all right?"

"Yes, Victory was just scared. Sometimes she is silly when she is scared. I am sorry I yelled at that woman."

"Don't be," the King said, gesturing to them to serve themselves. "Her behavior was inexcusable. I still can't believe you went in there with the horse thrashing around. That was incredibly brave."

"You do not like horses," Imogen said, remembering what Elspeth had said once. He flashed his blue-eyed gaze at her.

"Who told you that? I never said I didn't like horses," he said.

"Elspeth said it," Imogen said, blushing. *That's right, criticize the King in his own tent over his own dining table. Very politic of you, Imogen.*

"Well, you don't," Elspeth said, her mouth half full of food.

"I never said that. Just because I'm not a rider like Father—like other people. I think horses are beautiful."

"I would like you to meet Victory," Imogen said, "maybe in the morning."

"I—thank you," the King said. "Are you leaving for home then?"

"My mother should hear the news of the *banrach* immediately."

"Excuse me, I don't understand that word."

"It's a horrible custom that made Imogen married to Hrovald for five years," Elspeth said. "As part of the peace between the Kirkellan and Ruskald."

The King laid his fork and knife down. "*Who* did you say your mother was?"

"Mairen of the Kirkellan."

"Good heaven. The *matrian* of the Kirkellan. You were married to Hrovald?"

Imogen tried to explain the *banrach,* but eventually gave it up to Elspeth, correcting her occasionally. The King listened in silence, his eyebrows raised. "It seems we have more to talk about than I thought," he told Imogen when Elspeth wound down. "Would the *matrian* be interested in a treaty with Tremontane? It sounds as if you burned your bridges thoroughly when you left. Hrovald's the kind of man who would pursue war simply to avenge himself on you. Though I'm not sure who he'd be angrier at, the woman who humiliated him or the man who killed his heir. But even if he comes against us first, if we lose, he'll certainly take the fight to your people afterward."

"But we know nothing of Tremontane. Why would you want to fight with us?"

"I could use someone to put pressure on Hrovald's western flank so he can't prosecute full-out war against us. And I think we have more in common with each other than either of us has with Ruskald, if you'll pardon my presumption."

Imogen understood enough of his complicated words to know what he said. She looked at each of her tablemates in turn. "I cannot make a treaty myself," she said. "I can take your offer to the *matrian* and ask her. But I think, me, it is a good idea. I do not know if we can make peace before Hrovald brings his army against you, though."

"I have an idea for that," said the King.

CHAPTER THIRTEEN

A few days later Imogen and the *tiermatha,* along with the Tremontanan diplomatic envoy, topped a gentle rise and saw the tents of the Kirkellan spread out on the plains below them. Imogen's heart ached with joy. Finally, home, after so many dark months. Nothing had changed. She gestured for the others to follow her, and went down the slope toward the camp.

Three outriders peeled off from the horses milling about the outskirts of the camp and approached them. "Identify," they said. Imogen recognized one of them.

"Derry," she cried, "are you still riding sentry? Who did you piss off this time?"

Derry gaped at her. "Imogen? What are you doing back here? I thought we wouldn't see you for nigh on another four years!"

Imogen leaned across to grasp his forearm in greeting. "It's a long story the *matrian* should hear first. Will you escort us? I don't want any more challenges."

But it turned out being challenged wasn't something they had to worry about. Almost everyone they passed recognized someone in their little party, and the cheers and welcomes shouted at them grew in volume as they neared the *matrian*'s tent until the sound was almost tangible. As happy as she was, Imogen's nervousness as she approached the great tent grew. Suppose Mother didn't agree with the way she'd handled Hrovald? Suppose she was angry with Imogen for breaking the treaty? Imogen almost wished she'd stayed with Elspeth, though she had no idea what she'd do in Tremontane. Train horses? Breed horses? Do other horse-related things? No, there was nothing for her there and everything for her here.

She could see Mother standing outside the great tent long before she was close enough to speak to her. Mother didn't look happy to see her. She didn't look angry, either, which Imogen hoped was a good sign. Imogen pulled Victory up ten feet from her mother and dismounted.

"*Matrian*," she said, saluting formally.

"Inside," Mother said neutrally, and held the tent flap for her. Imogen thrust Victory's reins into the hand of a random bystander and followed. She'd seen no one else belonging to her family. Would Mother be gentler with her if Caele were there, or harsher?

The tent was empty. It looked no different than it had last summer. Mother brushed past Imogen, went to the central pole and leaned against it, looking at the floor. "Come here," she said. Imogen approached her cautiously, as if she were a cornered buck deer that might turn on her at any moment. Mother sighed deeply and turned around. "I don't know what it means that you're here," she said. "I fear something's happened that will mean disaster for the Kirkellan. But I am just so happy to see you I don't care." She reached out, her eyes filled with tears, and put her arms around her tall daughter, and Imogen, expecting anything in the world but this, hugged her and found she was crying too.

"I'm sorry if it turns out I've ruined things," she wept. "I did the best I could. I think I made the right choices. But I'm not you."

For a while, they held each other, unable to speak. Mother was the first to draw away. "I suppose you should tell me what happened," she said. She pulled up a fat cushion, sat, and added, "And don't leave anything out."

Imogen sat on a cushion of her own, thought for a moment, then told the story beginning with Elspeth North's arrival in Ranstjad. Mother interrupted a few times, asking for clarification, but otherwise listened intently. Her face went very still when Imogen explained Hrovald's plan to take power in Tremontane. When she got to the part where they escaped Ranstjad and made it to the Tremontanan camp, Imogen stopped, not wanting to explain the King's proposal until she knew Mother's thoughts on everything else. Mother's eyes narrowed and she propped her chin on her fist.

"You're right," she said eventually. "Hrovald broke the *banrach* when he violated the terms of our treaty. He had no right to start a war with a country we are currently at peace with. But you probably should have killed him."

"I was afraid it would make things worse."

"Internal conflict in Ruskald is to our advantage. The chiefs would have to fight for dominance, during which time they couldn't come against us. And whoever the new chief is might not be inclined to go to war against us. But it's done, and you made the best decision you could at the time. Unfortunately, it means Hrovald is going to batter at us until one of us is defeated, and there's no way I can make a peace with him now. So I hope those extra riders I saw with you represent a solution to our problem."

"I hope so." Imogen rolled her shoulders to ease the tension. "King Jeffrey of Tremontane would like to make a treaty with us. He believes we have more in common with each other than we do with Ruskald and that our respective military presences will put pressure on Hrovald so he won't be able to bring his full forces to bear against either of us."

"Did he send you with a proposal for me to examine?"

"Um. Sort of. But it's difficult to explain, so I'll have to show you." Imogen ducked out of the tent and beckoned to the Tremontanan soldiers at the back of the group. They dismounted and began to remove their bulky gear from their mounts.

"It's called a telecoder," Imogen said when the man and woman had set up the Device in the matrian's tent and retreated a short, respectful distance. "They're usually the size of a horse, but the military has these smaller, portable versions. This bar makes a mark on this paper. The marks are duplicated instantaneously by another telecoder Device, anywhere in the world. This one is set to communicate with a Device in the King's camp. I have the preliminary document he drew up, and you can read it and send him corrections or, um, argue technicalities or whatever else is part of making a treaty. There's a code the operators use that's faster than the alphabet, faster than writing. You could agree on terms within an hour."

"That's incredible. How does it work?"

"I don't understand it well myself. You could ask the operators. But...shouldn't that wait until the treaty is resolved?"

Mother fingered the arm of the telecoder. It went up and down at her touch. "How do I know what I say is transmitted accurately? I can't read this code. And suppose the—operator?—doesn't translate King Jeffrey's words accurately either?"

"I don't have any way to assure you of that," Imogen said. "But I've met the King, and I trust him. I think he wants this treaty very much. And he owes me two lives, so I think he's bound to deal honorably by me."

Mother stared at the Device for another long moment. "All right," she said. "Show me the document." Imogen handed her a folded sheet she'd been carrying inside her jerkin, then stepped aside to speak with the operators. Only one of them spoke Kirkellish, but she was reasonably fluent and Imogen was confident she and her partner would do a fine job of communicating with the King's camp, a hundred miles away. They left the tent to wait for instructions, and Imogen stayed, not sure what her responsibility was now.

Mother sat at her desk and read. Imogen hadn't known Mother could both speak and read Tremontanese, but nothing her mother did surprised her anymore. Imogen fidgeted. The King should have sent an actual diplomat along with the telecoder operators. He'd explained that sending a representative uninvited could seem aggressive or arrogant, but on their long ride Imogen had become convinced a treaty between their nations was critical, and how was she supposed to convince her mother of that? She picked at a loose seam of the tent wall. She scraped some unidentified dirt off one of the tent poles. Mother said, "Get out of here before we both go crazy." Imogen fled.

The crowd was now less a solid mass than a handful of clots, people greeting the *tiermatha*, even a few Kirkellan conversing with the Tremontanan soldiers, more with gestures than words. She accepted Victory's reins from—she stepped back in surprise—her own brother Gannen. "Did I give you Victory's reins without knowing it was you?" she exclaimed, embracing him.

"No, you gave them to Regan, but I told her I wanted to play a joke on you. Heaven above, but you look terrible, sister mine. When's the last time you bathed?"

"It was before I got divorced, outraced a good portion of the Ruskalder army, killed two men, and had supper with a foreign King, so I think I can be excused for being a little ripe."

Gannen's eyes widened. "Supper with a foreign King? What an exciting life you lead. Seriously, though, you look like you could use a rest. You want to come home and change, at least?"

"I can't. I'm waiting on Mother to approve a treaty with Tremontane so I can see if King Jeffrey will accept her terms."

"Good heaven. Did you bring him here too? Really, Imo, weren't you a chubby little girl in plaits just two days ago?"

"Time you started taking me seriously."

"Past time, apparently. So explain what's going on. Are you going to ride back and forth until Mother and this King come to terms? That seems like a waste of your abilities."

Imogen opened her mouth to explain, and Mother called, "Imogen, come back in here and look at this." Imogen shrugged and obeyed.

With Imogen's memory of what the King had talked about and Mother's formidable intelligence, it took them very little time to work out the changes Mother wanted to make to King Jeffrey's document. It took a great deal more time for the telecoder operators to encode and transmit the document. Mother and Imogen watched the process with interest at first, then boredom. After a longer wait—the Tremontanans had to decode the document, then the King had to read it, then he had to—

The key started tapping its arrhythmical beat. Imogen and Mother leaned forward simultaneously, then looked at each other and chuckled. As if their attention could make the message arrive more quickly. The tape sped through the Device and over the fingers of the female soldier, who read off the message for her companion to write. The reply was a good deal shorter than the original transmission, so either it was acceptable or King Jeffrey was furious at whatever Mother had said. The scribe finished writing and handed the page to Mother, who scanned it quickly.

"Hmm. Tell him…tell him terms will be in abeyance until the immediate threat has passed, negotiations to commence thereafter."

More encoding and tapping. Imogen got up to leave and her mother put a restraining hand on her arm. "Sit with me," she said, "and tell me about this King Jeffrey. What kind of man do you judge him to be?"

"I've only spoken to him a handful of times."

Gannen poked his head into the tent. "Imogen, I can't spend all day watching your oversized pony."

"Take Victory to the enclosure and see her settled," Mother said to Gannen. Imogen made a noise of protest, and she added, "Imogen and I have a great deal to talk about."

"But, Mother—"

"I know perfectly well you have nothing better to do, Gannen, and you should be happy to do a favor for your sister when she's done so much for all of us."

"Well, when you put it that way," Gannen said, and withdrew.

Mother nodded at Imogen. "You were saying?"

"He's decisive. His men and women admire him. He's far too young for his responsibilities, but he's not uncertain or foolish." Imogen wondered if the operators were listening to this and, if they were, what they thought of an outsider passing judgment on their King. "He's at war with Ruskald because Hrovald stole his heir, not just because he loves his sister. I don't think he lets personal feelings influence his actions. He has a sense of humor. And he understands about our horses."

"High praise indeed."

"It is for me. I liked him."

"I can tell." Mother stood and walked to the telecoder, which lay silent. "You know Tierani is expecting your brother's child?"

"Torin? How wonderful for them! Though I thought he had his eye on Gitta."

"It seems Gitta had her eye on Briony instead."

"Poor Torin. Though I like Tierani better."

"So do I. They intend to marry in a month or two." The telecoder chattered. Mother stood back to let the operators do their work, then again received a sheet of paper from the scribe. "It's acceptable," she told the woman. "Tell him the Kirkellan will set out in the morning." She dropped the paper on her desk, took Imogen's arm, and said, "Walk with me."

Only normal traffic remained outside the great tent. Imogen's *tiermatha* had disappeared. Imogen took a few steps toward their family tent next door, but Mother said, "I'd rather not go home just yet, if you don't mind."

They walked in silence toward the outer edge of the camp, Mother frequently saluted by the men and women they passed. "The Ruskalder army is on its way south," she said. "King Jeffrey's outriders estimate it will meet the Tremontanan Army in approximately five days. Hrovald claims a soldier of Tremontane entered the King's house at Ranstjad and killed his heir."

"That's almost entirely true. I'm not sure Owen would describe himself as a soldier of Tremontane, and he was enacting personal vengeance, but I imagine that's good enough pretext for Hrovald to call up his armies."

"The point is King Jeffrey and I have reached a temporary agreement for the duration of the conflict. They'll engage Hrovald's army from the front. We will strike the western flank. Hrovald won't expect us to throw in with Tremontane, which should give us the advantage and Tremontane a divided foe to attack."

"Why temporary?"

"We don't have time to work out the kind of details a peacetime treaty would require. I told him I'd be willing to negotiate again once the crisis has passed."

"You seem optimistic."

"You've seen Hrovald's army. We don't have better than an even chance, at most. But if things go sour, we'll withdraw and disappear into the plains."

"You mean we'd desert?"

"I mean if the Tremontanan Army begins to retreat in confusion, I'll take it as a sign we've lost." Mother shrugged. "My first duty is always to the Kirkellan, just as King Jeffrey's is to his people. We both understand that."

Imogen nodded. "How long will it take the Kirkellan to assemble?"

"Two, three days. We'll be cutting it close to arrive when Hrovald does, but I can't make our warriors move any faster than they do." She paused, then added, "I'm putting you in charge of a company."

"You are? Why me?" They'd walked a quarter of the circuit of the camp and were in sight of the track. A horse and rider came around the bend toward the hurdles and came up short, to the amusement of the bystanders.

"It's time you had some experience leading more than one *tiermatha* into battle."

"Thank you. I promise I won't let you down."

"I wouldn't give you the command if I didn't think you were ready." The rider dug his heels into his horse's sides and steered him around the hurdles toward the straightaway. Imogen would have to take Victory for some much-needed practice at the track.

Mother nodded. "I'll have to start summoning the companies. It's tricky timing, getting there just as Hrovald does, but I'll leave that to Kernen. I'll be following with the bulk of the camp." Kernen was the Warleader of the Kirkellan. Imogen intended to hold his position someday.

"I'll have to tell my *tiermatha,* but I'll join the family for dinner shortly."

Mother laid her hand on her daughter's cheek. "I feel as if all I do is send you away."

"At least I'm not going very far. And I'll be doing what I was born to do."

"Oh, Imogen," Mother said. "I hope that's true."

CHAPTER FOURTEEN

"I don't like going to war allied with people whose language we don't speak," Rhion said, peering ahead with her eyes shaded against the bright morning light. She and Imogen stood on a low rise, waiting for the rest of the companies to strike camp. They'd made good time the first day and Imogen estimated they'd be united with the Tremontanan Army by noon in two days. "Who knows what kind of confusion that might create?"

"I'm sure they use signals," Imogen said. "And I imagine they expect us to operate independently. It's not as if we'll have time to discuss strategy with them when we arrive. The Warleader thinks the battle might be underway when we get there.

"Yes, and I hate leaping into battle without time to assess the enemy's position," Rhion said. She was a dark-featured, dark-haired woman in her mid-thirties, lean to the point of skinniness. Imogen had never ridden with her before, but knew her to be precise and fond of details. She wouldn't be happy until she could see the Ruskalder spread out before her.

"Just five minutes more," Fionna said as she crested the rise. "They made good time."

"I wish we'd left five minutes *ago*," Rhion said.

Fionna shrugged. "Should've helped break camp if you're so eager."

Rhion snorted. Fionna tossed her short brown hair and stroked her horse's mane. She was of an age with Rhion and nearly as tall and thin. They had been best friends since childhood and had co-captained their company for nearly as long.

"So is it true the Tremontanans don't use cavalry?" Fionna asked.

"They have cavalry, they just don't fight the way we do," said Imogen. "They couldn't, really. Their horses are lighter and faster than ours, which suggests they use them for quick strikes rather than breaking the enemy line." She petted Victory's head so she wouldn't feel bad for not being a slim, speedy horse with thin legs and a narrow flank. "It's not like I know anything about their strategies, but I doubt they'll have us working together. Our strengths are too different. But it will be interesting to see them work."

Rhion looked around. "More interesting for *them* to see *us* work, I'd think."

"Chauvinist," Fionna said.

"When will any of them have had the chance to see a Kirkellan *tiermatha* thundering down on the foe? It has nothing to do with how much better our horses are. Which they are."

"Let's not be too vocal about that," Imogen laughed. "Remember, some of the Tremontanans speak our language."

"I'll be polite. I don't have to say we're better. I just have to let Charity prove it."

Imogen rolled her eyes, then prodded Victory ahead to join her *tiermatha*. They hadn't objected to riding out again so soon, were even cheerful about it, and were, if anything, more cheerful this morning, eating bread and cheese in the saddle, Dorenna tossing bits at Revalan who caught them in his mouth. "All right," she said as she rode up where Saevonna and Lorcun were making their horses dance together. "I want to know what the quartermaster put in your food. *Nobody* is this easy-going. And the odds against twelve people all being equally easy-going about the same thing are…I don't know what they are, but something ridiculously high."

"It's obvious, Imogen," Saevonna said, keeping her eyes on Lodestone's enormous, agile feet. "We spent nine or ten months trapped in a Ruskalder city, barely able to spar, hated and persecuted, and now someone tells us 'hey there, you're going to war, and by the way it's against those jackasses who hated and persecuted you.' I'd have *volunteered* for this."

There were nods all around. Kallum added, "Besides, I might have needed to get away from the camp for a while. A little misunderstanding about whose bed I was supposed to share two nights ago."

"Kallum, you're going to get in trouble someday, and then you're going to drag us into it," Dorenna said.

"Kionnal and I got married," Areli said.

A moment of stunned silence turned into exclamations and complaints. "What? When? You didn't tell anyone! We wanted to be there!" cried Imogen.

Areli and Kionnal exchanged a smug glance. "The night before we left. We thought this would be more fun, seeing you all excited," Kionnal said. "And we'll have a real celebration when this is all over."

"Aren't you even the least bit superstitious about getting married just before going into battle?" Revalan asked, throwing a hunk of bread at Kionnal's chest. He caught it and took a huge bite.

"You mean, now we're married one of us is going to be killed? Not really," Areli said, seeing her husband's mouth was full. "Our being married doesn't change how we feel about each other and it doesn't make us any more likely to put each other's welfare above the *tiermatha*'s than we were before. We've been talking about it for a while, but I was far more superstitious about getting married in that frozen Ruskalder city than now. Besides, I want to be married when I have my baby."

In the sharp silence that followed, Areli grinned and said, "Kidding."

She ducked and laughed beneath a hail of bread chunks.

Out of the corner of her eye, Imogen saw movement. The great banner rose above the Kirkellan host, giving the signal to move out. Imogen raised her fist and gestured to her company to fall in. They had a lot of ground to cover that day, and a battle to win the next.

By the curve of the land, King Jeffrey had moved his Army farther north and west since they'd last seen it. Like the border between Ruskald and the Eidestal, this land lay empty and unpeopled as far as Imogen could see, and she imagined its emptiness stretching all the way north to the pole, then spreading out just as empty from here south to the distant sea. It didn't look like anything anyone might want to fight over, though if Owen was right, the land was the reason they were here, Kirkellan, Tremontanan, and Ruskalder, whatever Hrovald might say about revenge.

Her company rode on the far right of the Kirkellan, loosely grouped behind Imogen, Rhion and Fionna. They rode without speaking, javelins couched at their right sides, long, straight sabers sheathed on their left. Imogen turned in her saddle to survey them; their expressions were solemn, but not fearful, and their bodies were loose without being too relaxed. Imogen judged them ready for battle, and she hoped they'd meet the enemy soon, before they became complacent.

The banner signaled a halt, then waved to summon the company captains to conference. Imogen nodded at Rhion and Fionna, then kicked Victory into a trot and swept around the front of the warriors to join the Warleader.

Kernan stood about fifty feet ahead of the body of the Kirkellan warriors, looking into the distance, while his aides cut a square of turf about four feet on a side from the ground at his feet. Imogen joined the growing circle of captains, ten men and women of whom she was the youngest and least experienced. Not that this intimidated her. Of course not. The aides removed the turf and Kernan squatted to draw in the moist earth it revealed.

"The scouts have found the armies, about a mile and a half from where we stand," he said. "The Tremontanans have already engaged the Ruskalder in battle, but they haven't been fighting long. I estimate we will make a timely and dramatic entrance." He grinned up at his captains, who grinned back. "The Tremontanan Warleader chose his ground well. The battlefield is at the base of a low rise that circles part of the field, like so—" and he drew with his finger an arc off-center in the square of earth. "Here lie the Ruskalder, grouped loosely. The scouts say they are drawn out into a long line and are trying to encircle the Tremontanans, who are here, here, and here. The Tremontanan cavalry are on their far right and won't interfere with us.

"Our men and women will divide into three groups. The first will join me in charging the Ruskalder rear. The second will hold back and observe the results of the charge, then ride to attack the left-hand flank. Once we engage the Ruskalder with the charge, Regan, Imogen, and Darian will make passes at the Ruskalder front with javelins to give our allies a bit of help, then return and engage with sabers; let's try to drive the bastards in and back. Questions? Then take word to your warriors, and may heaven bless the Kirkellan today."

Imogen rode back to her company with the two other captains of her formation. Regan was an old friend who'd taught Imogen to throw a javelin; Imogen didn't know Darian well, but he was a well-respected fighter in his early forties who'd been fighting Ruskalder long before Imogen was born. Now he said, "I think we should break the javelin passes down further, say a troop at a time? That way we're not stepping on each other's hooves."

"I agree," Regan said. "You, me, then Imogen?"

"I was thinking Imogen should go first."

"Me?" Imogen exclaimed. "I've never led a pass before."

"No better time to learn," Darian said. "But in truth the first pass is the easiest. Later passes, you have to judge which way to direct your efforts into a crowd that's been thrown into confusion by the first pass. And it might turn out we only need five or six javelin passes before we switch to sabers. I'll signal the switch, then it's every company for itself, yes?"

Imogen and Regan nodded. Darian held out his hand, and the other two took it in a three-way grip. "Confusion to the enemy," Darian said with a grin.

Imogen returned to her company and explained the strategies to Rhion and Fionna, who set about separating the troops so they'd be ready for their ride. The warriors around her donned their helmets and their gauntlets, elbow-length gloves with soft, sturdy cloth hands and hardened leather arm guards, worn on the left arm for protection from enemy swords when it came time for the thrust and parry of saber work. Imogen's gauntlet had been her father's once, and it fit a little too tightly, but she thought of it as her talisman whenever she went into battle. Behind them, Darian and Regan's companies formed up into their own troops, four blocks of fifty-five warriors each. Imogen petted Victory, who tossed her head, as ready to ride out as Imogen was. That was the signal—no, just a stray breeze. Surely it was past time to move out.

There. Imogen raised her gauntleted left hand and signaled, and behind her, over three hundred Kirkellan warriors and their formidable horses followed where she led.

It took them about ten minutes to cover the distance to the battlefield. They heard the cries of war long before they saw the warriors. A brisk, light wind blew the sounds of battle to them, shouts and shrieks and the dull metallic sounds of swords clashing that faded and then became louder at the wind's whim. The banner signaled a halt well before the crest of the rise, and the Warleader went forward to survey the ground. He nodded, as if he liked what he saw, then returned, and the banner gave the signal for positions.

Imogen loosened her first javelin in its stirrup. Her palm was damp; she wiped it on Victory's flank, her own personal battle ritual. The roughened surface of the javelin's haft would keep it from sliding with sweat, though Imogen knew from experience that once she touched Victory's broad flank, her nerves disappeared, replaced with a hot passion that would fill her veins with the joy of battle. She gave the signal to assume positions for the first run, and looked back to watch the troops separate and spread in preparation for their run. Then she gave the signal to advance.

They were behind the Ruskalder, probably farther behind than Kernan had wanted, but it was more important they be behind than that they be close. Then she realized being too far behind put her company, and Darian's and Regan's, far out of position. Without thinking, she gestured for the companies to move parallel to the rise and south, where they'd be able to strike their assigned position without having to run hard to get there.

Hooves sounded beside her. "What are you doing?" Darian asked. Imogen pointed to the battlefield. Darian said, "Hmm," then, "Well done. Let's stop about three hundred feet from here." Imogen nodded, but her heart was pounding. Her first real order as a captain, and she'd gotten it right.

They stopped at the appointed position and Imogen surveyed the field. She couldn't tell how the battle was going. All her experience with war had been as a fighter within a *tiermatha*, or a troop of four *tiermathas*, against similarly small bands of Ruskalder. But it was obvious even from this distance the Ruskalder far outnumbered the Tremontanans. Imogen grinned with glee. The Ruskalder had no idea they were coming. They were going to sweep down behind them—

—and speaking of sweeping, the banner went over the rise and a wave of Kirkellan war horses followed it, slowly at first, then gaining speed until they were about a hundred paces from the Ruskalder warriors, only a few of whom realized what was happening. A thousand throats roared defiance, and the Kirkellan crashed into the Ruskalder rear line and flowed over it like a boiling river. Riders nearer the rear of the charge turned aside to attack the line in each direction, and the tone of the battle sounded a higher, more terrified note.

Imogen was so enthralled with watching the charge she almost forgot she had a charge of her own to lead. She cried out to Victory, who took the gentle slope eagerly, straining at the bit to have her turn in the battle. Imogen risked a glance over her shoulder; the troop streamed out behind her in perfect order, the spacing between them precise, and she felt that hot flood of joy fill her, the horse beneath her, the wind in her face, the pounding contact that joined her and Victory to the earth. She took the javelin in her hand and leaned to guide Victory in a curve just as if they were on the track, and there was her target, and she threw and saw her javelin take the Ruskalder in the belly. Then she was away, making a long sloping curve that would bring her around again for another run. At the top of the curve, she saw Darian's second troop, and beyond them a mass of devastation that bristled with Kirkellan javelins. Darian's first troop had already pushed the Ruskalder back, and as Imogen watched, the line collapsed and fled, pursued by Tremontanan soldiers shouting their own defiance at the foe.

Imogen pulled Victory up and signaled to her troops to do the same. Soon Darian arrived, breathing heavily, and said, "That was quicker than I expected. Split into troops and let's go for containment. Watch out for the Tremontanans, though, let's try not to kill our allies."

Imogen nodded, and looked around for Rhion and Fionna. "Is that normal?" she asked as the two approached. "Four runs, no injuries on our side, and they flee? I hate the Ruskalder, but they're not cowards."

"They were being pressed on two sides, and we never came close enough to them for them to strike," Rhion said. "But if you're eager to be injured, you can join us in making a drive for the center."

Imogen surveyed the field. Now that she was closer and had a better idea of what to look for, she could see that even though the Ruskalder western flank had collapsed, the fighting was still strong in the center and on the east. Far on the eastern flank, she saw horsemen. "We'll circle around and help our brothers and sisters," she said.

Rhion and Fionna shielded their eyes. "They look like they're flagging," Fionna said. "Let's give them some relief."

Re-formed into troops, they set out at a canter, making a wide loop around the fighting so as not to interfere with their allies. They passed a company of riflemen and women, their jobs done, who cheered them as they passed. Near the center of the field, a couple of tents were set up far back from the fighting, and the King's banner flew above one of them. Imogen saw several figures looking out over the field, one of them holding something that glinted in the sunlight. A runner dashed away from the tents only to pull up sharply as Imogen's company passed between him and the battle. Imogen waved a closed-fist salute at the men, but didn't have time to see if it was returned, because they were coming up on the eastern flank.

The noise of swords clashing and the screams of the dying were almost deafening. There, that woman had to be the captain, shouting orders from a position where she could observe the movement of battle. Imogen reined Victory in next to her. "Let us take your place!" she shouted. "We'll give you time to rest!"

The woman looked at her with dull, tired eyes. It took Imogen a moment to realize she'd spoken in Kirkellish, and she repeated herself in Tremontanan and watched the eyes glimmer with understanding. "They're pressing us hard!" she shouted, leaning close to Imogen, "and I'm afraid if we withdraw we'll just pull them after us."

"Leave me to take care of it," Imogen shouted back, and gave the signal to break all the troops into their individual *tiermathas*. Then she dragged on Victory's reins until the horse rose heavily on her hind legs, and Imogen drew her saber and brandished it in a narrow circle: the universal sign for the *tiermathas* to attack independently.

A dozen *tiermathas* dove at the line, focusing their efforts on the places where the light cavalry were engaged with the enemy. With their longer, straight sabers, they used their superior weight to thrust at the Ruskalder, hitting less frequently than the light cavalry's curved blades with their slashing attacks, but doing more lethal damage. The cavalry captain's aide pulled out a horn and blew a short passage of notes, and the Tremontanan cavalry pulled back as the Kirkellan warriors filled the gaps.

Imogen waited only long enough to see the Tremontanans return behind the line to safety before waving her own *tiermatha* to take position along the furthest eastern flank and let fly with the javelins, then make one last run before their javelins were gone and they could go sword to saber with their long-time enemy.

This was the part Imogen loved. She knew the javelins were crucial, had seen them break a Ruskalder warband in minutes, but there was nothing to compare with feeling steel connect with steel to send a jolt through your bones and teeth into your brain. She thrust, and parried and thrust again, and lost her helmet, and shouted at the Ruskalder, who shouted back at her. Victory screamed fury at them, dancing to keep them away from the foe, snapping at anyone who came to close to her. Then she screamed a different note, and Imogen saw dark blood dripping down her horse's foreleg, and the battle fury took her. It was tempting, at those times, to leap off Victory's back and engage the Ruskalder face to face, but she brought Victory around and shoved and kicked her way toward Dorenna, who was covered in blood that was almost certainly not her own, and waved wildly for the *tiermatha* to form up.

Some of them wouldn't see her, but enough of them came, Kionnal, Saevonna, Revalan, that they could form a line and push the Ruskalder back, one step at a time. Kionnal, faster than anyone could follow.

Revalan, bigger than Imogen and heavier, prone to swinging instead of thrusting but capable of taking off someone's arm, or head, with that swing. Saevonna, cold and methodical, fond of taking the enemy in the throat. And Dorenna…it was better not to watch Dorenna in battle at all.

Their line stretched as they pushed their way forward, keeping the Ruskalder from reaching them from behind. Imogen, at the eastern end, was surprised to find another cavalryman there, a Tremontanan soldier. "They're falling back, ma'am," he shouted, and Imogen wiped sweat and blood from her eyes—when had she been hit in the head?—and realized he was right. She signaled again, and shouted, and her *tiermatha* grouped up, most of them, anyway. Dorenna dropped the dead Ruskalder whose throat she'd just slit and shouted, "Did they give up, the cowards?"

Imogen shielded her eyes and then wiped more blood off her forehead. Really, this wound was annoying. "The Army's in pursuit," she said. "I think we won."

The cavalryman said, "Ma'am, you're wounded." Imogen looked at him and realized he wasn't much younger than she. What did he see in her that rated a "ma'am"?

"It is nothing," she said. "I need to gather my people."

They'd lost a few riders, not many, but the Kirkellan were few enough in number to feel every loss. None of Imogen's *tiermatha* had been killed, though most were injured, and it turned out some of the blood on Dorenna was hers; a lucky slash had cut deep into her left shoulder and it required stitches. Imogen's scalp wound was long and shallow and she couldn't remember encountering anyone tall enough to have given it to her, but once it was bandaged she didn't care.

After her wound was tended to, she went about finding the rest of her company, all but the twenty-seven who weren't coming back and the twelve horses who'd gone down under their riders. She led them to a spot half a mile from the battlefield where they made camp with the rest of the Kirkellan, next to the much larger Tremontanan camp, and built up a fire in the middle of the day and told stories of their lost friends, human and equine alike.

Imogen pillowed her head on her crossed hands, lay back and

looked up at the sky. White puffs of clouds drifted past. Her muscles relaxed, leaving her drowsy. They'd won. They hadn't been destroyed. Mother could have her treaty with the King of Tremontane and Imogen could have…what? Would the Ruskalder come after them next? Hrovald wasn't going to forget how she'd humiliated him. Oh, how she wished she'd come face to face with him today. Mother was right; she should have killed him. How many Tremontanan soldiers had died today? How many Ruskalder? How many of them were dead by her hand? She thought of Anneke, and suddenly the idea of killing Ruskalder didn't satisfy her.

"Excuse me, I'm looking for Imogen of the Kirkellan," someone said in Tremontanese. Imogen opened eyes she didn't remember closing.

"Imogen, she said your name," Areli said, jabbing her with a sharp finger.

"Ow," said Imogen. She sat up. "I am Imogen," she said in Tremontanese.

The speaker was a young woman in what Imogen guessed was royal livery, dark blue and silver with the crest Imogen had seen on the second flag flying over the King's tent. "Madam, the King requests your presence."

Imogen cast her eye on her grimy, blood-spattered clothing, felt the bandage wrapped around her head that was probably already dirty, and reflected that the King was going to think scruffiness was her permanent state. She heaved herself to her feet. "All right," she said, and let the young woman lead her away.

She eyed her escort, who was short and blond, and that reminded her of something. "Where is the Princess Elspeth?" she asked.

"She went south three days ago, madam, she and Owen Hunter. The King married them the day before that."

"Oh." They were married? Not that she thought Owen was stupid enough to think less of Elspeth for having been raped, but was she really that emotionally recovered yet? A pang of regret struck her. She hadn't been able to say goodbye to her friend. Well, she could ask the King to pass along her good wishes, probably. Not that it was the same.

They'd moved the King's tent away from the battlefield and set it once again in the middle of the Tremontanan camp. This time, he was alone inside, seated at a desk writing on a paper in front of him. He looked up when she entered, and his smile turned to concern. "You're wounded. Let me call the camp healer for you."

"It is nothing large. Just much blood. Head wounds bleed."

"I've heard that. Please, sit down." He shut his inkwell and laid down his pen. "Your company came to the aid of our cavalry today," he said. "I saw you wave."

"You know that was I—it is to say, me?"

"No one else looks like you. Thank you. The cavalry commander tells me they were about to let that flank collapse, and we would have shored it up in time, but not without much loss of life. So—thank you."

Imogen shrugged. "It is what the allies do. Someday it will be you come to our aid."

"I hope it never comes to that, but I assure you we will." The King tapped the paper in front of him. "I'm making notes for meeting with your mother later. I know you don't do the negotiating, but do you think this treaty is something she wants?"

"I think so. The *matrian* is...practical. She wants no war with Ruskald. She prefer—prefers we have allies against them than to ally with them again."

"Not that Hrovald would want an alliance with you now."

"Hrovald would more like to have my head on a stick, I think."

The King laughed. "Probably. So, what will you do now?"

Imogen shrugged. "Go home. Train, ride Victory, train again."

"Is that—excuse me if this is personal—but is that what you always wanted to do?"

"Yes. No. I want to be Warleader. Someday it is what I will do. But that is far in the distance—in the future."

"I think you're well suited for it."

They both fell silent. Imogen wasn't sure what else to say to a King, especially one who wasn't a warrior. "Do you not fight?" she asked.

He shook his head. "I am not *allowed* to fight," he said. "Endangering myself endangers the Crown. And with just me and Elspeth…the North family has been small for many years now."

"I hear Owen and Elspeth are married."

"Yes. Four days ago. Elspeth asked me to say goodbye to you, and thanks. You have been the best of friends to her."

"I could not protect her from everything. I am sorry."

"That's not a guilt you should bear. It's all on Hesketh's head, and he's paid for it with his life."

"Is Elspeth…." She wasn't sure how frank Tremontanans were about sex, given Elspeth's extreme reaction and apparent inability to even say the word. "Is she entirely recovered yet?"

"I don't know." He ran his hand through his hair, disordering it somewhat. "When Owen came to me to ask if I'd marry them immediately, I told him I thought it was a bad idea. He said—did Elspeth tell you they were meant to marry at Wintersmeet? So their marriage was already several months delayed. Owen wanted it to be very clear his feelings for her weren't changed by what happened, as a reassurance to her, and he felt waiting to marry for any reason would make her feel the delay was her fault. He also said they'd discussed things and he'd told Elspeth he wasn't going to push her into anything she wasn't ready for—that sex would be her decision. So they're married, and Elspeth will see the palace healer when they arrive home, and I trust the two of them to work it out. Whatever that ultimately means."

"I think it is a good thing. She loves him very much."

"And he loves her. You should ask her to tell the story of how we met Owen. It's funnier from her perspective."

"I—" She felt awkward pointing out that she was probably never going farther into Tremontane than she was now. "It is good she was not here for the battle."

"That, and our mother was frantic over her by the time the Army went north. Telecoder messages that her youngest is safe are not the same as seeing her in the flesh."

"What is your mother like?" It seemed Imogen could think of things to ask, after all. And she really was curious about Elspeth's family.

"Smart. Beautiful. A good rider—not to Kirkellan standards, of course, but she likes riding. She's the Royal Librarian and the best one there's ever been. Elspeth looks like her. I look more like my—my father, what Mother calls the North good looks." He shook his head self-deprecatingly. "Me, Father, his sister Queen Zara…it breeds true in every generation, I hear." He certainly was attractive, with that dark hair and those blue eyes, but not when he was making the face he was then. Imogen wanted to ask about his father, but even her limited understanding of the language had caught that hesitation of the King's when he spoke of him, and she guessed it was not a subject he wanted to discuss.

"The *matrian* will be here tomorrow," he said, "for negotiations, but I was hoping you might have supper with me tonight. I'd like to understand more about your people before I meet with your mother."

"I like to," Imogen said, "but tonight is the time to mourn our dead. I am sorry."

"I understand completely," the King said. "Please give my regards to your Warleader, and my thanks." He seemed disappointed, which made Imogen feel bad at having to refuse his invitation. She liked him, and she thought he was a little lonely now Elspeth and Owen were gone. After she bade him goodbye and left the tent, she chuckled at the exalted circles she now moved in. Wife, and now ex-wife, of one King; friend and confidante of another. Well, now she could go back to being just Imogen of the Kirkellan, daughter of the *matrian*, sister and daughter and rider of Victory and Warleader in training. It would be such a relief to be herself again.

CHAPTER FIFTEEN

"I'm bored," Revalan said.

"Go for a ride," Dorenna told him.

"I'm bored of that too. Rohrnan's bored of it."

"I'm bored of your being bored."

"Stop squabbling," Imogen said. But she was bored, too. They were waiting for the *matrian* to conclude diplomatic negotiations so the Kirkellan warriors could return home. Some of the company captains had suggested leaving a few at a time, dispersing gradually, but Kernan had flatly refused to consider it. So the companies, disbanded into their *tiermathas*, sat, and argued, and ate, and waited.

"There's not even anywhere to go for some privacy," Kionnal complained.

"You only want privacy for one thing," Revalan said.

"Yes, well, it's something worth doing and I don't get bored of it," Kionnal retorted.

"Did no one hear me tell you to stop squabbling?"

"Imogen, squabbling is the only thing that's keeping us sane."

"Someone's coming out of the tent," Saevonna said. Imogen turned to look. Sure enough, it was her mother and the King of Tremontane emerging from the tent they'd set up an equal distance between the camps for the negotiations. They clasped hands, and the *matrian*'s honor guard escorted her back to the great tent. Imogen got to her feet and followed.

Inside, her mother shooed the honor guard back outside and kicked her shoes off. "Well?" Imogen asked.

"Do you always enter without being invited?"

"If I wait for an invitation, I never get to do anything."

"In some ways, you're worse than Caele." Mother took a water flask from a nearby camp chair and took a long drink. "Negotiating makes my throat dry. Yes, Imogen, we have a treaty. It is full of details I'm sure you'd find boring. We'll have a number of *tiermathas* joining with

Tremontane to assist them in establishing their new territory, for example. But...." She set the flask aside. "You might want to have a seat."

"What did you do? If it's another *banrach*, Mother—"

"Tremontanans are far too serious about their marriage vows to agree to the *banrach*. No, it's nothing so dire. I didn't realize how much of an impression you'd made on King Jeffrey."

"I helped his sister and his best friend escape from Hrovald, and I fought against his enemies."

"That, and he enjoys talking to you. At least, that's what he said."

"Mother, where are you going with this?"

Mother heaved a deep sigh. "Part of the treaty is an exchange of diplomatic ambassadors—"

Imogen sat straight up in her camp chair. "*Mother*!"

"You speak the language, the King likes you, and—"

"I'm no diplomat! I'm a warrior!"

"*Listen to me*," Mother said, low and harsh. "We are entering an era of peace. Hrovald won't come against our combined forces for at least a generation. There's no one left to fight. You could stay here and train to be Caele's Warleader, and I know that's something you've always wanted, but with no wars to prosecute, it would be a waste of your life. I know you're a skilled fighter. I also know you have so many other skills you've never even tried to use. I don't want you to look back ten years from now and regret giving those years up to a dream that can't be fulfilled."

"I am *never* going to regret being a warrior, Mother. It's who I am."

"It's not the whole of who you are."

"It's the part of me I care about."

"Because it's the only part of you that you know." Mother's face hardened. "You're going to be our ambassador to Tremontane. It's a temporary assignment, just one year, and you *will* do your best to learn those skills and you *will* represent the Kirkellan to the best of your abilities. Then you'll return home, and you can do whatever you want to with your life, and I won't say a word."

Tears of anger filled Imogen's eyes. "You can't force me to do this."

"Your mother can't. The *matrian* can. Do you wish to go against her authority? What kind of warrior would that make you?"

Imogen screwed her eyes shut. "I just wanted to come home," she said in a small voice.

"I know," said her mother, and she heard a rustle of fabric and felt a cool touch on her brow just below the bandage. "Oh, Imogen, I know. I sent you to Ruskald because you were the only choice. Now I send you to Tremontane because you are the *best* choice, and it is the best choice for you, and a far better opportunity than living in Hrovald's house was. The Tremontanans don't live like we do, you know, and being there will be a challenge, and you have never backed down before a challenge in your life. One year, to learn about those parts of you you've never discovered. You were willing to face five years in Ruskald, among enemies. What's one year among allies, if not friends?"

Imogen lowered her head. "I'm taking Victory," she said.

"And you're taking your *tiermatha*," her mother said. "And a full company of riders."

At first light, the camps began to pack up. Imogen had been packed since before dawn. Unable to sleep, she groomed Victory until the horse complained, then stood staring at the eastern sky watching pink light creep across the horizon. As soon as the pink turned to gold, she went around prodding lumps of groaning people until she had her *tiermatha* awake, fed, clothed and packed. She surveyed them, noticing in particular Dorenna's gory jerkin, Kallum's torn sleeve, their general grubbiness, and her own scruffy and slightly odorous appearance. "The Tremontanans will think we're refugees," she complained.

"It's not like we have water to spare for bathing, Imo. And we look like Kirkellan," said Dorenna.

"Then everyone will think the Kirkellan look like refugees."

"I don't see why you care what people think of how you look. It's never bothered you before," said Areli.

"I wasn't a diplomatic ambassador before. They're going to judge the Kirkellan based on what I do. It's an enormous burden."

"You're whining again," Dorenna said, and winced as she moved her shoulder the wrong way. "It's unattractive. So now you look like an *unattractive* refugee."

"And you're missing out on the adventure of this," Saevonna said.

Imogen went from glaring at Dorenna to glaring at Saevonna. "How exactly is this an adventure, and is there any way I can get you to stop being cheerful about it?"

Saevonna gave her an impish grin. "We get to introduce real horses and horsemanship to these backward Tremontanans. We get to be exotic strangers at a foreign court. And, best of all, as exotic strangers we get our pick of the best-looking men and women at court, and I don't know if you were paying attention, but some of those Tremontanan soldiers were *extremely* good-looking."

"Yes, but they also have those rules about no sex before marriage."

"Sex isn't everything. Besides," Saevonna said, blushing unexpectedly, "maybe marrying a Tremontanan wouldn't be so bad."

Areli and Revalan gasped together. Kallum said, "Do you mean to tell us you've got your eye on someone already?"

Saevonna shrugged. "Maybe. It's hard to tell when you don't speak the same language. I'm just saying I'm willing to keep an open mind."

"Maybe we need to make an effort to learn the language," Kallum said. "Not that I've ever had any trouble making my intentions clear."

"Might be a good idea to at least learn their words for 'no' and 'get away from me, you pervert,'" Kionnal said.

Kallum shrugged. "Like I said, maybe we should learn the language. It can't be too hard if Imogen learned it."

"Imogen," Mother called, and Imogen jumped. Her mother had approached silently, on foot, and on seeing her Imogen felt heavy of heart, as if her body were getting a head start on homesickness. She went to meet her mother a little way from the *tiermatha*, who in turn backed away a few paces to give them some privacy.

Her mother's face was serene, but her eyes were red and puffy. "I'm not going to apologize for sending you," she said, "because I don't think I'm wrong. But I'm sorry to send you off with such harsh words between us."

Imogen put her arms around her mother and hugged her, hard. "I don't want to go," she said, "and I'm not sure I agree with you. But you're right, I've never backed down from a challenge, and I think this challenge will make me a stronger warrior in the long run." She released her, and stepped away. "Besides, at least I'll be able to train in Aurilien," she added.

"Show them what a Kirkellan woman is like, warrior and peacemaker," Mother said, and saluted her. Tears streaked her face. Imogen swiped at her cheeks with the back of her hand, then turned and mounted Victory before she could burst into tears completely.

"Let's go," she said hoarsely, and signaled Fionna and Rhion to move their troops out. The *tiermatha* mounted and followed Imogen down the rise toward the Tremontanan camp.

It was eerily like, and completely unlike, the ride they'd taken through Hrovald's camp some ten months before. Like, because the camp was in the process of being broken, and collapsed tents and bundles lay everywhere. Unlike, because the men and women taking down tents and packing belongings waved and smiled at them as they passed. The Kirkellan smiled and waved in return, and Imogen's heavy heart eased somewhat. One year in Tremontane was a very different prospect than five in Ruskald.

The King's tent had already been packed away when they reached the spot it had stood. The King and a few of his advisers stood conversing nearby, a conversation that cut off when the King saw them. His face brightened. "Are you the ambassador, then?" he exclaimed. "The *matrian* only said she had someone in mind, but…this really is excellent news. I know Elspeth will be thrilled to see you again. Come, there are some people you should meet."

He offered his hand as if he meant to help her dismount, and Imogen, concluding it was a friendly gesture and not an insult, took it. "This is Marcus Anselm, commanding general of the Army…Colonel Henry Stubbs…Diana Ashmore, Baroness of Daxtry…oh, and Colonel Fred Williams. Gentlemen, Baroness, this is Imogen of the Kirkellan, ambassador to Tremontane."

Looking at these perfectly groomed and clean people, Imogen had never felt less like an ambassador in the whole short time she'd been one. But she held her head high, straightened her spine, and said, "I am pleased to meet you." There, her accent hadn't been quite as thick, had it? Not that she cared, but the way the Baroness looked at her made her feel at least seven feet tall with hairy toes. Imogen remembered her as the woman she'd seen in the King's tent that first night. She stood close to him as if waiting for his instructions.

"Fred's coming with us back to Aurilien with the Home Guard, and these other three will be establishing our new territory. The Baroness's lands abut these, and she's been a powerful force for keeping the Ruskalder at bay for years."

Imogen wasn't sure how many years that might be; the Baroness didn't look to be more than in her mid-twenties. She had an elegant face with a long, straight nose she now looked down at, or rather up at, Imogen. "It will be interesting having the Kirkellan for neighbors now," she said quietly, and smiled, and Imogen realized the Baroness's supercilious air was the unfortunate result of her eyes being too close to her very straight nose. She seemed quite nice when she smiled.

Marcus Anselm, on the other hand, just grunted and nodded when she was introduced. She wanted to ask him about the battle, but he intimidated her a little. The two colonels gave her friendly nods and gave skeptical glances toward the troops of riders. "I didn't realize the ambassador's retinue was so…large," Stubbs said.

"I do not understand retinue," Imogen said.

"The riders that accompany you as part of your household," he explained.

"These are for you," Imogen said, then shook her head. "It is to say, they are to increase the Army as a token of…of esteem."

Williams looked at the King. "Is that a good idea?"

"It's strategically sound," said the King. "I suggested we might develop tactics that will allow our armies to integrate more fully, if the Ruskalder decide they want to come back for another go. The *matrian* hopes this will also foster good will between our nations. Our diplomatic envoy will not be militaristic, but will serve the same purpose. I did insist the troops be under Fred's command—can you explain that to them, um...." He laughed self-consciously. "I don't know what to call you. Madam ambassador seems so pretentious."

Imogen didn't know what 'pretentious' meant, but she could guess his problem. "I am just Imogen," she said. "We have no titles the way you do. It is not—you are not disrespectful, just to use the name."

"Very well...Imogen...could you explain the situation? I didn't think about the language barrier, and I don't want to make this a jurisdictional nightmare. I just want your people to feel welcome in Tremontane, and I want Fred to be able to manage all the troops under his command."

Imogen turned to Fionna and Rhion, and said, "Apparently the *matrian* promised your troops would be under that man's command, as if he were the company captain. I have no idea what she was thinking, but he seems awfully nervous, so do you think you could manage to take orders from him?"

"I don't even speak his language, Imogen, how do you propose I do that?" Rhion exclaimed.

"Do not worry, she is just unhappy about the barrier of language," Imogen said to Williams, who didn't look any happier than Rhion did. "Rhion, *please* don't start an international incident before we've even left the camp. You'll be able to learn Tremontanan tactics from him, and he's supposed to learn Kirkellan strategy from you. It will...it'll be an adventure."

Rhion and Fionna looked at each other and laughed. "An adventure? All right, Imogen, if you're that desperate, we will put ourselves under his command. And I guess we'd better start learning the language."

Imogen controlled a sigh. "They understand. They say, they will start learning to speak your language and it will be an adventure."

Williams was still wary, but he nodded. "Guess we could stand to learn a word or three of Kirkellish," he said.

"Then we're going to head out. Marcus, I'll have two more telecoders to you by the end of the month. Diana, we'll see you in

Aurilien in a week or so, yes? Keep me apprised of any developments. I want to know if the Ruskalder even waggle their furry buttocks in our direction."

"Let me know if you need me there sooner," Diana said, laying her hand on the King's arm. "I imagine the Council is going to be very busy in the coming weeks."

"I will." He saluted the three, then accepted the reins of a very good black gelding and mounted without assistance, though he wasn't terribly graceful about it. Imogen threw herself back atop Victory and waited for him to signal the advance. He'd been glad to see her, that was something, and she already knew Elspeth and Owen, and she had one hundred and eighteen Kirkellan warriors at her back. Maybe she could see this as an adventure after all.

Part Two: Tremontane

CHAPTER SIXTEEN

Imogen's time in Ranstjad had not prepared her for her first sight of Aurilien. The city was *enormous.* It sprawled across the lowland plain like a lazy, sleeping cat, its golden wall failing to restrain the low-roofed buildings that spilled over into the green wooded landscape surrounding it. More people lived in this one city than made up the entire Kirkellan kinship. She was too overwhelmed even to gawk. The King, riding beside her, took in her silence and interpreted it correctly.

"I so rarely leave the city I forget what it looks like from out here," he said. "From inside, you only see pieces of it, and it's not so…so…it's had hundreds of years to become what it is, and it never fails to amaze me. I hope you'll like it. I know it's different from what you're used to."

"It is beautiful. And powerful," Imogen said. They entered another grove of trees and the city was lost to view. Forests were another thing Imogen had been unprepared for; the pines of Ruskald, the carpets of needles underfoot, were nothing like the great leafy variety of the southern forests, birch and maple and ash and oak giving way to one another as they descended out of the foothills of the Rockwild Range, as King Jeffrey called the Spine of the World, into the lowlands of Tremontane. Or perhaps it was simply that Imogen had lived in Ranstjad mostly in the winter, when all the creatures seemed to sleep. Here there were birds courting and challenging one another, and small animals darting between roots or up tree trunks, and occasionally a small deer would flit across the road. Imogen thought of the reindeer of the north, and remembered in a few months the hunts would begin, and felt a pang of homesickness so great she had to blink hard to keep from crying in front of the King, who would be embarrassed by her tears, which would make her cry harder.

When they emerged from the trees, the city wall loomed beyond a small settlement of those low-roofed houses. It was less intimidating than the sight of the whole city had been. The road, which until then had been a nice packed earth, was now covered with broad stones that had been traveled so often they were pressed deep into the ground, their faintly curving tops all that was visible of them. This could not be good for the Kirkellan horses' feet. She'd have to look into shoeing them, if they were going to live here for a year.

Men and women and children came out of the houses to stare at them, then to cheer as they realized who was passing. The King waved at them, smiling, but even though Imogen knew she was supposed to represent her people, she felt so uncomfortable at how they looked at her she could only straighten her spine and nod in what she hoped was a friendly fashion. By the expressions on their faces, it wasn't successful.

The crowds grew as they neared the gate, drawn to the King's banner that went before their extraordinary procession of marching soldiers and over one hundred giant horses. Imogen glanced at the King and realized with surprise his smile was strained and his eyes were glassy and focused on the far distance. "You are not well," she said in a voice she hoped carried over the sound of the crowd without being audible beyond the two of them.

"I'm fine," he said, continuing to wave. "Three years and I haven't gotten used to this. I feel—" He shook his head as if to negate his words. "I'm not good with crowds, is all. My father used to—that is, it was easier when there were two of us to be stared at."He looked at her and his smile became more genuine, for a moment. Imogen felt the pressure of all those eyes on him and on her and understood how he felt. *He's still grieving,* she realized, and felt a surge of compassion for him. Well, he wasn't alone now.

She put on her sunniest smile and waved at the people clamoring near her feet. To her amazement, they smiled back at her. She glanced at the King, whose fixed smile had disappeared into a look of astonishment. If he could manage it, so could she. She smiled at him even more broadly and went back to waving. "You are right," she said over the noise, "it is easier when there are two."

To her surprise, he laughed. "You are very wise, madam ambassador." He turned away to greet the crowds, but she knew he was still smiling.

The gate guards in green and brown saluted them as they passed. Imogen leaned over to the King and said, "Why is it some wear those colors and some wear the other? The blue and the silver?"

"Those are the colors of Tremontane," the King explained. "Green and brown for the mountains. Blue and silver is for the house of North, my family. The ones who wear it are in service to my family, not to the kingdom."

"The blue and the silver is prettier," Imogen said, and the King laughed.

"Don't tell anyone, but I agree," he said. He went back to waving at the crowd, and Imogen joined him. If anything, the throng of people lining the street was larger than the one outside the city, their cries deafening. It became impossible for her to speak to the King; even a shout would be unintelligible. She continued to wave and smile until her face hurt and her arm was sore. He was right; Aurilien was less grand once you were within her boundaries. It was nothing like Ranstjad, and not only because it was bigger. Everything seemed more cheerful here, possibly because of the warmer southern sun, but also because the buildings didn't seem to huddle together waiting for something to attack them. The roofs were more gently sloped, the wooden walls whitewashed or painted neatly, the doors stained dark colors to contrast with the lighter walls. Signs painted with pictures declared what was available inside: a foaming mug for a tavern, a candle for an inn, a bar of soap for…well, what could that be for? A bathing house? Imogen, accustomed to bathing in a tin tub in the privacy of her family tent, could not imagine an entire house given over to bathing people.

The crowds thinned somewhat as they passed into a district where the buildings were made of stone rather than wood, and now Imogen did gape at these tall, ornate houses like mountains with steps leading up to their wide doors and glass windows several feet across that lined their faces three or even four rows high. Plants grew in stone pots at the feet of the stairs, some of them flowering, some like tiny trees. Horses pulling wheeled, roofed carts pulled to one side as the procession passed, and men and women looked out of the carts and cheered and waved squares of white cloth. Carts for pulling people! The horses didn't look very cheerful about it. Perhaps they thought there were better things they could do, like be ridden properly.

They turned onto a road four times as wide as the rest, and it seemed this was where the rest of the city had come to wait for them, and cheer, and wave. More of the covered carts lined the road, people inside cheering, drivers sitting on top cheering, horses indifferent. Small children ran alongside the procession, though not too close to the Kirkellan horses, whose hooves were as large as some of the children's heads. Imogen waved down at them, and they beamed at her. How much of this did they understand, she wondered, how many of them knew why everyone was cheering? Come to think on it, did *she* know why they were cheering? Were they happy about the successful defeat of the Ruskalder army, or did they just like King Jeffrey? It was impossible to tell.

The road led to a high stone wall with an ironwork gate that stood open to receive them. The King reined in his horse, causing the procession to pile up behind him, and said, "Simon will take you to the embassy now. I'd like to invite you to dine with my family tonight. I know Elspeth is eager to see you."

"I am glad to come," Imogen said. He nodded to her and continued through the iron gate, leaving Imogen feeling a little lost. She stiffened her spine and gestured to the *tiermatha* to follow her and Simon Rettick, Imogen's diplomatic liaison and, she thought, nursemaid. He was a stout, red-bearded fellow with a pleasant smile who spoke Kirkellish with a strong accent.

"It's not far from the palace," he told Imogen, coming to ride beside her. "I hope there will be room. Your *tiermatha* may have to double up."

"I'm sure it will be fine. We're used to sleeping rough."

Simon glanced at her sidelong. "I don't think any of you will think of the embassy as 'sleeping rough.' It's quite comfortable, and fully staffed, though you may want to engage a lady's maid while you're here."

"Is that something you can help with?"

"Yes. Don't hesitate to ask for whatever you need, information or otherwise."

"And there's sufficient stable room?"

"I believe so. The North family purchased the estate from a wealthy family—I should say, formerly wealthy family—who were rather fond of horses. In fact, I believe the stables are more impressive than the house." He laughed. "I suppose you'll have to tell me if that's true."

"But the Norths—they didn't buy this estate just for our embassy, did they?"

"No. It's just one of a handful of properties the family owns in Aurilien. It was originally intended to house members of the extended royal family, a hundred years ago when the North family was much larger than it is now. It's been rented out for the last fifteen or twenty years and has been empty for almost two. So it was a fortunate circumstance you were in need of an embassy building."

The houses they passed now, while made of stone and lined with glass windows, were much bigger than the beautiful houses they'd seen earlier, most of them easily the size of the King's house back in Ranstjad. Some of them were set far back from the street, great stone walls topped with lacy ironwork spikes separating them from passersby. Through their gates Imogen could see gardens of well-trimmed shrubberies and beds of flowers she didn't recognize. She was so caught up in staring at their beauties she didn't at first realize Simon had stopped. "This is it," he said.

Imogen looked up. The house she faced was built of pinkish-grey granite blocks on a rougher granite foundation. Stairs led up to a polished oak door with brass fittings, beside which was a brass button set in a brass plaque decorated with scrollwork. There were no windows at street level, but the second and third stories were lined with glass panes that winked in the sunlight, all of them curtained off against prying eyes.

"We'll go around the back," Simon said, and they went around a corner, down an alley between the embassy and its neighbor, and behind the house to a wooden gate Imogen could almost see over. Simon rang the bell hanging to the left of the gate, and said, "They keep it locked. Even in these neighborhoods, there's crime. Wouldn't want your horses to be stolen."

Revalan laughed. "I'd like to see the thief who'd try it. He'd be lucky to get away with all the body parts he went in with."

"Nevertheless, just ring the bell when you return from a ride and someone will let you in."

"Where can we go riding?" Saevonna asked, casting a doubtful eye on the stone walls and pavement surrounding them.

"I'll find that out for you." He rang the bell again, more violently this time. "Certainly taking their time about this."

The gate cracked open. "What?" said a wiry woman dressed in old trousers and a sleeveless shirt that had originally been dark blue.

"The *Kirkellan ambassador* and her party would like to stable their horses, if it's not too much of an inconvenience," Simon said in Tremontanese.

The woman registered the presence of thirteen Kirkellan horses. Her mouth dropped open. "Sorry," she said. "I've had kids ringing the bell all morning. Come on in." She pulled the gate open wider and they filed in, two by two, through the relatively narrow space.

The stable yard hummed with activity and was, as promised, spacious. Sheds lined one side of the space and a long, low-roofed building occupied the other. "There's only ten stalls. Could you tell milady I'm sorry about that? We didn't know there would be so many of them."

"I speak your language," Imogen said.

"That's a relief. I was trying to figure out how to mime 'oats'." Imogen dismounted and took the woman's proffered hand. "Kate Fanshaw, milady, and I'm the stable mistress here."

"I am not milady. I am just Imogen."

"Begging your pardon, milady, but you're an ambassador and a diplomat and that makes you 'milady' as far as I'm concerned, and I'd better not hear of my people calling you otherwise."

Imogen shrugged. By the look of her, Kate Fanshaw was not a woman accustomed to losing arguments. "This is my *tiermatha,*" she said. "We will need three more stalls very soon."

"I'll get my people building a second stable right away. We should be able to knock together some temporary stalls until then. What's her name?"

"This is Victory. You may touch her if you wish."

Fanshaw stroked Victory's neck. "She's beautiful. They're all extraordinary. I never thought I'd see even one Kirkellan horse in my life, let alone thirteen. Good heaven, she's unshod. May I look at her hoof?"

Imogen nodded, and Fanshaw gently raised Victory's leg to peer at the hoof. "She doesn't go unshod all year, does she?"

"In winter she has shoes. But mostly she wears none."

"You might want to consider shoeing all of them. The streets around here are hard on hooves. I know an excellent farrier, can come in whenever you like."

"Thank you. We will want to meet him first."

"Naturally. Can I—but no, I've heard you care for your animals yourselves."

"Yes, though I think I will be busy…." Imogen felt embarrassed. Until she'd gone to Hrovald's house, no one had ever fed or groomed Victory but her. "I will need someone to help when I cannot be there."

"That someone will be me, milady, and I guarantee Victory will be well cared for."

The *tiermatha* chose stalls, Simon deferring to the diplomatic party, Imogen opting to wait for the new building, and Revalan and Lorcan losing the draw for the other two places. They removed tack out in the open, uncomfortable at the attention they got until a few of the younger stablehands hesitantly offered their services. Then it seemed everyone wanted to do something for the Kirkellan horses. Imogen saw her saddle and harness hauled off by a girl almost short enough to walk under Victory's belly, and hoped they were all as competent as Fanshaw, with her air of unconcern, implied.

Having seen an impromptu corral installed and Victory penned safely inside, she kissed her horse on her broad nose and turned to look inquiringly at Simon. "There's a back door," he said, "over this way, so you'll only use the gate when you go riding." The back door was small and unobtrusive. Inside was a narrow hallway with a polished wooden floor leading to a steep flight of stairs, at the top of which was a short landing about five feet on a side and a door with no latch that swung freely on its hinges.

Imogen pushed through the door and found herself staring in wonder at the room beyond. Its white walls stretched higher than any of the *tiermatha* could reach to a ceiling at least two stories tall. A lamp Device covered in crystals hung from the ceiling, casting glittering reflections on the walls. To the left and right were open archways through which they could see padded chairs, some very long, spindly-legged tables, and items of furniture none of them had ever seen, even in Hrovald's house. Flowers in tall vases gave off delicate, sweet scents. There was color everywhere, bright reds and golds in the cushions, deep blues in the rugs spread over the glossy wooden floors, and every color of the rainbow in paintings hung on the walls. The door directly opposite them turned out to be (when Saevonna opened it) the front door of the house. Beside them to the right was a wide, curving staircase, carpeted in white; directly to their left was another narrow hallway, which led to the back of the house, and beyond the stairway was a much wider hallway that did the same.

"This is…." Dorenna began, then trailed off.

Revalan wandered into the room on the left and squeezed the cushion of one of the long-seated chairs. "You could almost sleep on this."

"Excuse me for a moment," Simon said, and went down the narrow hallway. Imogen almost didn't register he'd gone. She ran her finger along the arm of a marble statue of a nude woman about two feet tall who seemed poised to take flight off her pedestal. The stone was cold and smooth to the touch. She couldn't imagine lugging it around from camp to camp; that was one advantage to living pinned down in a city, but at the moment, surrounded by opulence she'd never imagined existed, she missed her family tent and the friendly bickering of Torin and Neve over who would get the last piece of reindeer meat.

"This is Paula Schotton," Simon said, returning with a tall, thin, elderly woman in tow. "She's the housekeeper. Anything you need in the city, ask me; anything you need in the house, ask her."

Imogen didn't like the look of her. She had a stern face, thin lips and wrinkled, bony hands. "I don't speak your language," she said, and Imogen realized the sternness and thinness were caused by nerves, not a sour disposition.

"I speak yours, though, and we will all try to learn," Imogen assured her, coming forward to shake the woman's hand. It was every bit as bony as she'd imagined, but Schotton smiled, which made her look a lot more friendly.

"You can call me Mistress Schotton, then, and I'll be happy to help you with whatever you want. Sorry we didn't have the staff here to greet you, but I'm afraid we didn't have notice of your arrival."

"That is all right, Mistress Schotton, I will greet them when I go to supper at the palace tonight."

Mistress Schotton's mouth fell open just a bit, but she said, "Then I will arrange that. Let me show you to your rooms…I apologize again, but we weren't told how many of you there would be."

Imogen was starting to be annoyed with the King, who'd said all the arrangements had been made. He'd sent all those telecodes on the road; she'd thought at least some of them had to do with the Kirkellan delegation. Well, he *was* the King, maybe that was all beneath him and it was his underlings who'd failed.

Mistress Schotton seemed determined to make up for being so behindhand in her preparations by showing the Kirkellan every room in the house. Aside from the ones with chairs and tables, most of them made no sense to Imogen, though there was a room filled with books, more books than she'd ever imagined existed. She wished she could show it to her father, who treasured his five books and wished he had room to carry more. After a while the rooms began to blur together, so when Mistress Schotton opened a door and said, "I think the master suite is appropriate for you, madam ambassador," it took her a moment to understand the woman was addressing her.

The room was painted and upholstered in soft browns and muted golds, comforting to the eye. Two chairs were drawn up near a fireplace in which no fire had been laid, though since this was springtime in the south, a fire wasn't needed. A spindly-legged desk and chair stood near two tall windows, and another one of those elongated chairs had been placed at an angle facing the windows. An open door in the far wall showed a glimpse of another, brighter room.

"This is a sleeping room?" Areli asked doubtfully. "Are you supposed to sleep on that long chair? Kionnal, I hope ours is bigger than that."

"There were beds in Hrovald's house, there must be beds here," Imogen began, but Mistress Schotton, ignoring the conversation she couldn't understand, went to the far door while the rest of the *tiermatha* crowded in around the chairs and the fireplace.

"The bedroom," the housekeeper said, and Imogen went to the door and gasped. There was a bed big enough to fit two of Imogen, assuming another could be found and was willing to share. It was covered with a thick blue blanket and had half a dozen pillows arranged on it. Another table and chair were tucked into a corner, next to one of two other doors in the room. Imogen wondered what all the tables and chairs were for. It seemed Tremontanans were fond of tables.

"Closet," Mistress Schotton said, opening the door near the table. This turned out to be a tiny, empty room with a dresser and long poles running from wall to wall at head height. Imogen had no idea what it was for, so she tried to look nonchalant, as if closets were part of her everyday experience. "Bathing chamber," the housekeeper added, opening the other door and revealing a tiled room with an enormous ceramic tub over which a curved pipe protruded. Mistress Schotton twisted a knob on the pipe and water began to flow. "I'm sorry if this is patronizing, but I don't know that you have much indoor plumbing where you come from. Turn the handle and the water flows; turn it more, and the water heats up."

Imogen ran her fingers under the water, which was warm—no, it was almost hot enough to burn! She snatched her hand away and rubbed it dry on her trousers. "Come in here and see this!" she called out in

Kirkellish. The *tiermatha* crowded into the bathing chamber and made incredulous noises as she demonstrated the miraculous pipe.

"You realize this housekeeper thinks we're all a bunch of savages, right?" Kallum drawled.

"I feel like a savage," Dorenna said.

"Just remember how out of place she'd be roaming the Eidestal with the kinship," Kionnal said.

Imogen said nothing, but privately she wondered what more they were ignorant of. Eskandel and Veribold were at least as sophisticated as Tremontane. What kind of ambassador could she be if she could only gawk in wonder at the trappings of city life?

Chapter Seventeen

Between getting settled, explaining to Mistress Schotton that Areli and Kionnal were married—she'd looked appalled when the two of them started stowing their gear together—and washing in the beautiful big tub, it seemed like no time at all before Imogen was greeting the household staff, lined up in rows in the foyer, then getting into one of the carts Simon called a carriage, drawn by more unhappy horses, and leaving for the palace. Imogen had told Simon she could ride her own horse, but he insisted this was how people behaved in the city. Imogen filed that away for further consideration. Yes, they were in the city, but she was still Kirkellan; how much of her identity would she be expected to give up? Imogen stared out the window and felt a chill that had nothing to do with the evening air. Her mother had told her she had skills she'd never learned, parts of her personality she'd never explored, but she hadn't told Imogen to give up who she was already. She was a warrior. That wasn't going to change.

The palace was even more luxurious than the embassy, though Imogen wouldn't have thought that possible. It looked old, but in patches; Imogen knew nothing of architecture, but even she could tell it had been built by many different hands over time. She stared up at the dark tower extending high above the palace roofs, a long black finger pointing at ungoverned heaven like a warning, or possibly defiance. Directed by a guard, she walked dazedly through corridors and up stairs until she reached a hallway that led to a door guarded by two soldiers in blue and silver, fully armed and armored. Not knowing what else to do, she saluted them; the soldiers examined her closely, then opened the door and indicated she should enter.

Another hallway paneled in light wood below and painted a creamy white above led to a vast room filled with sofas (Mistress Schotton had supplied this word for the elongated chairs that had mystified them) upholstered in neutral colors and low tables of the same wood that covered the walls. There was a fireplace made of river stones, bare and swept clean of ash, and three other halls led off this room. Imogen inhaled a fresh pine scent that transported her to the forests of Ruskald, a pleasant memory untainted by everything else that had happened there.

"Imogen!" Elspeth squealed, and flung herself on her friend. Imogen hugged her, trying not to show her dismay at how thin the girl still was. Her full-sleeved shirt and loose trousers concealed how skinny her arms and legs were. "I was so happy when Jeffrey said you would be the ambassador! We'll have so much fun. It's not all stuffy diplomatic receptions and things."

"I did not realize there would be stuffy anything," Imogen said.

"Jeffrey says there's a lot of talking to people and making deals, but he actually likes that kind of thing. I like dances better."

"Jeffrey says much business gets done at dances," Owen said, saluting Imogen, warrior to warrior.

"Will the King join us for supper?" Imogen asked.

Elspeth shrugged. "He'll try to. He's been gone for about three weeks and he said the work had piled up. But I know he wants to talk to you again."

"Let us go in, then, and see if cook will bend his rule about not serving until his Majesty joins us," Owen said.

"What's this about his Majesty?" the King asked as he entered the room.

"Cook didn't listen to you about serving even if you're not here," Elspeth said, making a face. Imogen had never seen her so animated. Was it marriage that had done it, or just the freedom of being away from Hrovald's oppressive house?

"I don't think I'm going to change his mind. He seems to believe I don't take my rank seriously. Shall we go in?" The King extended his arm to Imogen, who looked at it blankly for a moment before accepting it. Why did King Jeffrey keep offering to help her, as if she were an invalid? *It must be some sort of custom,* she decided, *but it's a very odd one, showing respect by impairing a warrior's freedom of motion.*

The dining table was almost three times as long as Hrovald's had been and was made of a highly polished ruddy brown wood. As he had done in his tent, the King held Imogen's chair for her before seating himself at the head of the table, which put her on his right. Owen did the same for Elspeth, seating her at the King's left, then took his place on Elspeth's other side. Almost as soon as the King fully settled his weight in his chair, a door opened and servants streamed through, bearing covered platters and steaming tureens. "We serve all the courses at once, at these family meals," he told Imogen, sounding apologetic. "Saves interruptions later, makes it feel more cozy."

Imogen nodded, though she didn't understand what he meant by courses. This was just like a supper at home, or in Hrovald's house, which were Imogen's only other points of comparison. She should ask Simon if she needed some kind of instruction on fine dining in Aurilien.

There was a clear soup, and fresh vegetables, and some kind of roast, and tiny loaves of bread that were so soft Imogen could have made a meal out of them alone. She ate, and listened to Elspeth chatter about her day, and saw Owen watched Elspeth's every bite as closely as Imogen did. Elspeth didn't notice their attention.

"—and then I said—Imogen, are you listening to me at all?"

"I do not remember," Imogen said, making the men laugh. "You talked of people I do not know, and I lose track of who they are. But I am listening."

"I'm sorry," Elspeth exclaimed, contrite. "We should talk about things that are interesting to you. How do you like the embassy?"

"It is large, and my rooms are large. Even the bathing tub is large. It is big enough for me to sit down in it."

"That's the point," Elspeth said. "I love having a good long soak in the morning."

Imogen, who had had her bath standing up as usual, felt embarrassed at her ignorance. Of course. With hot water available at the turn of a handle, they wouldn't need to limit their bathing water by how much could be readily heated over a camp-stove or fire. "It is very nice," she said quickly, to cover her confusion.

"Don't be afraid to ask Simon for anything. I know, if I came to live with the Kirkellan, I wouldn't know how to do anything," the King said, giving her a look that said he understood perfectly the mistake she'd made, and sympathized. She ducked her head and took another bite of green peas.

"We'll have to go riding in the Park, you and I," Elspeth said, ignorant. "And I want to show you the hill, and the interesting parts of the palace, and—"

"Elspeth, love, stop overwhelming our guest," Owen said.

Elspeth blinked at Imogen. "Am I? I'm sorry, I'm just so excited to...." Her face went very still. "You were so good to me, I can't wait to repay the favor."

Imogen smiled at her. "I am glad to be here and for you to show me things," she said. "But I must also be ambassador. And I do not know how to do that."

"Didn't Mairen tell you what she expected?" asked the King.

"She said, tell everyone about the Kirkellan so they will understand us. And listen to people talk about themselves so I understand them. But I think there is more than this."

He nodded. "You will want to find out what other countries need and what you can give them. Then you discuss what they can give you, and then you put it into an agreement. You should always be careful what you promise." He tapped his finger against his lips, thinking. "And remember you are your country, when you're an ambassador."

"I think the *matrian* will decide what treaties I make, though. She is...experienced, and I am not."

"In either case, you're the face of the Kirkellan here in Aurilien." He laughed. "Sorry, that was more ominous than I meant it to sound."

"I understand." She wasn't entirely sure she did understand. He made it all sound easy. Imogen stirred the shreds of her meat around with her fork. "What do I call you?" she asked the King.

He seemed surprised. "Jeffrey, of course."

"But I do not think the other ambassadors call you that. And I am not your subject. So what I ask is, what is it the ambassador from the Kirkellan calls the King of Tremontane? Because I think if I say "King of Tremontane, pass the salt," everyone will see it is a joke."

"Oh, I see. You say 'your Majesty' just as I say 'madam ambassador.' But when you aren't being the ambassador, I'd prefer it if you'd call me Jeffrey." He smiled at her, the corners of his mouth quirking up.

"Thank you, Jeffrey, I will remember. But I will be the ambassador much of the time."

"But we're practically family, Imogen," Elspeth protested.

"I think it is not fair for the ambassador from the Kirkellan to be…." She couldn't think how to express herself in Tremontanese. "It looks like favoritism if I'm too friendly with the royal family," she explained in Kirkellish. "I have to be able to build relationships with the other ambassadors, and I don't want them thinking I can be influenced by Tremontane."

Elspeth frowned. "But I want to spend time with you."

"We can do that, but I can't look like I favor you, Elspeth."

"What are you saying?" Jeffrey asked, watching the conversation go back and forth between them.

Elspeth explained, and he said, "She's absolutely right, Elspeth. Don't expect Imogen to eat with us every evening."

"I don't expect that. I just want to be able to go places with her." Elspeth sat up straight. "There's a concert tomorrow night I want to take you to. Just you and me and Jeffrey. We were thinking it might be a good idea to introduce you into society slowly, before your first big appearance as ambassador at my wedding reception next week."

"I think—thought you are married already."

"Yes, but the marriage was private, so the reception has to be as public as we can make it. All the diplomats will be there, and there will be food and dancing and it's going to be *wonderful*."

"But it can also be overwhelming, and I say that as someone who's been dragged to these things his whole life," Jeffrey said, putting his elbows on the table and lacing his long fingers together.

"So going to the concert will give you a chance to meet a few people, see what society is like…will you come? That won't be too much like favoritism, will it?"

Imogen looked at Elspeth's eager face. "I will come," she said. "It will be interesting to see what life is like in Tremontane society."

"Wonderful! I'll call for you at seven o'clock tomorrow night." Elspeth leaned back as a servant came to collect their plates and bowls. "What's for dessert? Is it cake? Oh, you've never had chocolate before, have you, Imogen? You will *love* chocolate cake."

Imogen loved chocolate cake so much she had two pieces. Full and happy, she stretched out in the carriage and thought about how nice everything was here. Nice rooms, nice baths, nice cake. Nice bed with nice pillows. She was looking forward to snuggling into that bed. So much better than sleeping pillows on the ground.

The thought brought her out of her reverie. One day and she was already thinking how much better city life was than that of the Kirkellan. She would be going home in a year; she wouldn't be able to take that bed with her, or the tub and its tap. She could arrange to trade for chocolate—in fact, she needed to make a note about that—but she doubted they could cook cake in their camp-stoves. Everything she enjoyed here she would have to leave behind. *I am a Kirkellan warrior,* she reminded herself, *and that is the life I want.*

Imogen lay naked on her wonderful bed, her damp hair fanned out on the pillow behind her, and sighed with pure contentment at being clean. Elspeth had been right; lying immersed in hot water with her feet dangling over the edge of the tub (it wasn't *quite* big enough to fit her long legs) was wonderful. She felt totally relaxed, boneless, as if she were made of warm honey that puddled in the creases of her blanket and would pour off the edge of the bed if she weren't careful. She'd taken advantage of the limitless hot water to wash her clothing, scrubbing it with the scented soap she'd found in a cupboard with some thick, nappy drying cloths. She wished now she hadn't washed her shirt; it was the only one she had, and she was starting to feel cold, but it had been so filthy she couldn't bear to wear it one second longer. She crawled under the blankets and stretched. Her fears about getting too attached to city comforts were less urgent today. Surely it wasn't wrong to enjoy these pleasures while she had them? In fact, it might be considered part of her ambassador's position to respect the customs of the land she was in. That was an excellent justification. She'd have to remember it for later.

She rolled out of bed and padded into the sitting room—that was a name that made sense, you sat in the sitting room—to check on her clothes, drying before the fire she'd asked a servant to build while she was in the bathing chamber. And what a fireplace, too, drawing perfectly and letting no smoke into the room or, more importantly, onto her clothes. She fingered the fabric. Her silk undergarments were warm, her shirt was mostly dry now, and her trousers just needed to be turned again. She left her clothing where it lay and sat down on one of the chairs. The fabric was almost as soft as the blanket on her bed. She lay back and put her feet on the low table. It couldn't be for eating at, she realized; Tremontanans, like the Ruskalder, ate sitting on chairs, not propped on cushions. So she might as well make use of it this way.

"Imogen—*oh*!" Elspeth squeaked and backed out quickly, slamming the door.

"You do not to—you should not enter without being asked," Imogen called out, laughing. That was a surprise the Princess hadn't been expecting. She got up and put her clothing on, cringing at the dampness in the seams and crotch of her trousers. She opened the door and found Elspeth still standing there, her face crimson.

"I'm so sorry, I didn't think—why were you—" Elspeth stammered.

"I washed my clothes," Imogen said. "Now they and I are clean." She held the door open for Elspeth to enter.

"You washed—" Imogen looked at her in confusion. "Imogen, we have people to do that for us here. You could have…but then of course you wouldn't know. I'm sorry. I made assumptions."

"It is all right for me to wash my clothes," Imogen assured her. "I do—did—have done it many years."

"Yes, but you don't have to," Elspeth said. "We can—did you wash them in your tub?"

"Of course. And the soap is very nice." Imogen sniffed her own arm. Perfumed, like a flower. She liked the idea. Maybe she could introduce perfumed soap to the kinship. "But I will know now to ask Mistress

Schotton to wash them."

Elspeth closed her eyes. "You smell lovely," she said. "Do you need help getting ready? I was thinking you might want help dressing, tonight, your first appearance as ambassador of the Kirkellan and all that, and I didn't know if you had a lady's maid yet."

Imogen laughed. "I have dressed myself since I was a small child, Elspeth."

"Yes, but Tremontanan clothing is more like Ruskalder clothing, all those buttons up the back, and there are so many more layers."

"But I do not have Tremontanan clothing." Imogen was puzzled. Why should Elspeth expect her to have anything but what she'd brought with her?

Elspeth's face went from surprised to horrified. "You don't have any clothes."

"I have what I am wearing. My other shirt was torn in the battle, but this one is nice."

"No, I mean you don't have the right clothes for the concert."

"Why cannot I wear—it is to say, what is wrong with my own clothes?"

Elspeth shook her head. "Your clothes are good, they're just not right for a concert. Everyone will be dressed up, you see, and you'll…." She trailed off, her eyes anxious, then switched to Kirkellish. "They'll laugh at you," she said.

"I don't understand that at all," Imogen replied in the same language. "They know what I am. I'll look like what I am. What's the problem?"

"Look," Elspeth said, her slightly shrill tone contrasting with her obvious attempt to be reasonable, "you dress differently for different things, right?"

"I always dress the same."

"All right, *most people* dress differently for different things. We wear trousers for riding. We wear dresses for every day. We wear gowns for concerts and dances. If I wore a gown to go riding, you would think I was crazy, wouldn't you?"

"Of course."

"Well, they will think you're crazy for wearing your usual clothes to a concert."

Imogen's cheeks heated up. "But this is all I have. I'm not Tremontanan. The Kirkellan don't have fancy rooms to hold clothes; we have to carry everything we own. I don't see why I should change just so strangers won't laugh at me."

"Wouldn't you expect me to dress like a Kirkellan if I came to stay with your people?"

"That's different."

"How?"

"It just is!" Imogen shouted. It *was* different, though she couldn't have told Elspeth how. She'd worn Ruskalder clothing in Ranstjad because Hrovald had insisted on it, and somehow she'd believed it would be different here in Tremontane, that she could be herself and wear her own clothes and not be forced to conform to someone else's idea of who she was supposed to be. Apparently she was wrong.

"You don't need to yell at me," Elspeth said in an injured tone. "I'm just trying to keep you from looking ridiculous."

"You think I look ridiculous?" Imogen shouted, gesturing to herself. "Me and my clothes I wash myself because I don't know there are people to do that? Do you have people chew your food, too?"

"Now you're being stupid!" Elspeth yelled. "What makes you think you can come here and just…just keep on behaving like you're back on the plains? And make fun of us because we have things you don't?"

"I'm here to represent my people, not turn into some fake Tremontanan woman who's too soft to take care of herself!"

"If you're a representative of your people, they must all be stubborn and stupid," Elspeth yelled, and ran out of the room, slamming the door behind her.

Imogen stormed into her bedchamber and slammed the door behind her. It made a satisfyingly loud bang and rebounded against the wall. She wasn't going to cry. She was angry, and she didn't cry when she was angry, she yelled and threw things and made everyone around her miserable. Angry. She lay down on her bed and curled up, and let the tears fall.

She knew Elspeth was right, and it burned inside her. In Hrovald's house she'd submitted to his dictates, given up fighting and exchanged her warrior's garb for gowns, but she'd thought in Tremontane things would be different. That she wouldn't have to give up who she was to fit into someone else's idea of who she should be. A tiny voice inside her head said, *Are you really only you because of your clothes?* but she ignored it; it was small and stupid and so, for that matter, was Elspeth. She immediately felt guilty for the cruel thought. Elspeth just wanted to help. It wasn't her fault she didn't understand.

She got up and scrubbed the tears from her eyes. She would go and find someone to play the new game with, the one they'd invented with the green-topped table and the balls that went *tock* when they struck each other, and try to suppress the uncomfortable feeling that she was the one being stupid.

CHAPTER EIGHTEEN

Imogen woke with the first light, her head aching from a restless night. She went downstairs and found breakfast already laid out on the sideboard; she helped herself to bacon and eggs and toast and jam, poured out a large glass of apple juice and fell to. One of the nicest things about living in Aurilien, or maybe it was just the embassy, was there was always enough to eat. Hrovald had been stingy with food, although what there was of it was unexpectedly excellent. Mistress Schotton's cook was talented and she believed in cooking for an army. Imogen was happy to be part of that army.

She heard the distant sound of the front door bell. She had no idea what time it was, but surely it was too early for callers? In a minute a servant came in, bowed, and said, "Milady ambassador has a guest. Should I show her into the parlor?"

"Who is it?" Imogen asked, swallowing a mouthful of toast.

The servant hesitated. "The Dowager Consort, Alison North."

Imogen choked on her second mouthful. Elspeth's mother. What on earth was Elspeth's mother doing here at this hour? She felt guilty all over again, ashamed of the exchange she and Elspeth had had. Was the Dowager Consort here to chastise her for her rudeness? Imogen wiped her chin free of crumbs, brushed off the front of her shirt, and said, "Yes, please do have her go into the parlor and I will come soon."

She ate a few more mouthfuls of egg, drained her glass, then sat for a moment, composing herself. The Dowager Consort wouldn't be so ill-bred as to yell at her in her own embassy, would she? She knew almost nothing of the lady. Elspeth hadn't talked much about her family while she was Hrovald's hostage, and Jeffrey had said little more, so Imogen only knew Elspeth looked like her mother, that her mother was the Royal Librarian (whatever that was) and that she needed lots of coffee in the morning before she could truly wake up. Imogen disliked coffee, so they didn't even have that in common.

She entered the parlor and came face to face with a beautiful woman who was obviously Elspeth's mother. They shared the same pale blond hair, though Elspeth's was straight where the Dowager Consort's was a mass of riotous curls caught up at the nape of her neck, and they had the same heart-shaped face, porcelain skin, and enormous brown eyes. Unlike Elspeth, who always looked as if she were about to fly away and was, in Imogen's opinion, far too thin even when she hadn't been sick, this woman wore her weight well and carried herself with a calm assurance. She wore casual trousers and a full-sleeved shirt with ordinary work boots, an ensemble Imogen would never have expected to see on someone who'd been married to a King. She looked no older than Elspeth until she approached Imogen with her hand outstretched, and as she neared Imogen could see the fine lines around her eyes and lips, felt the inelasticity of the skin of her hand when she grasped it, and more than doubled her estimate of the woman's age. Of course, she'd have to be—when did Tremontanan women start having children, anyway?—in her late forties at least, to have a child as old as Jeffrey. Imogen hoped she would age as well as the Dowager Consort had.

"I'm so pleased to meet you," the woman said. "Elspeth told me you were an early riser, so I thought I'd take the chance you'd be awake at this hour."

"You have had your coffee, then," Imogen said without thinking, and the Dowager Consort laughed, a robust sound at odds with her delicate face.

"I see Elspeth has been telling tales," she said. "It's a sad truth I'm addicted to the stuff. Hot and sweet and milky, that's how I like it, and I'm usually fit to talk to people once I've gotten two or three cups of it into my system."

"Then I am glad to meet you. Please sit down, if you wish to talk, that is."

"I do, if you don't mind. I wanted to meet the woman my children speak so highly of." They both sat, Imogen facing the Dowager Consort, perched on the edge of her chair, still expecting a reprimand. "I don't have words to express my gratitude for how well you cared for my daughter. She was…very ill, wasn't she?"

Imogen nodded. "She is still not well. And I am afraid she will always get sick in the winter, now."

"So am I. We have good doctors here, and the palace healer, and…anyway, we'll do our best to keep her healthy." Imogen waited for her to bring up the rape, but the Dowager Consort blotted her eyes with her fingertips and said, "And Jeffrey tells me you led a rescue during the battle. He's very impressed by you."

Imogen blushed. "It is only that I did what is—was—should be done. War is like that."

"It seems we owe you thanks all around, then."

Imogen shrugged. "I am glad I can make things better. Elspeth is…." She couldn't think how to say it without seeming rude. "Fragile," she said finally.

"That's as good a word as any. She's sweet and intelligent, but she makes people want to protect her. Thank heaven she found Owen Hunter. He'd die for her if he thought his life would save hers."

"He did try to die for her, I think. Is he not now Owen North?"

"Hmm? Oh. No, they chose an indirect adoption. Owen's been accepted here in the city, but we didn't think Tremontane's acceptance would extend to seeing a Ruskalder adopted into the royal house." Seeing Imogen's blank expression, she explained, "It means they each maintain their status in their birth family and neither of them has a claim on the estate of the other. Their children, on the other hand, inherit both their parents' estates and both surnames. So Elspeth is still Elspeth North, Owen is Owen Hunter, and their children will take the name North Hunter."

"I am still not sure I understand the why, but I think I understand the what."

"Then you're doing better than half of Tremontane, I think." The Dowager Consort cleared her throat. "I…you probably know I'm not just here to say hello."

Imogen froze. "You are angry with me for being rude to Elspeth."

The Dowager Consort shook her head. "Oh, it's not you I'm angry with. I took Elspeth and Jeffrey both to task for making assumptions and then letting you believe it was your fault."

"It is not Jeffrey who does this." Imogen wondered at the kind of woman who could take a King to task for anything, even if she was his mother.

"Jeffrey has a responsibility toward you as the representative of a people we've just signed an important treaty with. It's in his interest to ensure you meet the diplomatic community as an equal, something that won't happen if you can't fit into society."

Imogen felt her anger rising again. "It is wrong to say I cannot be who I am. I am not of this society. Everyone knows this."

"And you think it would be foolish to pretend otherwise."

"Yes."

The Dowager Consort unexpectedly tucked one of her feet under her bottom, a casual gesture Imogen wished she could imitate. "I usually dress like this, you know," she said. "My work is sometimes dirty, all those old documents—well, I'm sure that's not interesting to you, and I have a tendency to talk too much about the Library. I hate dressing up for things. It used to be worse—do you know what a corset is?" Imogen shook her head. "It was an undergarment that shaped the body by lacing your waist and breasts very tightly, sometimes so tightly it was hard to breathe. One of the most satisfying things I did as Consort was to phase that fashion out completely." She laughed, and Imogen smiled even though she wasn't totally certain what the woman meant. "At any rate, I never felt comfortable in those gowns. Still don't, really."

Imogen waited for her to continue, but she just gazed at Imogen absently, as if she weren't seeing her. "You are talking about me now," she said, still feeling resentful.

"Every time I put on a gown, I'm still myself," the Dowager Consort said. "It's just a different side of me. It helped that my husband always looked at me as if I were the most beautiful woman in the room, no matter what I wore."

"You are the most beautiful," Imogen said, and she laughed again.

"To be honest, Imogen, I think if you stood beside me gowned the way Aurilien society expects a woman to look, no one would look at me at all. You are a remarkable woman."

Imogen blushed. The resentment began to fade. "I am beautiful however I dress," she insisted.

"You are *yourself* however you dress," the Dowager Consort said. "Don't let anyone tell you that you are defined by the way you look. You're not one person in riding gear and another one in a dress and yet another in your nightgown."

Imogen tried to hold onto her resentment, but it slipped away. It was stupid of her to feel her identity was tied up in her clothing. If she could remain Kirkellan in the midst of soft beds and hot running water, she could remain Kirkellan in a Tremontanan gown. "I think you are right," she said.

"Call me Alison," the Dowager Consort said, "and, Imogen, I would be so pleased if you let me help you with your wardrobe. Your clothing."

Imogen nodded. "I am grateful. I felt—" She didn't know the right word. "I shouted at Elspeth because I did not want to lose myself."

Alison tilted her head to one side and smiled. "Maybe we can help you find yourself instead."

Imogen's only experience with acquiring clothing, to date, had been visiting the Ruskalder seamstress who'd provided her with her gowns—that and sewing her own, as all the Kirkellan did. Alison North's idea of acquiring clothing began with a ride in a carriage drawn by a pair of unhappy horses. "We're going to need it," she said, but wouldn't explain further.

To Imogen's surprise, their first stop was not at a dressmaker's but at a shop selling undergarments of all kinds, plus some odd garments Imogen couldn't see the purpose of. The Kirkellan were being robbed, she realized, running her fingers over fabrics even finer than the silk her people traded with Veribold for. She was even more disconcerted when Alison presented her with one of those odd garments and demonstrated how to wear it. "It's beginning to replace the corset, for those of us with rather fuller figures. It's called a brassiere." Imogen was grateful it went on underneath her clothes. In the back room, she examined it. The stitching was so fine it was nearly invisible, and she'd never seen the fabric it was made of before. She felt embarrassed, and angry at herself for being embarrassed. She must look like such a…a barbarian to these people, in her clumsily-stitched shirt and the trousers she'd made herself. No wonder Elspeth had been ashamed of her. She put the strange garment on; it felt as awkward as she did. Surely everyone would know she was wearing it.

But Alison didn't say anything about it, didn't even comment on her appearance, just directed the shop assistant to wrap several of them, along with more undergarments than Imogen had ever owned in her life, and stow it all in their carriage. To Imogen's further surprise, their next stop was at a place displaying trousers and vests and shirts behind a glass window wider and taller than Imogen's arm span. "Well, it's *my* favorite kind of clothing, and I think they'll have things you can wear without any bothersome fittings," Alison said, and shepherded her charge up the stairs and into the shop. The idea of ready-made clothing, both here and in the undergarment shop, stunned Imogen. To think tailors—this was a word she learned from Alison—in Aurilien could afford to make clothing for no one in particular, hoping someone would buy it, and people actually did! She wandered around the shop, fingering the fabric, until Alison called her over and piled trousers and shirts into her arms, then directed her to another back room where she could put things on to see if they fit.

She came out wearing long trousers that fit better than her own and a loose shirt in a soft red fabric that reminded her of her favorite dress back in Ranstjad, and nearly walked into another woman before she realized the woman was her own reflection. The brassiere certainly did alter her figure, she thought, turning to see herself from all angles, and she liked the effect. She stood and stared, not at her body, but at her hazel eyes, her nose that turned up at the end, her round cheeks that were sallow from the long winter. She could be herself even in these unfamiliar clothes. In these unfamiliar undergarments. She looked back at her own clothes, discarded in the back room, and felt not embarrassment, but shame.

"Those look wonderful," Alison said when she saw her. "Go try some others on. I'm so glad they have trousers that fit someone as tall as you."

"But these are nice," Imogen protested. "I do not want others."

"Oh, you'll need at least six more shirts and another four pairs of trousers." Alison laughed at Imogen's dumbfounded expression. "You're a very active young woman and I hate to think of how hard your laundry would have to work to keep up with you if you didn't have a few changes of clothing."

The carriage was burdened with more packages. Imogen walked out of the shop in her new red shirt and trousers, with her old clothes bundled up under her arm where no one could see what they were. Alison eyed the little bundle, but said nothing. "I'm afraid this next stop won't be so much fun," she told Imogen when they were underway. "Lots of measuring tapes and fittings, but I assure you you'll like the results."

This shop, unlike the other two, had no glass windows of any size, just a discreet plaque next to the door with something in Tremontanese written on it. When Alison pushed the door open, a tinny bell rang out. "Julian?" she said. "I've brought you a wonderful surprise."

"One moment, milady Consort, I'll be with you shortly," a man's tenor voice said from a back room. Soon a little man, balding on top and wearing a length of measuring tape dangling around his neck, emerged from a dark doorway. "Now—" he began, saw Imogen, and went silent, his mouth agape. "Good heaven," he said faintly. He turned his faintly protuberant eyes on Alison. "Milady Consort," he said in the same faint tones, "please tell me you wish me to dress this young woman."

"I do, Julian. This is Imogen, she is the Kirkellan ambassador to Tremontane, and I think you can see why I brought her to you."

"I can't tell you how honored I am at your trust in me. She will be the greatest challenge of my career." Julian circled Imogen, muttering things she couldn't hear, until she became annoyed.

"I am not a statue," she said, "and I do not want to stand in one place for you to look at." She wasn't sure what the man meant by "challenge," but she bristled at the thought that he saw her body as strange and difficult.

"My dear young woman—Imogen, is it?—forgive me, but I simply want to examine your form."

"I am not strange."

Julian blinked up at her. "Good heaven, who said you were strange? You are *unusual*, which is far more interesting. I must understand how you are built before I design your gown. It must flatter your shape without making you look bulky, accentuate your height, keep that lovely bustline from being overshadowed by the rest of you…as I said, the greatest challenge of my career."

"Gowns, Julian, gowns plural," Alison corrected him. "The ambassador will have a great many social obligations and I'm sure you understand what that means."

The man raised his eyes to heaven. "A wonderful gift indeed. Now." He clapped his hands sharply, and a man and two women emerged from the back room and ranged themselves in front of him. "David, the samples book. Etta, bring my stool. The tall one. Sylvia, refreshments for our guests. We have a great deal of work to do."

It was nothing like Imogen's previous experience with being measured. The woman in Ranstjad had taken many notes and asked questions about Imogen's preferred colors, then sent her away and delivered the dresses three days later. Julian, by contrast, made no notes, and his measuring tape whipped around her so rapidly it dizzied her. "Yes," he said, "a bustle would be ridiculous, look at what heaven has already gifted you with," and "Proportions, it's all about proportions," and "No, milady Consort, I feel I must direct you away from the thicker fabrics; I know they're lovely, but we want them to drape." Imogen understood about two-thirds of what he said. She stood in the center of the flying tape, then sat and ate something called a cream puff and had to follow it with six more, they were divine and sweet and cold all at once, and stood again to be measured. Alison flipped through a thick book with David at her elbow, pointing at fabrics of all colors and textures. Imogen stopped her once and put her finger on an eight-inch square of red silk. "This is for wearing on the outside?" she asked in astonishment, and when David assured her it was, added, "Then I want this."

Julian detached the square from the book and held it up against her skin. "Yes, I think so," he said, and tossed it at Etta. "See if we have this in back. You'll have to get more sun, my dear, I can tell it's been a long winter for you."

Julian's assurances that the first of Imogen's dresses would be ready in two days followed them out of the shop. Imogen sat down heavily in the carriage and said, "Clothing is tiring."

"It's time for dinner," Alison said, pulling a round silver Device out of her trouser pocket and looking at it. "I know cook will be annoyed, but I don't feel like waiting for dinner at the palace. We'll go to a restaurant."

Imogen was amazed all over again that there were places in Aurilien where you could sit down without being expected and have food brought to you. That they could afford to take the chance the food might go uneaten astonished her. Clothes made with no one particular in mind. Food cooked for people who might not show up. A whole carriage-load of boxes only for her, more than Victory could ever dream of carrying. She looked down at her lap.

"Don't you like the chicken, Imogen?" Alison said.

"I do not think I belong here," she said quietly. "It is not that I fear losing myself. It is that I do not know what Tremontane wants from us that is not horses and warriors."

Alison sipped her cup of tea. "It is *because* we want more from you than horses and warriors that you belong here," she said. "I imagine our countries could have arranged a treaty of mutual aid, only meeting when danger threatened, but I believe Jeffrey felt that was a rather cold kind of relationship, and I'm sure Mairen agreed. We've had diplomatic ties to Veribold and Eskandel for years, but I don't think it occurred to anyone to look for a similar connection to the Kirkellan until Hrovald's aggression made it necessary. And how…again, the word 'cold' comes to mind…how cold to simply ask for your help and then behave as though you didn't exist."

"I am not sure I understand all of that. Tremontane wishes to be friends and not just allies?"

"There, you put it into the words I kept flailing around to find. You're already a better diplomat than I am." Alison smiled and took another drink. "You might ask that question of Jeffrey, if you can catch him when he isn't running around putting out fires. I mean, solving problems," she said, when Imogen's brow furrowed at the unfamiliar expression. "He's the one who made the treaty, after all."

"Thank you for telling me. And thank you for helping me stay myself. I like you very much."

"I like you too, Imogen. Shall we have dessert?"

They returned to the embassy in the early afternoon, carrying boxes and bundles from the carriage—"I see no reason to summon a servant when we both have two perfectly good hands," Alison said—and entered only for Imogen to drop parts of her burden when Elspeth leaped on her, crying, "I'm so sorry I said those things! It was terrible of me! Can you forgive me?"

"You can first forgive me for being stubborn," Imogen said, setting down the rest of her parcels to embrace Elspeth. "I am ready now to be ambassador."

"I'm so glad. Oh, Mother! What are you doing here?"

"We have been shopping." Alison set down her armload of packages.

"Without me? Unfair! You know I like it better than you do. Imogen, what did you get? Oh, I love this shirt. Did she take you to Julian? You are going to love—"

"Elspeth, love, take a breath. You really do need to learn to contain yourself."

"I'm sorry. I do love getting new clothes. How many gowns did you buy?"

Imogen looked sharply at Alison. "You did not say buy."

"How else did you expect we would get all of this?"

"But I do not have money."

"You do, actually. The embassy has a line of credit thanks to Tremontane's purchase of a large number of Kirkellan horses. You should probably outfit your *tiermatha.* They'll attend diplomatic events with you and will need proper attire, though I should think one or two items of formal wear will be enough."

"Oh! I'll go with you all!" Elspeth exclaimed.

"I am…overwhelmed," said Imogen.

Alison took her hand. "Don't be," she said. "You'll find people are the same wherever you go, even if society changes. Wait until you see the other ambassadors, and you'll understand when I tell you whatever small mistake you make will be overlooked. People want to meet you, Imogen, they want to know you for who you are. I predict you won't have any difficulty remaining yourself." She looked at her watch. "I'll leave you to Elspeth. Elspeth, Imogen won't want to do any more shopping today, so don't tease her. Imogen, I'll see you tomorrow at ten o'clock."

"Why will you see me then?"

Alison smiled mischievously. "Well, you'll need to learn how to dance."

The Kirkellan danced. There were dances for weddings and dances for the celebration of a good hunt, dances that told stories and even dances to remember the ones who had passed on. They were wild, lively dances with a strong beat, accompanied by the sonorous deep belling of the *kurkara,* the light birdlike whistling of the *balaeri.* They were not stilted, formal things in which you had to remember where your feet went all the time and where the music dragged you along, beat by beat, as if it too wished it were somewhere else. Imogen clasped Elspeth's hand and counted silently. She hoped this time they wouldn't run into the chairs that had been shoved back against the wall to make room for the dancers.

"…one two three, one two *back,* no, back, not forward," Elspeth said. "Mother, I don't think this is working. I keep forgetting I'm supposed to be the man."

"I do not understand why it is the man and the woman have different steps."

"Because if they both did the same steps, they would either walk away from each other or walk into each other," Alison explained. She pushed the large brass button that shut off the Device playing the dance music. Imogen regarded it with suspicion. Maybe Tremontanan dances were more exciting with live music, as Elspeth assured her there was. "Let's take a rest for a bit."

The four other Kirkellan couples relaxed and stepped away from each other. "This is much more difficult than hitting a target at speed," Dorenna said, massaging her foot where Kallum had stepped on it.

"If you didn't insist on taking the lead, this would go more smoothly," he replied.

Revalan, who'd sat out this round of dancing because there were only four women in the *tiermatha*, said, "I like it. It's smooth and flowing. Pity we won't do any dancing. Can you imagine trying to ask a woman to dance, or be asked, when all you can do is grunt and gesture?"

"Maybe we need to learn the words for 'Will you dance with me?' Saevonna said. She, like Revalan, had taken to dancing quickly. "One of you others needs to take a turn with me. Kalain, you've been sitting for far too long."

Imogen said, "At least you get to dance with a man. I don't think Elspeth is teaching me properly."

"I can understand your language, Imogen."

"I know. I wanted you to hear that."

"I'm sorry to interrupt," Jeffrey said from the doorway, "but I did clear my schedule to have dinner with you and none of you seem to be ready for it. I'm not sure the King is supposed to have to track his family down."

"Oh, Jeffrey, just in time," Alison said. "Come here and dance with Imogen. Elspeth simply can't keep up with her."

"And you already know the man's part," Elspeth said.

Alison pointed at Imogen. "Back to the center, Imogen, and let's try this one more time."

Jeffrey looked at Imogen. "I'm not a very good dancer," he said.

"Don't be ridiculous. You're a perfectly good dancer. You just don't like to do it," Alison said.

Imogen joined Jeffrey at the center of the room, and held out her hand stiffly. He took it and turned it over, examining it. "You should at least act as if you're pleased to dance with your partner," he said with a grin. Around them, the other couples formed up.

"I am tired and this is not enjoyable. But I am thankful you will help."

"It's just one dance, right, Mother?" He waggled his eyebrows at her, making her laugh. "There, that's better already."

"Hands on waists, right hands clasped, keep your elbow up, Imogen, and—" The tinny music started up again, and Imogen and Jeffrey both moved at once and bumped up against each other, then laughed together.

"Let's try that again," he said, "and this time do it backwards from what Elspeth incorrectly taught you."

"As if you could have done better, Jeffrey."

"At least I wouldn't have taught her the man's part, tiny." This time, they swung gracefully into the music, and after the first few steps Imogen stopped looking at her feet and could look at Jeffrey's blue eyes smiling back at her. "Much better," he said.

"It is more fun this way," Imogen said, and he laughed.

"I've never danced with anyone as tall as me before," he said. "It's interesting. In a good way, you understand."

"I do because I was dancing with Elspeth and she is tiny as you say."

"Hey! It's not my fault you're both giants. Everyone around me is a giant. Except Mother."

"Your father never complained about dancing with me," Alison said.

Because Imogen was looking at Jeffrey's face, she saw the shadow pass quickly across it before his smile reasserted itself. "Did I step wrong?" she asked.

"No, it was just a passing thought, nothing to do with you. You look very nice in your new clothes, by the way. Very much like a Tremontanan lady."

Imogen flushed. "How did I look before?" she demanded.

Jeffrey said, "Ah…also very nice?"

"I did not look nice. I looked like a warrior."

He raised an eyebrow at her. "Which suited you very well, as I recall."

His tone of voice, warm and admiring, made her flush even hotter. Alison said, "Jeffrey, stop implying Imogen's Kirkellan clothing made her look like a savage and pay attention. Imogen, keep your elbow up."

"I did *not* think you looked like a savage," Jeffrey assured Imogen, smiling at her more naturally now. "All right, you end by turning away, then coming back together—no, farther away, let's try that again—right." She turned and came face to face with those blue eyes again. They crinkled at the corners when he smiled. "I think you've got it."

"I think I should not dance with a shorter partner," Imogen said with a laugh.

"Then I'll have to dance it with you," he said. "I'd dance with the Veriboldan and Eskandelic ambassadors too, but they're both male and the ambassador from Eskandel has a very jealous harem."

"I do not know what harem means."

"Mother will explain it to you." He hesitated, then asked, "I don't suppose you'd like to join us for dinner? I'd like to hear what you think of Aurilien."

"I…one moment please." She turned to her *tiermatha*, who'd gathered around Saevonna to watch her demonstrate a complicated step. "Do you mind if I go to dinner at the palace?"

"Why not?" Revalan said. "You're the ambassador. It's probably an ambassador thing to do."

Areli and Dorenna exchanged knowing glances. "What?" Imogen said.

"Nothing," said Dorenna, giving her a look that said volumes.

"What?"

They exchanged glances again. "You and the King looked *very* good dancing together," Dorenna said in a low voice so Elspeth wouldn't hear. "*Very* attractive couple you made."

Imogen blushed. "Dorenna, stop trying to embarrass me."

"It's working, isn't it?"

"You're out of your mind."

"I don't know," Areli mused, "he does sort of get this light in his eyes when he looks at you."

"He does not. And *you're* out of your mind too. I'm going to dinner now with three people I consider friends, and I don't want to hear any more innuendo."

Areli and Dorenna looked at one another again. "Trust me, *you* won't hear any more," Areli said, grinning, and Imogen threw up her arms and turned away.

"Why don't you meet us behind the palace for sparring after your meal?" Kionnal said. "We can bring Victory along for you to ride back."

"That would be wonderful," Imogen said, relieved to hear the end of suggestive comments about her and Jeffrey. Out of their minds. "I'll meet you in the training yard."

"You should bring clothes to change into if you're going to spar," Elspeth said in Tremontanese when Imogen joined them.

"I will get them if you will wait," Imogen said, and ran to her room to get her Kirkellan clothing. When she returned, Alison was saying, "And I hope Bixhenta isn't too overwhelming."

"I don't want to think about Bixhenta before I eat," Jeffrey said. "It ruins the whole meal."

"Who is Bixhenta?" Imogen asked.

"The Veriboldan ambassador. He's…a little difficult."

"You'll meet him at the reception," said Elspeth. "You'll meet all the ambassadors and most of the provincial rulers and all sorts of lesser nobles and gentry. Just be sure to save time for dancing."

"Elspeth, you make it to be an enjoyable thing, dancing, and I am not sure I feel the same."

"Depends on the partner," Elspeth said with a twinkle in her eye, and in Kirkellish added, "and the short woman is right, you do look awfully good dancing with my brother."

"Elspeth!"

"All right, I'm sorry, I'm just teasing. You really don't have to dance often…oh, and did I explain about the two-dance rule? You only dance once with a man, because if you dance twice with him, it's like saying you're courting. And if you dance two in a row, that's a declaration of love."

"I'm not likely to dance two dances at all, let alone with the same man."

"Unless it's my brother!"

"Imogen," Jeffrey said, "what did Elspeth say to deserve being hit by you?"

Chapter Nineteen

The red silk gown flowed over the contours of her body, draping across her breasts and hips, fitting her at the waist but sweeping down from there into a skirt full enough to swish when she turned. Imogen turned now, craning over her shoulder to see her back. Her curvy backside still looked curvy, but didn't stand out the way it had in those Ruskalder dresses. She turned again just to hear the skirt swish. She'd never worn silk on the outside before and it made her feel uncomfortably conspicuous, as if everyone would be able to see through it to her skin. With her hair pinned high on her head, leaving her neck bare, she felt even more uncomfortable, as if she'd revealed it as a target for her enemies. She turned to look at herself full-front again and smoothed out some wrinkles over her belly. Even in her Ruskalder dresses, she'd looked like a warrior. Now, she looked like…what did she look like? A lady? A Tremontanan woman? She traced a faint scar that ran from the side of her throat to underneath her gown's neckline. No Tremontanan woman would have the scars of a warrior.

She went to sit on the edge of her bed. *You decided to follow the customs of this country,* she told herself. *Remember,* you *chose this. And you're still yourself.* She didn't feel much like herself tonight. She felt like an Imogen who'd been dressed up to be an ambassador, a responsibility she still wasn't sure she understood. *Talk to people. Ask them about themselves. Tell them about the Kirkellan. Be polite. Dance.* She sighed. Of all of tonight's chores, dancing would be the most difficult.

Elspeth had already drilled her on entering the reception room, how she would be announced and then have to make the long, slow descent down the broad stairs to the floor below. It had felt very far below when they'd practiced the day before; it would feel even farther away tonight. And now she would be wearing the too-thin dress that showed off every inch of her figure while hundreds of people stared at her. She looked at her reflection in the mirror, her face, not her body. She'd refused the offer of cosmetics, feeling they were unnecessary, and now she looked at her unadorned face and made herself smile. She ran her hands over the gown again, feeling the soft contours underneath, looked at her familiar curvy shape, her plump arms, and the smile felt more real. She liked her body. This was just a different way of showing it off.

Someone knocked at her bedroom door. "I think we're ready to go," Saevonna said. She wore a full-skirted gown of blue and gold and an unfamiliar expression.

"Is everything all right?"

"Kionnal and Taeron are complaining about how uncomfortable their clothes are, but I think everyone else is resigned. It's just…this is so far outside our experience, Imogen. We're not going to understand anyone there…are you sure we have to come?"

"You're my retinue, according to Elspeth, and all the other ambassadors will have attendants. At least I know my attendants are capable of killing anyone who tries to molest me."

"*You're* capable of killing anyone who tries to molest you."

"I know. I'm just not sure how appropriate that would be." She stood and smoothed her skirt again.

"You do look extraordinary in that gown, Imogen."

"Thanks. You're beautiful too, you know."

"I do. I'm embarrassed to say I like Tremontanan clothing. I feel…I don't know. Different, but I can't really say how."

"You don't feel like you're losing yourself?"

"No. More like discovering there's more to me than fighting."

Her words echoed Mother's so closely they raised goose pimples all up and down Imogen's arms. "Let's go, then," she said, and let Saevonna precede her out of her rooms.

The *tiermatha* were gathered in the foyer, looking like Tremontanans with varying degrees of success. Revalan was never going to look like anything but a Kirkellan warrior no matter how he dressed, and Dorenna…. "Dorenna, hand it over," Imogen said.

"What?" Dorenna looked suspiciously innocent.

"Whatever blade you have strapped to your thigh."

"You don't want me to be able to defend you?"

"They have guards for that. You don't need any kind of blade to kill someone. And it makes you walk funny." Imogen held out her hand, and Dorenna hiked her skirt up and unstrapped a seven-inch-long dagger from her thigh. Kionnal whistled appreciatively and Areli elbowed him hard in the stomach. Dorenna slapped the sheathed knife into Imogen's outstretched palm, scowling. "Thank you." Imogen set it on one of the ubiquitous tables, and said, "This is going to be difficult, I think, so remember to stay in groups of three or four with someone who speaks some Tremontanese in each group. And try to enjoy yourselves. At least you don't have to worry about remembering who is who."

"Am I allowed to ogle?" Kallum asked.

"As long as you keep it discreet. If you know how to do that." Imogen took a deep breath, and said, "Let's go."

They fit into three medium-sized carriages, Imogen sitting opposite Areli, who spent the journey looking out the window. Imogen would have believed Areli calm and relaxed if she hadn't seen the death grip she had on Kionnal's hand. She felt guilty, dragging her *tiermatha* into this, guilty because she felt so much happier knowing they were present even though they really weren't prepared for this. But then, neither was she. She faced the window, closed her eyes, and told herself it would be all right.

The herald at the top of the stairs looked astonished when the thirteen of them assembled to make their entrance, but announced them as "Imogen, ambassador of the Kirkellan" and left it at that. A hush fell over the room as Imogen descended at the point of a triangle that mimicked their fighting formation. If people were going to stare, she was damn well going to give them something worth staring at. They reached the floor, turned to the right, and split into groups to wander the room. Imogen watched the *tiermatha* go and felt bereft. She straightened her spine. She was a Kirkellan warrior and she would show these people no fear.

The people near her smiled and nodded and went back to their conversations, leaving her uncertain as to what to do or where to go next. A man wearing Tremontane colors swept past with a tray and offered it to her; she took one of the mysterious bits of food on it and bit into it, not very gracefully. Juice spilled over her fingers and almost onto her dress. She shoved the rest of the thing into her mouth and sucked her fingers, afraid of what the juice might do to her dress if she wiped her hand on it. The servitor looked at her with a bland, nonjudgmental expression, but she was sure he was laughing at her inside. "Where is it I can wash?" she asked, determined to act as if spilling food on oneself was perfectly normal at grand receptions.

"There is a door between those potted trees, if madam needs to refresh herself," he said, inclining his head to the left. Of course pointing would be undignified. Imogen moved as quickly as she could in the indicated direction, holding her sticky hand away from herself just in case. She found the room, which was lined with sinks and private stalls for the miraculous chamber pots that rinsed themselves, washed and dried her hand and hurried back out.

She had missed Jeffrey's entrance with Alison, but was just in time to see Elspeth stand with Owen at the top of the stairs, glowing with the applause of the crowd. She was beautiful and she was happy, and she wasn't dead of lung fever or trapped in Hrovald's house with his vile son, and Imogen's heart filled with joy. She turned her head away. The way Owen looked at Elspeth, that caressing, intimate look, made her feel as if she were intruding on a private moment. For the first time in her life, she wondered if anyone would ever look at her that way. It was a disturbing thought. She had always assumed she would have a lover or two, get married, have children, but the reality of what it might be like to be in love had never struck her until just now, watching (or trying not to watch) Owen and Elspeth in their private world. Areli and Kionnal's relationship was far more casual; whatever tenderness existed between them, they expressed it in the privacy of their bedchamber. She told herself it was just homesickness, but she suddenly wished she had someone to share those private looks with.

"Madam ambassador," someone said, and she turned with relief to see a man at her elbow. He was shortish and fattish and blondish and wore a brown dress coat over a black waistcoat. "Maxwell Burgess,

Foreign Relations chief," he said, offering his hand. "I apologize for not greeting you sooner, but I only returned from Eskandel yesterday evening. I trust we've treated you hospitably?"

"I am very happy to be in Tremontane," Imogen said. "Thank you for asking."

"We are glad to welcome our neighbors from the north," he said. "May I introduce you to your counterparts?" Without waiting for her assent, he took her elbow and steered her through the crowd to an ordinary-looking man dressed in the most extraordinary combination of colors Imogen had seen that evening, pale peach waistcoat with a peacock blue frock coat that fitted him much better than Burgess's did him, bright green trousers and shoes with brass buckles that shone as if he had someone following him around just to polish them. He bowed to Burgess, then looked at Imogen with great admiration.

"My lord prince, this is Imogen, ambassador from the Kirkellan. Milady, Prince Serjian Ghentali of Eskandel."

"What pity it is," said the princeling, "I was to ask you join my harem, you are woman of great remark." He took her hand and brought it to his lips, kissed the back of it gently. His accent was even thicker than hers, which made her happy; at least one person here was more obviously foreign than she was.

"I thank you for the great compliment," she said. Alison had explained about Eskandelic harems, that they represented the consolidated power behind the thinly-veiled fiction that the princelings ran the country, and being invited to join one *was* an honor even if it did mean sharing your bed partner with four or five other women. "How do I call you? Prince?"

"Ghentali is given to me as a name and it called am I," he said. "Eemogeen is hard to speak in my mouth, so I may call you madam ambassador, yes?"

"Excellent," Burgess said. "I see some people I must speak to, madam ambassador, but I hope you will reserve me a dance later? I am very fond of dancing, and I hope to make you feel welcome."

Imogen's heart sank. "I know few of your dances, but I would be glad to dance one of them with you," she said. She watched Burgess walk away, turned back to Ghentali, and found herself instead facing a redheaded woman whose gray eyes looked up at her with amusement. "You have met our husband," she said. "What do you think of him?"

Imogen thought quickly. "He seems friendly," she said, "and he likes his clothes."

The woman smiled. "If often you converse with him, you will find there is not much more to him than his love of the clothes. But he is kind and speaks well in public, and those characteristics are in a Prince of the most value. My name is Serjian Giavena. Please meet my sisters."

The Serjian harem turned out to be a group of intelligent, well-spoken women of whom Giavena was the leader. "I am the *vojenta*," she explained, "and I tell Ghentali what he should say after we decide what that is. We have made Ghentali one of the foremost in Eskandel of his peers."

"I know not much about Eskandel."

"Our countries are too far apart to have much to each other to give," said Giavena.

"But we are interested in how you live," said another woman, Donia. "We gather knowledge and preserve it. Our libraries and museums in the world the best are."

"I am interested in you too," Imogen said. "The *matrian* told me I am to tell others about the Kirkellan so we are not a mystery again—it is to say, anymore. And I think you should not be a mystery to us."

"I beg your pardon, Lady Giavena," Burgess said, arriving at Imogen's elbow, "but the Veriboldan ambassador has arrived and it's important madam ambassador meet with him immediately, so as not to cause offense."

Imogen again was grasped by the elbow and steered ruthlessly through the crowd. She began to feel annoyed with Burgess even as she was grateful to him for providing introductions. He could at least let her travel under her own power.

Burgess led her to the side of the room reserved for the royal family and then inexplicably abandoned her, pointing the way she should continue. She'd met Veriboldans many times before; traders came north to exchange food, silk, and spices for Kirkellan handwork and, of course, horses. These interactions did not prepare her for the sight of the Veriboldan ambassador, sitting as if enthroned near the seat of the King, which was currently empty. Alison sat nearby, conversing with an older man; she noticed Imogen and smiled at her, which gave her comfort as she faced the intimidating figure of the ambassador.

He was very old, his thin hair white and worn long around his shoulders. His bright hazel eyes were so sunken in wrinkles he appeared to be peering out of a dark mask, one with a short nose and very thin lips made thinner by the way he pressed them together, as if to keep words from escaping. He wore a long black robe of fine silk over a tunic and skirt of green figured silk, tied with a golden cord that looked like a slimmer version of the ropes that held back the curtains in Imogen's bedroom. The tips of his bare toes, which were lacquered bronze, protruded from the bottom of his skirt; the long nails of his left hand matched them. His hands were clasped in his lap, the fingers interlaced, and he surveyed the room without moving his head. As Imogen approached, his eyes flicked over her, then continued their journey. A slender, paler woman in her fifties stood next to him, dressed in similar fashion except her robe was green and her tunic and skirt were a muddy brown, and her nails were short and unpainted. She stared at Imogen without speaking.

Imogen was at a loss. Was she supposed to speak first? Was there some ritual they expected her to follow? Burgess had implied the Veriboldan ambassador demanded respect, but what should that look like?

Someone placed his hand low on her back and propelled her gently forward. "Bow at the waist and introduce yourself to the woman, not the man," Jeffrey whispered in her ear. In a louder voice, he said, addressing the man, "Bixhenta, welcome to my court." He sat down in a nearby chair that was almost a throne and spoke to his mother in a low voice; she laughed at whatever he'd said.

Imogen bowed to the woman and said, "I am Imogen of the

Kirkellan."

"I am the Voice of Bixhenta, Proxy of Veribold," the woman said in unaccented Tremontanese. "He bids you welcome in the name of our country."

Imogen doubted that. The Proxy's lips hadn't moved and he didn't seem aware of her presence. But she said, "My people are grateful for the relationship with Veribold we have made over the years."

The woman bent and said something to Bixhenta, probably translating Imogen's words, and he replied in Veriboldan. "The Proxy acknowledges the link between your people and ours. We respect your efforts in keeping the Ruskalder at bay, though Veribold needs no protection."

Imogen wanted to laugh. Keeping the Ruskalder at bay, as if the Kirkellan were in service to Veribold. Instead, she said, "If our positions were different, I am sure Veribold would do the same for us."

The Voice again spoke to the Proxy, who paused before responding. "Veribold does many things for the Kirkellan already. We hope you do not suggest we do more."

"I am just…acknowledging our relationship is one of more than trading partners. Which is *tradition*," Imogen said, emphasizing the word slightly. "We are especially grateful for silk. It makes the best undergarments."

She heard Jeffrey make a kind of choking noise. So he was listening in. Well, she wasn't going to bow and scrape to this Veriboldan Proxy, whatever that meant, and after all, it was true.

The woman's eyes widened. Imogen wondered how much of that she would translate for Bixhenta. Then she noticed the wrinkled face had changed, the lips more compressed, the eyes fractionally wider, and she realized Bixhenta had no trouble at all understanding Tremontanese. So he was using his translator as a diplomatic tool. Imogen wondered what his purpose was; putting people off guard, or giving himself more time to think of responses? She controlled her face. *Let's not give anything away.*

Bixhenta said something when the Voice finished, then, when she would have turned back to Imogen, took hold of her sleeve and said something else. The woman's eyes again widened, and she said, "Veribold wishes good relations with the Kirkellan." She wasn't doing well at concealing her emotions, anger and embarrassment at war on her face and making her cheeks pink. "We wish to discuss further trade arrangements. However, this is not the appropriate place. The Proxy wishes to invite the Kirkellan ambassador to tea at the Veriboldan embassy two days from now. This is a great honor and we hope the Kirkellan ambassador sees it as such."

Bixhenta twitched, and he glanced at the Voice so quickly Imogen would have missed it if she hadn't been looking at him rather than the Voice when she spoke. Imogen was certain that last sentence had been the Voice's own and guessed that some of Bixhenta's well-known snobbery belonged to someone else. She bowed, more deeply than was required, and said, "I am pleased to accept the Proxy's invitation. I hope we will have a...profitable talk about our two countries and how they benefit *each other*." She smiled sweetly at the Voice, who now looked as if she'd swallowed a lemon filled with tacks. "I am certain the *matrian* is—will be pleased to hear our relation with Veribold is still strong."

She bowed from the waist again, this time directly at the Proxy, and he surprised her by inclining his head in her direction. It felt like being dismissed by a King, and she had to stop herself curtseying the way Anneke always had to her. *Now what?* She took a step backward, then another, not sure how far she had to go before she could turn her back on him.

Once again, she felt a hand on the small of her back. "I beg your pardon, Bixhenta, but madam ambassador has promised me this dance," Jeffrey said, and guided her away from the old man toward the center of the room. It felt like a rescue.

CHAPTER TWENTY

Jeffrey's hand tightened on hers. "I had to get away from there before I started laughing," he said, grinning at her, his eyes crinkling at the corners. "You—oh, take my hand, there, and try not to think too much about the steps or you'll stumble. You impressed Bixhenta, and he doesn't impress easily. If only I'd known the key to breaking through his reserve was to talk about underwear, I'd have done that a year ago."

"It was only the truth."

"And he knew it. You realized he spoke Tremontanese, right?"

"Yes."

"It's a well-kept secret. An even better kept secret is that I speak Veriboldan. Comes in handy, since relations between our governments are rather tense at the moment. Would you like to know what they were saying?"

"I think perhaps it was not the same as what the Voice said to me."

"No. Let's see." He pursed his lips in thought. "She said, 'I think the fat girl—' I beg your pardon, it's what she said."

"It is all right. I am a fat girl. What did she say?"

"Oh. She said she thought you were too young for the position and the Kirkellan were disrespecting Veribold in sending you. And he told her to go on pretending Veribold cares about the Kirkellan, because they need your trade."

"I think they need us more than they say."

"I agree. Then he said, when you talked about mutual aid, that you were bold. He didn't sound upset about it. I don't know why; he usually hates it when people talk back to him. Then you said the thing about undergarments, and he told the Voice he had always wondered what the Kirkellan did with the silk they traded for. Apparently it has never occurred to the Veriboldans to use it for that purpose. And *then* he said if you were so clever, it would be interesting to see what uses you came up with for other Veriboldan trade items. So congratulations, madam ambassador, on your first diplomatic victory."

Imogen blushed. "It was an accident."

"Sometimes diplomacy is about capitalizing on those kinds of accidents."

"Then…thank you, your Majesty."

"I thought I asked you to call me Jeffrey."

"But I am ambassador."

"Yes, but we're dancing. We're allowed to be informal. Friendly, even." He winked at her, and she laughed.

"You are friendly to…Bixhenta, do I say it right?" she asked.

"It's a 'sh' before the 'ch' in the middle, but close enough."

"Bixhenta. But you say your countries are tense."

"I'm friendly because I don't want things to get worse. There are Veriboldan rebels along their eastern border we think are actually funded by the government. Now that Ruskald isn't a barrier between us, the danger that they might try to do more than just rattle their swords in our direction has increased."

"What is it you have that they want?"

"Devices. Tremontane has more magical source than any other country and we make better and more Devices. Bixhenta is here ostensibly to negotiate for freer trade, but I think he might be evaluating our internal stability. This conflict with Ruskald makes us look weak, and I'm friendly with Bixhenta so he won't realize how weakened the war has left us."

"And that is why you need rulers for the new territory."

"Exactly. We need to show a strong, united front."

"Then I do not understand why you took over territory from Ruskald when it was a barrier that protected you."

"Ruskald has always been more of a danger than Veribold. Having a shorter border with them is worth sharing a longer border with Veribold."

"Then they are afraid of you because you are the…the aggressor when you take this land."

"Too afraid to attack us, I hope."

"That is not a safe hope. It is when people are most afraid they forget to be afraid." She remembered saying the same thing to Hrovald, about his chiefs, and wondered if it had come true for him yet.

"Good insight. As long as I can keep friendly with Bixhenta and play along with his need to be superior and in control, Veribold can maintain its self-image and not fear Tremontane will take its preeminence away."

"Unless the government pays the rebels to be its secret standing army."

Jeffrey laughed. "Are you sure you've only been a diplomat for a week? You certainly seem to understand the situation well."

Imogen opened her mouth, closed it again, then after a moment said, "It seemed clear to me. I did not think it was diplomacy."

"Diplomacy is also about understanding the people you're treating with. I think—" He went silent and looked away past her ear.

"You think what?"

"It's not my place to say."

"Now you must say or I will step on your foot and pretend it is you who are clumsy."

Startled, he met her eyes again, then chuckled. "Your mother told me she thought there was a part of you that was no warrior. I'm beginning to see what that part is."

It was Imogen's turn to look away. His words disquieted her. Her mother had said much the same thing to her, that she was a warrior because it was the only part of her she knew. But she'd felt confident, talking to Jeffrey about his political situation and understanding it, as if something were waking up inside her. She pushed it aside and hoped it would fall asleep again.

"You continue to astonish me, madam ambassador," Jeffrey added. They turned away from each other, came back together, and the music ended. "And you dance very well." Imogen realized she hadn't tripped or lost count or done anything embarrassing or awkward. Jeffrey was an excellent partner. They bowed to each other, smiling, and Imogen let go of his hand. He immediately offered her his arm. "It's custom for the gentleman to escort the lady back to her friends."

"Then I should obey custom," she said, accepting the gesture without a hint of the discomfort she felt at having her freedom of movement impeded. It wasn't as if Jeffrey was going to lead her into an ambush.

"Oh, Jeffrey, I've been looking for you," said Diana Ashmore, emerging from the crowd. She laid her hand on his other arm. "Have you made a decision about the new territory?"

"Diana, is that really what you want to discuss?" Jeffrey said, amused. "At a wedding reception?"

"Why not? It's not as if it's your wedding." She laughed and squeezed his arm gently. "I know Howard Spencer is looking—oh, there he is." A tall, thin man with very sharp cheekbones was approaching at speed, as if he were racing some invisible opponent. He was followed by a woman whose attractive violet gown, embroidered all over the substantial bodice with crystals that caught the light and winked at Imogen, clashed with her red hair.

"No private discourse, Diana, we agreed on that," the man said. He sounded slightly out of breath.

"*You* agreed on that, Howard, and it's not as if we're in competition," said Diana. She released Jeffrey's arm. "Now we're both here, Jeffrey, you can stop being coy and tell us what you've decided."

"I was under the impression you were the one who answered to me," Jeffrey said. His words were pleasant enough, but there was a steely undertone to them. "Micheline, Howard, let me introduce the ambassador from the Kirkellan, Imogen. Imogen, this is Micheline Branston, chief of Internal Affairs, and Howard Spencer, Baron of Avory."

"I am pleased to meet you," Imogen said. Branston smiled politely. Spencer ignored Imogen. "It's obvious what the decision should be, Jeffrey," he said.

"That territory will take years to pacify fully," Jeffrey said. "I can't make this decision lightly. I appreciate your arguments that experienced leadership will benefit that process. I'm also conscious of your current responsibilities and have to consider whether adding the new territory to yours, making Daxtry and Avory counties, will stretch your resources too thin."

"I know I'm capable of increased responsibility," Diana said. "I've served Tremontane for many years—"

"And will continue to do so regardless of my decision, I'm sure."

"I don't suppose our desires have any weight with you," Spencer said.

"My decisions are based on what is best for Tremontane, not what is best for one man. Or woman." The steely note was back in his voice. "This discussion is over. I do not intend to turn my sister's celebration into a Council meeting, so I hope the two of you will enjoy yourselves. Micheline, I'll speak to you tomorrow morning in my office. Imogen, will you walk with me?" He strode away without waiting for her assent, making her take a few stumbling steps before matching his long stride.

"Sorry about that," he said in a low voice, though they'd quickly left Spencer and Diana behind. Imogen wished she could see both their faces, but turning around was awkward, so she just tried to keep up with her escort. "Howard and Diana will be the most affected by this decision, and I'm afraid they sometimes let their eagerness overcome their good sense."

"They wish more land?"

"The territory we took from Ruskald extends westward from their Baronies. They want their boundary lines extended. It's a possibility, but I'm still considering other options."

"You will make the right decision."

"I certainly hope so. Nothing I decide is going to make everyone happy."

"No, it is..." They stopped near the King's seat, and Imogen struggled to find the right words. "It will be the right decision because you are strong and will not let it be the wrong one."

Jeffrey put his hand over Imogen's where it rested on his sleeve and squeezed gently. "I thank you for your faith in me, madam ambassador."

His eyes were very blue and very intent on her, and Imogen blushed without knowing why. She looked away and saw Diana approaching them, smiling. Surely she wasn't going to bring up the territory decision again?

"Oh, Jeffrey," she said, "you're right, and I'm sorry for bringing business into this celebration. Can you forgive me?" She put her hand on his free arm again and smiled up at him. Imogen released him, feeling reluctant to let go.

"Of course, Diana," Jeffrey said. "I hope you are enjoying yourself."

"I will be, once you dance with me," she said, winking at him. "It *is* our dance, after all. I promise not to bring up politics if you promise not to back out. I know how you feel about dancing."

"Is it?" Jeffrey said. "I'd forgotten. Imogen, thank you for the dance, and please excuse me." He took Diana's other hand and moved into the figures of the next dance. Imogen watched them go. She had no trouble at all reading *that* interaction. Diana thought Jeffrey was hers, or wanted him to be. Jeffrey seemed oblivious to her attachment. Diana would be in for a huge disappointment, unless Jeffrey had a sudden change of heart. Imogen felt a little sorry for her.

Imogen saw Alison sitting alone, watching the dancers, and went to join her. "Would you care to sit?" Alison asked. "All the ambassadors have seats here, away from the crowds."

Imogen looked out at the chattering, dancing people and felt courage rise up in her. "I think I must be a diplomat now," she said, "but I will return again later." She'd faced down the Veriboldan ambassador. She could face anything now.

She danced, and talked, and danced again, and went into one of the small rooms lining the ballroom for some quiet only to back out quickly when she realized two other people were already using it. Diplomacy was exhausting work. She didn't know how many hours had passed when she began to feel tired and hungry for food that wouldn't try to explode all over her. She wondered if she was allowed to leave yet. That was something she could ask Jeffrey. She made her way to where he was sitting next to Alison. Diana stood near him, talking and laughing and occasionally touching his arm. Imogen wondered if Alison had left her seat all night. She didn't look as if she were having fun. As Imogen approached, Alison straightened up and smiled, a strained smile that looked as tired as Imogen felt.

"I do not know when it is all right for me to leave," she said.

Jeffrey pulled a watch Device from inside his coat. "It's rather late, isn't it?" he said. "But you can leave any time you like. One of the benefits of being an ambassador."

"Unlike being a King, which means you have to stay much later than you'd like," Diana teased, leaning close to Jeffrey. "Or a Consort, naturally," she added, nodding in Alison's direction.

"As I am merely a Dowager Consort, however, I can leave whenever I choose," Alison said coolly, directing an indifferent look at Diana that Imogen thought might conceal a different emotion. "Let me escort you to the door and summon your carriages, Imogen." She stood and kissed her son on the cheek. Diana had to move back to let her do it, and Imogen caught a glimpse of her face, which said she wasn't any fonder of Alison than Alison was of her. Yet another mark against Diana's chances with Jeffrey; he loved his mother very much.

Imogen circled the room quickly, gathering her *tiermatha,* then left the ballroom with Alison, who seemed more lively now. In the hallway, she said, "I think you like to dance but you do not. Why is that?"

"I'm sure I don't know what you're talking about," Alison said sharply. Imogen, abashed, went silent. After a moment, Alison sighed and said, "I apologize, Imogen. The truth is my husband was an excellent dancer and it was something we both loved. It's been three years, and the pain of his loss is mostly gone, but I still can't bear to dance without him."

"You loved him," Imogen said.

"More than I can say. Our love had a rocky start, which is why I never took it for granted. I think of him every day—fondly, not sadly, thank heaven."

"My parents are like that. My mother is sharp and hard and my father is softer and more gentle. And I think they make each other better because they have differences."

"That's very wise, Imogen. I hope Elspeth and Owen have that kind of marriage, and I hope it lasts a good long time."

"Why is Jeffrey not married? He is not too young?"

"He is rather plagued by women who would like to be the Consort. There are fewer women who would like to be the wife of Jeffrey North and none who see him for who he is. I wish he would marry. I know he feels the burden of having only one heir, and he and I both know Elspeth—and do not say a word of this to her, I don't want to hurt her or frighten her—Elspeth is not very strong and the odds of her having a child are not good. But having had the marriage I did, I can't encourage him to simply pick a healthy woman of the right temperament and do his duty." Alison sighed. "I have hope that someday he'll find the right woman. I'm not sure if he does."

"And I think Diana Ashmore is not the right woman even if she would like to be," Imogen said, daringly.

Alison looked at her, startled, then laughed. "Yes, she would, wouldn't she? Thank heaven Jeffrey doesn't see her that way. Doesn't see her at all, for which I should pity her, but I dislike her so much I only feel gratitude."

"You have not told him."

"Would you? Dislike her or not, I wouldn't embarrass any woman that way. And I fear, just a little, if I tell him she is interested in a relationship somewhat closer than the friendship they already have, it might incline him to think of her in the same way. Better for all concerned that he remain oblivious."

They reached the courtyard, where Alison said a few words to one of the runners lounging about the steps, then said, "I'm glad you're a friend to my children. There are so few people who can ignore their rank and form a more natural attachment."

"It does not—I do not think of that. I am glad it is not wrong to not think of them as better because they are King and Princess."

"Not at all. Respect is one thing, but servility is vile. I hope you think of me as a friend as well."

"I do," Imogen said, and impulsively hugged her. Alison hugged her back.

On the way home, Dorenna said, "Made friends with his mother, have you?"

"Dor, just shut up about it, all right?" Imogen knew she sounded harsh and didn't care. "I'm tired of hearing about how we look good together or that he's interested in me or whatever else you might come up with." Dorenna went silent, and Imogen instantly felt contrite. "I'm sorry, I didn't mean it to come out that way."

"No, you're right," Dorenna said from her dark corner. "No more."

Imogen settled into her own corner. Having told Dorenna off, now she found herself thinking about Jeffrey and how handsome he was, those blue eyes that crinkled at the corners when he smiled, how he always seemed happy to see her. *It wouldn't be so bad if he were interested in me, would it*? she wondered, and answered herself, *Not bad at all*. But it was foolish, because he looked at Elspeth and Alison and Owen the same way and he was certainly not interested in a romantic relationship with any of them. And even if he were, she was leaving in a year and, she realized with surprise, she wasn't interested in something temporary; she wanted to find a partner and ultimately a husband to build a family with. Jeffrey North was definitely not that man.

Chapter Twenty-One

The Veriboldan embassy was a four-story townhouse on a quiet street near the palace. Linden trees surrounded by tiny iron fences grew as if from the stony pavement, amazing Imogen. They were almost in full leaf now and cast fluttering shadows over her as she dismounted from her carriage. She spared a wave for the horses drawing the carriage, who didn't seem quite as unhappy as many of their fellows. Perhaps it was the driver, who was cheerful and friendly and asked after Victory's health. He agreed to wait for her, and she walked up the embassy steps, her strides awkward thanks to the full-skirted cotton dress she wore. Its several petticoats had been a point of contention between herself and Alison, and she'd only acquiesced to the dress because Alison had uncharacteristically stomped her foot and said, "Imogen, I am not going to be able to explain everything we do in a way you'll like, so just wear the dress and stop complaining!"

Now, even constrained by her skirt, she felt like a diplomat as she rang the embassy bell and was admitted by a short woman wearing a white robe over a black tunic and skirt. The high, arched ceiling of the entrance hall was supported by slim black pillars with capitals and plinths carved to look like crashing waves. The floor was tiled with irregularly-shaped tesserae in variegated shades of blue and green that made the floor appear to be moving, as if water flowed over it, which made Imogen feel a little nauseated. The white walls bore paintings that to Imogen's untrained eye looked like nothing more than blotches of color, albeit interesting blotches, all framed in the same black wood the pillars were made of. An archway at the far end of the hall revealed a wide staircase, its risers lacquered bronze, that led upward out of sight.

The small woman silently turned and walked toward the stairs, and Imogen followed, ascending about twenty steps before coming out on a landing. The floor here was plain, unvarnished wood, and while the walls were still white, they bore no decorations of any kind. A narrow hallway lined with white painted doors led straight ahead, while two other identical hallways extended right and left. The woman pointed to the left, and about halfway down the hall Imogen saw a doorway that was open just a crack. She went to it and let herself in.

Inside, the Voice of the Proxy sat at a small table bearing a tea set in jade glass and silver. She showed no sign of noticing Imogen's entry other than to lift the teapot and begin pouring. Imogen took the only other seat in the room, a chair matching the Voice's on the other side of the table, and accepted a cup of the hot, dark brown liquid. Veriboldan tea was one of the commodities their merchants wouldn't trade with the Kirkellan, so Imogen had never had it until coming to Aurilien, and then only once, because she disliked the astringent taste. She sipped politely and was surprised at its unexpected sweetness.

"We do not trade our best with the outside world," the Voice said in Tremontanese. "Veribold would be self-sufficient if it could. Trading with others is…uncivilized."

"I think I have no reason to be here, then," Imogen said. She drank more of the tea. If the Voice was going to be rude to her, she was damn well going to be rude back, so it was probably a good thing to drink the delicious beverage before she was shown the door.

"Not everyone shares this view," the Voice said. "And it is an impractical hope for perfection in a fallen world. I mean only to warn you."

"I see," said Imogen. She didn't, really. Was the Voice warning her Bixhenta was reluctant to trade, whatever he might have implied at the ball? Or was she saying Imogen's presence in the embassy was an embarrassment to all of them? She decided not to press the Voice further. Let her fill up the void with her words, and Imogen would see what she might reveal.

"You will speak when spoken to," the Voice continued. "Do not ask questions. And never reveal the content of whatever you may hear or speak of in this room."

Imogen raised her eyebrows, but said nothing. If she followed those rules, she wouldn't get anything out of Bixhenta. Well, what could they do to her if she refused to comply? Kick her out?

The Voice waited for Imogen to speak. Imogen simply nodded as if in assent. The Voice stood and cleared the tea things to a tray, then carried it away out of the room herself. The door she exited by swung back and forth as she pushed it open with her rear end, and Imogen caught glimpses of people sitting at desks or standing and conversing.

She looked around. The Veriboldans really liked white; this room, like the halls, was painted in that non-color. A large window with white draperies pulled to both sides filled most of a wall; smaller panes of glass ran down each side of it. Two more of the blotchy blobby messes of color hung facing one another, one in shades of red, the other in tones of brown. She tapped her toe on the bare wooden floor, tap-tap, tappity-tap-tap, until she got bored and decided to wander. A table under the window had a single drawer, which she opened; it was empty except for a soft gray puff of lint.

"I wondered how long it would take you to explore," said someone in perfect Kirkellish. Imogen turned to see Bixhenta, dressed in Tremontanan garb, his fingers laced together in front of him.

"I wondered if you would continue pretending not to understand anything but Veriboldan," she replied in the same language.

"No point, is there, when we both are aware of the ruse." Bixhenta closed the curtains, then took the seat the Voice had vacated and gestured for Imogen to sit as well. His voice was strong and sounded younger than his apparent years.

"The Voice gave me instructions I am planning to ignore," Imogen said, and Bixhenta smiled.

"Paoine is more of a stickler for custom than I am," he said. "She takes her role seriously and I think she is resentful I don't have a genuine need for her services."

"And you use her…why? To keep a barrier between yourself and your, um, supplicants?"

"Yes. It puts people off-guard. A trick of diplomacy, you might say."

"And yet you're willing to speak with me personally."

"We've danced the diplomatic dance long enough. I tire of the formalities. Let us treat together face to face, as it were."

"I appreciate it. My name is Imogen. May I call you Bixhenta, or is that too informal even for our new-found understanding?"

He laughed. "You even pronounce it properly. Very well, Imogen. I have asked you here on false pretenses."

Imogen frowned at him. "You don't want trade with my people?"

"No, I do, but that's not why I asked you to come. Do you understand what it means that we are in the Veriboldan embassy? This building is effectively Veriboldan territory. We have sovereign control over it and I can with some surety guarantee there are no unwelcome ears listening in."

"You're beginning to make me nervous."

"I wish merely to impress upon you the seriousness with which I take this conversation. Imogen, what do you know of the Tremontanan annexation of Ruskald territory?"

"I know they took it to prevent further Ruskalder invasions, and that it gives them a longer shared border with Veribold."

"They *say* they took it because of the Ruskalder threat. Are you aware of Veriboldan history with regard to Tremontane?"

"I only know what I've learned here, I'm afraid. That there are rebels along Veribold's eastern border Tremontane believes are funded by the Veriboldan government."

"The allegation is absurd, but I don't expect you to believe that simply on my say-so any more than I expect you to believe Tremontane's accusations." Bixhenta leaned forward in his chair and lowered his voice. "You will have to examine the evidence, and decide for yourself."

"With all due respect, why is your conflict with Tremontane Kirkellan business?"

"Such a bald-faced land grab can mean only one thing: Tremontane is preparing for invasion. No, I'm not saying they plan to invade right now, I'm saying they expect the necessity, if you can call it that, of invasion sometime in the future, and they're positioning themselves for it now. It shames me to admit it to an outsider, but...Veribold is not capable of defending itself against Tremontane's military. We keep to ourselves and attempt to be self-sufficient, though we acknowledge the benefits of trade. Yes, smile, young lady, and it's true we like to make it sound as if we're doing everyone a great favor by dealing with them, but we do appreciate our trading partners. But arrogance is not a justification for war."

"Why would Tremontane want to invade Veribold?"

"Our economy is thriving. Our coastline is more than double Tremontane's, and it's no secret they would like to increase their sea trade. And Tremontane has more than its share of unlanded, untitled gentry who would love to gain baronies or even counties of their own. Take a look at a map of the region sometime. You'll see Veribold is perfectly positioned to be an annex to Tremontane proper."

Now Imogen felt uncomfortable. "And you want a treaty with the Kirkellan against Tremontane. You know the *matrian* has already treated with King Jeffrey for mutual defensive aid."

"I'm not asking for the Kirkellan to break their treaty. When Hrovald went to war against Tremontane, it broke the *banrach*—yes, I have my resources—because the Kirkellan were not to be drawn into a conflict with a country they had no quarrel with. We wish simply to have the assurance that if Tremontane aggresses against Veribold, the Kirkellan will come not to their aid, but to ours instead."

Imogen sat silent for a moment. She was positive Jeffrey didn't intend to wage war against Veribold, so a treaty such as this one was harmless. But she didn't trust Bixhenta; who knew if he had ulterior motives? "What would Veribold offer in return?" she asked.

"Favored trading status. Better goods—you must know by now we don't send our best things north." Bixhenta smiled, in amusement, not malice. "An exchange of ambassadors, and that alone should assure you of our sincerity." Imogen nodded. If the haughty and meticulous Veriboldans were willing to send one of their own to live rough in the Eidestal, they were serious indeed. "I've taken the liberty of drawing up a proposal you may pass on to your *matrian,* though I'm afraid it will have to take the slow route. I cannot allow you to use palace telecoders and operators, obviously, and it would be bad form for us to code, send, *and* decode the messages we pass to your country."

Imogen nodded. "May I see the proposal? The *matrian* is the one who will approve it, but I should verify there isn't anything in it she would reject out of hand."

"Such as promising her second daughter in marriage to a Veriboldan land-holder?" Bixhenta's tiny eyes twinkled from the depths of his dark, wrinkled skin. He rose and pushed open the door the Voice had used. After a moment, a young woman entered, carrying a valise. "Don't worry, it's in Kirkellish," Bixhenta assured her. Imogen removed a thin sheaf of paper from it and read through it carefully. She wasn't a great reader, but she was able to tell that on the surface, at least, Bixhenta's offer was genuine.

"I think the *matrian* will welcome a treaty with Veribold," she said, returning the sheaf of paper to the valise. "Will you allow me to send a telecode telling her of your proposal and to expect its delivery?"

"Certainly." He held the door open for her and led her through a room filled with busy people into another room that was entirely given over to a telecoder. Imogen scribbled out her message and handed it over to be encoded and sent, then waited for the return message acknowledging receipt. The final words of the message were WELL DONE AMBASSADOR. Her mother's approval made her heart warm.

"I am glad we were able to come to a mutual understanding," Bixhenta said, offering his hand to Imogen. She shook it, feeling the dry, papery skin shift under her fingers. "And, Imogen? I suggest you look into my story. Find out for yourself what Tremontane intends. Don't let the King's smoothness of manner fool you."

She thought about that on the short carriage ride back to the Kirkellan embassy. Could Jeffrey really intend to invade Veribold? He'd said Tremontane was worried about Veribold invading *them*. It seemed the Kirkellan were going to be drawn into the heart of someone else's conflict. Whoever the aggressor was, Imogen was certain the Kirkellan did not want to side with them. She laughed to herself. What a strange chain of events, to lead to the Kirkellan allied with two major powers, and at the center of whatever peace was brokered, after being left to themselves for so many years.

She wished she understood the etiquette of being an ambassador better. Time to sit down with Simon and have him explain things. She had a feeling she should not discuss anything she worked out with Bixhenta with Jeffrey, and vice versa, but Bixhenta was right; she needed to find evidence that Tremontane's intentions were what Jeffrey had told her, and for that matter, she should find evidence that Bixhenta was telling the truth. The idea that Jeffrey might have lied to her made her feel ill. If he had, that would be the end of their friendship. Bixhenta had to be wrong. They both did.

Chapter Twenty-Two

Four days later she still hadn't come to a decision. She'd had a long conversation with Simon that ended with her entrusting the sealed valise to him to dispatch to Mother, but it had been inconclusive with regard to how she was supposed to prove the truth of either Jeffrey's or Bixhenta's accusations. In the end, she'd decided to stop thinking about it for a few days, see if her subconscious mind could come up with a solution, and waved goodbye to her *tiermatha* as they rode off to enjoy themselves with the Kirkellan company and the Home Guard. She, damn it, was spending the afternoon with members of the court at some kind of outdoor party. Her intimidating maid Jeanette helped Imogen dress in a form-fitting yellow muslin dress with a moderately full skirt, arranged her hair so tendrils curled down around her face where they would surely drive her mad, and fastened a wide-brimmed hat on her head that was intended to keep her face protected from the sun so it would stay sallow instead of bloom with color. She glared at herself in the mirror. She'd rather be sparring.

In the carriage with five giggling women, she stared out the window and wished she were riding Victory to this party, even if it meant using a sidesaddle. She knew she was sulking, but she didn't care; it was one of those days when she resented Mother for having sent her here, resented Aurilien for expecting her to behave like a Tremontanan woman, resented Jeffrey for…she wasn't sure why she resented him, it was irrational, but she did. She communicated with the other women in short, curt sentences, and eventually they left her alone. She felt uncomfortable at failing in her duties as an ambassador, but her bad mood was enough to let her ignore those feelings.

The park the carriages brought them to was outside the walls of the city and surprised Imogen with its natural beauty. She had expected a place as groomed as the large Park near the palace where people went to ride their horses or carriages and see people or be seen themselves.

There, flowers and trees grew in orderly beds and rows, the grass was trimmed daily, and artificial waterfalls and pools dotted the landscape in orderly randomness. Here, the natural features of the land had been exploited to produce a pleasing landscape, and if the trees and hedges had been placed there intentionally, they seemed unplanned. Imogen wandered by herself for a while, enchanted all over again by Tremontane's green beauty.

"It's quite the landscape, isn't it?" A young man she didn't know came to stand at her elbow, looking out over the same vista. "You know they had to move that entire row of trees seven feet to the left to block out the view of the road? Masterpiece of design, it was."

"It is impressive." Actually, the knowledge that the park had been that meticulously arranged made her irritable. They'd uprooted and replanted twelve trees just to block the view?

"Colman Winston," the young man said, offering his hand. "My mother is Henrietta Winston of the Stafford Winstons." He said this in an off-handed way that nevertheless sounded as if he wanted her to be impressed. Imogen obliged him, even though she had no idea who the Stafford Winstons were.

"Hope you're enjoying being an ambassador here," he went on. "Must be exciting, all these parties and dances and dinners, making treaties and such."

"It is fun and it is work," Imogen said. She was determined not to let her bad mood get the better of her, now that she was being an ambassador again.

"Hope you don't mind my saying, but your accent is simply enchanting," Winston said.

"It is how I speak. I think it will go away as I learn to speak better."

"I hope not. It sounds beautiful." He was looking at her with a definite suggestion in his eye.

Imogen began to have an uncomfortable feeling. "What is it you do for work?" she said, hoping to deflect the conversation.

"Oh, this and that. Not so much work as attend to business. You know."

"I do not know. What is business?"

"Oh…races, things to do on my estate. These days I go out to the track your Kirkellan have built on the parade grounds."

I wish that's where I was right now. "I think the track is wonderful."

"Yes, it's very popular. You know you're beautiful when you're enthusiastic like that?"

Imogen ignored this. "I will go to the track tomorrow," she said, mostly to herself.

"That's a wonderful idea. We could go together." He reached out to take her hand, but Imogen stepped aside and clasped her hands in front of her.

"I do not think so. I do not go to watch, I go to ride." She watched his smooth face register brief disappointment before going back to its old half-lidded sensual gaze.

"Then I'll be sure to cheer for you. I'd love to see you later. Perhaps you'd like to accompany me to supper sometime? Say, tomorrow night?"

"I do not think so," Imogen said, concealing her unease. "But it is nice of you to ask." She made her escape before he could press her further. Was he trying to court her? It certainly seemed that way. She felt even more uncomfortable. She didn't know what to do with this young man and his smooth if insincere compliments, except from what she knew of Tremontanans it wasn't acceptable to simply tell a person you weren't interested; you had to be subtle, and Imogen didn't know how to be subtle.

"Imogen! Come and sit with me," Jeffrey called to her. He was seated on a stone bench that looked out over what Imogen thought was a natural lake, but given the revelation about the trees she wouldn't be surprised to find it had been dug there on purpose. Two well-armed guards in North blue stood nearby, their eyes constantly scanning their surroundings as if they expected a shrub or a rock to sprout assassins at any moment. They examined her closely as she approached, tensing slightly, and Imogen noticed with satisfaction they clearly thought she was capable of being a threat to their King. She hadn't seen any evidence that anyone wanted to harm Jeffrey, but it was nice to know his guards were paranoid enough to defend him from any unexpected attack. She took a seat next to him, and together they watched the wind make ripples on the surface of the water.

"I like that dress," Jeffrey said. "It suits you."

"I am not sure about this hat," Imogen said, trying not to sound irritable. She found her imaginary resentment of him had disappeared.

"I have to say I agree with you," Jeffrey said. "Why don't you take it off?"

"But they are all wearing hats."

Jeffrey shrugged. "Maybe they all dislike theirs, too, and you'll free them from captivity to the tyranny of hats."

Imogen smiled. She removed the hat pins and put her hat in her lap. "Now I can feel the sun," she said, closing her eyes and turning her face up to feel its rays.

"Yes, you look much better without it," Jeffrey said. She opened her eyes and found him watching her instead of the lake.

"It is—it does not make my hair wrong?"

"No, not at all. You look lovely." Jeffrey looked back across the lake. "I'm glad for this excursion. I never get out here anymore. Too much work."

"I hope that is a natural lake and not a hole scooped out by diggers to fill with water," Imogen said.

He laughed. "No, it's been there for…probably longer than Aurilien's been around. The park was planned around it."

"I am glad. It is good they plant hedges, but moving a lake is—seems wrong."

"I agree."

"Jeffrey, is this where you've gotten off to?" Diana Ashmore exclaimed, coming up the low rise toward them. She sat down on Jeffrey's other side, forcing him to shift so Imogen had barely any part of the bench to sit on. "You're neglecting your guests."

"It's not that formal a party, Diana, and everyone seems perfectly happy." Jeffrey looked down at where Imogen sat and put his hand on her waist to keep her from sliding off. "Have you been enjoying yourself?"

"I am now I have such good company. Imogen, how do you like the park? I don't suppose you have anything like this in the Eidestal."

Diana's words were innocent, but behind them lurked a sarcastic and mean-spirited intent. "We do not have trees as you do," Imogen said, deciding to reply to Diana's overt meaning, "and we do not live in one place to make such a park. But there are places we go that are beautiful in a different way."

"Really? Tell me about some of them." Jeffrey turned his attention fully on Imogen, and Imogen, who was looking at Jeffrey and Diana both, saw unexpected anger cross the woman's face.

"There is a place where the river comes over hills very fast. It looks like it boils and it makes spray that tickles your face if you stand close. Then there is the plains and the sky makes a blue glass bowl over it, all the way in every direction you can look. And there is a lake where the reindeer come. It has trees with needles, not leaves, and it is in shade all year. The reindeer drink at it and they bring their children. We do not hunt there." Imogen felt tears sting her eyes and looked away. She was suddenly so homesick she wanted to leap up and run north until she was home.

She became aware of Jeffrey's hand on her waist, squeezing just a little as if trying to give comfort. "Your land sounds beautiful," he said quietly.

"Yes, very wild," Diana said with a laugh that had an edge to it. "Jeffrey, did you name Clare Goodwin to be the ambassador to the Kirkellan? Perhaps she's seeing these things right now! I know I wish I could be there."

"Speaking of being there, I thought you were leaving for Daxtry two days ago," Jeffrey said, his voice noticeably cooler.

"You're not eager for me to leave, are you?" Diana laughed again, a wobbly sound that would have made Imogen feel sorry for her if she weren't so annoyed at her rudeness.

"Since I feel better when I know you're in command of your forces, of course I'm eager for you to join them." His expression was placid, but there was steel in his words, and Diana recoiled, fear flickering across her face for the briefest moment before she regained control of herself and smiled broadly.

"How flattering! No, I've had word from my second-in-command and I've decided to stay another week so as not to neglect my Council duties. You won't be rid of me that easily!" She patted Jeffrey's cheek fondly, but she looked at Imogen as she did so and her eyes were angry and cold.

"I'm so glad to hear that. Imogen, would you like to see the lakeshore? There are sometimes ducklings in the rushes." He stood and offered her his arm, and Imogen took it; they left Diana sitting there, mute, and walked down the gentle slope toward the lake.

"I apologize for her rudeness," Jeffrey said quietly. They took a wide path that steered them away from strolling couples and groups chatting at the arched pavilions put there for that purpose, the guards following at a discreet distance. "She…" His voice trailed off.

"She does not like me," Imogen said.

He made an exasperated face. "She's in love with me," he said, "or wants to be Consort, at any rate. She's territorial."

"I think—thought you did not know."

"It's fairly obvious, don't you think? But we've been friends for years, and this…infatuation she's developed only happened about a year ago, so I pretend I don't notice so I won't have to ruin our friendship by telling her off."

"I think perhaps she has already ruined it by how she is."

"I just wish I knew a graceful way out of it. I need her focused on County Daxtry, not distracted by my rejection, and—well, you heard her, she's putting off returning to the border, probably because—" He stopped speaking abruptly and stared down at the edge of the lake. "Look, duck footprints."

Imogen wasn't fooled. "It is because I am your friend and I am a woman."

Jeffrey nodded. "Like I said, territorial." He put his hand on hers where she held his arm. "I'm sorry you have to be mixed up in this."

"I am not. I will still be your friend and it does not matter what Diana thinks."

He looked at her, unsmiling, his blue eyes serious. "Your friendship matters to me," he said. She was conscious of how close he stood, of his hand on hers, and she made herself smile and say, "I did not think I would be the friend of a King. You are much unlike Hrovald."

His eyes widened, then he laughed hard. "Unlike Hrovald," he said when he could breathe again. "Madam ambassador, that is high praise indeed. Shall we return to my guests, and see if Diana is right that they feel neglected?"

No one seemed to have noticed they'd been gone. Diana, too, had disappeared, rejoining the group just a few minutes before they were all to return to the city, coyly saying she'd found a new trail and followed it to its exciting end. On the return trip, Imogen's coachmates were more subdued, mostly speaking among themselves in quiet voices, but Imogen barely noticed, even though they frequently looked at her. She again stared out the window, but this time her thoughts were more confused than angry. She remembered his hand on her waist—that had been totally unnecessary—and on her hand—surely that indicated his sincerity and nothing more—and wished she knew what that serious look in his eyes had meant. Nothing, probably. The real issue was not what Jeffrey felt for her, it was that she'd experienced an undeniable attraction to him that afternoon, and that was unacceptable.

She returned to the embassy. No one else was back yet. She felt irritable again; it was too late for her to join them, and she really wanted to see the track the riders had built. She cadged bread and cheese from the kitchen staff and took it to her room to eat, sullen and alone. Tomorrow she was going to put aside the ambassador and return to being what she really was. Tomorrow she would be a rider of the Kirkellan once more.

Chapter Twenty-Three

Imogen wavered over what to do about investigating Bixhenta's claims for several more days. She told herself it was because she had too many demands on her time, between the track and sparring and social events and suppers and diplomatic functions, but the truth was she was afraid he was right, which would mean Jeffrey had lied to her, and that idea made her heart ache. Finally she decided she was being a coward. She considered sending a Kirkellan warrior to her mother with the message for security, but having made her decision, she didn't want to wait more than a week for a reply. So she set off for the palace.

The palace telecoders occupied a vast marble-floored room that had started life as a reception hall. The tapping of the brass arms, so tiny next to the wall-sized bases, echoed from the arched ceiling high above. It would be nice, she thought, not to have to send a message asking about Tremontanan military movements on a Tremontanan telecoder, but she was equally afraid to send the message by way of a public telecoder, so this was her only option. She sought out an inactive telecoder. Its operator sat in a narrow, battered folding chair, her hair pinned by two pencils, cleaning her fingernails with a pen nib. "Sign in for your turn," she said without looking up.

"This is for diplomatic business and I do not have to sign in," Imogen said. She'd dressed up in semi-formal gown and soft shoes and had Jeanette arrange her hair neatly on her head, thinking people were far less likely to challenge her right to use the telecoder if she looked like an ambassador than if she wore the scruffy trousers and shirt she planned to change back into for her ride after this. The operator looked up, blinked, and sat up straight.

"Madam ambassador," she said. "You have a message to send, or to receive?"

"To send, and then wait for a reply." Imogen held out the paper she'd composed her message on.

"I can't read this," the woman said.

"You do not have to read it as long as you can send it."

"I'll get a operator who can read Kirkellish."

"No, this is…confidential diplomatic business. I do not wish for it to be read."

"But that will take forever, sending it a letter at a time."

"Then it will take forever, and you should start now."

The operator shrugged, looked up Mother's telecoder in her book of codes, and began tapping out the message. Imogen looked around for another chair and prepared to wait. She was uncomfortable, being so secretive, but she instinctively felt asking the Kirkellan for information on Tremontanan troop movements was something the Tremontanans would not like, even if it wasn't exactly secret. After all, the Kirkellan were working with the Tremontanans, so *they* knew the troop movements. She worried about the telecoder operator working at the other end; he or she would read the message and would be in a position to pass along the information that Imogen was asking for military…again, how secret could this be if the Kirkellan knew about it? Even so, Imogen felt better not broadcasting her intentions.

Bixhenta claimed Tremontane was preparing for invasion. The disposition of troops would tell her if he was right. She hoped he was wrong. She crossed her legs at the knee and rotated her left foot. She could ask Maxwell Burgess about Tremontane's diplomatic relationship with Veribold. That couldn't be construed as nosiness, since the mutual aid clause in the Kirkellan treaty with Tremontane meant the Kirkellan could be pulled into a conflict with Veribold if Veribold attacked Tremontane first. The Kirkellan ambassador ought to know how likely a possibility that was. Burgess would probably also know what evidence Tremontane had for suspecting the rebels were secretly funded by Veribold. Having spoken to Bixhenta, Imogen's instinct was the rebels were independent, but he himself had told her to examine the evidence rather than take his word, and now that she'd decided not to accept the Tremontanan side so unquestioningly she felt she ought to do the same for the Veriboldan perspective.

She yawned. She hadn't realized how long "forever" could be. The operator looked as bored as Imogen felt. Several minutes passed before the operator sat back in her chair and said, "That's done. Now we wait for a reply. You could come back later, if you want," she added, with the air of someone doing Imogen an enormous favor. Imogen stood and stretched. It was tempting to go off for a ride, come back later for the message, but she didn't like the idea of what could be potentially damning evidence lying around where someone who could read Kirkellish might see it. So she said, "I do not mind waiting," and took her seat again.

It was over an hour before the telecoder began tapping out its message. Imogen impatiently stood over the operator's shoulder until the woman glared at her, then she went back to her seat and fidgeted. Finally the woman tore off the tape and handed it and the transcription to Imogen. "If it's so secret, you should probably keep the original," she said. Imogen thanked her and returned to her rooms in the embassy.

The message was long, and the woman had written all the letters down without spaces between them—naturally, since she would have no idea where the Kirkellish words began and ended—so Imogen took pen and paper and recopied it so it was legible.

TROOPS OF FIFTY ACCOMPANIED BY TIERMATHAS CONCENTRATED ALONG NEW BORDER NORTH. SOME DISPERSED INTO INTERIOR TO CONTROL RUSKALDER SETTLEMENTS. VERIBOLDAN BORDER NOT PATROLLED. TROOPS COVER ASSIGNED AREA AND OVERLAP WITH NEIGHBORING TROOPS. TIERMATHAS MAKE BROAD SWEEPS. OCCUPATION SUCCESSFUL TO DATE HOPE YOUR MISSION EQUALLY SO. GOOD WORK.

It was unsigned, but Imogen knew her mother's praise when she read it. She poked the fire into life and burned the folded paper and the tape. So Tremontane wasn't massing forces along the Veriboldan border. Of course, it could still mean Bixhenta was right, that Tremontane would turn its attention on Veribold after securing its Ruskald border, but in the absence of evidence she was inclined to believe his fears were unfounded.

She changed into her riding gear. Jeffrey hadn't lied to her. The thought cheered her more than it probably should have. *Let's not be attracted to the foreign King,* she told herself. *He's a good man, and a friend, and it doesn't matter that he has those blue eyes and those broad shoulders and that way he smiles at you like…and now I can't stop thinking about him.* She pounded down the back steps and out to Victory's new stall. She wished she was like Kallum—all right, not in the essentials, but he was so good at appreciating beautiful men without his heart getting involved. If it weren't for the stupid flutter she felt in her chest every time she saw Jeffrey, everything would be fine.

Her ride in the Park didn't calm her as much as she wished. The placidity of the other riders, the way the pedestrians ambled along the paths, made her, perversely, more restless. Her thoughts alternated between reminding herself she could be attracted to Jeffrey without acting on it and wondering what it would be like if he felt the same about her. She kept trying to suppress the latter thought, only to have it spring back up every time she saw a dark-haired man ahead of her. Finally she determined to think of other things entirely, like how Victory had been the first to take all five hurdles at the new track without tipping one, and whether her new gown would be ready in time for the Spring Ball. She had been invited to supper that evening at the palace and she would have to talk to Jeffrey without any of her inner turmoil showing.

When she returned to the embassy, she found a small pile of envelopes on one of the tables in her sitting room. She picked one up and turned it over in her hand. It had something written on it in curly script that, when she turned it around, might be her name. The others were variations on the first. Imogen broke the green wax seal on one and removed a piece of paper that had been cut to fit the envelope exactly. It smelled so strongly of violets it made Imogen sneeze twice. The paper was covered in curly handwriting she couldn't read. A message for her. She felt a moment's irritation at the sender for assuming because she could speak Tremontanese, she could read it too.

What was she supposed to do with them? Simon was out of town for a couple of days, and she didn't think this was something she should entrust to Mistress Schotton or one of the servants. She gathered up the envelopes into a neat stack. Elspeth could read them for her.

She'd been so impatient about her messages she was early for supper; the east wing sitting room was empty. She went looking for Elspeth. All the doors in the hallway looked alike to her, so she knocked, and waited, and moved on until a door opened halfway and Owen poked his head out. He looked mussed, as if he'd been wrestling with someone. "Imogen," he said in Ruskeldin. "Do you need something?"

Imogen held out her handful of envelopes. "Someone left these for me and I can't read them."

"Neither can I," he said. He didn't invite her in. The silence between them stretched. Suddenly Imogen understood. She covered her mouth to hide a smile and said, "Never mind. You…do whatever it was you were doing." He shut the door, and she fled, not laughing until she reached the sitting room.

Well. That meant Elspeth was unavailable. Imogen sat down on a sofa and tossed the stack of envelopes on the table in front of her. They slid and scattered, and one fell off the edge onto the floor. She bent to pick it up, looking at the handwriting as if she might miraculously become able to read the ornate script. Suppose these were important messages? She laughed. Important messages did not come drenched in scent.

"Something funny?" Jeffrey asked, entering the room. "You look lovely." He did not look lovely. He looked haggard and grim, lines dragging down the corners of his mouth.

"You told the Council your decision," she realized.

He nodded. "Two new baronies to the west of Daxtry and of Avory, Daxtry and Avory to gain land so the Snow River flows entirely through their territories. I may regret it later, but for now it saves me a jurisdictional nightmare and might ease Howard and Diana's disappointment at not gaining counties. Neither of them looked happy when I told them the news. Diana…." He ran a hand through his hair, disordering it and making it stick up in back. "Extending Daxtry's boundary all the way to the west would have made it a third again the size of our largest county, and I'm not going to weaken this country just to make her happy."

"I am sorry," she said. "It is hard to be the King, I think."

"Very hard," Jeffrey said, sitting down next to her. "I don't know how my father managed it. At least this decision was obviously the best choice for Tremontane. Sometimes you just have to pick from a host of good options—or bad ones—and weather the storm of disapproval." He vainly tried to smooth his hair down again. She half-lifted her hand to help, then felt uncomfortable at the idea.

"You are a good King," she told him instead, and the blue eyes met hers with a directness she found uncomfortable.

"I'm not so sure about that," he said with a smile. "Half the time I think my councilors just put up with me because fate handed me the Crown. I certainly wasn't prepared for the responsibility."

She shook her head. "I have watched you and them both. They argue, but then they stop when you speak. You have...." She struggled to express the word *charisma*. "It is to say, people listen to you even when you say things they do not want to hear. And it is not just because you are handsome and a King. It is because you are the person you are."

Jeffrey reddened and looked away. "Too much praise, madam ambassador."

"It is not praise. It is what is." Imogen felt annoyed at his diffidence. "I say Victory is the best because she proves it every day. I say I am a good fighter because I am here and my enemies are not. I say you are a good King because it is what I see. I will never tell you what is not true." By heaven, he was even more attractive when he looked like this. She quelled the urge to take his hand in reassurance.

He looked back at her. "No, you wouldn't, would you. I wish you could attend Council meetings. I could use your insights."

"I am glad I cannot. I will just yell at them."

"You'd fit right in." He sniffed. "Why does it smell like someone set a lilac bush on fire?"

"It is all these." Imogen gestured at the table. "They were in my rooms when I returned from my visit. And I do not read your language."

He picked up the envelope whose seal she'd broken. "They look like invitations." He slid the card out and went quiet, turning it over. "It *is* an invitation. To a party three nights from now in the city."

"Who is it inviting me?"

"Henry Scoggins. Youngest son of Mark Scoggins."

"That does not mean anything to me."

"He's just—he's a lesser noble, someone with more money than sense." He opened another envelope. "This one's to a concert tomorrow night, from a man I don't know. Someone else wants you to attend a dance with him, this man asks you to—hah—watch the Kirkellan race at the track. Two different people want you to go for a ride in the Park. Oh, this name I know, I won't even tell you what he wants because he's about fifty years old and hunting for a new wife." He gathered the cards together and tapped them to square them up. "It appears you've become popular," he said lightly.

"I do not understand."

"These men—" Jeffrey waved the cards at her—"think you're interesting and want to spend time with you."

Imogen scowled. "I do not like these—I do not know the word. These men who do not know me thinking I am interested in them."

"Well, to be fair, they're inviting you to do things with them because they want to know you better."

"I do not know how to behave. And I do not know if I will like them. I do not even remember these men."

"I know most of them. Do you want some help remembering?"

Imogen looked at Jeffrey, who was turning the cards over and over in his hand. "Will you tell me which ones I will like?" she asked him. "Because I think since you are a man, you will know the good ones."

He stared at the cards a while longer before he looked up at her, the blue eyes distant and thoughtful. "Well, most of these are people you should probably ignore, but I'm sure you might like some of them. Let's see." He glanced at the first one. "Oh, Michael Petty is a terrible choice. He'll drag you to a museum and then lecture you about the artist and what she was thinking and eating when she planned whatever awful piece you're looking at. Definitely not him."

"No. I do not think I like the sound of him."

"Hmmm. What is Anton Crowder doing sending you an invitation? He's almost betrothed to Penelope Winterbourne. Roger Crais…wandering fingers, according to Elspeth; Seth Hamilton, nice fellow, but there is that funny smell; Larkin Argyll, well, he's not a bad sort. Pity about the ears."

"What is it about the ears?"

"It's hard not to notice he has them, that's all. Then I don't know these other two, but Elspeth probably does. I have to say I don't think any of these men is worth your time, Imogen."

"Oh," Imogen said. "I feel strange. I am—was not interested in these men, but now you say none of them are good enough for me and I am disappointed."

"I'm sure there will be other invitations," Jeffrey said.

"It is not how we do it, we Kirkellan."

"How do you do it, then?"

"One gives the other a gift. If he takes it, he wants to know her better. They ride together and talk and share meals. If they are…if they fit well together, they will have sex to make them closer."

"That's definitely not how we do it."

"I do not understand why you choose to have sex only when you are married."

Jeffrey set the stack of envelopes on the table and rested his chin in one hand. "You said sex brings you closer. It's like that for us, only…when we make oath to one another, the lines of power tie us together, and sex with the person you're sworn to is even more powerful. And if you have sex often with someone you don't share a bond with, after a while it starts to…disorient you, I suppose. Makes you feel disconnected from other people and from the rest of the world. I'm not sure if that makes sense."

"I am not sure either, but thank you for explaining."

"Well, in the meantime, since you won't be accepting any of these," Jeffrey said, stacking the invitations neatly, "why don't you come with me to the theater tomorrow night? The play is a comedy, *Two Came to Kingsport*, and I think you'll really like it."

"I do not know what a play is."

"It's like a story where people pretend to be the characters and do and say everything that's in the story. This one's very funny. It's one of Mother's favorites."

"Thank you. I will come."

"I'll come for you at seven, then. Shall we go in to supper? This discussion has left me hungry."

"Me too," Imogen said. "Do I have to tell all these men it is 'no'?"

"It's polite, yes," he said. "I'd be happy to write those rejections for you, if you want."

Imogen nodded. "Then they will be rejected by an ambassador and a King both." Jeffrey's laughter trailed them all the way to the dining room.

She watched him covertly as he ate, his long, agile fingers nimbly wielding knife and fork, and wondered again that he seemed to be the only person who didn't realize what a good King he was. She didn't envy him his responsibilities; they made her grateful she only had to worry about treating with Bixhenta and understanding Ghentali's broken Tremontanese. Jeffrey was clever, and funny, and…she headed off that line of thought, reminding herself that however much more attractive his quick mind made him, he was still not the man for her. *But I can still look,* she told herself. *Looking never hurt anyone.*

Chapter Twenty-Four

Jeanette helped Imogen into her favorite red gown the next evening and arranged her hair low at the back of her neck. It was a look Imogen was dubious about, but she didn't have the nerve to challenge Jeanette, who wore an air of superiority that would not have been out of place on a Countess. "It is important you look your best when you are with the King, milady, because everyone will be watching you. You must always consider the dignity of your position."

"Would they not watch me anyway because I am beautiful?"

"What have I told you about immodesty, milady?"

"I do not understand how it is immodest if it is true."

"Because you're supposed to let others give you compliments, not compliment yourself."

"But I am the one who best knows if I am beautiful."

Jeanette sighed. "If I tell you this is a Tremontanan custom, will you follow it and stop asking questions?" Imogen nodded. "Then it's a Tremontanan custom. But between the two of us, I think you are beautiful."

Imogen stayed silent, but privately agreed. *And it has nothing to do with* him*, either.*

She waited in one of the parlors off the grand foyer, kicking her skirt to make it shimmer in the light. She'd been there for scarcely a minute when Revalan and Kionnal came in and sat near her. "So what's a play?" Kionnal said.

"I don't really know. I'll tell you when it's over."

Areli came in and sat on Kionnal's knee. "You look nice," she said.

"Thank you. Why are you all here?" More members of the *tiermatha* drifted in as she spoke. "This had better not be because I'm going to the play with the King. I think I told you I was tired of the innuendo."

"It's not you we're interested in," Dorenna said cryptically. She had her knife out and was cleaning her nails with it, conspicuously nonchalant.

The bell rang. Dorenna got up to answer it, shooing away the footman; since she shooed with the hand holding the knife, he turned and walked very fast back to the servants' door.

A young Tremontanan man stood on the doorstep. He had short blond hair and a blunt nose and was dressed in semi-formal clothing. He looked askance at Dorenna's knife, but otherwise seemed not put off to find her there. "Saevonna?" he asked.

"She's coming soon," Dorenna said in Kirkellish, and smiled when the man's eyes glazed over in incomprehension.

"I still think he's puny," Revalan said, leaving his seat and approaching the man.

"Everyone's puny next to you," Areli said.

"Oh, for heaven's sake, you are all so…*infantile*," Imogen said. She rose and offered her hand to the man. "I am Imogen," she said in Tremontanese, "and I think I have seen you at sparring practice."

"Marcus Oakes," he said, shaking her hand. Imogen thought he relaxed somewhat at hearing his own language. "Saevonna has agreed to dine with me this evening."

Nice work, Saevonna! "I am happy to meet you. We are all happy to meet you."

"Not to disagree with the ambassador, but I'm not sure that's true," Marcus said, eyeing Revalan while trying not to turn his back on Dorenna.

"For the love of everlasting heaven, I cannot *believe* you people," Saevonna said from the top of the stairs. She was dressed in her Tremontanan gown and appeared, to Imogen's shock, to be wearing cosmetics that looked very good on her. "If you're trying to intimidate him, it won't work. And if you're trying to embarrass *me*, you should all think very carefully about what you don't want to find in your bedsheets in the coming week."

"We just want to get a good look at him, Saevonna," Areli said.

"Well, twelve of you all staring at him at once is the same as intimidation, and Dorenna, don't think I didn't see that knife of yours." Saevonna descended the stairs and smiled at Marcus. "They know you," she said in heavily accented Tremontanese. "Not danger, just stupid."

Marcus grinned. "They care you," he said in equally accented Kirkellish. Imogen's eyebrows went up. Marcus really was trying hard, and Saevonna…yes, she *was* wearing cosmetics, how did she even know where to get them, let alone how to wear them?

"It is good to meet you, Marcus, and I hope you enjoy your food," Imogen said, glaring at Revalan, who had innocently moved to block the door. He stepped out of the way, grinning at Marcus in a way that was not entirely friendly. Imogen watched the two get into a carriage, then shut the door and expanded her glare to include all of them.

"Oh, Imogen, don't be so stuffy. Saevonna would do the same to us. Hell, she's done it to you," Dorenna said, sheathing her knife.

"Dor, she's really trying hard for this one. I don't think we should interfere, even if it would be paybacks."

"She did look nice," Revalan admitted.

"She looked *Tremontanan,*" Kionnal said disapprovingly.

"So do I. We're in Tremontane, Kionnal. Nothing wrong with dressing like the natives. You'd want them to dress like us if we were in the Eidestal, wouldn't you?" The bell rang again. "I'm leaving now. Why don't all of you find something more productive to do?"

The footman held the carriage door open for her and gave her a hand in assistance. She would never get used to that custom. "I like your dress," Jeffrey said. "Red suits you."

"I like it too," Imogen said, and refrained from saying anything about how beautiful she looked. If it was true, and it was, Jeffrey would know it without her having to say anything.

"Did I see another carriage leaving as we got here?"

"One of my *tiermatha* is courting with a soldier. A Tremontanan soldier. She is courting your way."

"You know, it never occurred to me that might happen, but it makes sense, doesn't it? Your people thrown together with our people, I mean."

"It is hard when they do not speak the same language, but Saevonna is learning."

"I suppose love finds a way no matter what language you speak."

Imogen was surprised. "I do not know that it is love."

"Did she dress in Tremontanan clothes?"

"Yes."

"Then if she changed her dress for him, learned his language, and went courting his way, I would say that's more than mere affection."

Imogen didn't know what to say. Saevonna couldn't be thinking of a serious relationship with a Tremontanan, could she? What would she do when the year was up? Stay here? Convince him to come home with her? She felt as if her *tiermatha* was breaking up in front of her. "I think we will have to see. It is only supper."

"True. Supper doesn't have to mean a commitment."

They talked of Victory and the new Baronies the rest of the way to the theater, which turned out to be a tall, windowless building, blazing with tiny lights outlining its roof and a sign probably taller than Imogen, with more lights tracing out words Imogen couldn't read. "That's the name of the play," Jeffrey explained as they exited the carriage. "My mother used to own this theater until she became Consort and Royal Librarian and couldn't devote enough time to it. I've been coming here almost my whole life."

"Then it is not something you do only once," Imogen said.

"Oh, no. There are always different plays. If you like this one, we could come back another time and see a different one." He offered her his arm. Perhaps she could learn to like that custom, after all.

With Jeffrey's guards flanking them ahead and behind, they entered, the stream of other theater-goers parting to let them through. Inside, soft blue carpets covered the floors, muffling their footsteps, and the walls were covered with a patterned golden fabric rather than paint. Imogen thought it looked like the inside of Elspeth's sitting room, which was pink rather than blue but had the same soft, unfocused look. Jeffrey led her up a wide staircase with very shallow steps and down a hall paneled in light brown wood to a door, where he stood back and let one of his guards open it and step through. After a moment, the woman said, "Go ahead, your Majesty."

Imogen and Jeffrey went through the door into a small room that looked out over an expanse of cushioned chairs on the floor below, most of them occupied. A quiet murmur like water rushing over a stream bed drifted up to Imogen's ears. Beyond the chairs stood a raised wooden platform shrouded in a dark red velvet curtain. The little room held six chairs upholstered in blue to match the carpet, arranged in two rows facing the stage as if they, too, were eager to see the play. The guard bowed and shut the door behind them. "I feel sorry for my escort every time I come here," Jeffrey said. "They have to stand all evening outside the door and never see a single play. Have a seat. It will begin soon."

Imogen thoroughly enjoyed the play. She laughed until she couldn't breathe at the broad physical comedy while Jeffrey roared at the wordplay Imogen couldn't understand. When the curtain dropped, she said, "That cannot be all there is. Miriam still has not found her shoes."

"This is intermission. You can use the facilities and stretch your legs if you like." Jeffrey stood and stretched as well.

Imogen decided to do as he suggested and went off to find the facilities. When she returned, Diana Ashmore was seated in Imogen's chair, leaning forward to talk to Jeffrey and laughing at something he'd said. "Oh, Imogen, what a pleasant surprise to find you both here," she said, and Imogen thought she put just the faintest emphasis on "both." "Jeffrey, how kind of you to introduce the ambassador to one of Aurilien's great cultural treasures. I really wonder that you've never taken *me* to the theater, when you know how much I love it. The view from your box really is excellent."

"I didn't realize you were such a theater aficionado, Diana," Jeffrey said.

"Oh, I go as often as I can." She leaned forward and put her hand on his arm. "Do you mind if I share your box for the second act? I'm with friends who don't appreciate the theater as much as I do. Help me convince him, Imogen," she added, looking over her shoulder at Imogen and smiling a pleasant smile that didn't reach her eyes.

Jeffrey glanced at Imogen, who wished she could read his expression; she couldn't tell how he felt about that. The idea of spending the evening with Diana annoyed her, but she couldn't come up with a reason to avoid it. She shrugged, hoping he could read her mind. "Of course we don't mind," Jeffrey said, and Imogen's annoyance increased. "Imogen, the second act's about to start, why don't you take your seat?"

Imogen looked at Diana, who showed no sign of vacating Imogen's seat any time soon. "I will enjoy this," she said, to herself more than to Jeffrey, and sat on Diana's other side. She wanted to shove Diana off her chair and, preferably, out of the box. Instead she clasped her hands in her lap and ignored both her companions. It didn't take long for the play to captivate her again, dispelling most of her irritation, though it reared up again every time Diana laughed her shrill, hideous laugh in her ear. Still, she enjoyed the play, even if the donkey didn't make a second appearance.

When the curtain came down a final time and they finished applauding, Diana still didn't rise. "Thank you *so* much for sharing your escort, Imogen," she said. "You understand how attached old friends can be." She put her hand on Jeffrey's knee and patted it. Imogen felt annoyed and angry all over again. How dare this woman treat the King of Tremontane like her personal property?

"I am sorry for you," she said, "because it is hard for you to find your own escort." Diana's face froze, and Imogen smiled brightly at her. Jeffrey's face was carefully blank. "Perhaps you should find other friends to be attached to." She put the barest emphasis on "other."

Diana opened her mouth to say something vicious, glanced at Jeffrey, and turned it into a smile. "We really should go together sometime, Jeffrey," she said, and kissed him lightly on the cheek in the manner of an old friend. The smile she bestowed on Imogen as she left was not even a little bit friendly.

Jeffrey raised his eyebrows at Imogen when the door shut behind Diana. "I had no idea you could be so catty," he said.

"I do not—did not like her behaving to me as if I am intruding on *her* evening."

"I'm sorry I told her she could stay. It was because of the territory decision. I hated to tell her no tonight when I essentially told her the biggest 'no' you can imagine yesterday."

"I know she is your friend, but she is not a nice person sometimes."

"She certainly has been more obvious in her, um, bid for my affections lately." He touched his cheek. "Shall we go? I doubt Diana is waiting around downstairs to accost me again."

"And if she is you can have your guards carry her away." That made him laugh.

Back in the carriage, Imogen watched Jeffrey restlessly look out the windows, at the floor, in every direction except at her. She wondered what was going through his mind. She herself was thinking about Diana, who now she was safely elsewhere seemed more like a figure to be pitied than hated. Imogen didn't think Diana was actually in love with Jeffrey, but if she was, how sad, to love someone who cared nothing for you. Then she remembered the look on Diana's face as she sat in Imogen's chair, that cruel, triumphant look, and decided Diana wasn't worth wasting sympathy on, however tragic her circumstances.

"I'm trying to figure out how to ask you something in a way that won't insult you," Jeffrey said abruptly, and Imogen froze. What under heaven could he possibly have in mind?

"You will ask and then I will not be insulted even if it is insulting," she said lightly, as if his words hadn't thrown her into turmoil.

Jeffrey laughed. "Well, you can't say I didn't warn you in advance." He leaned forward. "Mairen told me there was a part of you that wasn't a warrior," he said. "I've seen you become a diplomat and a part of Tremontanan society, and I think maybe that's what she was talking about. But it seems to me you're still clinging to the warrior part of you, and not allowing yourself to see what it's like to truly become this new self. I was wondering why that is."

She froze again, but for a completely different reason. How dare this Tremontanan man challenge her like that? She looked out the window, her eyes burning with angry tears. She was a warrior. Living in Aurilien and dressing like a Tremontanan woman and going to dances and parties wasn't going to change that—

—but it should, shouldn't it? It was what she'd promised Mother. One year, to learn those things about herself that had nothing to do with war. One year, and she'd already broken her promise by refusing to admit these new things she was learning had anything to do with who she really was.

"Oh, heaven, that wasn't meant to make you cry," Jeffrey said, moving to sit next to her and putting his arm around her shoulders. "I shouldn't have asked such a personal question."

"It is a true question," Imogen said, blinking to dispel her embarrassing tears. "I made a promise to learn and I did not keep it."

"Why is that?" He grinned at her startled expression. "I've already made you cry; I don't see how anything I say can make it worse."

She smiled and shook her head. "I am fighting with myself, all the time I am here. I think I know, inside me, I am only a warrior because I know nothing else, and I am afraid I will want to be another thing when I know what that is."

"Would it be so bad, being a diplomat instead of a warrior?"

"I am leaving behind everything I know."

Jeffrey looked out the window again. "I was never meant to be King," he said quietly. "I was going to go into business. All my life, I knew—I was such a kid, but I'd already decided I was going to run a theater like my parents did before Father became King. *That* theater, if I could, bring it back into the family. I knew all about the business, how it worked, the finances, everything. Father still made me go through all the lessons Sylvester did, all that stuff about running a kingdom, but I never gave it more than the minimum of my attention because it wasn't who I really was." He sighed. "But the day came when I realized not only was I good at those lessons, I was better at what it took to run a kingdom than I was at theater administration. I was devastated. It was like I lost everything that made me who I was."

"What did you do?"

"Threw a temper tantrum that lasted three days. Then I went and asked Father for a job in one of the departments. It's how Zara trained him, back in the day."

"Then you think I should not be a warrior."

"I think you should be whoever it is you really are. I think there's nothing wrong with losing one dream if you end up living a better one."

She was increasingly aware of the weight of his arm across her shoulders, his hand gripping her upper arm. "I do not know which is the better one," she said.

"Live them both, live them well, and find out," he said. He turned so he could face her more directly. "I can't tell you to do more than that."

He sounded so sad, so regretful, that impulsively she took his free hand in hers, startling him. "Jeffrey," she said, then couldn't think of anything else to say.

He looked down at their joined hands, then looked up. "You're the most remarkable person I've ever met," he said. "Warrior, diplomat...beautiful woman."

Imogen couldn't look away from his eyes, colorless in the low light. "You think I am beautiful?" she said.

He removed his hand from hers and caressed her cheek, smiling. "From the moment I first saw you," he said, and leaned in to kiss her.

She was only startled for a moment, and then the feel of his lips against hers, his hand gently touching her face, overrode her surprise with desire. She put her arms around his waist and felt him slide his hand from across her shoulders to the nape of her neck, under her hair, holding her steady against the movement of the carriage. She returned his kiss, enjoying the softness of his lips and his warm breath on her cheek. She'd been kissed before, stolen kisses in the shade of the tents or near the horses' enclosure where no one could see, but she'd never felt this heart-pounding excitement, this blissful awareness of his hands and his mouth and the heat of his body as he drew her closer. He kissed her again, then pulled back just enough to rest his forehead on hers. "I hope you don't mind," he said in a low voice, "but I've been thinking about doing that for several days now and this seemed the perfect time to take advantage of you."

"If take advantage of me means you kiss me again with your wonderful mouth, I like it," she said, and he grinned and kissed her again, this time playfully, tracing the line of her ear with his gentle fingers and making her shiver with delight.

The jolt of the carriage coming to a halt banged their heads together gently. Jeffrey's teeth grazed her lower lip, which made them both laugh. "I'm not quite ready to stop, are you?" he said.

"It has only been two minutes. That is not long enough," Imogen said.

Jeffrey knocked on the roof of the carriage. "Go once around the Park," he commanded, then took Imogen in his arms again and said, "So how long would be enough?"

She trailed a finger along the hard edge of his jaw, feeling the faint roughness of stubble overlaying the smoothness of his skin. "If you always kiss the way you do just now, I do not think I could put a number on that."

"I do have to take you home sometime."

"But sometime is not now. And I think I will have to kiss *you* because you seem not interested now."

"No?" He swung her around to recline across his lap, making her giggle, and proceeded to nuzzle his way along her neck toward her lips, saying between kisses, "I am *very*… interested… in everything… about you."

She laughed, and for a while they forgot about speaking.

Later, they sat hand in hand watching what little was visible of the Park pass by their window, and Imogen said, "If you think about kissing me for many days, I do not know it."

"I've always been good at hiding how I feel. It's a survival trait when it comes to the Council."

"Then you are courting me when you ask if I want to see the play."

"I hoped it wasn't obvious. I sort of panicked because of those damned invitations. I knew they would just keep coming and eventually I'd run out of reasons for you to turn them down. So I decided to court you secretly, give you time to get used to the idea before I declared myself."

"I do not see how I could be used to a courtship I do not know happens."

"It's been about three years since I courted a woman. I think I might have forgotten how."

"But you could just say you are interested. I would not be cruel if I do—did not care for you."

"Three years, remember? I was afraid you'd say no and then things would be awkward between us, and I really didn't want that. This way, if it turned out my charms didn't appeal to you, we were just two friends who happened to enjoy the same social activities."

"We Kirkellan do not do things that way."

"You said. The trouble is, if I gave you a gift…in Tremontane that means a lot more than just an interest. In the eyes of the kingdom we'd practically be betrothed."

"I see." She squeezed his hand. "I like how your way worked."

"I'm surprised it worked at all."

"I feel sorry for those men now."

"Oh, I was telling the truth about every one of them, so don't waste your sympathy."

"You do not make their flaws bigger?"

"Exaggerate? Maybe a little bit. But tell me you wouldn't rather be with me right now than with Larkin Argyll and his ears."

Imogen looked at him in the dimness. "Maybe his ears are handsome."

Jeffrey grabbed her around the waist with one arm and pulled her close. "I don't think so," he whispered, and kissed her again, his fingers once more caressing her cheek. She kissed him for a moment, then drew back. "This is not kissing time. This is you talking time. I think you cannot want to kiss me very long."

He twined his fingers with hers again. "I think I wanted to kiss you from the time you told that stable mistress you'd make her eat her own Device if she didn't apologize to Victory."

Imogen laughed. "That is a very long time, Jeffrey. I think I do not believe you."

"Well, maybe that's an exaggeration. But I can tell you this," he said. "When you sat next to me at the lake, with your face turned towards the sun and those strands of hair blowing in the breeze, I knew I would do almost anything to have my arms around you and feel your lips on mine."

Imogen blushed. "I think you know how to talk to women," she said.

"Just you." He kissed her again, slow and sweet. "Will you dance with me tomorrow at the Spring Ball?" he asked as the carriage again came to a halt.

"Of course."

He kissed her again. "Just one dance. I'm not ready for the world to know how our relationship has changed, madam ambassador."

Imogen frowned. "This is something you are embarrassed about?"

He ran his finger down the side of her neck and along her shoulder, traced the pale line of the scar that emerged from her gown's neckline. "No, but the political implications of the King of Tremontane becoming romantically involved with a high-ranking diplomat from another country are…complicated."

"Then you should not have kissed me," she said, pretending anger.

Jeffrey recoiled slightly, his eyes registering hurt and surprise before he realized she was teasing him. "You—" he began, and she threw her arms around his neck and kissed him once more, playfully. "You should not have everything your own way all the time, I think," she whispered.

"I think there's little danger of that with you around," he whispered back.

He helped her down from the carriage, escorted her the few steps to the embassy door—it really was unnecessary, but even a few moments more with him was heaven—and kissed her hand, his lips lingering longer than was necessary. "Good night, my dear… ambassador," he said with a smile, and was gone almost before she was inside.

The foyer and parlors were dark, the few Devices that were still lit turned down low. Someone moved in the left-hand parlor. "I need to talk," Saevonna said. She was still in her Tremontanan dress and in the dim light her eyes looked enormous.

"Did something happen?" Imogen came to sit next to her on the sofa.

Saevonna shook her head. "But I think I want it to. Oh, Imogen, I really like him, and I think he likes me, but…I never thought anything like this was possible. I can't even really talk to him!"

"Well, you know what Kallum says—"

"Kallum isn't interested in a steady relationship with anyone but himself. I just feel so confused…maybe I shouldn't have kissed Marcus, but it felt so wonderful…."

Imogen put her hand on Saevonna's shoulder. "I know *exactly* how you feel," she said.

Saevonna's eyes went wide. "You, too? But, Imogen, he's the *King*. That makes it a hundred times more complicated."

"He's still just a man. That's all the complicated it takes." Imogen didn't feel as certain as she sounded. Now that the pleasure of kissing Jeffrey was a sweet memory, she wondered if it had been a stupid thing to do. "I'm going to go to bed and think about this in the morning, and I suggest you do the same." They ascended the stairs together, silently, but when they were about to part company, Imogen said, "Saevonna?"

"Yes?"

"Would it be so bad, falling in love with him?"

Saevonna was silent for a moment. "I think what's bad," she said finally, "is that I don't have a ready answer for that question." She turned and went down the hall toward her room, her head bowed.

Back in her sitting room, Imogen rang for Jeanette and let her undress her, pleading fatigue when Jeanette questioned her silence. So Dorenna had been right; Jeffrey was interested in her. She climbed into bed and touched her lips. He was *very* interested in her. The question was, was it a good idea for her to be interested in him? *Too late for that,* she thought, *you know you don't care that he's a King and you're a Kirkellan warrior.* But it was true their being romantically involved had complicated political implications. If Bixhenta, to take a not totally random example, learned she'd just spent an hour in the arms of the King of Tremontane, he'd think she was firmly in the enemy camp and would never trust her again. No, she wasn't going to think about it now. Time enough in the morning.

She burrowed into her many pillows and closed her eyes. She could still feel his arms around her, his hand in hers. Damn. They couldn't go on, could they? He'd said it himself; she was the face of the Kirkellan here in Aurilien, and the face of the Kirkellan had no business having such intimacy with the face of Tremontane, however attractive that face might be. She was supposed to remain impartial.

She rolled onto her side and stared into the darkness. *Wait until morning. It's not as if you can do anything about it now.* It was hours before she finally fell asleep.

CHAPTER TWENTY-FIVE

She came late to the breakfast table the next morning, bleary-eyed and aching as if she'd slept on the bare ground instead of her too-soft mattress. Dorenna and Revalan sat at the table, placidly eating, and Areli stood at the sideboard helping herself to eggs and sausage. Imogen dropped into a chair and put her face in her hands.

"*Somebody* had a late night," Dorenna said.

Imogen peered out at her through her fingers. "You have no idea," she said.

Dorenna sat up straight and stared at her in astonishment. "You didn't," she said. "Imogen, you barely know the man. Did you—was it in the *palace*?"

"By heaven, Dorenna, I didn't have sex with him," Imogen said, exasperated. "He kissed me. I kissed him. Many, many times." Her cheeks flushed at the memory even as her heart felt heavy. "And now I don't know what to do."

"What is it Tremontanans do when they're courting, anyway?" Revalan said, and broke a piece of bacon into three sections, stacked them and stuffed the stack into his mouth. "Bad enough they have to dance around the issue of whether or not they're interested in a romantic relationship," he went on, his voice muffled.

"It probably doesn't matter. I don't think I'm allowed to find out," Imogen said.

Areli took a seat next to her. "Why under heaven not? He's not married, he clearly wants to pursue the relationship, you're attracted to him—"

"And he's the King of a foreign country. And I'm an ambassador."

"So?"

"So suppose we have to go to war against Tremontane? She'd be compromised," Revalan said.

"We're not going to war against Tremontane. Imogen, this is crazy. You can't just give up," Areli said.

"Why not?"

Areli and Dorenna exchanged glances. "Stop it," Imogen said. "You've been teasing me about Jeffrey practically since I met him. All you know about him is he's handsome and tall and a King. That's not enough to build a relationship on and certainly not enough for me to risk my reputation as the representative of the Kirkellan. I'm better off telling him—" Her stomach clenched. She rose from the table and started putting food on her plate. Nothing smelled good. She must be coming down with something.

"Imogen," Areli said carefully, "we may not know him, but we certainly know you. We've seen the way you look at him and we've heard how you talk about him. This is not some passing physical fling, and you know it, or you would if you'd let yourself think for five minutes."

Imogen set her plate down on the sideboard and bowed her head. Now her chest ached along with her stomach. "That's ridiculous," she said.

"Is it?" Dorenna said. "Any time you come home from one of these social things, half the things you tell us are about what your King did, or said. Have you heard us teasing you about him lately? It stopped being fun the minute it was clear you really did care about him."

"It doesn't matter," Imogen whispered. "It doesn't matter," she repeated in a louder voice. "I have a responsibility that's more important than how I feel." As she said the words, she felt her perspective shift. The warrior would pursue Jeffrey and damn the consequences. The ambassador would put her people first. And she was the ambassador.

"Imogen, think. What if this never comes again?" Areli said. "What if—"

"I'm barely twenty, Areli. I'll find someone else." She felt as if she were going to be sick. "Someone who's Kirkellan, probably, someone who grew up the way I did, someone I can talk to without groping for words all the time and who rides well and doesn't have all these—" She left her plate and walked away.

Safely in her rooms, she lay on her unmade bed and stared at the ceiling. She couldn't tell him in a message, even if it weren't a cold thing to do. She'd have to see if she could get him somewhere private at the ball tonight. Maybe he wouldn't be terribly disappointed. It was just kissing, that was all, nothing binding on either of them. They could still be friends, couldn't they? She remembered his gentle touch on her face, his lips on hers, and went to the bathing chamber to scrub those memories away.

She and the *tiermatha* were late to the Spring Ball. Imogen didn't want to spend any more time there than she had to. She still dreaded the moment when someone would ask her to dance and she'd have to turn him down because she didn't know the steps. She took a tall glass of straw-pale wine as soon as she reached the floor, reasoning that having her hands full might deter any would-be partners.

She did not see Jeffrey. She did see Diana almost immediately, as if the woman were picked out by a ring of lights. She was conversing with a man and a woman Imogen didn't know, though her attention seemed divided between her conversation and the rest of the room; her eyes roved constantly, as if she were looking for someone, probably Jeffrey. Imogen felt a sharp pang of jealousy and suppressed it. She had no right to feel jealous. On the other hand, she felt she had every right as Jeffrey's friend to wish Diana would find a large hole and jump down it headfirst.

"Madam ambassador." She turned to find Maxwell Burgess at her elbow. At least he hadn't taken hold of it. Yet. "The ambassador from Veribold would like a moment of your time." He wasn't smiling, and for a moment Imogen was afraid something awful had happened. Bixhenta had found out about her evening with Jeffrey and wanted to break off all diplomatic ties with the Kirkellan. He wanted to break off ties with *Tremontane*, and Burgess blamed her even though Jeffrey had kissed her first.

"Madam ambassador, are you well?" Burgess asked, and now he did take her elbow and his expression was of normal concern. He smiled at her. "Bixhenta is intimidating, but he's not going to eat you."

Imogen managed a smile at the weak witticism and let Burgess steer her in the direction of the ambassador's seat, near—oh, heaven, there Jeffrey was, he was sitting on the chair that wasn't quite a throne, and he was talking to his mother so he hadn't seen her yet, but any moment now he'd turn his head—she fixed her eyes on the Voice of Bixhenta, who was staring at her as if wishing she were somewhere else, preferably the Eidestal.

Imogen bowed to the Voice, barely aware of what she was doing. It probably wasn't a very good bow, but it was the best she could manage in her barely-concealed agitation. *You're behaving like a child having her first courtship. Grow up, Imogen.*

"Madam ambassador, the Proxy of Veribold greets you," the Voice said, the coolness of her voice belied by the tightness in her jaw.

"I am pleased to be welcomed by the Proxy. I enjoy our meetings," Imogen replied. She smiled pleasantly at the Voice and saw the tension in the woman's jaw increase. She really shouldn't torment the woman so, but it was too easy and Imogen was tense enough herself to feel the need for some kind of release.

The Voice bent to speak to Bixhenta and receive his words in return. "The Proxy invites you to attend on him at the embassy tomorrow morning to continue the conversation you had on your previous visit." Imogen by now knew to watch Bixhenta's face for clues, and aside from a slow blink on "attend" it seemed the Voice had relayed his instructions exactly.

"I am pleased to visit with the Proxy tomorrow," she replied, keeping her eyes on Bixhenta's face. So it had something to do with the treaty. Could Mother have signed and returned it so soon? Anxiety over her personal problem subsided in the thrill she felt at the thought of further negotiations. She could think of a number of trade items she'd like to see the Kirkellan embrace, starting with chocolate.

"Then you are dismissed," the Voice said, and Imogen raised her eyebrows in surprise, because the woman hadn't conveyed her last words to Bixhenta or received any instructions from him. Bixhenta continued impassive, but Imogen would bet the Voice would get an earful when they were back at the embassy. If she were Bixhenta, she'd find another Voice, one who wasn't so prone to delivering her own ultimatums.

"I think it is for Bixhenta to say if I am dismissed or not," Imogen said, and bowed directly to the Proxy. To her shock, Bixhenta stood, moving each joint independently as if he were unfolding, then bowed to Imogen, not very low, but unmistakably a bow. Imogen was peripherally aware of the few people around them becoming motionless, but Bixhenta's eyes remained fixed on her and she couldn't look away. She bowed again to cover her confusion, then backed away three steps and turned to go at the fastest pace she could manage that wasn't a run. She didn't have a destination in mind, just a desire to get away. Bixhenta had bowed to her. Yes, it was probably just to humiliate the Voice, but he'd still bowed to her, and who knew what that meant in Veriboldan culture? Well, yes, she could think of one person who would know what it meant, but she wasn't ready to face him yet.

She bumped up against someone who said, "Clumsy—" and at the familiar voice, Imogen's heart sank. Only one other person at this affair she wanted to see less than Jeffrey, and she had to run into her. Diana turned, and her anger instantly became much nastier. "I should have known it was you," she said. "Tell me, are you awkward because you're fat, or is the awkwardness something you were born with?"

The unexpectedness of the attack left Imogen groping for words. "I—I am sorry to bump against you," she said, and stepped out of Diana's way. Diana moved to intercept her.

"I suppose I should congratulate you on your conquest," she said, and sipped her wine. It was the exact shade of her gown and her carefully rouged lips. Someone might have called her beautiful if they couldn't hear her voice, smooth and filled with bitter spite. "I wouldn't have thought Jeffrey so desperate, but then I suppose I never really knew him."

"I do not understand you. I do not make the conquest." Wonderful, her grasp of Tremontanese was deserting her. She struggled to remember how angry Diana had made her just the night before. She could fight her if she could find something to hang onto, something to remind her she wasn't ugly and bare-faced and wearing a dress that made her look lumpy.

Diana grasped her forearm and squeezed, an innocent gesture that felt like the claw of some kind of raptor. "Oh, I won't tell anyone," she said in a low voice. "Heaven forbid I should embarrass the King of Tremontane when he's doing such an excellent job of it himself." She took another sip of wine. Her lips looked bloody in the brilliant light of the Devices hovering high above. "His loss, if he preferred you to me."

"I do not think he love you ever," Imogen stuttered. "You are desperate and want his Crown and not him. That is not the fault of anyone but you."

Diana's claw gripped harder. "I've been his friend for *years*," she hissed. "I know him better than anyone does. You have no idea what you're interfering with, the relationship we've built. Jeffrey will come to his senses and you'll be *nothing* again." The hand holding the wine glass began to tremble, sending waves of ruby liquid splashing up the sides of the glass.

Nothing. Diana's words shook Imogen out of her stupor. As if she only had value because Jeffrey cared for her. She was a warrior of the Kirkellan and Diana couldn't take that from her no matter what she said. She grabbed Diana's claw with her free hand and broke her grip effortlessly. This deluded woman couldn't hurt her with her words. Imogen, on the other hand, could break every bone in her claw with one twist. The thought tempted her, but she merely released Diana with a force that sent her hand swinging. "I am not a threat to you," she said. "If your relationship is weak it is because you stomped on it with your giant feet and your hands that cannot keep to themselves. I am sorry for you but it does not mean I will not be friends with Jeffrey. I cannot make him love you because you make yourself unlovable."

Diana was motionless, only her trembling hand and the splashing wine showing she hadn't been struck dead. Imogen circled around her, her eyes never leaving the frozen Baroness. As unstable as Diana was, she might decide to attack Imogen, or at least throw her wine on her, and Imogen didn't want a conflict that would end with one of them, not her, bloody on the ballroom floor. As soon as she was far enough away, she turned and fled again. This time, she stayed alert, not wanting to run into any more enemies. Surely Diana was the only one she'd made in Aurilien? The image of Hrovald showing up in the palace ballroom, wielding his sword and screaming for her head, amused her briefly.

"Saevonna," she said with relief, seeing her friend turn in her direction. She was eating something that dusted her lips with crumbs—good heaven, Saevonna was wearing cosmetics again. Imogen wished the world would stop spinning for just five minutes, just long enough for her to find her footing.

"Imogen," Saevonna said, "you look like you're being chased."

"I feel like I'm being chased. Do you know who Diana Ashmore is? Yes? Is she following me?"

"I don't see—no, she's talking to that man who's always hauling you around by the elbow. Why, did you insult her?"

"She insulted me first." Imogen closed her eyes. "Do I look lumpy in this dress?"

"What? Of course not. Your dressmaker is a marvel. Is that what the bitch told you? You realize we can make her disappear, right?"

Imogen laughed weakly. "I almost broke her hand."

"I suppose it would have looked bad, but think how nice it would have felt. All those bones, so close to the surface...."

"You're so bloodthirsty." Imogen took a deep breath, then registered the carefully blank look on Saevonna's face. "She's coming after me, isn't she?"

"Not her. But I hope you've made a decision, because you're going to have to tell him something." Saevonna's blank look vanished, replaced by a smile and a bow. "Your Majesty," she said in Tremontanese.

"Good evening," Jeffrey said. Imogen turned to face him. He'd been addressing Saevonna, but his eyes were entirely on Imogen, and his smile...everything that had passed between them the previous evening was in his smile. Without thinking of what he might make of it, she smiled back, and his smile broadened. "I believe you know this dance?" he said to her, and offered his hand. She took it, and felt the faintest of squeezes before he drew her along to the center of the floor and took her in his arms.

She looked past him, over his shoulder at the other dancers. If she met his eyes, it would be all over for her. There was that young man who'd propositioned her at the garden party, whatever his name was. There was, ugh, Diana again, talking to a woman with some intensity and again glancing around the room as if looking for someone, or afraid someone was looking for her. At some point even the self-absorbed Diana would have to realize Jeffrey was never going to make her his Consort and give up her ridiculous attempts to gain his affection.

"You're not looking at me," Jeffrey said. He turned her once and brought her close to him again.

"I am afraid my eyes show everything," she said, trying to remember the next steps.

"You're right. I know I'm having trouble controlling mine." They danced in silence for a moment longer, then he said, "I've been completely useless all day. I haven't been able to stop thinking of you."

"I have thought of you as well." True, though not the way he'd interpret it. She should have practiced what to say. Her fumbling command of Tremontanese was inadequate to expressing anything this important.

"I'm glad. I'd hate to be the only one who found last night memorable." He laughed, quietly. It felt as if they were dancing in an invisible sphere, their words audible only to themselves. "Will you attend the violin concert next week with my family? I'm sure I can find a coach that only seats four to take Mother and Elspeth and Owen home, and then I'd be forced to escort you myself, such a pity."

Here it was. "I cannot," she said.

"Really? That's too bad. Well, I can think of some other pretext so we can be alone together. There's always another play, of course…the trouble is I'm watched almost everywhere I go, so privacy is hard."

"It is to say I cannot go with you to be private. We cannot be a relationship." That sounded wrong, but she didn't dare look at his face for a clue.

Jeffrey said nothing. His hand went rigid in hers. Imogen blurted, "I am ambassador and you are King. I cannot—it is that I am the face of the Kirkellan to all the nations and not just to Tremontane. If I am with you I cannot treat with Bixhenta and that is why I am here, to treat with the nations and to be...I cannot remember the word, but it is when you do not put one above the other."

"Impartial," Jeffrey said, his voice distant.

"That is the word. Impartial." She wasn't doing this right. She should have gotten him somewhere alone instead of doing this in the open, where anyone could see whatever it was her words were doing to his face. "But I don't want to," she said in Kirkellish. "I want you. I want you to kiss me again, over and over, and look at me with those eyes that find me beautiful. I want to discover if something more than physical attraction can grow between us, because I think it already has. But I am the ambassador and what I want doesn't matter. And if I'd known this was what it meant to learn about the part of me that isn't a warrior, I...I still would have done it."

She turned to look at Jeffrey finally. He, naturally, looked confused. "Can you translate that for me?" he said.

Tears came to Imogen's eyes. "It is that I do not want to, but I must if I am ambassador. But what it is I want is to take you into one of the little rooms where lovers go and kiss you more. So I am sorry I cannot do this."

Jeffrey suppressed a smile. "That has to be the most heartwarming rejection I've ever received," he said.

Imogen blinked the tears away. "I am sorry," she repeated.

"So am I. Imogen, I never thought of the position I was putting you in. I think of you as a woman first and an ambassador a far, far distant second. You're right, you can't stay impartial if we're courting, and I can't change that just by making sure no one finds out." He looked away from her, out across the room. "Much as I might wish otherwise."

"I am afraid I hurt you."

"I won't say I'm not incredibly disappointed, but that's not your fault." He looked back at her. "I think you should know one thing," he said. "In less than a year, you won't be an ambassador anymore, and when that happens, I will take you in my arms and kiss you until you beg me to stop."

"Which I think I will not do." The weight on her heart vanished. He was smiling at her, he wasn't angry or hurt and he understood, and he still wanted her.

"Fortunate for both of us." He went back to scanning the room. "Not to destroy this not-so-tender moment we're having, but is there a reason Diana is glaring at me?"

"She thinks I steal you from her. We had a fight. I did not break her hand which I think is good for me that I show…restraint."

He snorted with laughter. "Restraint indeed. I'm sorry she feels so hurt, but I'm not going to follow her wishes just to make her happy."

"That is what I tell—told her. She did not like that."

Jeffrey snorted again. "I'm surprised you *didn't* get into a fist fight, talking like that."

"She is crazy but not stupid enough to fight a Kirkellan warrior with no weapon. She is thin enough I can break her with my one hand. Do not laugh, I am serious."

"I know you are, it's just…as beautiful as you are, I have trouble remembering you're a warrior too."

"You think perhaps warriors cannot be beautiful?" She warmed all over at his words.

"I think I should stop talking now before my mouth gets the rest of me in trouble."

"I think you are wise. And I think you should call me beautiful again, since it must last a whole year."

His blue eyes met hers. "You are beautiful," he said, "and I'll never forget what it was like to kiss you."

She shivered with pleasure. "I will not forget either, because I have never been kissed like you kiss before.

He pulled her closer as the music came to an end. It was goodbye, but she felt like she was flying.

CHAPTER TWENTY-SIX

The Voice didn't greet Imogen when she returned to the Veriboldan embassy; the room where she'd spoken to Bixhenta before was empty. She stood and waited for a few minutes before the door opened and Bixhenta entered. "Forgive my tardiness, but I wished to conclude some other business so I could give you my full attention," he said. "I apologize for my rudeness."

"Thank you," Imogen said. "I was admiring this…it *is* a painting, isn't it? I don't understand much of Veriboldan art yet."

"It's meant to convey a feeling rather than represent something," Bixhenta said. "The viewer's response reveals his or her character. What do you feel when you look at this piece?"

Imogen studied it again. "Confusion," she admitted.

"Then an interpreter of Veriboldan art would say you have an open and honest mind, and do not fear change."

"And are you an interpreter of Veriboldan art?"

"No, but I feel confusion when I look at it, too, and that's what I was told that response means." They laughed together. "Will you sit? This shouldn't take long."

Imogen took the seat she'd used before, and Bixhenta lowered himself into his chair and steepled his fingers. "The *matrian* and I have come to an arrangement," he said. "She asked me to give you the terms of our treaty, to help you in your dealings with Veribold. I will have a copy for you before you leave."

"Thank you," Imogen said. Surely he hadn't called her here just to tell her that.

"I believe I told you not to take any assertions made by me or King Jeffrey at face value," he continued. "Did you investigate?"

"I did," Imogen said. The way he looked at her made her nervous, as if she were a two-year-old filly and he was sizing her up for purchase.

"So you have learned Tremontane is poised to invade Veribold."

She hesitated. What was appropriate to say, here? "I do not believe so," she said carefully, watching his face to see which way to step next.

"Impossible. What proof do you have?"

So *that* was the trap. "I don't think I should give you that information. I'm sure you have your own sources."

"My sources tell me nothing. Are we not allies? Come, girl, this information could save two countries a great deal of bloodshed."

"Bixhenta, I apologize for being blunt, but my sources are confidential and I don't believe it's my responsibility to do the work your people have failed to do."

His ancient face turned a delicate pink, possibly the closest he could come to displaying anger. "I insist you tell me how you gained this information."

Imogen rose. "I think this conversation is over. If you'd bring me my copy of the treaty, I'll leave. I'm sorry to have to disappoint you, but I'm sure if our positions were reversed, you'd do the same."

Bixhenta stood in that same slow unbending of joints. "You are fortunate we have already signed the treaty," he snarled. "I did not think the Kirkellan would be so ungrateful."

Imogen said nothing. Bixhenta glared at her once more, then shoved the swinging door open hard; it struck something, and Imogen heard a cry of pain that swiftly cut off. She stood facing the windows, clasping her hands together to control their trembling. Bixhenta had wanted her to spy for him. So much for all that noble talk about learning for herself. That could mean Veribold *was* planning to invade. She ought to tell Jeffrey—no, she couldn't, she had to remain impartial. And his intelligence sources were far better than hers. If Veribold were planning to invade, he would know.

A woman dressed in silk robe and tunic came through the swinging door bearing a sheaf of paper. She handed it to Imogen and was gone almost before Imogen could take hold of it. No valise this time; apparently Kirkellan who disappointed the Proxy didn't rate that high. She tucked it under her arm and carried it that way back to the embassy.

It didn't contain anything new, she discovered, and squared the papers together and put them in her dresser drawer. There ought to be somewhere more secure to put them. Simon would know. He was due back tomorrow, and they'd be safe in the drawer until then. It wasn't as if there was anything particularly sensitive in the treaty. Even so...she worked out a message to take to the palace telecoder. It was probably a good thing for Mother to know Bixhenta had tried to make her spy for him.

Diana left for the front two days after the Spring Ball, relieving Imogen's fears that their mutual hostility would increase to the point that violence would erupt. Imogen spent her days riding and her evenings attending dances and concerts and even an art display at the Veriboldan assembly. Apparently Bixhenta's anger and disappointment hadn't lasted, or maybe he just didn't want to appear to be at odds with the ambassador from the Kirkellan. She was surprised at how much she enjoyed the show despite not understanding anything about Veriboldan art. The presenter, a short, fat woman with long black hair, spoke with great eloquence, her translator spoke with considerably less, and Imogen sat back and let the words wash incomprehensibly over her. She stared at the pictures, feeling surprise and anger and regret, and wondered what those reactions said about her.

The invitations, as Jeffrey had predicted, continued to pour in. Imogen tried to be impartial and asked Elspeth's help in reading and winnowing them. She refrained from asking Elspeth what her brother thought of her "swains," as Elspeth called them. She could hardly remain impartial if she hung on Elspeth's every mention of him. Her *tiermatha* provided help of a different sort.

"I didn't like the look of him. His hair was too blond," Dorenna said the morning after Imogen had gone to dinner with one of her swains.

"Nothing wrong with blond. Or brunet or red-headed," Kallum purred.

"I mean it looked like he'd done something to it. If he isn't confident about what heaven gave him, I'm not sure I'd trust him."

"He was very pleasant," Imogen protested.

"*Pleasant?* You might as well say he's got a nice personality, for all the praise that is."

"He's got that too."

Dorenna rolled her eyes and sighed dramatically. "Don't you want someone more exciting? Someone who makes your toes tingle when he kisses you?"

"I didn't let him kiss me, so I don't know if they do." *And I already had someone whose kisses made me want to melt.*

"I think she's taking the safe choices because her heart's already given elsewhere," Kallum said, his eyes twinkling. "To someone tall, dark, and unattainably gorgeous, at least to me."

"I've already said the King and I are not courting. It would be improper."

"Doesn't mean you're not still thinking of him," Dorenna said.

"I'm not. I'm thinking of the concert tonight and wishing I hadn't accepted an invitation from Larkin Argyll. He seems nice, but it's really hard to look at him and not think *Ears!*"

She saw Jeffrey twice during this time, once from behind at the concert where she sat next to Larkin Argyll and passed the time twiddling her thumbs and wondering if the performer was going to saw at his instrument so hard it would break in half, and once at dinner in the east wing with Elspeth and Owen. He behaved naturally, holding her chair as usual and asking after her *tiermatha* and Victory, and she thought they were doing well until she caught Elspeth's suspicious eye cast her way. *It's our eyes,* she thought as she drew figure eights in the leftover sauce with her fork, *our eyes give us away, and I don't know what to do about that.* She smiled sweetly and unselfconsciously at Elspeth, and didn't look at Jeffrey through the rest of the meal. When dessert was over and Jeffrey had gone back to work, Elspeth said, "Let me walk you to the door, Imogen, I want to talk to you."

They hadn't gone very far before Elspeth said in Kirkellish, "What's going on between you and my brother?"

Imogen, unprepared, gaped, and said, "What do you mean?"

"I mean the way you managed to say more with your eyes than you did with your mouths. Then you stopped looking at him altogether and he couldn't keep his eyes off you. If you were courting, you'd tell me, yes?" She sounded hurt and a little angry.

"We're not courting, Elspeth, I promise."

"But I can tell you want to."

"Well, we're not. And we're not going to." She could have explained it all to Elspeth, but she knew her friend too well; Elspeth wouldn't be able to stop herself from telling Imogen how unfair it all was, and wouldn't it be nice when the year was over, and building up their relationship until she had Imogen and Jeffrey safely married with a child on the way. Imogen would have enough trouble staying impartial without Elspeth's "help."

"Everyone's going to believe otherwise, you know."

"Then you'll have to convince them of the truth."

"*I* believe otherwise." Elspeth pouted.

"Pouting is unattractive, Elspeth."

"I would really like it if you *were* courting, Imogen."

"Elspeth, I promise if that ever happens, you will be the first person I tell. Now, how are things with you and Owen?"

Having safely deflected Elspeth, she returned home to find Dorenna, Saevonna, and Areli in the left-hand parlor. They stopped talking when she entered, Dorenna trying to conceal a smirk, Areli looking composed and Saevonna looking guilty. "What are you three talking about?" she asked.

"Birth control," Dorenna said, her smirk no longer concealed. "Turns out Saevonna may have a need for it."

"Has it gotten that far?" Imogen exclaimed, sinking onto a nearby sofa.

Saevonna was crimson. "Very far," she said. "I thought these Tremontanans had rules about sex…but I've had to stop him twice, now, because I wasn't prepared, and now I'm worried if we sleep together he'll regret it afterward. And suppose he's a virgin? I've never been with a virgin before. It's intimidating."

"Suppose he thinks *you're* a virgin?" Dorenna said. "You plan to tell him otherwise?"

"Thanks, Dorenna, now I have something else to worry about. How under heaven do you propose I tell him that? I can barely say *I love you.*"

They all went silent. "Do you?" Imogen asked.

Saevonna nodded. "I know it's insane. *I'm* insane. But I have never felt so…I don't know. So content as I do when I'm with him."

More silence, broken by Areli saying, "I knew Kionnal was the one for me after three days. Sometimes it happens like that. And we've been together for over three years now and I've never felt a moment's doubt. Of course, it took *him* over a year to realize the truth, so I don't know what the moral of the story is."

"You're making me feel like an unromantic old maid," Dorenna complained. "I think it would take me a hell of a lot longer to learn to trust someone that completely."

"I think we're abnormal," Areli said. "So don't worry."

"Oh, you're abnormal, all right. What about you, Imo? You and that King of yours?"

"We're not courting," Imogen said, trying not to let her blush give her the lie.

"Oh, I forgot." Dorenna winked broadly at the other two, who grinned.

"I told you, there isn't anything between us because that would be inappropriate for me as the ambassador."

"I think the ambassador had better tell that to her rosy red embarrassed cheeks," Dorenna said.

"Stop teasing, Dorenna, Imogen's made her choice and there's no sense bringing it up again," Areli said, but her expression as she looked at Imogen was curious, as if she were trying to solve a complicated puzzle. "Anyway, Saevonna, Tremontanan birth control is more sophisticated than ours, but it works on the same principle. I'll give you the name of my supplier; he's very friendly and he speaks Kirkellish, so you don't have to worry about mix-ups."

Imogen sat silent for a while, waiting for her blush to subside. First Elspeth, now her *tiermatha;* it seemed the only person who believed there was nothing between her and Jeffrey was herself, and she didn't think herself was very convinced either.

She went to Prince Serjian Ghentali's birthday party two days later with Darin Weatherby, a young man who'd passed Elspeth's rigorous screening process as well as the scrutiny of the *tiermatha*. He was a solid, pleasant man who enjoyed hearing Imogen's stories of the Kirkellan and diffidently shared his own stories of his work in the assessor's office, "which is as boring as it sounds," he told her on the ride to the Eskandelic embassy. "Really, I'd rather hear about your *tiermatha*. Is it true you join one and then never leave it until death?"

"That is only part true," Imogen said with a smile. "It is more true you are part of *tiermatha* until you change your life. That means, get married or do a trade skill, or sometimes it does mean die. Though not as much now we have peace with Ruskald."

"And then if someone leaves, you take on a new person? How long have these members been in your *tiermatha*?"

Imogen counted on her fingers. "Some of them are new just from a year ago, before I go to Hrovald's house, because of war deaths. I know—knew Saevonna and Revalan since five years ago, and Dorenna and Areli and Kionnal nearly as long. Kallum three years. The others are all much newer and I do not know them as well, but I trust all of them with my life."

The carriage came to a halt. "I don't know even one person I'd trust my life to, let alone twelve," Weatherby said. He was well-informed enough not to offer her his hand to assist her out of the carriage, which should have pleased her, but instead left her comparing him unfavorably to Jeffrey. She smiled brightly, pushing Jeffrey's image to one side. She was at a party with a pleasant young man and she was going to enjoy herself.

The Eskandelic embassy was in an older part of Aurilien, where single-story buildings presented a blank front to the street. A brass plaque affixed to the wall next to the gate announced this was the Eskandelic embassy, or at least Imogen guessed that was what it said. The door stood wide open, watched over by four men wearing traditional Eskandelic garb, long skirts with two deep pleats and full-sleeved jackets open over bare chests. Imogen passed them to enter the foyer, which was small and cramped. She hoped the rest of the building wasn't similarly proportioned.

A woman in traditional clothing, down to the jacket over her bare chest, took Imogen's wrap and Weatherby's greatcoat. Another woman gestured for them to exit the room through the door opposite. They emerged, not into the salon Imogen expected, but into a garden lit brightly by white globes that hovered about a foot above Imogen's head. Low yew hedges defined alcoves containing black ironwork tables, above which hovered miniature versions of the globes overhead, and matching chairs. A path picked out with smooth, disc-shaped tiles and star-like tesserae wove around the hedges and out of sight beyond taller walls of evergreen. Men and women sat and conversed at the tables, or spoke to one another over the hedges, while others strolled along the path and disappeared around the corner.

"Shall we sit?" Weatherby said.

"I want to see where they go," Imogen said, pointing. She took his arm and drew him along after her, not waiting for his assent.

They found themselves in a maze, quite alone, with the voices of other guests fading into the distance. Even more curious, Imogen continued to follow the path, towing Weatherby with her, taking turn after turn without seeing anyone. The globes were fewer here, and the ones remaining painted strange shadows across the living walls. It was unsettling, and Imogen had almost decided to turn around and go back to the party when she entered a clearing where several paths met. A statue of a nude woman, her back arched painfully so her breasts and hips were thrust forward, stood at the center of the clearing, and Serjian Ghentali sat on an iron bench beside it. Other wanderers admired the statue, or emerged from their paths to greet Ghentali, and Imogen decided to do the same.

"Madam ambassador, I greet many time your face!" Ghentali exclaimed, rising and coming to meet her. "I birthday is have much… parthy? Party! Who is this?" Imogen introduced Weatherby, who bowed.

"Many better is people, yes? Good that you come, here, you I give now." Ghentali took her hand and pressed into it something small with many hard edges. "Birthday is I give to all, yes?" He took a breath, and said, slowly, "Welcome to my parthy. Party!"

"Thank you very much, Ghentali," Imogen said, bowing. "I hope it is enjoyable for you as it is for me to be at your party."

"Thirty-six!" he exclaimed proudly. "Go, eat, drink. Great fun I have!"

Someone else approached the ambassador, and Imogen retreated. "He's an odd fellow, isn't he?" Weatherby said. "Friendly, though. What's that he gave you?"

"I do not know." At the mouth of the path they'd entered by—at least she hoped it was the same path—she stopped under a light globe and looked at what Ghentali had given her. It was a faceted stone the size of her thumbnail, clear and colorless in the harsh white light of the globe, set in a silver or white-gold bezel and hanging from a long silvery chain. As she shifted her hand, it twinkled at her with rainbow flashes.

"Good heaven, Imogen, I think that's a diamond," Weatherby gasped. "May I?" He took the chain from her and held it up so the stone dangled free. It caught the light of the globe, which transformed it into twinkles of color. "Almost certainly."

"It is not diamond, Ghentali not give out diamond even if it is his birthday. It must be…." She didn't know the Tremontanese word for "crystal," but she tapped it with her forefinger and watched it spin, and marveled at how beautiful it was.

"You really shouldn't accept this," Weatherby said, handing it back to her.

"It is rude to give back a gift," Imogen said, "and on his birthday as well. And it is not diamond. You will see." She fastened the chain around her neck and admired how pretty the crystal was, dangling between her breasts and continuing to catch the light.

They returned to the alcoves and found food and drink being served. Weatherby fetched her a plate full of tiny sandwiches and a glass of champagne, and they retired to a table where they could watch the other guests. The harem was present, acting as hostesses, and Imogen reminded herself to speak with them before she left. She nodded and smiled at people she knew, spoke to a few, but mostly sat silently observing. It was a pity Jeffrey wasn't here. They could exchange comments on the other guests, and he would wander from group to group, listening to complaints or discoursing on the territorial acquisition with equal ease. She did like watching him work. She hoped someday to be as comfortable a diplomat as he was. Damn. She hadn't even gone a full half-hour without thinking of him. And at a party with another man, no less.

She drained her glass and looked around the garden. There was Maxwell Burgess; she should greet him. "Please excuse me, I will speak with the department chief," she said, and rose from the table.

Burgess greeted her politely, but without enthusiasm. "I hope you are enjoying the evening," Imogen said with equal politeness.

"Of course," Burgess said with a shrug. "And you, madam ambassador?" His eyes roved the garden, never resting on her.

"I am well. Ghentali is a generous host. I do not know it is Eskandel tradition to give gifts for a birthday."

"Yes," Burgess said.

His continued indifference surprised her. Usually he was a good conversationalist. "He has given me this," she said, and lifted the pendant to show him. He glanced down, then took it in his hand to examine it.

"That is a valuable gift indeed," he said, sounding surprised.

Imogen shook her head. "No, it is…I do not know the word. It is a hard stone you can see through. They make regular shapes like sticks with six sides."

"Crystal. You may be right." He dropped the stone and looked beyond her. "Excuse me, madam ambassador, I must speak to Mister Godalming. Have a pleasant evening."

Imogen watched him go, surprised at his abruptness. Of course. He was a friend of Diana's; Imogen had seen him speaking with her at the Spring Ball. Well, if her *tiermatha* hated Diana on her behalf, it made sense that Diana's friends would share her resentment of Imogen. She was just surprised the Foreign Relations chief wouldn't remain impartial. She was growing to hate that word.

She continued to visit with friends and acquaintances, occasionally crossing paths with Weatherby, who was doing the same. A Deviser approached her for a meeting to discuss trade options; a young woman wanted to know about the possibility of working together on a breeding project for Kirkellan horses. The Kirkellan were becoming part of the wider world. Victory might want to bear children someday, and suppose they were sired by a Tremontanan horse? She might not be insulted by the idea.

Weatherby escorted Imogen to the door of the embassy without attempting to kiss her or do anything more than bow over her hand. She rather liked his company and hoped he wasn't developing a romantic attachment to her, because she wanted to see him again. She dropped her pendant into her dresser drawer and rang for Jeanette. She wanted to see him again because he was safe, she wasn't attracted to him, he wasn't likely to take a place in her heart. Damn. She wasn't going to be impartial, was she?

When Jeanette had gone, Imogen lay in her bed, staring blank-eyed at the ceiling high above. There was only one man she wanted to be with wholeheartedly, and that wasn't going to change just because she dutifully pretended not to see him when they were in a room together. Being apart had only made things worse. She sat up, punched her pillow with some ferocity, and lay down on her side. She could write to Mother, ask to be relieved of her position…no, she'd made a promise, and now that promise was making her burn with thwarted desire. She rolled onto her back again. She wanted him in her bed, lying naked beside her, running his hands over her body…she took her pillow and held it over her face, trying vainly to block the vision.

"I don't know how you can stand to do that," Elspeth said, lounging on one of the sofas in the east wing drawing room with her feet on the armrest.

"It is soothing," Imogen said, selecting another needle bearing a different colored thread.

"It's *boring*."

"You do not have to be bored. You can read a book. Or draw me sewing. Or knit."

"I hate all those things. Isn't it time for dinner yet?

"I do not know. I do not have one of those Devices that shows what the time is."

Elspeth took her watch out of her pocket. "Twenty minutes. I'm hungry *now*." She sat up. "Can I look at your pendant again?"

Imogen set her needle aside and removed the pendant from her neck. Elspeth took it and held it up to the light. "It's awfully pretty for crystal. Are you sure it's not a diamond?"

"I do not think Ghentali would give me a diamond as big as that no matter how much he likes his birthday and me." Imogen stitched the hindquarters of a tiny horse, knotted her thread and bit it off.

"That's disgusting. You have scissors."

"And I have teeth as well and they do not need hands to work." With another color she sketched in the horse's mane.

Elspeth slipped the pendant back over Imogen's head and freed her hair from the chain. "I do like the horse," she admitted. "Needlework is pretty so long as I don't have to do it." She turned her head at the sound of footsteps. "Jeffrey! And Mister Burgess." Her enthusiasm faded at the second man's entry. They were followed by four guards in blue and silver uniforms. "Jeffrey, can we have dinner early? I'm starving."

"Not now, Elspeth." His face was grim, his lips set in a straight white line.

"Madam ambassador," Burgess said, "would you stand, please?"

Imogen stuck her needle in her fabric and laid the hoop down. Burgess looked impassive. Jeffrey looked angry. Her heart thudded against her ribs. "What is this about?"

"Madam ambassador, you are accused of espionage against Tremontane for having given confidential military information to the Proxy of Veribold."

She felt faint. "I do not understand," she said.

Burgess removed a telecode tape from inside his coat. "Madam ambassador, did you receive communications detailing Tremontanan troop movements from the Kirkellan camp?"

"I did," she said, "but I did not—"

"Following your first meeting with Bixhenta, you used the palace telecoder to send this message to the Kirkellan camp. You met with him a second time after receiving an answer."

"How do you have that? I burned it."

"The palace telecoders keep a duplicate of all messages sent and received," Jeffrey said, his voice low and angry. "The message you carefully concealed from the operator wasn't hard for our translators to decipher."

Burgess said, "The message is a request for information about troop movements in the occupied territory. The reply clearly states the Tremontanan border with Veribold is undefended and there is no one in the area who could raise an alarm when Veribold invades."

She stared at Jeffrey, frightened of the furious look in his eye. That he could look at her that way…. "Bixhenta told me to investigate the truth and not to just believe his words," she protested. "I did not tell him what I learned. He want me to, but I do not."

"Investigate the truth of what?" Jeffrey asked. "That Tremontane lies open and ready for invasion? I fail to see what need you had of that information."

"Bixhenta refuses to speak to us," said Burgess. "I take that for confirmation. If he were innocent, he wouldn't need to hide in his embassy; he would want us to know the truth."

Imogen looked from Jeffrey to Burgess. "It is a mistake," she insisted. "I did not tell him."

"And there's this," Burgess said, taking the pendant in his hand and yanking on it to break the chain. It cut into her neck and she cried out in pain. "We asked Ghentali about his 'gift'. He confirmed it is a ten-carat diamond and he gave it to you 'out of friendship.'" His sarcastic emphases made her heart beat more painfully. "I wonder what secrets you sold to him to deserve what I can only call a princely gift."

She shook her head, hoping her dizziness would pass. "It is his birthday," she said. "He say he gives gifts to all."

"I didn't receive a gift. Neither did your escort, Mister Weatherby, who confirmed Ghentali's account. It seems very few of the Eskandelic ambassador's guests received a gift from him, and none were given anything nearly so valuable as this." He tucked the telecode tape and the diamond into his coat. "Madam ambassador, I am placing you under arrest."

"*No*!" Elspeth exclaimed, grabbing Burgess's arm. "Imogen would never do anything like that. You're wrong!"

"Don't interfere, Elspeth," Jeffrey said in a flat, hard voice. "This has nothing to do with you."

"But—"

"I said *enough!*" he shouted, turning his glare on her, making her flinch and drop Burgess's arm.

"Jeffrey—" Imogen pleaded. He had to believe her.

"I don't want to hear anything from you," he said, still in that voice that made him a stranger. "You may have helped Veribold invade my country, which makes you my enemy."

"But I did not do this—"

"Shut up. I'm done talking to you." He turned to Burgess. "Have her taken to the prison. I'll interrogate her later. We might be able to contain the damage if we find out exactly what she told Bixhenta."

"Madam ambassador, I would prefer not to bind you. Will you agree to go quietly?" Burgess said.

Imogen assessed her chances. Four men, fully armed…it was almost a compliment. "I will go quietly because I am innocent and I will show you," she said, but her voice was weak and she felt on the verge of tears. Elspeth burst out crying. "It will be all right," Imogen lied, "you do not need to cry for me." The guards led her away, and she wondered if she was allowed to cry for herself. That thought brought her to her senses. She would not cry. She straightened her spine. She was innocent. And she would show these men no fear.

Chapter Twenty-Seven

It probably looked, she thought, as if the guards were escorting her somewhere perfectly normal, like the ballroom or a waiting carriage. She was too angry and frightened to pay much attention to the route, but she was aware they were moving steadily downhill. At one point she realized they must be underground, and yet they continued to descend. They passed through an old wooden door and were suddenly in a much newer building with tile floors that echoed with the tread of the guards' boots. The pale yellow bricks of the walls looked bluish in the glare of the light Devices embedded in the ceiling.

They turned a corner and entered a small chamber with an iron-bound door that looked as if it had been there longer than the rest of the building. One of the guards knocked on it. They waited. Eventually Imogen heard the creak of a key being turned, and a small woman holding a large ring of keys pushed the door open. The guards led Imogen through the door into another small chamber with another ancient door, which the woman also unlocked and opened. Beyond this door lay a long, poorly-lit corridor lined with age-blackened wooden doors. Each had a small barred window at the top and a metal slide at the bottom.

The woman went to the fourth door on the left and unlocked it. One of the guards prodded Imogen, who turned on him, snarling, before she remembered she'd agreed not to fight them. "I am *innocent*," she growled, then gasped as the guard backhanded her across the face.

"No talking," he said, and shoved her more forcefully. Imogen felt as if she could cheerfully kill him, but she turned and walked through the door and heard it close behind her, then heard the rasp of the key in the lock.

The cell was small but clean and comfortably appointed, illuminated by a round Device fixed in the ceiling that shed a flickering yellow light over the room. There was a cot against one wall with a blanket and a pillow, a sink with a tap, a mirror, a small chest and a chamber pot. The chamber pot was empty and didn't stink. The blanket, which was a washed-out red, felt scratchy, but there was a clean sheet underneath and the pillow was unstained. The floor was solid granite worn smooth; she wondered how many generations of prisoners the cell had seen.

She sat on the cot and stared at the floor. Jeffrey had looked at her with such anger that remembering it made her stomach churn. He *couldn't* believe Burgess's accusations. That she could be condemned on such slim evidence as Bixhenta's refusal to talk and Ghentali's innocent gift…good heaven, what was the man thinking to give her something so valuable as casually as that? He'd been so cheerful, so happy to see her, and he could have had no idea how his gift would be used against her…or had he? Was he in on this plot to discredit and condemn her too?

It had to be a plot, but to what…oh, by thundering heaven, would Diana go to such lengths to see her humiliated? To break Jeffrey free of her clutches? She absolutely would. And Burgess was her tool. Imogen covered her face with her hands and gave out a huge, shaking sigh. He would have had access to the telecoders, though how he'd found out about her messages she had no idea. The operator? Someone he'd had watching her? Had someone been watching her everywhere she went? She wanted to be sick, but couldn't bear the thought of sharing her tiny cell with the stench of her vomit.

She stood and paced again. Three long paces one way, three long paces the other. Plenty of room. Four paces, even, if she made short steps. It only felt tiny. She sat on the chest and felt the rough wood dig into her rear end. No one knew where she was. No, Elspeth did; would she think to tell the *tiermatha*? She pictured Dorenna and Revalan leading an attack on the prison, screaming and slashing and dying at the hands of gun-wielding soldiers, and hoped Elspeth would have the good sense not to run crying to the *tiermatha* for help. She shifted from the chest to the cot, curled up on her side atop the blanket, wrapped her arms around her knees, and stared at the door. Someone would come, eventually. She would figure out what to do then.

She had no way of knowing how much time had passed. At one point the slide at the bottom of the soot-stained door opened and someone pushed a dented metal tray through the slot. She rushed to the door, but the slide closed before she could do…what, exactly, had she planned to do? Fight her way out through a narrow slit barely three inches high? The tray contained two slices of thick brown bread, a flat bowl of watery soup with tiny chunks of carrots and dull green peas, and an equally flat tin mug of water. She snatched up the bowl, draining it without resorting to the spoon with its oddly flattened bowl. The whole thing looked as if it had been set beneath a giant paving stone and pressed. She used the bread to mop up every drop of the soup, then drank the water, which tasted unpleasantly of loam. Then she sat cross-legged on the floor in front of the slot and waited, buttocks aching from the cold that seeped through her muslin dress. Shortly it slid open again and a man's deep voice said, "Pass it over."

"I am innocent. Let me out. I will prove it," she demanded.

"Don't make me come in there t' get the tray."

"I think you should come in here and we will see which of us leaves."

"Just hand the tray over and stop causin' trouble."

"No." She was being stupid, she knew, but being trapped in this little box of a room had all her nerves on edge.

"Fine. Keep it." The slide snapped shut. Imogen stood and kicked the tray so bowl, cup and spoon scattered everywhere with a clatter. She paced the room again. Two strides in each direction. It had been larger before she ate. The wall the door was set in was shorter now, she was certain of it. She curled up in a ball and stared at the door, willing it to open or fall over or burst into flames.

The light flickered out, then came back on as a faintly glowing circle of gray light in the ceiling that illuminated nothing. Nighttime, unless this was some nasty trick to confuse the prisoners, make them more compliant. Imogen got under the blanket and tried to make herself comfortable. The cot was too short for her; her feet in those useless crepe-soled slippers dangled off the end so the frame cut into her ankles. She drew her knees up and stared at the glowing circle. She couldn't see the point of it. Maybe it was to give you hope that the light would come back on again someday, so you could see the wonderful glories of your prison cell and be grateful you weren't in complete darkness.

She stared at it some more until she could no longer tell how far away it was. Three feet? Three inches? It hovered just above her nose. When she exhaled, she could taste her own breath, as if it were reflected back at her. She blinked up at the blackness she knew was only inches from her face. If she tried to sit up she would dash her head against cold stone as the ceiling lowered itself upon her, crushing her as flat as the dinnerware. That's what had happened to her tray. She couldn't stand. She couldn't breathe. Imogen screamed and threw up her hands, ready to pound futilely at the stone, and felt nothing but air. She leaped off the bed and swatted at the circle, clawing at it with her fingertips, panting in her desperation to knock it over or turn it off or somehow make it disappear so it would stop staring at her like a lidless eye. Finally, her breath gone, her shoulders aching, she fell back onto the cot and lay on her side with her arm over her face.

Tears slid down her cheeks. She could still see Jeffrey's furious face, could hear him telling her to shut up. He was supposed to believe her. He was supposed to at least listen to her, though she didn't know why she expected that from him. They'd known each other barely two months; he'd known Burgess for years. Of course he'd take his Foreign Affairs chief's word over that of an illiterate barbarian he had nothing in common with.

She sank into a restless sleep, waking at every imagined noise—why were there no cries from other prisoners, no demands for release? Was she the only one here? Could she be trapped here forever? She woke fully, her teeth clenched on a scream, and buried her head under the pillow. She felt as if the blackness was closing in on her again; she squeezed her eyes shut and tried to breathe slowly, calmly, and eventually fell asleep again.

The light woke her, flickering back into life, its meager brightness blinding her dark-acclimated eyes. Imogen lay unblinking, taking in every detail of the room. It was no smaller than it had been the day before, but now she felt suffocated. She ran to the door, screaming, "Let me out! Let me out of here!" She banged on the door, but the noise her fists made was muffled by the thick oak that had absorbed centuries of screaming. No one came. Finally, her throat raw and aching, she gave up. She used the chamber pot, washed her hands and face, and again sat cross-legged on the floor watching the slot. After a while, she heard footsteps coming down the hall, and the metallic sound of the slides scraping open and shut. The footsteps became louder and then stopped outside her door. "You hafta give the tray back if you want more food," the deep-voiced guard said.

"I am innocent," Imogen said wearily, her voice scratchy from screaming.

"I'm not the one to tell that to," the guard said. The slide opened. "D'you want food or not?"

Imogen stood and gathered the tray and dinnerware, such as it was, and slid it through the slot. "Thanks," the man said, and pushed another tray under the door. It was identical to the one she'd been given the night before. She pulled it toward herself and ate. It wasn't enough. She wondered if the plan was to keep the prisoners underfed so they wouldn't have the energy to fight back. It was working.

She returned the tray without comment when the guard came back to collect it, then sat on her cot, staring at the floor so she wouldn't see how the walls leaned in toward her. She didn't know how they'd constructed it, making the walls curve inward without collapsing on themselves. Perhaps they sagged a little more every day. Had the ceiling shrunk? Would the walls eventually meet at the center of the room, blocking out the light entirely? She wouldn't be able to stand upright if that happened; she already felt as if the top of her head brushed the ceiling. She stood and reached up. No, she still had to stand on the tips of her toes for her fingers to reach it. An illusion. The designers of this prison were evil geniuses. She already felt as if she were going mad.

More footsteps, approaching her cell. It was too soon for her to be given her meal like a rat in a cage. Two people. She waited for them to pass by, but they stopped at her door and the key turned in the lock. She leaped up, heart pounding. They'd realized Diana had played a horrible prank on her and were here to let her out. Then she heard Jeffrey's voice, saying, "Leave her to me," in that cold, horrible tone, and her stomach roiled. She clenched her back teeth together to keep from vomiting. The last thing she needed was to lose even the scanty meal they'd served her.

Jeffrey pushed the door open, nodded to someone Imogen couldn't see, and the door closed behind him and was locked. He was unshaven, his clothes disheveled, and he looked as if he'd had as bad a night as she had. He held a finger to his lips to silence her, though she hadn't been about to speak—she couldn't think of anything she wanted to say to him—and cocked his head, listening to the receding footsteps. Silence, and a minute passed before he turned to face her. He didn't look angry. He looked devastated.

"Imogen, I am so sorry," he said quietly. "I couldn't think of anything else to do."

"I am innocent," Imogen insisted.

"I know." He took a step in her direction, then stopped, his fists clenched at his sides. "Somebody wants me to believe Veribold is on the verge of invading us, so I'll draw the troops south. They want it badly enough they drew you into the plot, made it look like you were working with Bixhenta. Max was so insistent…I had to pretend I believed him, Imogen, because I need to find out why he's so desperate for me to believe the lie."

"It is Burgess who planned this because Diana hates me."

"I thought of that, but the plot Max 'uncovered' goes much farther than you. He might be working with Diana, but honestly, I don't see what she'd gain from this." He began to pace, seemed surprised by how quickly he came up against the prison wall, and stopped. "I think you looked like a good candidate to pin it on because we're…friends, and I'd be off balance thinking you'd betrayed me." He laughed, one short mirthless sound. "Max's bad luck that he picked the one person outside my own family I'd never believe it of."

The knot in Imogen's stomach began to relax. "You believe me," she said.

"Imogen, I would sooner doubt myself. I'm sorry, but I wouldn't have warned you even if I'd had time. I couldn't count on you reacting properly. I didn't mean anything I said to you in the drawing room. It was all part of the plan." He took another step toward her, then returned to pacing in a tight circle. "I swear I'll make Max pay for this."

"You are certain he does this?"

"I'm certain. He's smart, but he's sloppy. Why didn't you give the diamond back to Ghentali? That's more damning than Max's claim you colluded with Bixhenta."

"I do not know it was a diamond!" Imogen shouted, ignoring Jeffrey's attempts to shush her. "It was present from nice man and I think it is crystal and it would hurt his feelings to give it back! You—"

He clapped his hand over her mouth. "I'm supposed to be interrogating you," he hissed. "I don't want anyone coming down here—ow!" He yanked his hand away and examined the place where Imogen had bitten him.

"You do not touch me," she snarled, and backed away to sit on the cot. "You say cruel things and you let them put me in this tiny room with walls that curve in and then you tell me it is all your plan. I hate your plan. I hate—" She buried her face in her hands and shook with the effort of suppressing her sobs.

She felt his arms go around her and his head rest on her shoulder. "I'm sorry," he whispered into her ear. "It took all the discipline I had to watch those guards take you away and do nothing. I wanted to kill Max for forcing me to do that to you. He's going to suffer for this, I swear it."

She leaned into him, her anger forgotten in the comfort of such simple human contact, and let her hands fall to her lap. "I am sorry I bit you," she said, mostly meaning it.

"It was my own fault for underestimating you," he said, and kissed the side of her face. She turned and put her arms around his neck and then they were kissing, hard, desperate kisses that felt to Imogen as if they'd been stoppered up inside her for far too long. She felt his long fingers tangle themselves in her hair and the sick feeling vanished. *This* was what she had longed for, all this time, this was what she had needed without even knowing it, and she drew him closer and heard him groan, quietly, deep in his throat and slide his hands from her hair to her waist to pull her hard against him and kiss her so fiercely she felt she might lose herself in him completely. When they finally broke apart, breathing heavily, Jeffrey brushed the hair away from her face and said, "So much for impartiality."

"I was not impartial even when we do not court," Imogen said. "I do not care about impartial anymore. I do not care about the other men. I care about you."

He smiled and ran his forefinger along the line of her cheekbone. "I suffered the most agonizing jealousy whenever you accepted an invitation from one of those men who, I should point out, are not worthy of you."

"I liked some of them. Darin Weatherby was nice."

"Darin Weatherby told Max you knew Ghentali had given you a diamond and you refused to give it back even though you also knew it was an inappropriate gift."

"I think I must find him now and beat him until he bleeds."

Jeffrey laughed. "I probably shouldn't let you enact vigilante justice on people, but the idea has some appeal." He kissed her again. "I wish I could stay longer, but I think Max is starting to suspect I don't believe him, and I don't want him running."

Imogen's heart pounded. "You cannot leave me here again."

"Imogen, it's just for a little—"

"No, you cannot, the room is getting smaller and I do not want to be crushed!" She tried to stand, to pound on the door and shriek again, but Jeffrey pulled her down and held her until her breathing returned to normal.

"I'm sorry," he whispered, and kissed her forehead lightly. "I need you to endure this for just a few hours more. As soon as I find out what Max is planning, I'll send for you. I promise."

"You must do it soon," she whispered back, "because I think I cannot tell what is real anymore."

He turned her in his arms to face him, and kissed her again, his lips lingering on hers. "*That* is real," he said, "and I will think of you every moment until this is over, and then I will go on thinking of you because you make me happy."

She nodded, and smiled a weak and watery smile. "I will remember this and not how you looked when you said those things to me. No, do not make that face," she said, because Jeffrey looked as if she'd struck him, "it is that I could only remember that before, and now I have something much better to think of." She stroked his stubbly cheek. "And I think it will be nice if you shave before you kiss me again," she said, smiling more firmly this time.

He laughed. "I make no promises," he said. He hugged her tightly, then released her and stood. "Someone will come for you," he said. "Soon. I swear it."

She nodded, unable to speak because her throat was closing up. Jeffrey put his face to the window and shouted, "I'm done here," and soon someone unlocked the door, and he walked away without looking back. She curled up on her cot again and tried to remember being kissed so she wouldn't see the walls curving in on her. He'd promised to get her out; she hadn't been abandoned. She could endure a while longer.

Time passed. A tray came through the slot, this one bearing chopped, dark meat she couldn't identify, but she wolfed it down and finally felt full. She went back to her cot and drowsed restlessly. Another tray. Thick white soup and black bread. The lights went out. She stared at the dim circle of light until her eyes hurt; when she looked away, a black circle hovered in front of her eyes, radiating darkness. She whimpered and closed her eyes until it went away.

She became aware of her own breathing, in and out far too quickly, then realized she could hear it echo, as if someone else were in the room, breathing in rhythm with her to conceal itself. She held her breath and heard nothing. It was clever, whatever it was; she breathed again in an erratic pattern, and it matched her every breath. "Who's there?" she shouted in Kirkellish. "I know you're there!" More breathing, faster now to match hers. It could be anywhere in the darkness. It could be anything. She pressed herself up against the corner of the walls and shook so hard her head bounced off the stones. "Come and fight me if you dare!" she shouted, but her voice shook as hard as her body, and she cursed herself for showing fear.

Light gleamed in the far wall, warm, flickering light. A lantern. The glow brightened until it made Imogen's dark-adapted eyes hurt. A key turned in the lock, and the door swung open, letting in even more blinding light. "You're free to go, madam ambassador," said the deep voice.

Imogen looked around. The room was empty except for her. She scrambled off the cot and past the man with the lantern, feeling like a small animal fleeing the fox's den. "Where do I go?" she asked.

"Someone's waiting for you," the man said. "I'm glad to know you were innocent after all."

Imogen blinked at him in the lantern light. He had a kind face. "Thank you," she said, and bolted for the exit.

She had to wait, fidgeting, for the small woman to open the two doors, but finally she darted through the second door and ran squarely into Kionnal, who caught her before she could stumble. She looked around in amazement and saw Saevonna and Kallum standing just beyond him, looking nervous and uncertain. "Imogen!" Kionnal exclaimed. "I almost thought we'd been sent to the wrong place."

"What are you doing here?"

"The King sent us to retrieve you," Saevonna said.

"But—how? You barely speak Tremontanese."

"This," Saevonna said, and held up a man's ring, silver with a dark blue stone, "and a note for the prison warden. I think he said something like, his authority, and not being challenged, and how you'd trust us more than some North guard." She handed the ring to Imogen. "You take it. It makes me nervous, holding who knows what kind of power. I might accidentally command a legion to jump off the city wall."

Imogen examined it, patted her body looking for a place to put it, and finally jammed it onto the middle finger of her left hand, which was the only one it fit. "So I'm not guilty anymore?"

Kionnal shrugged. "I assume so. We were told to bring you to the north wing quickly and not much more. You should see it up there.

Looks like someone kicked an anthill and then set it on fire. Whatever your King learned, it's got a lot of people upset. Follow me."

"Do you know the way out?"

"More or less."

They ran down corridors Imogen vaguely remembered. "What happened while I was locked up?" she said.

"Elspeth came to find us," Saevonna said. "It took us a while to make out what she was saying, she was so hysterical. Then we argued about what to do."

"Some of us wanted to storm the prison and make them release you, but cooler heads—and by cooler heads, I mean mine—convinced them that was suicidal," Kallum said.

"It would have been. I was so afraid you'd try it anyway," Imogen said.

"It was Marcus who told us how to reach the King," Saevonna said, thumping Kallum on the arm. "I think he was expecting us, though, because Marcus didn't have to do a lot of explaining about what we wanted. Everyone just passed us on to the next person."

"And didn't your King look *angry* when we reached him," Kallum said. "He's unspeakably beautiful when he's angry. I never thought I'd be jealous of you, Imogen, but...by heaven, he's something to look at."

"Shut up, Kallum," Kionnal said mildly. "Where were we? Right. He was interrogating that shortish man you're always talking to at diplomatic events, looked like he'd been using a stick or something, but he looked glad to see us. He asked the three of us—well, he asked Marcus to ask us—to come fetch you, and I don't know where he sent everyone else."

"And you just went?"

"We did. There's something about him that makes you want to do as he says, even if you don't understand what that is." Kionnal looked over his shoulder at Imogen. "If he locked you up, why'd he send us to free you?"

"It was part of his plan. It wasn't a good one, but I think he was improvising."

Kionnal looked as if he wanted to say something else, but subsided. "What?" Imogen asked.

"He's trying to tell you we approve of your King, even if he is a Tremontanan," Kallum said.

Imogen turned around and ran backwards for a few steps. "I'm sure he'll appreciate that."

"Imogen, I think you should give up on pretending he doesn't mean anything to you, because no one believes it," Saevonna said.

"I can't—"

"You're not doing a very good job of being impartial, if that's what you're about to say," Kallum said.

"Is this really the sort of conversation we ought to be having right now?"

"What better time than when you can't go anywhere?" Kallum laughed, breathily.

"All we're saying," said Saevonna, "is it looks like he makes you happy, and we want that for you."

"Even if he is a Tremontanan," Kallum repeated.

"Even then."

Imogen shook her head. "It's not that simple," she said.

"So work out the details later. Just know you have our blessing," Saevonna said.

"Did I need your blessing?"

"Of course you did. Heaven only knows what trouble you'd get into if you didn't have your *tiermatha* at your back."

It took several wrong turns for Kionnal to lead them out of the prison complex and into the palace proper, but once there, it was easy to reach the north wing. It was less easy to find Jeffrey, or anyone who could tell them what was happening. Kionnal was right; there was some desperation in the way people ran from place to place in near silence, as if events were too dire for speech. Imogen led her people through the maze of hallways, occasionally stopping to ask for assistance that was never forthcoming. Imogen had nearly decided to seek out the rest of the *tiermatha* so they could face the disaster together when she saw Frederick

Williams ahead of her, talking to someone she couldn't see. "Colonel Williams," she began, then realized as she neared him that the person he was talking to, standing just inside a door, was Jeffrey.

"*Imogen,*" Jeffrey said, and though he didn't reach out to her she could read everything he couldn't say in his eyes. "Fred, give me a minute. Imogen, will you ask your *tiermatha* to wait?" He pulled her into the room and shut the door behind her. He startled and raised her hand wearing his ring.

"Did you—" he began, and shook his head. "You couldn't have meant—Imogen, you don't know, do you—"

"Do not know what?" She removed the ring and presented it to him. He took it and slid it onto his ring finger, still staring at her hand in a distracted way. She expected him to kiss her, but instead he ran his hands through his hair and turned away. "This is so much worse than I'd thought," he said. "Max was plotting with Diana, after all—I'm having trouble believing it of her, but—they wanted me focused on Veribold so I wouldn't realize Diana had pulled her troops out and was coming here until it was too late. It may *be* too late."

"I do not understand why she brings her troops to here."

Jeffrey faced her again. "She wants to kill me and Elspeth and take the Crown," he said. "She wants to be Queen."

Part Three: Rider of the Crown

Chapter Twenty-Eight

"Based on the timing of the telecode we received, we've got only hours, possibly much less than that, before Diana's forces arrive," Jeffrey told his captains and Imogen, gathered in his office. "It's hard to say for sure because Burgess's woman in the telecoder office prevented the warning message from reaching me immediately, but this is the timeline we've reconstructed: Just over two days ago, Diana Ashmore left the border with Barony Daxtry's detachment of the Tremontanan Army and headed south. It took several hours for the Army to notice her absence and connect that to the sudden loss of communication with the palace. General Anselm sent several companies after her, but Diana has a head start of over a day on those forces. Maxwell Burgess's information is that she's coming here to take the Crown. We have to assume she'll try to storm the palace; we have to hold out until the Army arrives. The bad news is even with our Kirkellan allies, we're outnumbered by more than two to one, and the palace isn't the most defensible of structures. The good news is we found out about Diana's coup attempt before she actually arrived, and we're better armed than she is." He paused and surveyed the attentive faces. "Thirty-six hours, ladies and gentlemen, we have to hold out for thirty-six hours, and I can't think of anyone better suited to the task than the Home Guard and a company of Kirkellan warriors."

Colonel Williams spread a hastily-sketched map of the palace on Jeffrey's desk, shoving books and papers to the floor without an apology. "The palace has too many levels for this to be truly accurate," he said, "but it should give you an idea of what we're dealing with." He pointed at spots irregularly spaced around the perimeter of the building. "These are the exits," he said. "The main door is obviously where we'll have to concentrate our forces, but I'm guessing the Baroness is too smart to push through there. She's more likely to feint and make her real attack here, at the west door, or here, at Ansom's Gate. The other two are small enough that we can easily barricade them and defend them with only a handful of soldiers, with runners in case I'm wrong and she tries to enter through one of them."

"What about the Justiciary?" asked one of the captains, a woman with white hair and an unlined face.

"Already sealed off," Jeffrey said. "Those doors are meant to stop a prison riot. Diana won't get through that way."

"When you get your orders, take your troops and go immediately to your stations," Williams continued. "The goal is to keep them from entering the palace at all costs, but we have to be prepared for the possibility they'll overwhelm us. Remember, most of the side routes will be blockaded; if the Baroness's troops get through and you have to fall back, don't head down one of those blind hallways or you'll be trapped. Any time you do fall back, send a runner so we can keep track of where you are. Don't give up ground unless you absolutely have to. And stay out of the rotunda; we'll have riflemen there to pick off the Baroness's soldiers if they're stupid enough to try to cross that big open space." He mopped his forehead. "The arrows show where you should go in the event you're pushed back. Memorize those routes. We're depending on having soldiers at certain points if the Baroness pushes too far in. Don't deviate from the route unless you have orders from me or from his Majesty."

"That's all. Gather your troops and dig in to your positions," Jeffrey said, "and may heaven bless us all."

Imogen lingered after the captains had dispersed. "Where is Elspeth and Alison?"

Jeffrey's eyes went blank momentarily, and Imogen remembered what Elspeth had told her about his magical talent. "Mother is in the north wing, and Owen took Elspeth and went to ground in the city. It's essential Diana not find her, and Owen is as good at hiding as anyone I've ever known."

It was just as essential Diana not find Jeffrey, but then there was no point in Imogen mentioning that. "And you will be where?"

Jeffrey scowled. "I'm putting a small force right at the entrance to the east wing as a decoy, just in case, but I will be locked in the north wing. I hate being so vulnerable, but if she kills me…I wish I understood what drove her to this. She wasn't obsessed with power when we were younger."

"People are not the same their whole life."

"I know. I shouldn't be worrying about this. Too many other things to worry about." He took her hand. "I want you to take your *tiermatha* and one other, preferably one that isn't as fluent in Tremontanese, and guard Ansom's Gate. I know you heavy cavalry types are trained to thrust rather than slash, and with the narrowness of that entrance I'm counting on you having an advantage over Diana's infantry if they break through. By heaven, I wish we had more time."

"We have enough time to be ready, and that is a good enough wish," Imogen said. "But I think my *tiermatha* is slow because I want my saber and it is not here yet."

"That's not what I meant."

Imogen raised her eyebrows. "You mean that you and me have more time? What will you do with this more time?"

"This." He hugged her tightly, laying his bristly cheek against her soft one. "Imogen, you know our chances aren't good, right?"

"I know. But they are not so bad either. You have good fighters who will die to keep you alive because they love their country and do not want it to be ruled by a crazy bony person."

He laughed. "She is rather bony, isn't she?" He released her and stepped back. "Don't die if you can help it."

"I cannot promise what will happen, but I know my enemies will shake to know my saber is at their throats. And I will not die if I can help it. So you will not either." She didn't say what they both knew, which was if Jeffrey died, it would only be because Imogen was already dead. "I must go," she said.

He looked as if he was about to say something else, then shook his head and held the door open for her. She saluted him, then went to find her *tiermatha*. They had work to do.

Sharp-edged granite blocks, fitted together so tightly they made a sheer cliff eighty feet tall, formed the northern wall of the palace. No windows pierced the cliff, which extended to the left as far as Imogen could see before curving out of sight. To the right, Imogen's view was blocked by the irregular jutting block of the north wing, whose large windows would offer a too-easy entrance if they weren't some thirty feet above ground level. They were dull in the moonlight, blocked from the inside by improvised barriers of planks and upended desks. One of those windows belonged to Jeffrey's office. They'd probably turned that enormous claw-footed desk of his into a shield. He would be farther inside, in one of those smaller meeting rooms with no outside access, no hopelessly indefensible windows. She allowed herself one more thought of him, then went inside.

"There's no movement, but then it's unlikely they'll try this door," she told the *tiermathas*. "There's no gate in the outer wall on this side, and the west door is bigger. But that means it's even more important we stay alert, because this is the entrance where the enemy can do the most damage if it's not secured. Excuse us." This last was directed at several men and women carrying boards and hammers. They began securing the door as neatly as if they'd been trained to defend the palace against intruders. Imogen gestured for her troops to move farther down the passage, away from the noise of the hammers.

"The goal is to keep the enemy from entering for as long as possible. Once they get inside, the advantage is theirs. We don't want to fight a defensive battle if we can help it." She held up one of the gun Devices they'd been issued. "These are only for short-range fighting. They each have six shots. Point, squeeze the trigger, use it up, toss it aside. They only have enough source for those six shots. Try not to shoot any of your friends." A murmur of laughter went up. "If we can block the door with their bodies, so much the better. If not, then it's saber work, and you all know the drill. We can fit three across without falling over each other. Front rank fights until the second rank takes over, then retreat to the rear. Third rank pulls out anyone who falls. Keep moving and keep fresh.

She didn't tell them that even if they kept moving so no one tired, every time they switched positions they would lose ground. No sense discouraging them before they'd even met the foe. "When I give the command to retreat, the two first ranks hold position while everyone else moves, then those six run like hell and get down, because our fallback position is manned by riflemen who will hold them back until we're ready to come at them from the side corridors. Beyond that, we'll have to improvise. Any questions?" No one spoke. "Then let's get ready for a long day."

The carpenters had finished nailing up thick planks and were now carrying in furniture which they slotted together neatly to make a barricade bristling with chair legs and finely polished table tops. The barricade would make things more difficult all around; the enemy would have trouble forcing their way past it, but it would also make it hard for the *tiermathas* to get clear shots at them. "Don't shoot unless they get past this," Imogen called out. "Let's not waste our Devices."

She leaned back and stared at the opposite wall. The waiting could kill you, so she'd learned to let her conscious mind slip away, to become nothing more than a pair of eyes, a pair of ears, a pair of nostrils just waiting for a signal that it was time to meet the foe. The wall was covered with fuzzy red paper; she reached behind herself and rubbed it as if she were petting Victory. Victory would be disappointed to miss this battle, but it wasn't a fight for horses. If Imogen rode her into the palace, she'd have to lie across Victory's neck to keep from cracking her head against the low ceiling of this narrow hall. Still, the idea of Diana's soldiers breaking through the door to come face to face with an enraged Kirkellan war horse made her smile.

"Thinking of your enemies lying on the floor under your feet?" Dorenna asked.

"Thinking of Victory trampling their skulls under hers," Imogen replied.

"That would be something to see, wouldn't it? I wish we weren't trapped in here like rats. So much better to be free to scatter them as we rode through."

Imogen remembered the cell walls closing in on her and closed her eyes. "Let's not talk about being trapped, all right?"

"We have plenty of space to fall back, plenty of provisions, and a good communications network. I'm confident in our chances," Saevonna said, leaning against the wall opposite Imogen and sliding down it to sit on the floor.

"That's because you're disgustingly optimistic," Dorenna said. She scuffed her toe against the bare stone of the corridor and said, "So where's Marcus?"

Saevonna looked up at her. "In the rotunda. He's a rifleman," she said in an emotionless voice. "He's probably safer than I am, unless they get up to the second floor. He's…not the best swordsman, but he can take care of himself."

"Of course he can," Imogen said. "Thirty-six hours. Thirty-five, now. Probably less than that. We can hold out that long."

Saevonna nodded. She looked as if she was wrestling with some inner enemy. "Is anything wrong?" Imogen asked.

"He asked me to marry him," Saevonna said, still in that flat, emotionless voice.

Imogen gasped. Dorenna dropped to squat beside Saevonna. "What did you tell him?"

"To ask again when this was all over. I didn't…it was too unexpected." She closed her eyes and banged her head gently against the wall behind her.

Imogen and Dorenna exchanged glances. "What are you—do you know what you're going to tell him?" Imogen asked quietly.

"No," Saevonna said, her eyes still closed. "I wish the enemy were here. I need something uncomplicated I can point my saber at. At least then I know what I'm doing."

Imogen and Dorenna looked at each other again. "You know we'll support you, no matter what you choose," Imogen said.

"That's what I'm afraid of," Saevonna said cryptically. She pushed herself up. "I'm going to check the fallback route again. Please don't tell anyone else. I don't want them distracted."

"She doesn't care about *us* being distracted," Dorenna murmured when Saevonna was gone.

"Shut up. She clearly needed to tell someone. Dor, what if she leaves?"

"She won't leave. We're family. She'll make him come home with us."

Imogen shook her head. "She's adapted to life here better than anyone else. I know her Tremontanese is better than his Kirkellish."

"Shut up. I can't think about this right now. I wish she'd kept it to herself."

"No, you don't."

"No, I don't." Dorenna went from a crouch to a sitting position. "What happens if the enemy breaks through somewhere else?"

"We wait for new orders and join the fight, probably."

"You don't think they'd make us wait here in case they try to enter at more than one point?"

"I don't know, Dor."

Dorenna cursed. "I hate this part."

"Me too."

Revalan came down the passage, balancing long rolls of bread in his arms and a basket of fruit over his elbow. "Breakfast," he said. "Early breakfast, anyway."

The bread proved to be stuffed with meat and cheese. The three of them ate in silence, Imogen preoccupied with Saevonna's predicament. Saevonna loved Marcus, but did she love him enough to give up everything she knew for him? She'd be a foreigner in Aurilien her whole life. Her children would grow up city-dwellers who knew nothing of riding free across the plains, knew nothing of what it was to hunt the cunning reindeer or cuddle with their family inside their tent against the howl of a winter storm.

She had a brief but vivid memory of watching Jeffrey at a time when he wasn't aware of her scrutiny, telling Elspeth some story. His whole face was alight with humor, his long fingers gesturing as he illustrated a point, and she remembered how she'd wished he'd turn that look on her—and then he had, and it had warmed her down to the core. *He loves me,* she realized, and fear filled her at the thought. She didn't know if she returned his affection, didn't know if she even wanted to. Being a diplomat was one thing; letting go of her life entirely was very different.

She heard a scrabbling at the outer door. "Wait," she said, holding up a hand. There it was again. Then the door shook with the faintest of tremors.

"They're trying to break it down," Revalan said, "but they don't have a battering ram."

The tremors came regularly for a short while, as if several people were slamming into it with their shoulders. Imogen was joined by Dunevin, captain of the second *tiermatha*. "Sounds like it's holding," Dunevin said, sounding uncertain, but Imogen had learned Dunevin always sounded uncertain no matter what he actually felt or thought.

"For now," Imogen agreed. Neither of them had to say *until they get a battering ram*. Imogen tried to think if she'd seen anything on the palace grounds Diana's soldiers could press into service to batter down a door. Even if they did, they'd probably use it against the main entrance, where they could pour through into the entry hall and down the wide corridor toward the rotunda, all of which were too vast to be successfully blockaded. Imogen thought of Marcus, waiting on the second floor. Heaven help him if he was as distracted as Saevonna was.

Hours passed. Occasionally someone would try and fail to beat down the door. Imogen ordered the *tiermathas* to walk around, stay relaxed and rested. They'd have plenty of warning if Diana's troops managed to break through.

A young runner trotted up the hallway to Imogen. "All the entrances are still holding firm," she said, "but the main doors are starting to weaken. Hold your position for a secondary assault." She ran off the way she'd come.

Imogen passed the word. They waited. Her warriors paced the length of the hall, or talked quietly, or napped in the way experienced fighters did, catching rest when and where they could. Imogen's runner, a boy no more than twelve, curled in a ball off to one side, sleeping the sleep of someone who hadn't fully grasped the precariousness of their position. Imogen let him sleep. With luck, they wouldn't need him. She knew better than to count on luck.

The pounding on the door began again. This time, it was louder and more rhythmic. "This is it," Imogen called out. Warriors stood and stretched and unlimbered their gun Devices. She prodded the runner with her toe. "Warn Colonel Williams they are trying to break through here."

Another runner came up the hall, breathing heavily. "They're through the front doors," he said. "Hold position here."

Imogen nodded, but both boys were already gone. "We may have to fall back to support the others," she said, "so be prepared to retreat even if we haven't lost our position." She drew a deep breath. "These soldiers have no idea what it's like to face a Kirkellan warrior in battle. We have a reputation for ferocity and I want us to live up to it today. Fight well, fight long, and let your sabers drink deep."

They roared in response, and for a moment, the pounding against the door ceased. Imogen grinned. *That's right, you poor deluded fools who think you're justified in fighting against your own King,* she thought, *just you think about what's waiting for you on this side of the door.*

Chapter Twenty-Nine

The pounding resumed. Whoever had built Ansom's Gate had built it well, and the carpenters had made it stronger. It was a long time before they began to hear the creaking complaint of wood stressed almost beyond its capacity. Then they heard the door splinter beyond the wooden barrier, and the planks shuddered. Every eye was fixed on the barricade, whose spindly-legged tables and delicately carved chairs seemed like nothing more than a gossamer web the enemy could brush aside without a thought.

The planks splintered and exploded inward. A soldier in Tremontanan green and brown struggled through the gap, kicking at the remnants of boards and door to widen it. A shatteringly loud clap, a spark of light, and he fell, his throat a gory mess. Imogen looked at the warrior who'd fired the shot, who looked as stunned as the dead man did. "There's a hole," she said lamely, and pointed at the barricade. "I didn't know it would do that."

"Well, keep on doing it," Imogen said. Another soldier clambered over the broken wood and the broken body of his comrade and began tearing at the barricade, followed by more soldiers until the area between the door and the barricade was filled with enough of them that they were getting in each other's way. The Kirkellan fired more shots, but few of them struck soldiers because the barricade, except for that one lucky hole, was well-built and without many gaps. Another soldier went down, then another. Their comrades were pulling them out as fast as they could, and the Kirkellan shot at those rescuers and managed to take down a few more.

The barricade shifted. "It's coming apart!" Imogen shouted. "Ready sabers!" Ranks of Kirkellan warriors formed up, the first two ranks still armed with gun Devices and taking shots at anything they could see. A soldier incautiously raised his head over the crumbling barricade and took a bullet in the forehead; he fell forward over the barricade, making it shift further. Then it came down entirely, and soldiers clambered over it only to be met with the massed gunfire of the first ranks of the Kirkellan. They fell, injured or dead, and more soldiers climbed over their bodies and dropped to the ground in front of the barricade, drawing their swords.

It was a massacre. So many soldiers came over at once they didn't have room to swing their swords without hitting an ally. The Kirkellan, accustomed to defending themselves and their horses against such strokes, parried and thrust, and thrust again, going for the soft tissues of the stomach and groin, or feinting at faces and throats. More soldiers went down, creating obstacles for their comrades to avoid or get over. The Kirkellan forced them back against the barricade, then over it, then, to Imogen's amazement, back out the door. "Stand down!" Imogen shouted, hoarse from screams she didn't remember making, and they all stood for a moment, heaving great breaths of weariness. "Stand down," Imogen repeated dully. It was a heaven-sent miracle, an impossibility, and it wasn't going to happen twice. The next time, Diana's soldiers would be prepared. The next time....

She looked around. Two Kirkellan dead, two more injured. One of the dead was Lorcun of her own *tiermatha*. They would mourn him later. For now, they had to move the bodies somewhere out of the way. "You two," she said, too tired to remember their names, "take our fallen dead to one of the side corridors, out of the way. You—" she shook her head to clear her eyes, "I mean, Maeva, help get the wounded out of the way and see if they can continue, or take them to the infirmary. Everyone else, let's heave the bodies—oh, damn."

One of the enemy soldiers lifted his head and looked directly at her. "Don't kill me," he pleaded.

"I should, traitor," Imogen said in Tremontanese.

"I'm no traitor. I'm trying to return the kingdom to its true ruler."

Imogen groaned. "And I think Diana told you it is her."

"She's fought the Ruskalder for years. She's earned our trust. What has the false King ever done for us?"

Protected this country? Ruled wisely? Worked long hours to make decisions you couldn't bear to shoulder? "I am not going to argue with you and I am not going to kill you even though I should. Maeva," she said, switching to Kirkellish, "as long as you have to take Aemen to the infirmary, take this fellow along too. Dorenna, tie his hands—better yet, you go along, and hurry back."

"You should kill him," Dorenna said.

"His only crime is believing that frothing bitch's lies. But if he tries to escape, cut him down." She looked around. "Get moving, everyone, they'll be back."

Her runner came back as they were repairing the barricade and heaving bodies over it. "Colonel says report on damages and hold your position. The fighting's reached the rotunda and the enemy forces have split. So far they're contained."

Imogen heard Saevonna take in a sharp breath. "Tell them we have pushed the enemy back for now. We still hold our position and we will send word if we fall back." *If, not when.* She stopped to tie her hair back more securely, then shouted, "They're coming!"

The second wave was much cannier than the first. Two soldiers kept low, protected from the guns by the barricade, and began dismantling it from the bottom. The Kirkellan exhausted their guns and could only watch as the barricade disintegrated before them. Realization struck Imogen and she shouted, "Take the battle to them! Tear the barricade apart!"

The Kirkellan set to ripping apart furniture and flinging it at the soldiers, forcing them back, but eventually it was gone and they were back to saber work. These soldiers had learned the lesson of their dead comrades; they didn't crowd together and block one another, but had plenty of room to swing their swords, and now the Kirkellan did far more parrying than they did thrusting. Men and women on both sides fell. Kionnal, in the first rank, dropped his saber and went to one knee, clutching his stomach; Areli and Dorenna both screamed his name and dove after him, Areli to pull him to safety and Dorenna to take his place. She fought like the wind, screaming and unstoppable, and in the face of her vicious attack the soldiers faltered and stepped back. "Somebody help me!" she shouted, then grunted and fell backward. Two Kirkellan rushed to take her place, and Imogen, cursing, got her hands under Dorenna's armpits and hauled her out of range of the soldiers.

She was unmarked. Imogen couldn't see any wound that might have killed her, but she lay ashen-faced and limp on the floor. Imogen felt for a pulse and couldn't find it because her hands were too shaky, that was it, not because there was no pulse to find. She tried again, and Dorenna opened her eyes and startled Imogen so much she screamed and flashed on a memory of Dorenna doing the same thing to her when she'd nearly died of lung fever. "Don't *do* that!" she said, and slapped Dorenna hard, her hands shaking even more from the rush of fright.

"Blow to the head," Dorenna whispered. "Just let me sit a moment."

"Stay down," Imogen told her, and went back to the fight.

More Kirkellan had fallen. Areli sat with Kionnal's head in her lap, both of them white. Areli held a wad of cloth to Kionnal's side; it was already streaked with blood. "I'm not dead yet," Kionnal joked, his voice too faint for comfort.

"He needs to get to the infirmary," Areli said.

"We need every wounded warrior out of here, because we'll have to fall back in a few minutes. Can you take them?"

Areli nodded. "Get everyone moving."

"And tell Dorenna she's helping you. She won't go if she thinks she's on the wounded list."

"Is she—"

"She got hit on the head and I think she's concussed. She'll just get in everyone's way if we let her stay." Imogen looked toward the fighting. "It's my turn in the front rank. Go."

She slipped past her comrades and ducked into an open slot where a warrior had just fallen, his throat slit so deeply his head bounced as he hit the floor. Imogen slit the belly of the woman who'd killed him and kicked her backward into another soldier. She parried a blow aimed at her head, ducked under it and slashed across his thighs, making him stumble right into her return strike. This was what she was made for. She was a good diplomat, but she was a phenomenal fighter, and her saber ran red with the blood of her enemies, and she laughed in their faces as power surged through her, setting her on fire. She was unstoppable. She was—

—she was fighting nearly alone, had pressed the soldiers too far and was now separated from her comrades, and she had to back up or risk being cut off completely. Dunevin was shouting at her, words she couldn't make out, and then someone took her place and she backed away into the other *tiermatha's* captain. "We've lost half our force!" he shouted in her ear. "We need to fall back!"

Imogen screamed at him wordlessly, feeling the need to kill overpowering her, and he struck her across the face. It brought her to her senses. She looked around and saw only fourteen warriors remaining upright. "Fall back! Fall back!" she shouted, and took up a position in the front rank to protect the retreating warriors. There were only three of them, and Imogen fought mechanically, counting the time it would take them to reach the fallback position, then the time it would take for them to take shelter and for the riflemen to ready their weapons. "Strike hard!" she roared, and the three of them cut down their opponents, turned, and ran as hard as they could.

The fallback position was an intersection where a large corridor met two smaller ones. Imogen and her fellow warriors pelted into the intersection and went to their knees, then crawled as fast as they could to either side. Diana's soldiers raced after them and ran into a solid wall of gunfire. Rifle balls and Device bullets riddled them, and they collapsed, screaming, while the Kirkellan crawled behind the barricades on either side and fell to the floor, spent.

The weapon fire went on for a while. Imogen sat up and surveyed her warriors. There were nine on her side, counting herself, Kallum, Saevonna, Revalan, and five of Dunevin's *tiermatha* whose names she didn't know. "Did everyone make it to the other side?"

"I think so. They were carrying the wounded. Jathan got hit pretty hard, maybe three others wounded slightly."

Imogen counted. "We've only lost three. Eight, if you count the ones too injured to fight."

"Is Kionnal...."

"I don't know. It looked bad. If Areli doesn't come back, that's a bad sign."

The rifle fire stopped. They heard shouting from the hallway, then more shouting from farther away. "That's not good," Revalan said.

They leaped to their feet, sabers drawn, as people came running down the hall behind them. "No, we're friends!" came the call, and several men and women in blue and silver appeared, swords in hand.

"We are glad to see you," Imogen said, coming forward and shifting her saber to her other hand so she could clasp the leader's. She had dark hair bound severely back at the nape of her neck and an elegant profile. "I am Imogen."

"I know who you are," the woman said with a smile. "Connie Anselm. Lieutenant Anselm. We're here to provide relief. Is this all that's left of your command?" Behind them, the rifle fire began again, and someone screamed. Anselm's smile grew broader.

"The others are across the intersection. What is happening?"

"The Baroness's troops were stopped at the rotunda. They had to find another way around, except we blocked all the other exits. But Colonel Williams said to tell you he thinks this is where the Baroness is making the real push. Do you know where your secondary fallback position is? You're supposed to join the troops back that way." She pointed in the direction of the north wing. "The rest of your warriors will have to go to the other fallback position, down that way. We'll hold this point as long as we can."

"We can help here," Imogen began, but Anselm shook her head.

"Orders," she said. "They want you to take command back there. You know what the colonel said—they depend on having you where you're told to be."

Imogen hesitated. More rifle fire sounded, telling her the attack had resumed. "Good luck," she said, and collected her warriors.

The corridor rose gently as they ran east. They passed several corridors, all blocked, and came to a place where their hallway crossed another. Imogen's heart sank. She knew the cross-path; it led directly to the north wing. Thirty or forty soldiers holding gun Devices relaxed when she came into view. "Ma'am," said one of the men, a short fellow with graying hair and a square, craggy face, "what are your orders?"

Imogen looked around. "No barricade?"

"They want us to have clean shots, nothing to get in the way. There's a barricade down there—" he pointed east, down a dark hall—"and the other hall leads to the prison complex, which is sealed off. So it's just that hall you came down we have to worry about, though we're watching the other way just in case."

"Then let us do that, and hope they do not pass Lieutenant Anselm."

"We'll know if they do because the lieutenant will haul ass in this direction."

"Good." A light went on. "Is she related to the general?"

"His only daughter. She's on her way up, and not because of who she's related to, either."

Imogen nodded. So Tremontanans went to war as families, too. "What is your name?"

"Trell, ma'am."

"Trell, send your runner to the lieutenant to tell her turn right when she gets here, into the prison corridor. We can set up an ambush. I will report to the north wing now."

The hall to the north wing was paneled in dark wood, somber and weighty, with a blue carpet that matched the North colors and muffled her footsteps. Steps rose to a short landing, then rose again to a broad hallway which opened up into the north wing. There was no door to bar entrance; there was no barricade; there were only doors lining the halls, and the reception desk, and about fifteen soldiers who lowered their weapons at her approach. "I want to see Colonel Williams," she said, and was silently allowed past the guard.

She had to poke around before she found the room the colonel had retreated to. Several runners sat on chairs or the floor in one corner; as Imogen watched, a woman handed one of them a note and the girl scampered off without waiting for instructions. Other men and women were gathered around a military telecoder with the air of people waiting for something. The colonel and Jeffrey looked up from the map they were studying. The colonel frowned; Jeffrey looked tense.

"I take it your people are outside the north wing now?" Williams asked. "Come look at this, see if there's anything you can add."

It was the sketch map of the palace, but now it was covered with circles and X's and lines drawn in red and green pencil. "This is the ground we've had to give up," Williams said, pointing. "And this is what we blockaded so they couldn't get at it easily. We've funneled their attack into just a few choke points and have managed to keep them there for far longer, frankly, than I'd hoped."

"What is this?" Imogen asked, tapping Ansom's Gate.

"Ansom's—oh, you mean the markings." A red X crossed through a green circle with some violence. "Your people held out longer than anyone else. It was green until just half an hour ago. Congratulations."

"I am only sorry we had to give way. We killed many of them and sent one to your—the place where the injured go."

"You sent an enemy soldier to the infirmary?" Jeffrey was incredulous.

"He is here because Diana tell—told him she is Queen and you are wrong. He wants what is best for Tremontane and I think he can learn you are that."

"I wondered why they'd turn on me." He turned a red pencil over and over again in his long fingers. "I would rather not execute them all for treason."

"Time to worry about that later, your Majesty. Madam ambassador—I suppose you're not that right now, are you?"

"Today I am a warrior. Tomorrow we will see." But the ambassador seemed more distant every moment.

"Well, Imogen, we're holding at these spots. The rotunda's finally clear, once they realized it was a death trap. I don't think I have to tell you how crucial your defense is."

"I see it—saw it when I came here. There is no barricade or door. There is only us."

"And that small handful of soldiers, yes. If the rest of the Army is to make a difference, they need to be here in the next few hours." He glanced at the telecoder. "They *have* to come."

"Something is wrong," Imogen guessed. "More wrong than Diana attacking you."

The telecoder began chattering. "Wait," Jeffrey said, holding up one hand. He went to stand over the operator, who was scribbling as fast as her pencil could move. Imogen saw his face go very still. When the telecoder went silent, and the operator laid her pencil down, Jeffrey said, "Fred, we have less than half a day."

"Half a day for what?" Imogen said. Jeffrey and Williams ignored her. "Half a day for *what?*" she insisted.

Williams shook his head. Jeffrey said, "She might as well know." He took Imogen's arm and drew her to an unoccupied corner of the room. "You know Max had someone in the telecoder room blocking the Army's messages about Diana's movements," he said quietly. "Then we had to abandon the room when we were preparing for the siege because it was indefensible. We didn't regain contact with the Army until about half an hour ago." He ran his hands through his hair, a now familiar gesture of frustration. "Diana's troops were at the far eastern edge of the new border, just outside Barony Daxtry. When the Army discovered she'd abandoned her post, the detachment just west of hers broke off to follow. It left a gap—"

Imogen cursed.

"Exactly," Jeffrey said. "The Ruskalder army is marching on Tremontane."

CHAPTER THIRTY

"But that is too convenient," Imogen said. "How could they be ready so soon?"

Jeffrey let out a long, deep breath. "Hrovald's army must have been gathering for a month, watching for a weakness in our border patrols. I can imagine what he thought when that gap appeared. It seems he started moving south when the troops chasing Diana had barely disappeared over the horizon."

"I do not understand. Burgess wanted you to move the troops south into Veribold. Did he and Diana want Hrovald to invade?"

"Max says they had no idea Hrovald's army was even there. He's nearly dead with terror—Max, I mean. Colluding with Diana *and* clearing the way for an enemy invasion, even by accident...anyway, the main body of our Army figured it out and started pursuing Hrovald, but...what it comes down to is Hrovald's army is going to be here in a matter of hours, twelve if we're lucky."

Imogen felt faint. "He will overrun us."

"The main Army is several hours behind Hrovald. It's absolutely imperative we end this now, so we can prepare to defend Aurilien. I've got people looking for Diana—she can't be so unreasonable as to want the city to fall."

"I do not agree with you."

"I have to take the risk. I can offer her exile rather than execution if she gives up. She *has* to see reason."

"I hope you are right. But I think you are not. It is more likely she will fight until she is dead."

"She'll come here either way," Jeffrey said. "She's always had a turn for the dramatic, so I imagine she'll want to gloat before she—"

"Do not say it," Imogen commanded, cutting him off. "You must not think this way."

He gave her a wry, bitter look, and turned away. She grabbed his wrist.

"This is for you," she said. "If you do not believe it is worth it then there is no point in us believing it."

"Imogen, I'm helpless," he said in a low voice. "Men and women have died, are dying, to keep me safe, and it's not going to be enough. It just seems ridiculous, that all of this stupid conflict is over one man's head."

"Then what will you do? Go to Diana and say, here I am, cut off my head and stop killing people? This is not about one man's head. It is about a country and two heads. Diana is bad for Tremontane. You are good for it. We fight to keep the country alive and you are just…I do not know the word. Your head is that of the country and I will die before I let it fall."

He looked at her in wonder. "It's not even your country."

That staggered her. Yes, Mother had sent the Kirkellan for just this reason, though she couldn't have foreseen these circumstances, but she had sent Imogen to be a Kirkellan in Aurilien, an observer and not a participant in Tremontanan matters. How Imogen's heart had become tangled up in Tremontanan affairs was…. She looked at Jeffrey's haggard, unshaven face. So it wasn't such a mystery after all. "Then I will fight because I like your head where it is," she said lightly.

He smiled at her. "Then I'm not helpless as long as I have you to wield that saber on my behalf. It's still covered in blood," he pointed out. Imogen pulled out the tail of her shirt and tried to wipe it off, but it had dried tacky and her shirt caught on the smears.

"It will pass when I again trample my enemies beneath my hooves," she said.

He grinned. "Pity we can't bring the horses indoors. We'd have half again as many warriors, and Diana's troops would all wet themselves in terror."

"I thought it too. The palace was not designed with horses in mind and perhaps it should have been."

"I'll pass that along to the palace architect." He took her free hand and squeezed it. "Go. Fight this battle."

"I will *win* this battle. You will see."

"And, Imogen?" He caught at her hand when she would have left. "Don't tell them about Hrovald. I don't want them falling into despair. Time enough to worry about it when this threat has passed."

"Then you do not fall into despair either, King of Tremontane." She grinned at him and ran back to her troops, her bloody saber dark red in the light of the Devices lining the walls, candles burning without flame. "The Army is coming in a few hours," she told them, "and we must stand firm until then." Another burst of rifle fire, another burst of screams, then silence. "We are better than they are and we have better position. We cannot let them pass. Rest, and be ready."

She couldn't take her own advice, was too restless to sit still. She paced the too-wide corridor, trying to become nothing but a pair of feet, a pair of legs, until Revalan stood in her way and refused to move. "You're making everyone nervous," he said, shifting his bulk to block her path again. "Especially those Tremontanans. Don't make me tie you to a chair."

"You don't have a chair."

"There's a barricade just down that way."

"All right! I'll stop." She said to Trell, "Sorry, I have extra energy because I wish to again bloody my saber."

"Hope you don't mind my saying this, ma'am, but none of us is that eager," Trell said. "We're fighting our fellow soldiers who are just in this because the Baroness told 'em lies. Don't think we're not prepared to do our duty, and all of us would die for the King if we had to, but it doesn't make us like it."

Imogen bowed her head. "I am sorry," she said. "It is not the same for us but I should have thought of how you would feel. You know you are doing the right thing."

"We do, ma'am, and we're glad to have you Kirkellan with us. Is it true you held out for three hours against the invaders?"

"I do not know how long it was. I think I need a Device that says what the time is. But it was long and tiring. So I should sit and rest now, I think."

She sat down next to what was left of her *tiermatha*. "How's your King holding up?" Revalan said.

"He's not my King. I'm a warrior of the Kirkellan," Imogen snapped.

Revalan held up his hands in self-defense. "That's not at all what I meant."

Imogen sighed. "Sorry, Rev."

"Where did that come from, anyway?" Saevonna said.

Imogen rubbed her eyes, which were dry and scratchy. "I don't know. Forget I said anything. The King is holding up about as well as you'd expect. I'd hate to have to sit somewhere and let someone else protect me."

"Remember when I broke my arm while we were on long patrol and the crag-wolves came?" Kallum said. "Nearly drove me crazy to have to sit by the fire while the rest of you hunted."

"I remember you bitched about it long enough we thought about sitting on your head to make you stop," said Revalan.

"Still, I feel for him. He's not a bad fighter, either. Did you ever spar with him, Imogen?"

She shook her head. "Never came up."

"Well, I did. He's damned fast, if a little undisciplined, though I was probably distracted by how good he looks with his shirt off."

"Kallum—"

"I'm not making suggestive comments! I'm just stating a fact."

Imogen slapped him upside the head. "Keep your facts to yourself, then." Kallum grinned at her and rubbed his head.

"I wonder how Kionnal and Dorenna are doing," Saevonna said. "Areli can't return to us even if…well, however Kionnal's doing, because that route's blocked off. I wish we had them here."

"So do I. Does it seem too quiet to you?"

They listened. No sounds of combat came from the western passage. Imogen got to her feet. "I'm going to check on them," she said, and then the distant shouting began again, this time louder. "Everybody take your positions," she said, and went to stand in the cross-hall leading to the north wing as if she could block it with her body alone. They waited, listening to the sounds of fighting rise and wane. Imogen's hand gripping her saber hilt was numb; she made herself relax again. Two eyes. Two ears. One heart that pounded too hard in her chest however relaxed she made herself. Two lungs that took in air and expelled it, calmly, regularly. He was depending on her. Two legs, balanced lightly on two feet. Two hands, one white and bloodless, the other streaked with too much blood, none of it hers. Whether she'd be able to say the same when this was all over was heaven's care and not hers.

Silence again, then shouts. It was driving her mad. "Stand down—" she began, then realized the shouting was coming closer and wasn't fading away. "This is it! Hold this position!" she shouted in Tremontanese, then repeated herself in Kirkellish. Across the way, Trell and most of his soldiers backed farther down the hall, staying out of sight of whoever was coming from the west. Another handful of Tremontanans faced the western hallway; the rest, including the Kirkellan, blocked the way into the north wing. Imogen flexed her fingers on the hilt of her saber, and waited.

Blue-coated soldiers emerged at a flat run from the western hallway and flung themselves toward Trell's group. Lieutenant Anselm flew past, turned, and took up a guard position in the eastern hallway. "They're coming!" she panted, unnecessarily, and Imogen's heart raced with the need to fight. *Now,* she thought, *they need to come* now.

As if in response to her thoughts, the first green and brown soldiers emerged from the hallway, their momentum great enough to carry them into the arms of the North soldiers opposite. Lieutenant Anselm swept her sword around in an arc that nearly cut the first one in half, and the soldiers behind her stepped up to join her. "Trell, *hold*!" Imogen shouted, and held up her hand to the Kirkellan. Not yet time to attack, hold…*hold*….

"Now!" she screamed, and she and Trell leaped forward at the same time, pressing the attack on three sides. It was close work, too close, not enough room to move, and Imogen saw some of Diana's soldiers working their way toward her position, trying to skirt the conflict and sneak past. She stepped back and they smiled, thinking she was

retreating. She bared her teeth at them—they might think it was a smile, but she had learned it from the crag-wolves, who were as merciless in battle as she was. She blocked the first swing contemptuously and spitted the soldier with her return thrust, raised her foot and pushed him off her blade and into his comrade hard enough to make him stagger. "You should go home," she told the second man, "there is nothing but death for you here."

The second man came in swinging more carefully than the first, and she blocked his first swing, then the next, brought up her saber toward his eyes and thrust for the heart; he blocked, and she grinned more widely. The rush of battle-lust rose up inside her, filling her with strength and agility that felt like nothing else in the world, it felt like life itself even as she brought her saber around, chopped at the man's knees and thrust hard at his chest when he tried to dodge. Bright red blood bubbled up around his lips as he slipped off her blade. He looked so surprised she nearly laughed, but had to save her attention for the next woman who came at her, sword raised incautiously; she sliced into her belly and saw the woman fall, clutching herself. She was so young, even younger than Imogen, with her eyes wide as if she couldn't understand where she was or how she'd got there—

—and Imogen had to duck and raise her blade quickly. That moment's inattention had nearly cost her her head. She thrust and parried and thrust again, shoving aside the compassion that had no place on the battlefield, even if that field was a palace hallway. Time to think about the morality of war later. Now was simply the fight, and the battle-lust, and stroke after stroke until her arm tired and she had to step back and let someone else take her place for the moment.

She squatted to catch her breath, laid her saber across her knees, and surveyed the scene with eyes that stung with sweat. The initial counterattack had worked; fighters on both sides were having to tread carefully because so many soldiers, blue and green, had fallen in the center of the intersection. But now Diana's soldiers had gotten their bearings and were pressing hard against the defenders of the north wing hall. There were enough of them that they'd managed to turn the pincer strategy against them, half the green soldiers engaging Trell's group, the other half fighting Imogen's, back to back, with Lieutenant Anselm's people hacking desperately away at the enemy, trying to drive a wedge between them.

One of Imogen's warriors fell, and she dragged the woman aside and took her place. Her throat felt raw from screaming defiance at the foe, the saber dragged at her arm, but she pressed forward, she would not let him down would not let him down *would not let him down*—

A familiar face startled her so much she dropped her guard for a split second. Diana was just as surprised to see her, which was all that saved Imogen from having her heart riven in two. She blocked Diana's thrust, shoved her hard so she stumbled back a few steps, then drove in for the kill, which Diana blocked. "Fat girl," Diana sneered, though her malice was diminished by how heavily she was breathing. "Thought I'd find you—" *oof*—"at your lover's side."

"My place is here, and here you are to fight me," Imogen panted, and struck again. She was so tired. If Diana had appeared two hours ago, this stupid little fight would have been over already.

Diana sliced at Imogen's throat, and Imogen parried, though not easily. "I would have been content to be Consort, you know," Diana said, breathing hard, "rule through the King, I would have been satisfied with that. But *you* came along—" she parried a blow that would have taken her head off— "and I realized that wasn't enough for me. Any King who thinks a foreigner is worthy to share the Crown deserves to have it taken from him."

"You are too wrong even for me to tell you all the wrong you are," Imogen said. She didn't have the breath to spare, but she couldn't help herself. "I am not Consort and I not become Consort. You do not deserve the Crown." She would not die here. She would not die by this woman's hand. She was so tired.

"Deserve? That doesn't enter into it. I can take it, that makes it mine." Diana swept Imogen's blade aside, and all at once her left side erupted with pain. She tried to scream, but her throat had closed up. She was so tired, and now she hurt. Diana's sword, bright with blood—with *her* blood—passed before her eyes. She tried to collapse, but Diana's claw gripped the neck of her jerkin and pulled her close, eye to bloodshot, maniacal eye. "I wanted to arrange for you to die in front of him," Diana said, "but just you dying will have to satisfy me." She shoved Imogen away; Imogen, her arms and legs weak with exhaustion and pain, couldn't keep herself from falling hard against the wall. She tasted blood, pain shot through her head, and she remembered nothing more.

Echoes of voices. She was at the bottom of a deep well. Far above, light and shadow and noise, but here at the bottom of the well…no, she was rising, floating upward, the black sides of the well going gray and then rolling up on themselves, vanishing. She was lying on the floor at an awkward angle—no, she was lying on someone's body, and the awkward angle was because her back was arched painfully across the corpse. Everything was too bright and echoed too loudly. People were fighting all around her. She couldn't remember how she'd gotten there. Fighting, growing tired, Diana—

Imogen tried to sit up, her heart pounding in terror, but her body wasn't responding. Her side was on fire. Diana had stabbed her. Eyes prickling with tears, she fumbled around her clothing until she could feel her side. Bloody, painful, but…it was fairly deep, but wasn't anywhere near her vital organs. Stupid Diana and her stupid love of the dramatic hadn't bothered to see just how solidly she'd connected. Imogen tried to rise again, and this time managed to get to her feet. Her vision went black for a moment, and she leaned heavily on her saber, making it bend alarmingly. She breathed deeply, making herself remain calm even as terror sped like a knife-edged wind through her brain, *hurry hurry hurry she's got him now, capture the King and you win the game*—

The fighting was confined to the cross-hall; the route to the north wing was absurdly clear, as if someone had drawn an invisible line and said "thus far, and no farther" to the combatants. Only the bodies of soldiers here and there along the way revealed there had been fighting in this hallway at all.

The blue and silver soldiers who'd been the last line of defense were gone, mostly, though one slumped against the reception desk as if he were taking a nap. He looked up at her as she passed and mouthed a word she couldn't understand. The only sound came from the fighting, far behind her. Her heart felt as if it were trying to smash its way through her ribs, her side hurt, and she was still having trouble seeing. She dragged her way toward Jeffrey's command room. She had no idea what she would do when she got there, since she didn't think she could lift her saber more than waist high, but she could…she could throw herself on Diana, crush her under her weight, pity she didn't weigh twice as much as she did, *this saber is getting really heavy and the lights shouldn't be flashing like that, should they?*

The door to the command room stood open. She could hear Diana speaking in that swooping way she did when she was telling someone how wonderful she was. That meant Jeffrey was still alive. Her exhausted heart tried to react to this with joy, but she felt only weariness.

"…too late for any other solution."

"Diana, we have a common enemy here. Don't be a fool. Hrovald will destroy the city if we don't stop him, your forces and mine together." That was Jeffrey, sounding unharmed if a bit tired.

"But with you still in command and your ass firmly placed upon the throne. You think I don't know what it means if I give in to you now?"

"You don't have to die. You can go into exile. I'll even pardon your officers. Just let this end."

Diana laughed. "You forget who has the upper hand here."

"I'll admit you have me outnumbered. I'm counting on your officers—*my* officers—being unwilling to murder their King."

"My officers are loyal to me, not to you, Jeffrey. It's what happens when you fight together, day after day, for years on end."

Imogen came out of her reverie, blinked away the grayness at the edges of her vision, and pushed the door farther open so she could see into the room. Diana, her back to the door, stood opposite Jeffrey. They both had their swords in a rest position. Between Diana and Imogen stood five men and women in green and brown Tremontanan uniforms. They were armed as well, but held their swords ready for an attack. Colonel Williams lay collapsed on the map table, blood pooling beneath his body, and a couple of blue and silver soldiers ranged themselves around Jeffrey, their swords also drawn and ready to attack. They looked tense and afraid. She couldn't tell how Diana's officers felt. She stepped into the room a few paces, then stopped, uncertain what to do.

Jeffrey saw her. His eyes widened, and his lips parted in amazement. *"Imogen,"* he said.

Diana laughed. "The fat bitch is dead, Jeffrey. That's a pathetic ruse."

"The fat bitch is right here and thinks your aim is bad," Imogen said.

Diana's head whipped around. Quick as a snake, Jeffrey's sword was up and plunged into Diana's stomach nearly to the hilt, angled upward to strike the heart. Unlike Diana, Jeffrey's aim was excellent. Her head came back around, and she stared at Jeffrey with the same amazed look he'd just given Imogen. She looked down at the hilt of his sword, at his hand spotted with her blood, then sagged at the knees. Jeffrey withdrew his sword and let her collapse onto the bloody floor. "This ends now," he said in a cold, cutting voice. "Drop your weapons and you won't hang for treason. One chance. Now."

Swords thumped to the floor, bouncing hollowly as they struck the soft carpet. "Good," said Jeffrey. "Go out there and tell your soldiers to stand down. They won't suffer for their leader's idiocy either, but if the killing doesn't stop *now,* they're going to suffer for their own. Go!" he shouted, and they scrambled to flee. One of them bumped into Imogen, who rocked unsteadily, then collapsed. She closed her eyes and felt the world steady beneath her.

Arms, lifting her up. "Imogen, Imogen, sweetheart, look at me," Jeffrey said. She opened her eyes and blinked at him. It must be the blood loss that made him seem so far away. "She said you were dead. Did she injure you? All right, I see it, just—how stupid, I was going to say 'stay right there'—"

He went away, and she heard a tearing sound, then he came back and pressed a wad of cloth into her side. "Can you hold that? You, yes, both of you, get her to the infirmary immediately. *Now!*"

Two sets of hands supported her to her feet and helped her walk.

Her vision was clearing. "I guess we won," she murmured.

CHAPTER THIRTY-ONE

She wouldn't have made it down the steps to the ballroom without their help. Cots occupied every inch of space that wasn't taken up by bedrolls. Her assistants half-carried her to a bedroll and helped her lie down. That was so much better. The ceiling, high above, was painted to look like a starry, moonless night. How strange that she'd been in here so many times and never thought to look up.

"Let's have a look," said a woman wearing a doctor's tunic, and removed the cloth from Imogen's clutching fingers. She bit back a yelp when the woman accidentally jabbed her side. "Sorry about that. We can have it bound up in no time. Edmund, bring my kit over here, please! I don't have anything for the pain, it has to go to the more desperate cases, so I apologize for how this will hurt."

It hurt, but not badly, and when the deep wound had been packed with gauze and bandaged Imogen felt so much better. She lay staring at the starry sky, working out familiar constellations, until Dorenna said, "Some people will do anything for a lie-down, won't they?" She sat down by Imogen's head.

"I see your brains are still where they should be," Imogen said.

"Nice that you acknowledge I have some. Kionnal's going to be fine in a few weeks. Probably piss red for a while, but the doctor was able to patch him up. Saevonna isn't doing quite as well. Got hit in the chest and it collapsed her left lung. She's waiting on the palace healer, who seems well past overworked...Imogen, Marcus is with her."

"Good. She needs that kind of support, given that we seem to have abandoned her."

"No, it's...she.... He asked her again, and she said yes." Dorenna clenched her fists in her lap. "She's staying here."

Imogen felt as if Diana's sword tore through her body again. "It makes sense," she said, her voice wobbly. "It's the best choice for her."

"It's a *stupid* choice," Dorenna said. "What is she supposed to do here? Sit around and have his babies and tend his house and never fight again? *We* are what she is, Imogen, and she's going to regret this choice forever!"

"Dorenna, keep your voice down!"

"We have to stop her, Imo. She has to see reason."

"Dor, stop. You know Saevonna. She never does anything without thinking it through."

"She's also sickeningly optimistic. She sees her handsome lover and thinks because they're in love, it will make everything all right. It doesn't work that way."

A tear trickled down the side of Imogen's face. "You haven't been paying attention. She's *thriving* here, Dor. It's not just Marcus. She speaks the language and she's comfortable with the society. It's like there was this whole side of her waiting to appear."

"But she's Kirkellan. That's no less her than this ridiculous fantasy."

"She had to choose. She didn't choose—" Imogen's throat closed on the words. She swallowed, painfully, and said, "She didn't choose us. And we can't make her change her mind."

"I thought I could count on you in this."

"I'm not going to tell Saevonna how to live her life. And you aren't either. How happy will she be if we force her to stay with us?"

"But she's going to regret it!"

"That's not our concern."

Dorenna scowled. "Imogen, you're not going to lie there and tell me you think she really made the right decision? Leaving behind everything she knows?"

Another tear crawled after the first. "I don't know."

"Well, you'd better figure it out," Dorenna said, "because I'll bet my horse your King is going to ask you the same question."

"Dor, I—"

"I can't talk about this any longer, Imogen, I'm sorry." She pushed herself to her feet and almost ran away. Imogen lifted herself on one elbow and watched her go, then lay back and wiped the wet trail from her cheek.

That wasn't a bet she would take. She was certain Jeffrey loved her and was equally certain he wouldn't want her to leave when her year was up. Her own feelings were far less certain. Yes, she cared for him; yes, if she had to she could make a life for herself in Tremontane. But the idea of leaving the wild plains, of condemning Victory to a life on hard cobblestones and laps around the parade ground.... She closed her eyes tight and clenched her fists. *It will be easier*, she thought, *if I can keep him from asking the question. Maybe mother will understand this, if I tell her I need to come home early.* Then she thought of leaving Aurilien, of leaving him and Elspeth and Owen and Alison behind, and her heart ached. There would be no easy choice. Better all around if he didn't ask the question.

"Are you in pain? I'm sure they can give you something for that." She opened her eyes and saw Jeffrey bending over her. She shook her head and relaxed her fists. He still looked terrible, even upside-down as he appeared from this perspective, and her heart beat faster at the sight of him.

"I am only thinking of not pleasant things. I do not hurt much."

"I'm glad. What not-pleasant things?"

"They are not pleasant so I think I will not tell you. And I feel better to see you."

He sat cross-legged on the floor near her head and took her hand in his. "When she told me she'd killed you, I didn't believe it—couldn't believe she could overpower a warrior like you—but she was so triumphant...and then you appeared in the doorway and I felt all that fear and uncertainty just disappear."

"You killed her. It is a good thing."

"I've never felt so certain of anything in my life. It felt as though—no, never mind."

"That is not a no never mind face."

He sighed. "It felt as though I was finally King in my own right, and not because of my father. It just seems callous for that feeling to come at the cost of someone's life."

"You have always been King in your own right. You have only just learned it is true. When you tell them, drop your weapons now, I hear it and they hear it in your voice. And I am callous too because I think if

Diana does anything good with her life it can at least be to make you see truth finally."

He laughed. "Madam ambassador, you are very wise."

"I only tell you what is true. If that is wise, then I must be wise."

"I depend on you to tell me the truth." He smiled at her, his blue eyes crinkling at the corners. Then he looked up at something she couldn't see, and said, "I have to go now. I'll see you later."

Hrovald. "Then I am coming too," she said, and struggled to stand. Jeffrey pressed her back down onto the bedroll with ease.

"You're in no condition to fight," he said. "You need to stay put."

"This wound is nothing. It is a scratch."

"You won't do me any good if you collapse again."

"Then I will not collapse. Move your arm."

Jeffrey swore and stood up. "I won't help you."

"I do not need help." She stood and the room turned a slow circle around her. She felt Jeffrey's hands support her. "You said you would not help," she said faintly.

"You said you wouldn't collapse." His face swam into focus in front of her. "Imogen, this is madness."

"Do you have enough soldiers that you can waste even this one?"

"I— " He looked over her shoulder again. "I really do have to go. For the last time, will you please rest?"

"I will rest when I have received my orders."

He sighed. "Then you might as well come with me. Fred—damn." His eyes went distant. "I keep forgetting Fred is gone. Colonel Haverson's a good man, but…well." He offered Imogen his arm. "Don't think this means I approve of you trying to kill yourself," he said.

She patted his hand. "I will show you I am well enough when I cut down my enemies before me."

"If we do this right, it won't come to that," Jeffrey said.

Imogen held herself straight in the saddle. Her side throbbed, but no one needed to know that. Unfortunately, she couldn't conceal it from Victory, who jigged restlessly and had to be calmed every five minutes.

"Glad to be back where you belong?" Revalan said.

"Ready to wet my blade with Ruskalder blood, is more like it."

"It does feel more natural, fighting them," Kallum said. "I rather like some of these Tremontanans."

"Not as much as *some* people do," Dorenna muttered. Imogen glared at her. They hadn't told the rest of the *tiermatha* what Saevonna had chosen. No point distracting them from the job at hand.

"What was that?"

"Nothing," Dorenna said. "I hate waiting, is all."

"You understand the best outcome is for us not to fight at all?" Imogen said.

Dorenna scowled. "Best for who?"

"You're bloodthirsty today," Kallum remarked.

"*You* didn't have to sit out the last fight thanks to a purely imaginary injury."

"You were seeing double," Areli said, "and bumping into things and apologizing to things that weren't there."

"Fine. It was a real injury. The point is now I'm better and I'm ready to do what we do best."

Imogen petted Victory again. Fighting was what she did best. The life of the ambassador seemed so far away she could barely remember what it was like, let alone compare it with that of the warrior. She remembered the heat of battle filling her skin to bursting with power, but instead of joy at the memory she felt only emptiness. Impatience overcame her, and she said "Wait here" to her company and trotted toward the main gate. She didn't have any reason to be there, but she needed to move, needed to do *something* to keep from driving herself crazy.

The defenders had closed the iron-banded, iron-studded gates and levered two vast wooden bars into place to hold them shut. Soldiers ran up and down the stone stairs on either side of the gate that led to the top of the city wall. Riflemen took up positions behind hastily erected wooden battlements that lined the wall-walk. Marcus might be one of them, though he could just as likely be at one of the other two gates.

Imogen thought of Saevonna, still lying in the infirmary, and of Kionnal, whose condition was just bad enough that the doctor had forbidden him to rise. She'd tried to prevent Imogen from leaving too, but Jeffrey had said, "Don't bother, doctor, she's too stubborn to make it worth your while," and Imogen had held her head straight and pretended not to be in pain until the room was far behind them.

Colonel Haverson looked up as she approached with a faintly puzzled expression. "Can I help you with something, commander?" Haverson was a slender man with a slender mustache whose pale brown eyes never settled on anything for more than a few seconds.

Imogen cast about for something to say. "I am just curious about the defenses," she said, hoping she sounded confident.

"Are you sure you don't want to fight on foot? This strategy seems pretty dangerous," he said.

"We are more comfortable in the saddle and there is not enough room for all of us at the gate or on the wall. We are…experienced at harrying a larger force. Do not worry about us."

"I saw you Kirkellan in action the first time we faced this bastard. I'd believe just about anything of you. We should have the runners here shortly. Good luck, commander."

He saluted her, and she returned the gesture and rode directly up to the gate. It certainly looked solid enough to keep out an attack, but Hrovald, no doubt furious at his earlier humiliation, would be even more determined than Diana to have his revenge. Could Hrovald turn those thick-trunked trees with their curving branches into battering rams? She went close enough to the gate to lay her palm against it. No, it would hold. It had to hold long enough for the Tremontanan Army to reach them. As confident as she'd sounded talking to Haverson, she wasn't at all sure it was a good idea for their diminished company to assault Hrovald's army from behind. They would be like gnats worrying a stallion's flank. But it was either that or wait, impatient and useless, as part of the masses of foot soldiers preparing to defend the gates and walls, and Kirkellan were not, in general, good at waiting for things.

She rode back to her *tiermatha*, sadly reduced now, and the other *tiermathas* under her temporary command. "Try to stay focused," she told them. "When Hrovald's army arrives, it's likely he'll set all his warriors at the main gate, but runners will come from the other two to report on whether he's striking at them as well. We'll clear one of those smaller gates and use it to attack his flank—out of the gate, make our run, then back for a breather. When the Army gets here, we'll provide as much support as we can. But it may be some time before they arrive, so rest, eat something, walk around on your own feet for a bit."

"You going to take your own advice? You're awfully keyed up," Areli said as warriors dismounted all around them.

"Just eager for the fight to start."

"I think she's afraid if she dismounts, she'll fall over," Kallum said, eyeing her speculatively.

"I will not. I'm not badly injured. Everyone needs to stop making such a fuss."

A murmur went up from the battlements. All heads turned in that direction. "Here it comes," Imogen whispered.

They waited for an agonizing eternity before a roar went up from outside the gates. Imogen glanced at Revalan; the sound was familiar to them, but another murmur went up from the soldiers manning the wall-walk, this one with an edge of fear to it. Imogen cantered to the gate and rode back and forth across the road, shouting, "They are just men! They will bleed and die at your swords! You are soldiers of Tremontane and *you will not fall!*"

Another roar went up, ragged but loud, this time from the defenders. "Make them fear you!" Imogen screamed, and the defenders on the wall and the men and women waiting on the ground roared out with one voice, shouting defiance at the enemy.

Imogen returned to her *tiermatha*, and said, "What?"

"You know what," Kallum said. "You realize they have leaders for that sort of thing, right?"

"Leaders who don't know enough about the Ruskalder to know how to respond. They needed my help."

Dorenna scowled. "You're not one of them, Imo."

"You think the Ruskalder are going to let us walk out of here unharmed just because we aren't Tremontanans?"

"I think you've forgotten—" Dorenna began hotly.

Areli punched her on the arm. "Shut up," she said. "The Ruskalder army is about to overrun this place. Let's fight them and not each other."

"No, I want to hear this," Imogen said, pitching her voice over the sound of rifle fire and the shouts of fighters on both sides of the gate. She took hold of Rapier's reins just above where Dorenna held them bunched loosely in her fist and tugged. "What have I forgotten, Dorenna?"

Dorenna cast a bitter glance at Areli. "You think like a Tremontanan now," she said. "You've already made your choice."

She felt as if she'd been slapped. "What did you just say?"

"I told you to shut up, Dorenna," Areli warned.

"Why, because I'm the only one willing to point it out? You weren't acting like a foreign auxiliary in that palace battle, Imo. You were planning strategy and giving orders like any other Tremontanan captain. You've already picked a side. You're just not willing to admit it."

Imogen barely kept herself from striking her. "Don't you *dare* tell me I don't know my own mind," she snarled. "You and Areli were the ones who told me I should pursue him. Didn't it occur to you this is where it might lead?"

"I sure as hell didn't think it would lead to you forgetting who you are."

"What is *wrong* with you, Dor? Battle's been joined and you want to pick a fight over some hypothetical future choice I'm going to make?"

"Because it shouldn't even *be* a choice!" Dorenna's face was flushed and furious. "You are *Kirkellan*, Imo, not some skirt-wearing city dweller. I don't care how well you think you've adapted, this is not who you are. You think love is going to be enough to make up for everything you'd have to leave behind, your family, your *tiermatha,* your training? It's not true for Saevonna and it's a hundred times worse for you."

"Wait, what about Saevonna?" Revalan said.

Imogen ignored him. "I am not in love—"

Dorenna threw up her hands. "Thundering heaven, Imogen, would you for the love of all that is holy wake up and take a look at your life? You are in love with Jeffrey North and you look to be the only one who doesn't know it."

Imogen looked at the others, stunned. Revalan wouldn't meet her eyes. Kallum shrugged and nodded. Areli reached out to grasp Imogen's hand. "It's really obvious," she said.

"*Think*," Dorenna pleaded. "You don't belong here. None of us do."

Imogen shook her head. "It's not that simple."

"Then explain it to me. Explain it so I can understand how you can even contemplate choosing him over us."

"It has nothing to do with Jeffrey," Imogen began.

"It has something to do with him," Areli pointed out.

"Is someone going to explain what's going on with Saevonna?" Revalan asked.

"Please stop talking!" Imogen said. "It's not about him. It's about who I am. I was born to be a warrior and that's all I was, and then I came here and I learned there are so many other things I can do, things I am, that I never would have guessed existed. And, Dorenna, those things are just as much me as fighting and riding are, so yes, it is a choice, and it's not an easy one, and no one's actually asked me to make it yet so I'm not sure why we're even fighting over this!"

Dorenna yanked Rapier's reins away from Imogen's hand. "We're fighting," she said, struggling to keep her composure, "because I don't want you to throw your life away like Saevonna did. And I'm not going to sit silent and let you make the wrong decision. I may not have blue eyes and a chiseled jaw, but I care about you too." She jerked on her reins and wheeled around to join the rear ranks.

"What in the hell is wrong with Saevonna?" Revalan exploded.

"I should go after her," Kallum said, but Imogen held up her hand.

"Let her be alone for a bit, Kallum," she said. "Saevonna agreed to marry Marcus and stay in Aurilien with him. What with Lorcun and Maeva dead, and Kionnal being so wounded, I think she thinks our *tiermatha* is falling apart."

"She made it sound as if Saevonna had done something awful,"

Revalan rumbled.

"You don't think she has?" Areli said. "She's more or less abandoning us."

"No more than if she'd decided to marry and raise a family in the Eidestal. She'd have to leave the *tiermatha* for that, too," he said. "So what if she chose to marry a foreigner instead?"

"I—" Areli began, then shook her head. "It just feels wrong, that's all."

"Your feelings shouldn't be the basis for Saevonna's life," Revalan pointed out.

"Is it wrong for me to wish the Ruskalder would just smash that gate in?" Kallum said. "Because that is just the kind of uncomplicated thing I could use right now."

As he spoke, something cracked into the gate from the other side with a hard, thudding noise. "Axes," Imogen said. She turned Victory so she was facing the gate. "Stand ready!" she shouted.

The rifle fire redoubled. The axes struck again, but more raggedly, as if some had dropped out of the chorus and the others had lost the beat. Peripherally, Imogen was aware of someone coming up beside her. "Do you think they'll break through?" Dorenna asked.

"Depends on if those riflemen can shoot straight down. I'm more worried about keeping the Ruskalder off the walls." She was tempted to leap down and run up the stairs to see what the army looked like, but she curbed the impulse. It wasn't as if she'd never seen the Ruskalder army before.

"I told the third *tiermatha* to spread out. They were bunched up to one side."

"Thanks."

"Rapier's feeling restive. I guess he needed to calm down some."

"I think Victory wishes she'd taken a walk, too."

"She looks good. Ready for battle."

"So does Rapier."

They waited silently, listening to the thud of axes and the screams of men shoved off the wall by its defenders. "I wish life could be more like a battle," Dorenna said. "Everything's so clear and unambiguous."

Imogen nodded. "No worries about maybes and mights. Just your saber in the other man's belly."

"Exactly."

"Commander?" A young soldier ran toward them, breathing heavily. "Colonel Haverson says to take the west gate, it's nearly clear."

The thud of the axes was joined by a tearing sound. "They're breaking through," Imogen said. "We'd better hurry. Form up, everyone, and follow me!" she shouted, maneuvering Victory through the horses and riders thronging the broad street. Behind her, the tearing sound grew louder. She wondered if the soldiers left to defend against the incursion would be demoralized by what looked like a retreat. No time to worry about that. She cleared the mob and nudged Victory into a trot, the fastest gait she was willing to risk on these slick cobbles. Behind her, the deserted buildings echoed with the sharp *clack* of iron-shod hooves on stone as seventy Kirkellan warriors fell into step behind her, drowning out the shouts of battle as they trotted through the streets toward the west gate. Citizens had fled their homes and businesses to shelter in the palace, which thanks to Diana's assault was no guarantee of safety. Jeffrey was in there somewhere, as was the rest of the North family, all of them depending on the Army to stand fast. Depending on her.

The west gate was a smaller version of the main gate, wide enough for two horses to pass abreast and blackened from a long-ago fire. It was also unnaturally still. Even the soldiers stationed on the wall were silent, without even the quiet sounds of armor shifting with its wearers' movements.

Imogen dismounted and ran up the wall to speak to the captain. She looked out over the nearby woods and across to the untrodden fields; not a sign of movement, enemy or otherwise.

"You can see they haven't bothered to come here," said the captain, his head cocked as if listening. Imogen held still and heard the faint noise of battle drifting toward them.

"It is the main gate they want," she said.

The captain turned to face her. "Heaven help them if they can't hold out," he said.

"They will," Imogen said, praying it was true. "We are ready if your soldiers will open the door for us."

He nodded. "Ready the gate," he shouted, and said to Imogen, "Good luck, commander."

They exchanged salutes, and Imogen returned to her company. She mounted Victory, feeling a rising excitement her horse picked up on. The horse underneath you, the saber in your hand, a scream of defiance on your lips, these were things she understood.

"Would you have believed, a year ago, that today we'd be leading a charge against a Ruskalder army from inside a Tremontanan city?" Kallum said, taking a position on her left.

"It's hard for me to believe any of the things that have happened to us since last summer," Imogen said. The bars were clear and two teams stood ready in front of the doors. "But right now, right here, I know exactly who I am."

She waved at the teams, then raised her fist and shouted a command. The gates swung ponderously open, and the Kirkellan set out to find the enemy in a wild chorus of screams and a thunder of giant hooves.

Chapter Thirty-Two

They cleared the woods that came nearly to the gate and spread out across the wide, green fields, grouped loosely by *tiermathas*, though most of them had so many members missing they couldn't fall into standard formations. It took them nearly five minutes of cantering to come within sight of Hrovald's army, at which point Imogen signaled the *tiermathas* to pull up and wait while she examined the field of battle.

"The army's smaller than it was when we fought them before," Kallum said.

Imogen nodded. "Still several thousand strong, but…look at that. Five banners."

"So?" Revalan said.

"There were nine last time. Hrovald's lost the support of some of his chiefs. Hah! I told him that would happen. I like being right."

"He's still got enough warriors to overrun the city," Kallum said. "And here we are just standing around."

"Right." She scanned the field until she found what she wanted. "Left rear banner, the one with the…I don't know what that is, it looks like a hand with seven fingers. Looks like he's hanging back a bit. Let's encourage him to flee. Running strikes on the diagonal, wait for the group ahead of you to get clear before going in—no point us stepping all over ourselves. Riders with javelins first, two passes, then sabers take three runs and back here to catch your breath. Any questions? Then *forward, Kirkellan*!"

She shouted a command to Victory, who leaped to obey, her speed increasing until they were flying over the ground toward the Ruskalder army. Every jolt sent a spike of pain through her side, and Imogen gritted her teeth and squeezed the hilt of her saber so hard she felt it should crumple under her hand. This was nothing. Barely worth noticing. She could give in to the pain later. Now was the time to pass that pain on to others.

The air was filled with war cries and the screams of the dying. The great gate hung open awkwardly, one half dangling from a twisted iron hinge, the other flung wide, and the entire Ruskalder army pressed forward, every warrior intent on forcing his way through the gap. They had no idea the Kirkellan were upon them until the first hail of javelins flew. Men fell and died and were trampled by their panicking fellow warriors, who fell in turn under the second wave. Imogen swept in, saber raised, raked a man across the face with a short slash and drove her saber through another man's heart. Two more strokes, and she was out and circling around for another pass. She laughed, throwing her head back and letting the sun warm her body, for the moment pain-free. She—

--there had been another time, the sun on her face and loose strands of hair blowing in the wind, only she hadn't been alone—

--and she blinked the memory away. She was preparing to ride down more Ruskalder warriors, and *that* was the memory her pain-addled mind dredged up? She clenched her teeth against another spike of pain. Thinking of Jeffrey wouldn't win this battle. She looked back over the battlefield and felt a moment's dismay. There were so many of them, and so few defenders. From here she could barely see the highest tower of the palace, its old stone dark in the afternoon light. She swiped loose hair out of her face. It would not fall. She would not allow it.

The Ruskalder recovered from their initial shock and were ready when the next wave of attacks came, and Imogen traded blows with one without doing more than wind both of them before she had to disengage. She was tiring already, damn Diana and her damned sword. Her vision was graying at the edges, but she continued her third pass, swept by without engaging anyone, and rode off in the direction of the rendezvous point, desperately clinging to her saddle. Victory, thank heaven, was smart enough to stop in the right place without being told. Imogen fumbled for her flask and drank deeply, wishing it were something a great deal stronger than water.

"Imogen, go back to the city," Areli said.

"I'm fine."

"You think we didn't notice that last pass of yours? You nearly fell off Victory."

"I did not. And I'm fine now."

"You said that. We don't believe it," said Revalan.

"I'm not leaving this battle."

"The hell you aren't," Dorenna said. "You think you're doing us any good, us watching all the time to see you don't collapse and get yourself and Victory killed? I don't know what you think you have to prove, but *I'd* go back if I were in your condition, so that ought to tell you something."

Imogen shook her head. "All right," she said, "I won't fight. But I can still command from here."

Kallum shrugged. He looked at the other three. "I think that's the best compromise we're going to get out of her. Don't leave this spot, Imogen."

"I won't. Falling into a Ruskalder horde and getting hacked to pieces isn't how I want to end my days." Imogen dried her saber on her trouser leg and sheathed it. "Five minutes' breather, and then back in," she called to the assembled Kirkellan. "Press harder this time, but be careful—they might pursue you when you retreat."

She and Victory went as close as they dared to the army for another look. The chief whose men they'd attacked wasn't watching the main gate anymore. He was too distant for her to make out his expression, but she would bet he was considering turning his warriors loose on them. If he did, they'd have to flee to the gate and barricade it, because they couldn't take on four or five hundred Ruskalder with only the seventy—she turned and quickly counted—yes, seventy riders, they hadn't lost anyone yet. On the other hand, Hrovald didn't like his chiefs to show initiative, and he might view the chief's opportunism in the same light as desertion. Time to make this chief even more conflicted.

"Ride, Kirkellan, ride!" Imogen shouted, and the riders flew out across the fields once more. No more javelins; now it was strictly saber work. The *tiermathas* came at the Ruskalder in groups, now, spaced out along the enemy's line. A horse went down, its rider caught up by another Kirkellan. A rider took an unlucky blow to his sword arm and was pulled down by the Ruskalder who'd struck him; his horse reared up, struck, and the rider scurried dangerously beneath his mount's hooves to safety. They were making inroads against the Ruskalder, and the chief stood up on his mount—a beautiful black Kirkellan stallion, they really should take it away from him—and waved his hands. If he shouted anything, it was lost in the noise of battle, but immediately there was a surge as the chief's part of the Ruskalder army turned to attack the Kirkellan instead of pressing forward to the main gate.

"Fall back!" Imogen screamed, but they didn't need to be told. They ran toward her, chased by the Ruskalder, and Imogen, satisfied that they'd outrun the nearest pursuit, turned and led the retreat to the west gate.

The soldiers had hauled open the doors for them before they arrived. Imogen pounded full-speed through the gate, skidding on the cobblestones, and got Victory turned around just in time to see the gate swing shut and the bars drop down to secure it. She trotted back to the gate and listened to the furious cries of the Ruskalder pounding at the door. "They do not have axes," she observed to the captain.

"Nor rams nor ladders nor grappling hooks," he said. "You must have pissed them off royally. They're mostly just screaming and beating their fists on the wood like a drunken husband come home late wanting his wife to open up."

"Does this wall-walk go all the way around? I want to see the army."

"It's not in the best repair, but you might be able to walk far enough to get an eyeful."

Imogen dismounted. "Watch Victory," she said, handing her reins to Kallum. "I'll be back soon."

"Imogen—"

"I'm *fine,* Areli. I'm just going to stroll along the wall and see how Hrovald reacted to his chief's defection. No straining myself." The pain had dulled to a throb, though tiny shooting pains still flared as she ran—no, better walk—up the steps to the wall-walk. She looked over the wall at the teeming mob of Ruskalder shouting below. One of them saw her and pointed; she waved, and the pointing turned into a much ruder gesture she returned cheerfully.

She made it nearly a third of the way around the wall before she reached a gap she couldn't cross, not without tearing something. She leaned out as far as she could and watched the distant battle. The army looked distinctly ragged, particularly on the side they'd assaulted. She wished she could see Hrovald's face right now, and then put her saber through it.

A light winked at her, far off under the afternoon sun. She shielded her eyes and squinted. Something was moving. Something big. Something that glinted with the light of the sun reflected off thousands of armor plates and hundreds of harnesses. The Army had come, and it had brought the Kirkellan with it.

She ran, her hand pressed against her side, until she was almost back to the gate, then slowed her pace so her *tiermatha* wouldn't yell at her. "The Army's coming!" she shouted as soon as she was within earshot. "I saw horses with them. They're almost here!"

Cheers overwhelmed the sound of the Ruskalder beating impotently on the gate. "We can't get out," Revalan complained. "We'll have to wait until the Ruskalder leave to rejoin the fight."

Imogen threw herself onto Victory's back and stifled a grunt of pain. "I'm going to make sure the defenders at the main gate know about this," she said. "They were hard pressed and I'm not sure anyone's aware of anything beyond the fight at hand."

"We'll come with you," Dorenna said.

"Why bother? This will keep me out of the fight. Suppose the Ruskalder withdraw while I'm gone? You wouldn't want to miss that."

Dorenna scowled. "This had better not be a clever plan to get yourself killed."

"If I were clever, would I have let that bitch inside my guard? I'll be back."

The sound of fighting never disappeared as she crossed the city; the noise at the west gate faded and was replaced by a much harsher, higher-pitched chorus of fury and pain as she neared the main gate. She didn't remember it had been breached until she turned a corner and found herself in the middle of a war. The Ruskalder had forced their way through the main gate and were being held in check only barely; dozens had made it past the choke point at the gate and were fighting, or lying dead, along the main road. Soldiers still battled along the wall, trying to keep the Ruskalder from breaking through that way. Far too many soldiers in blue and silver, or green and brown, lay crumpled in death at the gate or along the base of the wall.

Imogen found Colonel Haverson standing halfway up the stairs on the right side of the gate. She shouted her news to him, but he shook his head indicating he couldn't hear her and came down the stairs to meet her. She repeated herself, and he looked grim. "Might not matter unless they can get here in the next half hour. We won't be able to hold them much longer. We should fall back to the palace while we can."

"But the palace gates are all destroyed. The Ruskalder will run over you and everyone there." *Elspeth, Owen. Alison. Saevonna and Kionnal. Jeffrey.*

"They're about to overrun us here. Unless you have another suggestion?"

"Please hold her," Imogen said, sliding off Victory and thrusting her reins into the surprised colonel's hand. She went up the stairs at a fast walk and found a place where she could watch the battlefield without getting in anyone's way.

The bright sun made it impossible for her to judge how distant the Army was, and she had no way of calculating how quickly they could bridge the distance to Aurilien. But it looked strange. Surely Tremontane's Army wasn't that large, even with the addition of the Kirkellan? And they were short the companies of soldiers here in the city. She shielded her eyes and stared until her eyes watered, but still couldn't tell what was different.

She looked down at the Ruskalder army. The narrowness of the gate had funneled them into a spear point thrusting into Aurilien's side, relentlessly driven home by the mass of warriors behind it. The sight made her chest ache. They could not be allowed to take the city. She wouldn't let them do it. She looked out over the army, noting the position of the banners. The seven-fingered hand was still gone.

Hrovald's banner…sweet heaven, there it was, the howling crag-wolf of Ruskald, not a hundred feet from the gate. And there was Hrovald, sitting his horse, urging his men forward with great slashes of his sword. There was a clear space some five feet around him as a result. At the rate his men were going, he'd be inside in less than the half hour Haverson had predicted they'd need.

She came back down the stairs and mounted. "We will distract them," she said to Haverson, and rode off toward the west gate, thinking furiously. If she could get Hrovald's attention…he no doubt hated her enough she could be a distraction all by herself, but would that stop the army? They might not even be able to get out, if Seven-Fingers still had his army surrounding the gate. The Tremontanan Army and the Kirkellan were so close, they just needed a little more time….

The Ruskalder were still at the gate, though they'd stopped pounding and had started singing a war song that seemed to have a hundred verses, each one about a different part of the body the Ruskalder would cut off or crush or maim in some way. Since they were singing in Ruskeldin, the Tremontanan soldiers listened in curious ignorance, and the Kirkellan just rolled their eyes. "The Ruskalder are so childish," Revalan said when Imogen drew up beside him.

"We've got to get out of here to harass the Ruskalder army again," she said. "If we can take the pressure off…the Tremontanan Army is so close, they just…." She fell silent.

"What good can we do? There's only sixty-five of us left," Dorenna said.

"There's no way the whole Ruskalder army can get inside the city before the Tremontanans get here. They'll be crushed against the city wall, the more so because they still have no idea the Tremontanan Army is coming," said Kallum.

"Maybe they should," Imogen said, an idea forming.

"Should what?"

"Know the Army's on their heels." Imogen slid down again—her side was really starting to hurt now—and went slowly up the stairs. The jeering redoubled when the Ruskalder saw her on the wall, but she ignored them and looked off into the distance, where the oncoming Army was now clearly visible. "Look!" she shouted at the Tremontanan soldiers nearby. "The Army is on its way! They'll be here in minutes. Tell everyone!" She waved and shouted and jumped, once, before realizing it was a bad idea. The soldiers near her caught the idea and ran with it, jumping and shouting and waving and pointing until the soldiers on the other side of the gate joined in. It didn't take long for the Ruskalder to turn and look at what had gotten the defenders so excited. Then the seven-fingered banner dipped and wheeled, and the chief cursed at his men and rode off toward the main body of the Ruskalder army, the warriors following at a run.

Imogen came down the stairs and stood, breathing heavily, leaning with her hand on Victory's flank for support. "We can ride out again."

"What was the point of that?" Revalan asked.

"They'll spread the word that the Tremontanan Army is on its way. The Ruskalder will have to turn and prepare to fight, or at least most of them will. That means fewer people trying to get in the main gate, which will ease the burden on the defenders. Mount up, riders, and let's chase some Ruskalder!"

"You're *staying*," Areli said when Imogen tried to follow her own order. "You've already exerted yourself too far."

"I swear I won't enter the fighting. I just can't bear to be left behind, Areli, you should understand that."

Areli glared at her. Dorenna said, "If you fall, one of us is going to have to carry you back, and if that someone is me, I'm going to put a few more holes in you just for spite."

"Understood." Imogen pulled herself into the saddle, carefully not grimacing, since Areli and Dorenna were both still watching her. "Captain, I think you must bar this gate after us and go to help them at the main door. They are not doing well."

"I don't think we should leave our post," the captain said, though the gleam in his eye told her he wished otherwise.

"If you do not, then I think perhaps this post will not matter."

The captain's lips twitched. "You could make it an order."

"I am not your superior."

"Ma'am, after the day we've had, I think you've earned the right to give orders."

Imogen wasn't sure it worked that way, but she said, "Then I order you to help the soldiers at the gate." *If nothing goes wrong, neither of us will be in trouble. Though, come to think on it, if things do go wrong, no one will be around to get either of us in trouble.*

She led the diminished company through the gates and around the curve of the city wall as before. Ahead of them, the seven-fingered banner made straight for the army and another one of the banners, this one of a fist wielding a sword point-down as if stabbing his enemy's back. Imogen held up a hand. "Let's watch for a bit."

Ripples passed through the army. The first spread outward from the seven-fingered banner, as if it were a stone dropped into a pool. The second ripple began at the farthest edge of the Ruskalder army and spread, more slowly, toward the city wall. Warriors turned to face the new threat, which now seemed only minutes away. And a third ripple arose, trailing another banner that moved from near the gate to the rear, or now the front, of the army. Hrovald. Imogen's heart raced. "Go, keep them busy until the army arrives," she said, and watched with impatience as her riders darted away.

The Ruskalder were waiting for them. This time, riders engaged the enemy and had to pull away quickly or be overcome. Some Kirkellan were overcome, their horses slaughtered as they themselves fell. Imogen's hands clenched so hard into fists her nails cut deep into her palms. She had to get closer. Just a little, not close enough to be drawn into the fighting. She might need to pull someone out, heaven forbid. Maybe a few feet closer.

Then she saw Revalan's Rohrnan founder, saw Revalan fling up his hands as he disappeared into a mass of Ruskalder warriors, saw Dorenna, screaming, launch herself and Rapier into the mob, and without a conscious decision Imogen kicked Victory into a gallop. Dorenna was laying about her with sword and knife, forcing the Ruskalder back, and Imogen rode in to where Rohrnan lay unmoving and Revalan lay beside his horse, his chest a gory mess, his eyes open and sightless. Imogen heard herself screaming at Dorenna to get clear, used Victory's mass to shove her way past two Ruskalder to grab her friend's reins. She nearly lost her head when Dorenna turned on her before realizing who it was. Dorenna only needed one look from Imogen to know what had happened. Together, they fought their way clear of the mob and rode some distance away, silent, then without another glance Dorenna rode back toward the battle. Imogen was too numb to cry. *Later. We'll mourn later.*

The seven-fingered banner dipped, steadied, then dipped lower and finally fell. The Kirkellan raised a shout that despite her sorrow warmed Imogen's heart. One chief gone; that left several hundred Ruskalder warriors without anyone to give them orders. If only they could do the same with Hrovald's banner.

She looked around to see where it was. There, near the edge of the army, moving back and forth to follow the pacing Hrovald on his undeserved Kirkellan mount. He was *right there* and not a single Kirkellan warrior was nearby. Again without thinking Imogen rode in his direction, staying well clear of the army and moving quickly to discourage anyone who might see her as the easy target she was. Hrovald turned to watch her as she rode by, close enough that she could see his face contort with fury when he realized who she was. He viciously slammed his heels into his mount's sides, shouting something at his warriors she couldn't make out, and rode directly at her.

Chapter Thirty-Three

Stunned, she at first didn't realize no one was riding out after him. She thought, *That's interesting, I wonder if he wants to come to terms,* then realized he was bearing down on her with his sword upraised. She nudged Victory into a gallop and steered her wide of the army. Hrovald changed his course to follow her. Of course he wasn't interested in peace. He wanted her dead.

His horse was gaining on Victory. She didn't have time to lead him in the direction of the *tiermathas;* she needed to find a place to stand and face him. She looked around and saw the fields extending in every direction, toward the army, toward the woods, toward the city. *This is as good a place as any.* She wheeled, drew her saber, screamed a battle cry, and charged.

Their blades met with an arm-numbing clash, and Imogen rocked back in her saddle and barely recovered before Hrovald swung at her again.

"Greetings, wife," he said, grinning at her.

Imogen bared her teeth at him. "Don't you remember? I divorced you."

"Only husbands can divorce wives." He parried a stroke and returned a blow that rattled Imogen's teeth.

"Does your first wife know that?" She drew in a breath and parried his blow. "Why would you want a wife as unwomanly and *violent*—" this with a jaw-cracking blow of her own—"as I am?"

"I'm going to make you submit—" he gasped for breath— "like a good Ruskalder woman."

He slashed at her face, and she ducked, then thrust at his navel. Her side throbbed wetly with what she hoped was sweat.

"I am Kirkellan, and a warrior. We do not submit." Imogen parried, struck, parried again, and swung a great chopping stroke at the man's head. "And let me tell you—" she thrust at his stomach— "what I told the last man you sent after me." She swung at his head. "Until you win, just—shut—up."

They went silent, then, no wasted breath, the only sounds the block and parry and thrust of combat. Imogen wiped sweat away from her forehead, a momentary inattention that got her a shallow slice on her left biceps. Her side was definitely bleeding now. Jeffrey was going to kill her when he saw her. *No. No thinking of him.*

Hrovald's gaze flicked to her side, and his grin broadened. "I'm not the first one to try to gut you," he said. He thrust at her side and Imogen barely deflected the blow. She turned to put her injured side away from Hrovald and took another cut across the shoulder. "Weak, like any woman," he snarled.

Imogen thrust for Hrovald's stomach; he deflected it poorly, and her saber ran deep into his thigh. "Good thing I'm a weak woman or that would really have hurt," she said, making Hrovald redouble his efforts, ignoring the blood his trousers were soaking up. Flecks of foam speckled the corners of his lips, and his eyes were so wide Imogen could see white all around his dark irises. He screamed profanities at her until he was hoarse, but showed no sign of weakening.

Imogen felt drained. She knew she was losing blood, though her side was numb. Her vision was blurry and her arm hurt from blocking Hrovald's mad swings. She was going to tire first, and then it would be over. She wished she knew how close the Tremontanan Army was. She just had to keep him occupied until the Army came, and then they could take over. Her exhausted arm was parrying and striking on its own. *Wouldn't it be nice if I could leave it here to finish the fight and I could go have a nap somewhere else?*

She gave Victory a signal and Victory reared up and slashed at Hrovald's mount with her iron-shod hooves. Hrovald's horse squealed and danced back a few steps, and Hrovald's next swing connected with nothing but air. Imogen, breathing heavily, maneuvered Victory out of the way and lowered her weapon to a guard position. "Pity you don't know how to make that horse a weapon," she said.

Hrovald screamed and rode at her; Victory sidestepped and Imogen swung hard at Hrovald's back. The blow glanced off his armor, and in her weakness she fumbled and nearly dropped her saber. Then Victory screamed in pain, a long high sound that cut to Imogen's heart as surely as Hrovald's sword might. Her rear legs buckled and Imogen tumbled to the ground, landing hard on her backside. High above her, Hrovald grinned and ran his tongue along the flat of his blade, which was dark with blood. "Broke your weapon," he said.

Imogen rolled over and found Victory struggling to rise, blood streaming from a deep, broad wound in her flank. "*No,*" she said, then had to duck and roll again as Hrovald's sword came whistling toward her head. Victory cried out and thrashed her legs. Imogen came to her feet and, circling, drew Hrovald away from her wounded horse. "Why don't you come down here and make this an even fight?" she shouted.

"Fighting women is beneath me," Hrovald said.

"Then you don't mind your entire army knows you can't kill this one woman? Weakling. Coward. You entered into an agreement with one woman and were humiliated by another. How did you explain it, when your people found you tied up in that little room? Did you lie to them about being overcome by six huge men with axes? Anything to keep their respect—"

Hrovald roared and leaped off his horse, stumbled, and ran at Imogen, flailing wildly. Even though she'd expected it, even though it had been her plan, the ferocity of his attack surprised her, and she barely deflected the first of his wild swings. If she'd been fresh and unwounded, the fight would have been over in seconds, but her reflexes were slow, her brain muddled, and she fought a defensive battle, parrying and blocking and never seeing an opening to make an attack. *He's going to kill me*, she thought, and an image came to mind, not of her *tiermatha* or Victory or her family or even Jeffrey, but of that lone dark tower rising high above Aurilien. "You can't have it," she gasped, and shoved him back, hard, following with a slice across his midsection he had to leap back to avoid.

Now she pressed the attack, feeling strength rise up like a golden tide within her. She laughed in Hrovald's face as that power filled her, thrusting at his belly, slashing at his face—

—but there were too many people now, jostling her, driving her and Hrovald apart. The Army had arrived, and she was caught up in the middle of it. They were both going to be crushed. She had to get free. She saw Hrovald mount his horse and slash at the fighters surrounding them, turning violently in his saddle as he looked for her. Imogen shoved and kicked and struck with her saber, wading after him, deflecting blows and trying not to be drawn into combat. Hrovald continued to flail about, screaming obscenities, and still didn't see her even when she pressed against his horse's flank. "Sorry," she whispered to the animal, and drove her blade deep into its side.

It reared and twisted to get away, and Hrovald, his grip firmer on his weapon than on his reins, fell to the ground. Without thinking, Imogen raised her saber in a two-handed grip and drove the point of it through Hrovald's chest and into the ground beneath him with all her failing strength.

Hrovald gasped, his mad eyes still wide. He reached for the blade with both hands and pulled at it, bloodying his hands on its sharp edges. Imogen, panting, leaned on the hilt so she wouldn't fall over. "Kill…you…" Hrovald choked out, blood staining his lips, then the light in his eyes died, and his hands fell limp to his sides. Imogen breathed in deeply, watching sparks of light cross her vision. *I should say something,* she thought, but no words came to mind.

A blow skittered across the shoulder of her leather armor. She ducked to avoid the next one and tugged hard at her saber to free it. It was stuck fast in the ground. She hadn't realized she'd had so much strength left. She dodged another blow and punched her attacker in the throat, and when he staggered, choking, she ran. She and Hrovald had been nearly at the edge of the fighting, and she stumbled into clear ground and kept running. She was cold and aching and dizzy, her earlier battle rage evaporated. She turned; no one had followed her. She staggered to a nearby copse of trees and lowered herself to the ground, and let unconsciousness claim her.

Imogen woke at twilight to the sound of birds in the trees above her.

They seemed to be arguing, different voices taking up the fight at top volume. The roots of the tree she lay beneath dug their giant knuckles into her back and neck and, most painfully, her wounded side, which felt as if it had been torn open and filled with molten iron. Her trousers were unpleasantly damp where her buttocks had rested too long on the earth. Standing took several tries and finally the assistance of the tree she'd fallen unconscious next to. She looked around, but found no convenient stick to use as a cane, so she walked, one slow step at a time, away from the copse and toward the battlefield.

To the south, the city was lit by a thousand lamps, glowing as golden as if struck by the summer sun. The oak and iron gate still sagged, but the wall was empty of attackers and defenders both. No smoke rose above the roofs and towers of Aurilien, no screams drifted on the chilly wind to her ears. They'd won, though where the victors had gone was a mystery. Nothing moved on the battlefield. There were no signs of either army. It was as if ungoverned heaven itself had reached out and swept everyone away, soldiers, warriors, horses and all, leaving nothing but the dead.

Too many bodies lay where they'd fallen in grotesque poses. Now the battle was over, she found herself regarding them with nausea. She'd been happy enough to kill when she was fighting for her home, but in seeing the result of so much bloodshed she could only think of the waste. If Hrovald had been content to stay at home, if he hadn't been so driven by pride and a desire to conquer, this field would be empty of everything but grass.

"Help me," one of the bodies said. Imogen fell to her knees beside a woman in a green and brown uniform whose face was a mask of blood and whose hand clutched at her stomach. "Water," the woman added, her voice nearly a whisper, and Imogen patted her sides until she remembered she'd left her flask on Victory's harness. *Victory. Is she even alive?* "I'm sorry," she told the woman.

"Help me," the woman repeated, and coughed up more blood. Imogen carefully lifted the woman's hand away from her midriff and tried not to recoil at the stench of the wounded soldier's exposed stomach and entrails. The woman whimpered.

"I can't—" Imogen began, then scooted around to get her hands under the woman's armpits and lift her. The woman tried to scream, then fainted. Imogen gently laid her down and felt for a pulse. She found one, thready and weak, and then it was gone. Imogen sagged beside the body and cried. She had gone to war against the Ruskalder for years, had killed their warriors and brought back the bodies of fallen Kirkellan, but she'd never sat on a battlefield beside a woman whose life she had no way of saving. She looked at the distant city gate, lit by a dozen Devices hovering like oversized fireflies, and thought, *You had better be worth the sacrifice*, without knowing who or what she was talking about.

She painfully got to her feet and again resumed her slow, limping pace toward the distant lights. Tomorrow they would bury their dead, assuming there was anyone around to do so. The missing armies puzzled Imogen. Hrovald's might have fled, but where had the Tremontanan Army gone? She saw no camps or even the marks of the passage of a large number of people.

Imogen realized she was on the ground. She didn't remember falling. That was a bad sign. She needed to get to a doctor, quickly. She pushed herself up and resumed her journey. *No one knows where I am, or they'd have retrieved me by now. Jeffrey will be frantic. He was right. I should have stayed behind. But who would have killed Hrovald if I had?* Had it even made a difference? It didn't seem as if anyone had noticed the King of Ruskald impaled by her saber, stuck to the ground like a bit of paper skewered with a pin.

Music and shouting and brassy light clamored at her as she neared the city wall. The doors had been cleared of bodies, and she passed through with no trouble. Inside, people danced and sang through the streets, musicians played on every corner, and she could smell alcohol and the sharp, lingering scent of gunpowder. An explosion went off nearby, and she cried out and threw herself to the ground before she realized she wasn't dead. A shower of blue-white light rained down from the sky, evaporating before it reached the street. Another explosion, and green and red sparks blossomed high above. A celebration, not an attack.

How odd, and how beautiful.

Imogen leaned against a nearby building, stared up at the colorful sparks, and caught her breath. *The palace. They have doctors there. Sweet heaven, it's so far away.* She was so discouraged she wanted to cry.

"Hey, sweetheart, come and have a drink with us!" a man shouted, and Imogen was dragged painfully away from the supportive building and handed from one person to the next until, dizzy and nauseated, she jerked away from their hands and clutched her side, weeping with pain.

"Oh, heaven, she's injured. Fellows, we have a war hero here! Ma'am, we're sorry, had no idea, let us get you a doctor."

Imogen shook her head. "I need to get to the palace," she said through tears and gritted teeth.

The man's face swam in her teary vision, but he seemed kind. He shouted, "We need a coach for the war hero, right now!" and soon Imogen was handed from person to person again until she was tucked into the dark, cool interior of a carriage which trotted away over the cobblestones. Imogen wedged herself into a corner, trying to minimize the jolting. The pain was so great she retched and had to lean far out the window to keep from vomiting inside the carriage. Afterward, she sagged onto the seat, clammy drops of sweat erupting on her forehead, a bitter taste of bile on her lips. *Just a little farther. He's going to kill me. Just a little farther.*

She fell into semi-consciousness, waking only when the carriage came to a halt. She opened the door and staggered out, hanging tight to the handle to keep from falling down. She heard running feet, then hands supported her up the steps, then they were carrying her awkwardly, one person on each side, and her head rolled back to watch the ceiling hurry past. Just as the vaulted ceiling gave way to shaped stone, she closed her eyes and knew nothing more.

CHAPTER THIRTY-FOUR

She woke in a strange bed with a dark blue canopy speckled with silver. North colors. Sunlight flowed like honey through tall windows opposite the bed. She felt numb all over—no, she felt well all over, completely free from pain for the first time in as long as she could remember. She moved to touch her wounded side and realized she was naked under the blankets. Her side bore a ridged scar that felt as if it was at least six months old. She ran her fingers over the bumpy scar tissue, then over the rest of her body, wondering what other miracles might have been worked on it.

"*Lilia*," her mother said, and Imogen looked and saw Mother seated a short distance away, holding a book. She set the volume down face-first and rose, her arms outstretched.

"Mother," Imogen said, and then her mother enfolded her in her arms, and they were both crying, though Imogen wasn't sure why—she wasn't dead, was she? Mother stroked her hair, and Imogen sobbed tears of relief and joy.

"You must be starving. You slept for two days," Mother said, releasing her daughter and pulling the bell rope. "The healer said it's as if your body experiences the normal healing process at an accelerated rate, and it exhausts you, but when you didn't wake up right away…we were all worried, as you can imagine."

"Where is this place?"

"One of the rooms in the east wing. King Jeffrey insisted, when it became clear you couldn't be moved to the embassy. He's been very accommodating. Yes, thank you, would you ask the kitchen to send something for the ambassador?" The servant who'd appeared in response to the bell bowed and shut the door behind him. "Any pain? Dizziness?"

Imogen shook her head. "Nothing but hunger. I feel as if I…well, exactly as if I hadn't eaten for two days."

"The healer says you're to eat as much as you want and sleep as much as you can. No visitors for another day or so, but you have many friends who are worried about you and would like to see you back on your feet."

Imogen sat up straight and had to adjust the sheet to cover herself. "Victory. Is she all right? Mother, Hrovald stabbed her, the bastard, and—"

"Shh, shh, she's fine, the healer's seen to her too. He was almost stunned—I don't think he'd ever worked on an animal before, but the King said she was no less a hero than you." Mother's eyes grew misty. "They found your saber, stuck through Hrovald's heart, and you nowhere to be seen. We were just about to send out a second search party when those soldiers came in carrying what everyone thought was your body. It was…." Mother shook her head and wiped her eyes. "I'm just glad you're well. What happened?"

The door opened and the servant came in, laden with two trays bearing several covered dishes. Imogen's stomach growled. "Put them here," she instructed the servant in Tremontanese, patting the bed next to her and diving onto the dishes almost before he'd set the trays down. "Oh," she moaned, "roast beef and baked potatoes and butter and…I can't talk, Mother, you'll have to tell me about the battle instead." Her last four words were indistinct, her mouth full of meat.

Mother laughed. "Don't choke, Imogen, I'm not sure the healer can fix that. Well. I should start at the beginning, a month ago." Imogen made an incredulous sound, and Mother waved her to silence. "After that battle, I was approached by Ingivar—oh, I see you know him. He brought me an intriguing proposal. He told me Hrovald was unstable, which I knew, and that he was mismanaging the country, which I'd guessed, and that he, Ingivar, wanted to overthrow Hrovald, which was a complete surprise. I've always considered Ingivar an honorable enemy, and the idea of dealing with him instead of Hrovald had great appeal. So we sent messengers back and forth, and the result was, when Hrovald called up his army a second time, Ingivar and three other chiefs pleaded indisposition and refused to come."

Imogen looked an inquiry at Mother. "What are you asking? Who were they? No. What did Hrovald do—oh, yes. Not much he *could* do without displaying weakness, even though he knew they were in rebellion against them; he was trying to fight a war against Tremontane and he was either unwilling to give that up or didn't feel he could maintain his reputation if he had to force the issue with his rebellious chiefs. So I suppose he just pretended everything was well. He still outnumbered the Tremontanan Army even without those four chiefs.

"The thing he didn't know was that Ingivar, as soon as Hrovald was committed to the march on Aurilien, brought the other three chiefs and added his forces to the Tremontanan Army the way we Kirkellan did."

Imogen swallowed. "I saw it. I didn't know what was different, but I thought the Army was bigger than it had been before."

"Yes. With Ingivar's forces, we were easily able to overcome the Ruskalder army, aided by the fact that someone had skewered Hrovald and left him to rot on the battlefield. Ingivar took control of the remaining chiefs, told them he was the King now, and that was it. The war is over."

"Where did the armies go? I was so confused, wandering around the battlefield and seeing nothing and no one."

"The Tremontanan Army, and our warriors, are camped around on the east side of the city, near the barracks. The Ruskalder made camp on the far side of the forest. Well out of sight of the city—truce or no, nobody in Aurilien wanted to see Ruskalder camping just over the fields. And out of sight of the battlefields. It will be grim work, burying the dead, and far too many dead at that." Mother looked grim herself. "But I think the truce is holding."

"Ingivar struck me as honorable, too. I think he'll be a much better neighbor than Hrovald."

"He has some things to discuss with you. He won't say what. If you want, I can tell him to negotiate with me instead."

"No, why shouldn't I speak to him? But later. Let me tell you what happened." She gave her mother the complete story, beginning with the siege of the palace that had led to her being wounded, then her part in the battle up to Hrovald's death, then her return to the palace. Mother listened intently, and when Imogen was done, said, "For an ambassador, you make an excellent warrior."

It was a joke, but it made Imogen uncomfortable. "I make an excellent ambassador, too," she protested.

"I know. I should never have sent you those troop movements. I should have realized how they could be used against you."

"It was my good fortune Jeffrey didn't believe I would betray him. Anyone else, it might have meant my head."

Mother nodded. "I'm looking forward to meeting these other ambassadors. From your few letters—" she glared in mock-severity at her daughter—"they seem fascinating characters."

"I'll be sure to introduce you." Imogen pushed away the last of her dishes, feeling over-full and slightly sick, but far preferring that condition to hunger. She also felt sleepy. "Mother," she began, but Mother was already pushing back her chair from the bedside.

"I should go spread the good news," she said. "Someone will fetch the dishes, and then you should sleep." She kissed Imogen on the forehead. "Welcome back, daughter."

Imogen snuggled back into the pillows and pulled the blankets around her chin. But despite her weariness, sleep didn't come. She stared up at the canopy. North colors. She'd fought Hrovald and nearly died for the sake of what those colors represented. The saber in her hand, the horse beneath her, the ground rushing past—it was who she was, who she was meant to be. Could a diplomat have stabbed Hrovald through the heart? A diplomat wouldn't have been on the battlefield at all.

She thought of Bixhenta and Ghentali, of treaties and receptions, thought of Jeffrey and what he'd said the first night he'd kissed her—something about how there was nothing wrong with giving up one dream in favor of a better one. He was right, though he'd been talking about a different dream. What she'd done in Tremontane...she had so many skills she'd never dreamed of, but none of them could compare to her abilities as a warrior. As a commander of troops. She could never be truly happy here, no matter how much she loved Jeffrey; she was a Kirkellan warrior, and that was where her destiny lay. As if her resolve had turned a switch inside her, she began drifting off, waking only when the servant returned to collect the dishes, then falling deeply asleep.

When she woke again, it was full night. Imogen rolled onto her side and began feeling around for the light Device switch. "Don't get up," Jeffrey said from the darkness at her side. Imogen pulled the blankets close around her chest just as light bloomed, blinding her briefly.

"How long have you sat there?" she said.

"Longer than I'd like to admit," he said. "I apologize for the intrusion." He'd shaved and was dressed in clean clothes, but he still looked tired. The lamp cast unattractive shadows across his face. "Are you well?"

"I am hungry again," she said.

"I can have someone bring you food," he said, but made no move to pull the bell rope. "No pain? The healer said you should be perfectly recovered."

"I am not in pain. I do not feel tired now either. Just hunger."

Jeffrey rested his interlaced fingers on his knees and studied them. "That's good. I—we were all very worried. Victory wounded, your saber left behind…it was as if you'd simply vanished."

"Thank you for tending to Victory. She is my dear friend."

"Well, yes, I know how much she means to you, so I didn't think she should suffer."

Silence descended between them. He was so distant. Could he really be so angry that she'd ignored his warning and nearly gotten herself killed? But if he was, why was he here? "I am sorry," she blurted. "I do—did not listen and you were right."

"Right about what?" He sounded startled.

"That I am too injured to fight. I killed Hrovald because I was lucky. He nearly killed me. I should listen to you. Please do not be angry."

"What? Imogen, I'm not angry with you."

His words should have been a comfort, but they only deepened her confusion. "Then what are you angry at?"

"Nothing. It's just been a long couple of days, not knowing when you'd wake up." His tone of voice substituted "if" for "when," and

Imogen felt a pang of compassion for him.

"I am glad you care," she managed.

"Of course I care. Imogen...." His words trailed off into silence. Compassion turned into a stomach-churning dread. She had to tell him quickly, before he said something that would make this situation truly heartbreaking. This was far, far worse than the Spring Ball.

"I think the Kirkellan will return to the Eidestal soon," she said. "I am looking forward to the hunts."

Jeffrey's face went very still. "You're going back with them."

"I am a warrior of the Kirkellan. It is my home."

"I see." He didn't look angry, or sad, or anything but completely emotionless. "It's true, you're a natural commander. I've had the reports of Colonel Haverson and Major Randulf. Haverson says you roused the troops against the Ruskalder when our own commanders didn't know what to do. Randulf told me you took command at the west gate and brought down one of the enemy banners with no help from anyone else. People look to you for orders and they trust what you tell them to do. You're going to be the greatest Warleader the Kirkellan have ever had."

"I think not. There is no more war for me to be Warleader." The ache in her stomach had turned knife-sharp. She'd expected...what? Whatever it was, she hadn't expected him to agree with her.

Jeffrey shook his head. "The Ruskalder won't stay peaceful for long. Ingivar is strong, but there are others who see his progressive policies as a threat and will do whatever it takes to stop him. I give it another five, possibly seven years before Ruskald becomes a threat again. And your current Warleader—Kernan is a strong leader, but Mairen told me he's getting to an age where he's ready to lay down his saber. After what's happened in this war, no one's going to question your qualifications to take his place."

"I...think you are right."

"Thank you for wielding your sword on my behalf. I would be dead now if not for you."

"It is what I want to do." Everything seemed distant now, Jeffrey's voice, his face swimming in front of her, her hands clutching the blanket.

"I do not belong here," she said.

Jeffrey nodded. "I know. I think I've always known." He stood. "I don't know if we'll have another chance to speak before your warriors leave—there's a lot to do still—but just in case, I want you to know I...feel honored by your presence here in Tremontane. Madam ambassador."

The sharp pain moved upward to her chest. "I am glad I came," she said, knowing it was a lie. "I think I must sleep again now."

"I thought you said you were hungry."

"I was wrong. I am just tired."

"All right. I'm glad you're well. Good night, Imogen."

"Good night."

He switched off the Device, then the door opened and closed again, and Imogen was alone. She realized she was still sitting up with the blanket wrapped tightly around her chest and relaxed her fingers until it fell away, then lay back and closed her eyes. Of course Jeffrey wouldn't try to change her mind. It was why he was such a good King; he saw the truth beneath all the irrelevant details that clouded it and he had the courage to act on what he saw. She was a Kirkellan warrior, above all else. The wind in her face, the horse beneath her, her saber in hand, those things made sense. They were what she was born to. Nothing about her was shaped to fit into Tremontanan society; she barely spoke the language, for heaven's sake. She ran her fingers over the ridged scar on her belly. No Tremontanan lady would have the scars of a warrior.

Here in the darkness, staring blindly at the invisible canopy above, she could admit to herself she loved Jeffrey, she'd started to dream of a life with him, but he couldn't follow her to the Eidestal and she wouldn't let him if he was able to. Love couldn't solve everything, not for either of them. She hugged her pillow to her chest and stared into the darkness until dawn touched the tall windows, when she finally fell asleep.

"You've lost weight," Areli said, eyeing Imogen critically.

"I have not."

"You have so. That dress is almost hanging off you."

Imogen plucked at the fabric, which was undeniably loose on her. "This dress is supposed to be close-fitting. I'll have to pick something else."

"No, don't, it's so pretty, and I know Saevonna will appreciate it."

"She'd better. I don't know how Tremontanan weddings are normally conducted, but we put this one together awfully fast."

"Had to," Areli said, hitching up her skirt and examining her hemline in Imogen's mirror. "They're practicing the Tremontanan tradition of celibacy until marriage."

"I can't imagine how hard that is." Imogen ran a brush through her hair. Areli had helped her dress, but couldn't put her hair up, and rather than ring for Jeanette, Imogen decided to leave it down, shining chestnut tresses hanging halfway down her back. It made a nice contrast to the deep red of her gown.

"Can't you?"

"Can't I what?"

"Imogen, I thought you were going to stop pretending you're not in love with your King." Areli took Imogen's face in both her hands and leaned so close the tips of their noses touched. "It must be so frustrating for you, being the ambassador and seeing him all the time. Have you thought about talking to Mairen?"

"About what?" Imogen pulled out of her friend's grasp.

"Yes, about what?" Dorenna said as she entered the room. She was gowned as haphazardly as ever and looked uncomfortably warm, even though her pink and white dress was suitably light for spring.

"About Imogen being released as ambassador."

"Really?" Dorenna grinned. "So we can go home? Yes, Imogen, talk to Mairen. Nearly getting killed on behalf of a foreign government ought to count for something."

"No, Dorenna, so she and King Jeffrey don't have to hide their love anymore."

Dorenna stopped grinning. "And then what?" she demanded of Imogen.

Imogen shook her head. "Then we go home."

"Imogen!"

"Don't yell at her, Areli, she's finally making sense."

"She is *not* making sense. Imogen, what are you saying?"

Imogen sat carefully on the sofa to avoid wrinkling her gown. "I'm saying love isn't enough to build a life on."

"Which is what I've always said."

"*Shut up,* Dorenna." Areli knelt in front of Imogen and tried to catch her eye. "That's not what this is about, is it. Something else happened."

"Nothing happened. I'm a warrior of the Kirkellan, not a diplomat, and I'm ready to go home."

"Imogen, you can't just throw this away. I think you belong here, with him."

Dorenna slapped her hand down on the fireplace mantel. "Stop trying to influence her, Areli!"

"And you weren't? Imogen—"

"Just...stop, all right?" Imogen put her hands over her ears, then took them down when she realized how childish she looked. "We're supposed to be celebrating Saevonna's marriage, not arguing over my life and the poor decisions I seem to be making about it. Dorenna, stop gloating. Areli, I don't want to talk about this anymore. And now we're going downstairs, and Saevonna's going to be married by the King, and then we'll have a party and everyone will stop worrying about the future for a few hours, or by heaven I will start breaking heads!"

The *tiermatha* was smaller by four people, Lorcun and Maeva and Revalan having been buried and mourned the week before, Taeron still in the infirmary, but it was still large enough that with the addition of Marcus's family, the large parlor with its many spindly-legged tables seemed small. Marcus's parents were both dead, and Saevonna's family was far away on the Eidestal, so Imogen had asked Jeffrey to officiate, hoping it wasn't too presumptuous, hoping that whatever had passed between them had left them still friends. She ignored the ache in her chest when he nodded politely and thanked her for the honor. Just like a friend would.

Now she stood just behind him on his left, Marcus's older sister and his aunt and uncle standing to the right, and translated the words of the ceremony for Saevonna and the *tiermatha*. When it came time for the two to make what Jeffrey called their hearts' oaths to each other, Saevonna hesitated. "Imogen, I want to say this right. Will you translate for me?" So Imogen, in her best and most careful Tremontanese, told Marcus that Saevonna would love and honor him and be the strength to his weakness, all the days of her life, and she found herself crying out the tears she hadn't the night she made her decision, hot, bitter tears of regret for a life she couldn't live. Since half the *tiermatha* was crying, too, no one had any idea anything was wrong.

Jeffrey left after the ceremony, though Imogen asked him to stay. "This is a family matter, and I'd just make things awkward," he said.

"I do not think so," Imogen said. "I think they like you."

"Yes, but I think poor Marcus is overwhelmed. He's far more class-conscious than you Kirkellan are. It's refreshing, being surrounded by people who don't care that I'm the King."

"It is that you are not their King, I think."

"I've seen them behave the same way toward your mother. I think it's a Kirkellan trait." He nodded to her and stepped into the waiting carriage, leaving her grasping for something else to say.

Mother arrived just after Marcus and Saevonna had departed for their wedding trip, the details unknown even to Saevonna, who'd told Imogen, "I made Marcus promise not to tell me, so there was no chance of it leaking to the rest of the *tiermatha*. I want my wedding night to be private, with no nosy Kirkellan hanging around offering advice."

"I suppose it's a good thing you have servants," Mother said, gazing around the two parlors, littered with the detritus of the celebration, china plates and wine glasses of crystal and gold and a very relaxed *tiermatha* entertaining Marcus's relatives with Kirkellan dances and songs. "It's all lovely, but it makes me yearn for the simplicity of our family tent, wouldn't you agree?"

"I suppose," Imogen said, absently, thinking, *How much longer do we have to stay here? I wish I were home already.*

"I meant to ask you what Ingivar wanted," Mother said.

"What? Oh. It was about Hrovald's fortune. Seems I earned it by right of conquest. I told him to give it to Elspeth as reparations. I won't have much use for it, and he certainly abused her enough." She picked up an empty wine glass and tilted it, watching a last pale rosy bead trickle down the inside toward the lip.

"You seem distracted," Mother said.

"I—what? I'm just thinking about Saevonna, I suppose. Wondering what kind of life she'll have. In three days she takes oath as a Tremontanan citizen and officially joins the Army. It's just so different here."

"She seems content with her choice."

"She has someone who loves her. That makes a difference."

"Indeed." Mother looked around again. "I'd like to talk to you about something. Can we go somewhere private?"

Imogen led the way to her suite, where she sat across from Mother, who took the sofa. "Before I say anything else, I want you to know I've been satisfied—more than satisfied—with your work as ambassador here. You've opened the way for us to build relations with other countries, and both the Veriboldan and Eskandelic ambassadors speak highly of you."

Imogen sat up straight in her chair. "What do you want me to do *now*, Mother?"

"Imogen, calm down. This isn't that kind of conversation. Well, actually, I suppose it is, in a way. But this time it's entirely up to you."

"I'm not joining the Serjian harem. I know it's an honor, and I like the women, but…no."

Mother laughed. "Harem? No, daughter, I have no intention of forcing you to do anything, nor do I plan to manipulate you into doing something you'll hate." She cleared her throat. "I'm told you were thinking of asking me to release you from your ambassadorial duties early."

"Who told you that?"

"More than one person, actually, but that's not important. Is it true?"

Imogen hesitated. "I'd…considered it, yes."

"Would you like to tell me why?"

"No."

"So it doesn't have anything to do with the fact that you've fallen in love with the King of Tremontane?"

Imogen's mouth fell open. Mother laughed. "Give me some credit for having eyes, Imogen. And based on what I observed when you were missing, he's more than a little in love with you."

She shook her head. "It doesn't matter. I'm a Kirkellan warrior, not a Tremontanan lady. There's no room for me in this society. I just don't want to spend the rest of the year being constantly reminded of that fact."

"Imogen, I asked you to learn—"

"I know. I did. And you were right, there's more to me than being a warrior. I was a good ambassador. I'm just far, far better a fighter than I am anything else, and I think I've just proved that on Hrovald's body. I know what I want now, mother. Tremontane isn't it."

Mother regarded Imogen so steadily she had to look away. "Are you certain that's what you want?" she said. "Because I'm inclined to grant your request, but I don't want you to choose rashly. This isn't something you'll be able to come back from, daughter."

"I know." Imogen drew a deep breath. "I want to go home, if you'll let me."

"I will. I've missed you. Your family has missed you." Mother stood. "I'll need to name another ambassador before I can relieve you of your duties, but you can make preparations to leave. I imagine your *tiermatha* will be happy to go home as well."

"Dorenna's been ready since we arrived."

"Ah, Dorenna. She doesn't much care for Tremontane, I hear."

"She was very upset about Saevonna's marriage, too."

"No doubt she sees it as a desertion."

"Yes."

"And how do you see it?"

"Saevonna's more herself than she's ever been," Imogen said. "She's going to make a wonderful life for herself with Marcus. How can that be a desertion?"

"It's hard to leave everything you know behind. Frightening, even. But when you leave it for something better—"

"And now we're talking about me again."

"Merely making conversation. You've made your decision, and I'll support you."She kissed her daughter's cheek. "I'll be at the palace if you need me. The King and I have some things to work out."

Imogen sat back down on the sofa after her mother left and studied her clasped hands. The thought of joining the *tiermatha* downstairs wearied her. She'd take Victory for a ride outside the city instead. She might even come back.

Chapter Thirty-Five

"We wish you safe journey, *matrian* of the Kirkellan," Jeffrey said, saluting Mother. He stood a few steps up from the foot of the palace stairs, their black granite glinting in the noon sun, putting himself at eye level with the *matrian* on her horse. He wore a formal coat and dress boots that were probably too hot for this weather and looked like a stranger. "Good fortune to you."

"Thank you for your hospitality, your Majesty," Mother replied. "I look forward to many years of good relations with Tremontane."

Imogen looked at the back of her mother's head, at Victory's ears, anywhere but at Jeffrey's face. Three weeks had passed since the battle, three long weeks of waiting for their wounded to be well enough to travel, and she'd seen him at a handful of official functions and once at supper when he'd invited her and Mother to dine with his family. Elspeth had chattered, oblivious to the silence between her brother and her dearest friend; Owen had glanced between Jeffrey and Imogen, puzzled, but said nothing. Alison had been silent for most of the meal, but Imogen had caught her looking reflectively at Jeffrey, then had to turn away as Alison transferred her gaze to Imogen. She felt guilty somehow, as if she should have chosen differently, been a different person, and that made her angry.

"Madam ambassador," Jeffrey said, and Imogen, startled, realized he was addressing her. "Thank you for your service to Tremontane on behalf of your country. We owe you a great debt."

"I am pleased to do it," she said stiffly. "I love Tremontane and it is dear to me so I am happy to keep the country safe." Elspeth wasn't there, had refused to see her off when she realized Imogen really meant to go, and Imogen was torn between wanting to say goodbye to her friend and being grateful that Elspeth's presence wouldn't make things worse.

Mother called out a command, and their little party turned down the long driveway toward the city. They would join the rest of the Kirkellan warriors outside the gates. Imogen focused on the space between

Victory's ears, which flicked first in unison, then separately, then in unison again. She stroked her horse's mane and tried to block out her surroundings…the smell of fresh pastries told her they were passing her favorite bakery, which meant Julian's shop was just beyond that down the street to the left. Running water to the right…that would be the inn whose drains never worked right, so when the stable master sluiced out the stalls the overflow ran into the street. The innkeeper had been fined for it, but nothing had changed. Behind her, the *tiermatha* exchanged loud greetings with Ed Veres, owner of the Box of Roses tavern where they'd spent several evenings drinking and starting friendly brawls. Imogen had only gone once before deciding it wasn't something the ambassador ought to do, but it had been a memorable evening.

"Imogen! Tell Areli Tim Overson still wants to marry her!" Ed shouted. Imogen smiled and waved at him, pretending not to hear.

"What did he say?" Areli asked. "He said my name."

"Just that that drunken blacksmith you won a bet from is still in love with you," Imogen said.

Areli laughed. "That's one person I won't be sorry to leave behind. Made it nearly impossible to have a quiet drink in there."

"You should have let me beat him up," Kionnal said. "I think it's my husbandly duty."

"He was harmless. And I can beat up my own drunks, thank you."

"Imogen, tell Areli to let me defend her honor."

"Imogen, tell Kionnal not to meddle."

Imogen ignored them. She twined her fingers in Victory's mane and prayed they'd stop talking to her. The sounds of merriment died away in the face of her silence. She transferred her gaze to Mother's back, ahead and slightly to the left. She'd never realized her mother had sloping shoulders and a very short neck. With her hair wrapped into a bun low on her head, it looked as though her head sat directly on her shoulders. What an odd optical illusion.

"Imogen?" She realized Areli had addressed her directly and, by her tone, had done so several times already. "What?" Imogen said, and knew she sounded surly.

"Never mind," Areli said. "Sorry."

Kallum struck up a traveling song that faltered when everyone remembered Revalan had always sung the low part. Imogen was sorry that her bad mood had soured the trip before they'd even passed the gates, so she said, "I wonder where the hunts will take us this year." The others gratefully took up this conversational thread and pulled to see where it might lead. Imogen fell back into silence. The hunts. That was something to look forward to. Her family. Maybe Torin wasn't married yet, maybe she hadn't missed that. She ought to practice with the javelin more, now that the Ruskald border didn't need to be patrolled—but then, what was the point, if the war was over? Unless Jeffrey was right about the possibility of renewed hostilities in a few years...but then that's what she was going home for, wasn't it? She gripped Victory's mane so hard the horse tossed her head in protest, and Imogen let go and wiped her palm on her trousers.

Outside the gate, the air carried the scent of wildflowers and hundreds of horses, a warm, pleasant musk so familiar Imogen bent low and sniffed Victory's skin, inhaling a thousand memories. Victory didn't deserve to be cooped up in the city, she should be free to ride the plains like a Kirkellan warhorse instead of trotting through the nasty cobbled streets like some rich woman's pampered pet. Imogen looked to the far distance and pretended she could see the Eidestal already. "What are we waiting for?" she asked Mother, who turned in the saddle to look at her. An expression passed over her face too quickly for Imogen to read it.

"We have to wait for the wounded to arrive," she said. "You know how slowly they travel. Imogen, what's wrong?"

"Nothing's wrong. I'm impatient to get home, that's all."

Mother brought her horse around and came forward so her knee pressed against Imogen's. "Go check on the wounded," she told her daughter. "It will give you something to do, if you're so anxious to be moving."

Imogen left her place in line and trotted past the main body of the Kirkellan. She didn't realize she had a companion until she reached the long, high-sprung wagons that had been a gift from Tremontane for the transport of those Kirkellan still too injured to ride. The palace healer had done his best, but even the *cadhaen-rach* had its limits. "Going to check up on Taeron?" Dorenna said, referring to the last member of their *tiermatha* still badly injured.

"Yes," Imogen lied. She hadn't even remembered Taeron was here until Dorenna brought it up. "And to see if there's anything I can do to help move them along."

"I'll keep you company," Dorenna said, and stuck to Imogen's side like a short, well-armed burr throughout Imogen's visit to Taeron and her conversation with the woman in charge of the wounded, who didn't conceal her annoyance at Imogen's presence well. Imogen hovered, annoying the woman further, in the hope that Dorenna might get bored and leave, but eventually the woman's irritation flowered into hostility, and Imogen had to go.

"She wasn't very friendly, was she?" Dorenna said as they rode back to the head of the procession, which hadn't moved very far. "She could at least have thanked you for your concern."

"I don't know anything about sick people, and she knew it. I was just getting in the way."

"Still, it would have been polite. Imogen?" She overrode Imogen, who'd been about to ask Dorenna when she'd ever cared about being polite, and continued, "I know this has been hard for you, but you've made the right choice, coming home."

"Have I?"

"You're a warrior. You have family and friends who need you. Your whole life is with us. You and I both know it's too much to give up. Who would you even be, in Aurilien? It's not as though they need your warrior's skills."

Dorenna's wheedling tone, like that of a mother coaxing a recalcitrant child, irritated Imogen. "It's not as though the Kirkellan need the skills I mastered in Aurilien," she said, feeling contrary.

"What are they? Talking to people. Getting them to agree with each other. Of course you can use those skills for your own people. All right, maybe the war is over. Maybe you won't be Warleader after all. But there will still be, I don't know, disagreements and quarrels that need a person who can settle those things. Maybe that's what you'll end up doing. And you'll want to breed Victory—"

"Dorenna," Imogen said, "what is this about?"

Dorenna reined in Rapier. "I can see you're unhappy," she said, "and I know you're afraid it's because you're doing the wrong thing. I want you to realize you've made the right choice. I want you to remember all the reasons why it's the right choice. Imogen, your sadness will pass, and someday you'll look back and be so glad you didn't stay in Tremontane. I know it."

Imogen looked at her friend's anxious face. "I think you don't want me to go because it will break up our *tiermatha* further," she said. She felt hollow inside, remote, as if Dorenna's anxieties were all for some other Imogen living a parallel life. "I think you're more concerned about that than you are about me. I'm glad Saevonna didn't listen to you, because she's going to have a long, contented life with Marcus, far away from us, and you know what, Dorenna? The sadness we feel at losing her? That's going to pass too. Stop being so afraid of things changing, Dor."

Dorenna had gone from anxious to white-lipped anger. "I'm doing this for your own good, Imogen," she said. "You'd be miserable there, all alone with no one but that King and his family—"

"Stop talking now, Dorenna, before you say something we won't be able to come back from." Imogen rubbed her too-dry eyes. "In case you hadn't noticed, I've already made my decision, and I know it's the right one, so I don't know what you think you're proving by trying to argue me into making it again. You get your wish. I'm coming home. And your fears have nothing to do with it." She nudged Victory into a trot. "Stay away from me for a while," she said, "or we won't be able to stay friends."

She rode beside Mother for several miles, neither of them speaking. Imogen fell back into her waiting state, becoming a pair of eyes, watching the horizon, a pair of ears, listening to the footsteps of hundreds of horses on the dirt road. She felt nothing now, not sorrow nor anger nor even longing, just a weariness of spirit that dragged at her until she was sure

Victory would complain at the added burden. Towards evening, Mother gave the signal to camp for the night, and Imogen helped her put up the *matrian*'s traveling tent with the minimum of words needed to accomplish the task. Imogen stayed with her mother while they ate their supper, hardy fare that had come from the palace kitchens, then took her bedroll and spread it inside the *matrian*'s tent, ignoring the surprised and hurt looks she got from her *tiermatha*. She would only continue to dampen their spirits, and sharing a tent with Dorenna that night was more than she could bear.

She crawled fully-dressed inside her bedroll and lay there stiffly, unable to relax into sleep. She'd slept too long on those Tremontanan mattresses, that's what it was, had gone soft in the more than two months she'd lived there. It was a good thing she hadn't stayed longer, or she wouldn't have been able to go home at all, what with growing accustomed to soft beds and endless hot water and the like. How embarrassing for a rider of the Kirkellan to become so dependent on such things.

It was dark enough now that she couldn't see the roof of the tent or the walls to either side of her, and for a moment she was back in her cell with the roof and the walls curving in on her, and she sucked in a breath and sat up, hugging her knees and trying to get her heart to slow down. It was in her imagination, it wasn't real, and she remembered sitting with Jeffrey on that awful, tiny bed, remembered him kissing her and saying *That is real,* and grief hit her so hard she curled up on her bedroll, put her arms over her face, and sobbed. *It's the right decision, it is,* she told herself, but she no longer believed it. How could it be the right decision if her whole self was crying out for something else?

She howled out her stored-up misery soundlessly into her sleeves, nearly convulsing with the force of her sobs, unable to stop herself, and felt hands gently lifting her head into a soft lap, circling her about her shoulders as they'd done since she was a toddler sobbing in terror at her first thunderstorm. "Cry it out," Mother whispered. She clutched at her mother's arms and wept until she was wrung out and exhausted. When her sobs subsided to deep, shaking breaths, Mother helped her sit and hugged her tightly. "I thought you were not as well-adjusted as you seemed," she said with a wry smile.

"I thought I was more well-adjusted than that," Imogen said, wiping her face with her sleeves, which were already soaked with her tears. "I'm sorry."

"For what? Having desires? No need to apologize for that." Mother sat cross-legged before her. "Imogen, what is it you really want?"

Imogen sighed. "I want to go home," she began, but Mother shook her head and placed her fingers over Imogen's lips. "I mean, what do you *really* want? If you could make this world bend to your needs, what would it look like?"

Imogen closed her eyes. "I want to live in Aurilien," she said. "I want to marry Jeffrey and be his Consort and have children with him. I want to breed Victory and see what I can make of those spindly Tremontanan horses. I want to talk to people and figure out how we can both get what we want." She opened her eyes. "But it's ridiculous. I was born to be a warrior, Mother, trained to be one, and I've just proved I do it better than I do anything else. I ought to do what I'm best at."

"No," Mother said, "you ought to do what you *love* best. Your father is still a better rider than either of us, war wound or no, and a better trainer of riders, but what he wanted was to raise you children, and neither of us has ever regretted that choice."

"This is much bigger than the difference between riding and childrearing."

"The size of it isn't important. You think we're only allowed to make choices when the consequences don't matter? Maybe the choice means more *because* you're choosing between two lives. Though I think, aside from the issue of the people involved, those lives are not so mutually exclusive as you'd imagine."

The people involved. "But Jeffrey told me he knew I was a warrior. He wanted me to be Warleader—he didn't say a single word about wanting me to stay!"

Mother made an impatient noise. "Jeffrey North is a brilliant man and an excellent King, but he has a tendency toward self-sacrifice.

Understandable, given his history, but I don't think you should let him ruin his life just because he wants to suffer nobly. And I don't think it's his choice to make."

"But now I can't go back. You said it yourself."

"I just said that because I wanted you to take me seriously. You need to go back, Imogen. Talk to him. Maybe there's no hope for you. But I would bet my horse that's not true."

Imogen stood and began packing her things. Mother reached up and grabbed her hand. "In the morning," she said. "It's full dark already. You want to wander around and kill yourself before you see him again?"

Imogen stood still and took a deep breath, then another. "I don't think I can bear to wait that long," she said, but sat down on her bedroll again and began taking off her boots.

"Patience is a good quality in life and in marriage. Probably more important than honesty, though I'll never admit it to your father."

"I think Father already knows it, what with living with you all these years."

Mother swatted her on the top of her head. "Disrespectful child. Get some sleep. And, Imogen?"

"Yes?"

"When you tiptoe out of here at the first light of dawn, don't bother waking me to tell me where you're going."

It was the longest night of Imogen's life, longer even than the ones she'd spent watching Elspeth and Dorenna fight for their lives. She napped, dreamed sunrise had come, and snapped awake, then drowsed again only to dream of Jeffrey angry with her, Jeffrey not angry with her, Jeffrey married to Diana, Jeffrey a distant stranger. The last time she woke, she realized she could see the outlines of her fingers, and rose and began to dress hurriedly.

Gear in hand—she might have been forsaking her old life for a new one, but some habits were hard to leave behind—she set out for the picket line only to stop as she passed the place where her *tiermatha* camped. She had one other thing to do.

She crouched to enter Dorenna's tent, careful to kick the knife away from where it lay by Dorenna's hand; Imogen had seen her nearly gut a rider who'd incautiously tried to wake her. She shook Dorenna's shoulder and whispered her name. The woman came instantly awake, closed her fist on a knife hilt that wasn't there, then looked up at Imogen. Even in the not-quite-dawn light, Imogen could see confusion in her eyes. "Imo? What's going on?"

"I'm sorry we fought, Dor. You wanted what was best for me and you weren't wrong. I *am* a warrior of the Kirkellan. It's just not who I'm going to become."

Dorenna rubbed sleep from her eyes. "I don't understand."

Imogen hugged her. "Oh, Dorenna, I'm not sure I do either, but I couldn't leave without asking you to forgive me for going."

Dorenna froze. "You're not leaving."

"I am. And maybe I'm wrong, maybe he doesn't want me and I'll be back in a few hours. But you have to trust me that *this* is the right decision, going back, and I'm truly sorry it hurts you so much, but you know I can't live my life to suit you anymore than Saevonna could. I'm leaving the *tiermatha* to you. Take good care of them?"

She turned to leave, and Dorenna said, "Wait. Please." Imogen turned back. Dorenna's face was mostly shadow in the dimness, all except the white parts of her eyes and her teeth when she spoke. "I'm sorry," she said. "I know it's the right decision. I could see it coming from the moment we set foot in that embassy. I just didn't—I thought if I could convince you, you'd change your mind. I shouldn't have done that. I do just want you to be happy, you know."

"Dor—" Imogen flung herself on her friend and heard her sniffle. "Don't cry."

"I'm not crying. You know I never cry." Dorenna grinned at her and wiped away tears. "Now get out of here. Go find your King and have a long and happy life together."

Imogen ducked out of the tent and trotted toward the picket line. Victory was awake and greeted her with a snort and a streak of slobber down her chest. "That's right, we're going home," Imogen whispered as she freed her from the picket line and began saddling her, no easy task in the dimness even as the sky continued to lighten. She mounted just as a line of light illuminated the eastern horizon. "Let's go," she said, and Victory trotted around the camp until they reached the road, where she set off at a ground-eating gallop.

Color flowed into the landscape as the sun rose, grays and browns turning into vibrant greens and blues. The delicate scent of wildflowers filled the air, borne by the fresh morning dew that made everything brighter. The road went through the forest, here and there, and gray squirrels dashed across the road to chitter at their brothers; birds sang at her and swooped past her head, making her grin. She felt better than she had in weeks, her heart light, and she would have sung with the birds if she knew the tune.

She came out of the forest into a long stretch of open road and saw, ahead of her in the distance, a rider on a Tremontanan horse coming her way. He, or she, appeared to be moving even faster than she was. *Jeffrey*, she thought, then laughed at herself. Even if he had decided to come after her, he certainly wouldn't be without his escort, and he didn't like horses, anyway. She rode on, preparing to pass the other rider, then to her shock realized it was Jeffrey, after all.

He seemed even more stunned to see her than she was to see him. "Imogen," he said.

"Jeffrey," she said, then so many words rushed into her mouth she couldn't choose between them.

"Why are you here?" he said.

She swallowed. Why hadn't she worked out what she'd say to him in advance? "I am…coming to see you. To talk. Why are you here?"

"To correct a mistake," he said. "Don't leave. Stay with me. I love you, Imogen, and I don't want to lose you."

She had to grip Victory's reins more tightly so she didn't fall off her horse. "You do—did not want me to stay."

"No, I did. I desperately wanted you to stay. But you so clearly belonged with the Kirkellan I felt like a fool asking you to give all that up just to be my wife. Then I woke up before dawn today the way I have every morning for the last three weeks, with my stomach in knots and the memory of your kiss on my lips, and I realized I didn't give a damn what you were best at." He drew in a deep breath. "I know it's selfish and I have no right to ask it of you, but I want you to marry me and I don't want you to leave me ever again."

Stunned, Imogen found herself standing on the ground with no memory of dismounting, looking up at Jeffrey. There was so much hope, and so much fear, in his eyes that her heart felt as if it would burst from everything pent up inside her. "I came to tell you I am not leaving," she said. "I do not give a damn either."

Jeffrey slid down off his horse and took a few tentative steps toward her, as if he were waiting for her to bolt. "Are you sure you want to give all of that up? It's your whole life, and I don't want you ending up resenting me for it."

She thought of everything she and Mother had talked about, and words deserted her. "It is only part of my life," she tried, "and this is another part, and I want to live in the part that has you in it, because you are my home."

He closed his eyes briefly and let out a long breath. "You are my home," he echoed, and looked at her with those blue eyes that now showed no fear nor hope but only joy. "Imogen—"

She closed the distance between them, put her arms around him, and was pulled into his embrace. "I love you," she whispered, then his lips were on hers and they kissed, slowly, as if it were the first time. Imogen sighed with pleasure, and felt him smile against her mouth, then his kisses became sweeter, more intense, and she breathed in the sharp woody scent of him and the last of her doubts fell away. Jeffrey put his arms around her waist and kissed her again, then drew back, caressing her cheek with his long fingers. "I do not believe I begged you to stop," Imogen said.

He laughed. "This is just a pause while I look at you in amazement that you came back. I thought my cause was hopeless, but I had to try."

"Not hopeless, because I love you," Imogen said.

"You've never said that to me before."

"I will say it again if you want, because it is true."

"I hope so, if you're going to marry me."

She tightened her arms around him. "I love you," she said, then he kissed her again and made more words impossible.

Eventually, Imogen became aware of Victory standing patiently behind her, and stepped away from Jeffrey, who made an unhappy noise. "We must not stand here in the road anymore."

"Oh. Yes, we should probably go back before they send out a search party. You have no idea how hard it is for me to slip away from my escort. They're not going to be happy with me."

"Do they know where you went?"

"I left a note." He mounted his horse, only a little awkwardly. "It wasn't a very informative note, but at least I tried. It probably didn't help that I didn't want them following me. When a man is going to beg a woman to love him, he doesn't need an audience."

"You do not need to beg me. I loved you before. You just had the face that says you do not want to speak to me." Imogen swung herself onto Victory's back and led the way back toward Aurilien.

"That was actually the face that says I want you to have what's best for you even if it kills me, which I thought it might."

"You do not decide what is best for me, Jeffrey. But I chose to give up what I love, so we both were stupid."

He laughed. "At least we figured it out in time. I didn't think about what might have happened if I had to chase you all the way to the Eidestal. I didn't even bring food."

Imogen's stomach growled. "I did not eat breakfast."

"Then, back to the palace, where I will be shouted at by my security chief, then breakfast, and then you and I and Mother will plan the quickest royal wedding this kingdom has ever seen."

"It must be quick?"

"Oh yes." His eyes twinkled. "The night I waited for you to wake up—the memory of you lying there, naked except for a few thin blankets, those bare shoulders with your hair hanging loose over them—I can wait for our wedding night, but that memory makes me want it to get here as soon as possible."

She threw back her head and laughed, and at just that moment they came around a curve in the road and Aurilien lay before them. The morning sunlight struck the stone walls and made them glow as if they were made of gold, and Imogen caught her breath at the beauty of it. "Something wrong?" Jeffrey asked.

She shook her head, and smiled. "Let us go home," she said.

EPILOGUE

One year later

Imogen woke, stared at the ceiling, then leaped out of bed and dashed for the water closet, where she didn't quite make it to the toilet before vomiting all over the floor. She retched and gagged until she thought she might turn herself inside out. Gentle hands pulled her hair back from her face, but too late; the bitter, sharp smell of bile clung to strands of hair and drifted up from the tiles below. Spent, she wiped water from her eyes and tried to breathe normally.

"That sounded worse than the last time," Jeffrey said.

"It is unfair. Elspeth weighs as much as a wet kitten and she was never ill. I cannot even bear the smell of food. I think I have lost five pounds since yesterday."

Jeffrey put his arms around her and pulled her to lean against his chest, heedless of the smell. "It will pass."

"You have said that for three weeks. I think I will never be well again."

"Give it another seven months. I think childbirth will cure it." He helped her to stand. "I'll draw you a bath, and you can wash your hair and then try to eat something. The midwife said keeping your stomach full will help."

Imogen made a face. "I cannot fill my stomach with dry toast and cheese."

"I don't blame you. At least by dinnertime you can bear something stronger." He turned the tap and hot water began to fill the room with steam.

Clean and dressed, she lay in bed with her wet hair piled on her head and nibbled the hated dry toast and watched Jeffrey dress. "I didn't realize I was so interesting," he said, buttoning his coat.

"You are always interesting to me even when you do boring things," she replied, and he grinned at her.

"You are interesting to me when you float naked in the bathtub," he said, "and I would show you how interested I am if I weren't late and you weren't ill." He brushed crumbs from her lips and kissed her. "You taste of cheese. I won't be at dinner today—too much to do before the reception tonight."

"I cannot believe Bixhenta has been recalled. It will be so different without him."

"Strange to me, too. He became ambassador just before I became King. But four years is always the limit of their ambassadorship, so this day was always coming."

"I look forward to meeting the new Proxy."

"I'm sure Bixhenta has warned her about you."

"What about me needs warning?"

"That you're not respectful of Veriboldan superiority and you are learning to speak their language."

Imogen frowned. "I do not see what is wrong with any of that."

"Nothing, so long as you're Veriboldan." He kissed her again, and then his eyes went blank for a moment. "Elspeth's coming," he said. He'd told her about his magical talent on their wedding night and been irritated that Elspeth had given away his secret months before.

"She will want to talk. You should go before you are drawn into the conversation."

He nodded and opened the bedroom door just in time for Elspeth to walk through it. "Thank you!" she said cheerfully. "It's as if you knew I was coming." She winked at her brother, who rolled his eyes and left.

"You look as if you've been sick again. I'm so sorry," Elspeth said, sinking onto the bed. "Would you like to hold Telaine?" She held her baby out, and Imogen took her, gingerly. She had no experience with infants, but reasoned she should get as much practice as she could before she had a baby of her own. The four-month-old Princess regarded her with unblinking eyes of an indeterminate color. Privately, Imogen thought Telaine looked like a monkey, with her thin face and wispy brown hair, but Elspeth and Owen thought her perfect, and who was she to argue with parental affection?

"Will you be well enough for the reception tonight?" Elspeth said, picking up a piece of toast and putting it down again with a look of distaste.

"This always passes before dinner. I will rise soon and go to see Victory."

"How is she?"

"It will be another two or possibly three months before she has her baby. She is comfortable but you can see her belly is swollen. I think she is smug because she will have her baby before I do."

"I'm excited to see it. The first cross between Kirkellan and Tremontanan horses. What do you expect it will look like?"

"I expect it will look like a foal. Beyond that I do not dare to imagine. As pretty as Victory, I hope."

"Me too. Let me take Telaine, she needs to go to her nurse." Elspeth took the baby and perched her on her hip as naturally as if she'd been doing it her whole life. "I'm going for a walk with the Hayneses in about half an hour. What else are you doing today?"

"Resting. I will sew in the afternoon and be read to. I am tired all the time."

"Oh, I'd join you, but that sounds so boring I would just drive both of us crazy."

"I enjoy it."

"Warrior of Tremontane, wielding a needle instead of a sword." Elspeth smiled. "Rest well, sister dear, and I'll see you at dinner."

When Elspeth had left, Imogen pushed her tray to one side and stared at the ceiling again. It was white and high above and showed no signs of curving in on her. What with the vomiting and the constant tiredness, her activities were limited, and she resented her weakness. She had given up being the warrior, had embraced being the Consort, but she hadn't realized how much of her was still Kirkellan until she had to give up riding, however temporarily. She couldn't tell Jeffrey, but sometimes she felt like a stranger to herself. There were nights when she woke, tears in her eyes, remembering the Kirkellan and fearing she'd made the wrong choice. On those nights she tucked herself against her husband's side and listened to his soft breathing; he was a heavy sleeper and never woke, but in his sleep put his arms around her, and she would drift off again, comforted. Then she would wake in the morning to feel his hands caress her body, and they would lose themselves in each other, and she would know she'd made the right choice after all.

Her stomach felt as settled as it was going to get. She pushed the blankets aside and stretched. Victory, then dinner, then sewing. Then the reception. Elspeth was right, her life was boring. She smiled. Boring wasn't so bad.

"Will not the nobles be angry?" Imogen asked. The smell of roast beef nauseated her, and she had to content herself with green beans and stewed peaches, soothing to her stomach.

"Not if they don't find out," Jeffrey said. He took another bite of beef, then added, "They all spy on each other anyway. I'm just late to the party."

"If it means you aren't surprised by the next person who wants to take the Crown, I'm in favor of your spy network," Alison said.

"Thank you, Mother. It's a complicated process, but Micheline is fully behind it—actually, Internal Affairs has been nagging me for more than two years to set up something like this. We have confidential agents in the other countries, even Ruskald, but it was hard for me to accept there might be a need for it here."

"It is because you want to believe everyone is as honorable as you," Imogen said.

Jeffrey grimaced. "That's true. I never believed I'd become so suspicious, but being nearly overthrown by a power-crazed Baroness will do that to you." He pushed back his chair. "It's later than I thought. Imogen, we should probably dress for the reception. Mother, you're not coming, are you?"

"I am not. I intend to settle down with a book, but I promise to think fondly of you all in your stiff and uncomfortable formal wear."

Alison was only partly right; Imogen's gown was soft and flowing and only slightly uncomfortable for being too loose. Jeanette fastened it up the back and said, "You'll need new clothing soon, milady Consort."

"I know. Julian can talk of nothing else. I am tired of being described as a challenge." She settled Ghentali's diamond around her neck. She didn't care if it was an inappropriate gift; she wore it as a trophy, a sign of vindication, and if Jeffrey sighed and shook his head when he saw it, he never told her to take it off.

She and Jeffrey wore North blue and silver tonight and made, she thought, a striking couple as they entered the reception hall. The new ambassador was not there, but Ghentali and the harem were. "Madam ambassador!" he exclaimed, holding out both hands to greet her. He'd never grasped the change in her status, and after several months Imogen gave up on trying to correct him. "Beautifulest in this tonight! And a diamond lovely as you!"

"Thank you, Ghentali." He'd also forgotten he'd given her the diamond. She'd long ago worked out how it was his harem "guided" him so easily.

"I not have met this Proxy who is the new, and you? She like Veriboldans is by herself alone."

"I have not met her either. I am curious about her."

"The curiosity I have too." He bowed to her. "Speak again, will we?"

"I hope so, Ghentali. Good evening to you."

"And you, madam ambassador."

Giavena stopped to speak to her as the rest of the harem moved on. "May I congratulate you on your condition?"

"Thank you, Giavena."

"I have heard you in the mornings ill are. I wish a medicine that will very well cure your symptoms to give you."

"Giavena, if you can make me stop vomiting I will be in your debt."

Giavena smiled. "It is a thing our doctors use often, very safe, and I happy to help am. I used it with all my pregnancies and it made better my life. I will send it to the east wing in the morning with instructions." She patted Imogen's arm and followed her sisters.

"Milady Consort, the new Proxy is here and wishes to meet you," Miles Thorpe said. Thorpe, Burgess's successor as chief of Foreign Affairs, always seemed nervous around her, as if he thought she might blame him for his predecessor's sins. Smiling at him only made things worse, so she simply nodded and followed him through the crowd.

The new Proxy sat beside Bixhenta in his usual place, near the King's seat, which was currently empty. She was in her late thirties, almost as dark-skinned as Bixhenta, and wore robes of blue and gold, and her long nails were lacquered a deep blue that matched Imogen's gown. Both stood as Imogen approached. Bixhenta's Voice, a much nicer woman than her predecessor, came to meet Imogen and bowed to her; Imogen, now the equivalent of a queen in Veriboldan eyes, inclined her head.

"Milady Consort, the Proxy of Veribold greets you and wishes to introduce his successor," the Voice said.

Imogen again inclined her head, this time toward Bixhenta. "We are sorry to see you go, Bixhenta," she said.

Bixhenta said something to the Voice that included the words "sorry" and "impertinent." She knew that last word well because Bixhenta often used it in regard to her, usually with a smile. "The Proxy is pleased with the success of his embassy here and hopes milady Consort will travel to Veribold one day. He is certain she will make an impression on the court."

Imogen smiled sweetly at the Voice. "Perhaps someday. May I know the new Proxy's name?"

"She is called Catalhin, milady Consort."

Imogen nodded at the new Proxy. "On behalf of my husband, I welcome you to Aurilien, Catalhin. I hope we may deal as well together as we have with Bixhenta."

Unlike Bixhenta, Catalhin had a humorless face. Imogen guessed she did not see this posting as an honor. She spoke briefly to the Voice, who looked shocked, but said, "The Proxy thanks you for your consideration and wishes you good health in your expectant state."

Imogen stayed expressionless. The Voice hadn't correctly translated a single word of Catalhin's comment, which had been rude nearly to the point of unforgivable offensiveness. Veriboldan women were cloistered from the moment their pregnancy became known to the day they gave birth, and what Catalhin had said about Imogen's character for appearing in public in her state, even as little as Imogen had understood of it, was both crude and vicious.

Bixhenta himself remained as expressionless as Imogen hoped she was, but she knew him too well to miss the deepening of the wrinkles around his mouth and eyes that said his muscles were tight with anger. He said something in a pleasant-sounding voice, but spoke too rapidly for her to make out any words other than "Consort." Catalhin responded dismissively, "I will (something) shames herself (something) no respect for Veribold (something else, including a rude word Bixhenta probably thought she didn't know) should leave now."

"I have great respect for Veribold, Catalhin, or I did before I met you," Imogen said pleasantly, hiding her anger, which surged through her with a wild joy as if she were going into battle. *In a way, I suppose I am.* "I did not realize ambassadors were allowed to speak so of the Consort of Tremontane."

Catalhin's gray eyes went wide with surprise. Bixhenta was smiling and didn't trouble to hide it. Imogen continued, "I am sorry for you to leave us so soon. I think when my husband hears what you have said he will agree with me that Veribold is not well served by your presence here. I am certain your government will understand you wanted only to allow your customs to override those of your host country."

Now Catalhin's eyes were wide with terror. She gabbled something in Veriboldan Imogen couldn't understand. The Voice, who was shaking slightly, said, "The Proxy wishes…requests…she would regret giving up this assignment so soon—"

In clear and precise Veriboldan, Bixhenta said, "If Catalhin were to return to Veribold under these conditions, she would never hold public office again and her career would be destroyed."

"That is pity. I no care," Imogen said in the same language.

Catalhin stood and bowed deeply before Imogen. To Imogen's amazement, she said in heavily accented but intelligible Tremontanese, "I humbly beg your forgiveness. I should not have been so rude simply because our customs are different. You deserve the respect we would expect you to give to our King and I have failed utterly to show that respect. Please allow me to continue to serve my country as ambassador."

Bixhenta looked shocked. The Voice was in tears. Imogen wondered briefly if it was because Catalhin had just made her unemployed. "I choose to forgive you because of the goodwill *Bixhenta* has created between our governments," Imogen said. "He is a model you would do well to follow."

"Thank you, your Majesty," Catalhin said, her head still bowed.

"Bixhenta, I will speak with you again before you leave for Veribold, if that is agreeable," Imogen said.

Bixhenta laughed and shook his head ruefully. In Tremontanese, he replied, "I look forward to it, milady Consort." He winked at her, and she winked back.

She had only gone a few steps when someone grabbed her elbow and steered her toward the far end of the room. "I want to know what just happened there," Jeffrey said. "You made the Voice cry and I'm almost certain I heard the new Proxy speak our language."

"You did." Imogen told him the whole story, leaving out the specifics of the insult Catalhin had given her. When she was about halfway through, Jeffrey started having difficulty not laughing. By the end, he had covered his mouth with his hand and was making little snorting noises.

"I do not think it is all that funny," Imogen said.

"It's *hilarious*."

"Well, maybe it is very funny. But I do not know what will happen now."

"The Veriboldans will have trouble maintaining their superiority. Our relations with them may cool somewhat. On the other hand, the Proxy is going to be *very* respectful and the Voice will be out of a job."

"I am sorry for that. She is much nicer than the old one."

"They'll find something for her to do. Veriboldans aren't wasteful." He looped her arm through his and they began to walk the circuit of the room. "You don't still have doubts, do you?" he said abruptly.

"Doubts about what?"

"About this choice. Imogen, it's not like I'm complaining, but I can guess what it means when I wake up and you're clinging to me like you're afraid you're going to fall."

"I will not change my mind."

"Of course not. But I hate to see you uncertain of who you are."

She thought of Bixhenta and Catalhin, of pregnant Victory and the life growing inside her own body, of the family she'd left behind and the family she embraced now, and the last of her doubts faded. "I know who I am," she said. "I am Imogen. And this is my home."

He squeezed her arm. "Don't forget that."

"No," she said, "I won't."

Glossary and Pronunciation Guide

balaeri (BAH-luh-ree): a Kirkellan musical instrument, a reedy kind of flute.

banrach (BAHN-rock): a marriage in name only that provides kinship ties but does not allow sexual relations. Outdated.

cadhaen-rach (CAD-en-rock): Inherent magic, as opposed to magic manipulated by outside forces or Devices.

kurkara (kur-KAH-rah): a Kirkellan musical instrument, similar to an oboe.

matrian (MAH-tree-ahn): leader of the entire Kirkellan people. Always a woman.

Samnal (SAHM-nahl): a gathering of Ruskalder chiefs, part council, part war games.

skorstala (skor-STAH-lah): a large central room in a Ruskalder chieftain's house, used for eating and entertaining.

tiermatha (teer-MAH-tha): a combat unit/clan group of thirteen Kirkellan warriors.

tinda (TIN-dah): a memorial ground for fallen Kirkellan warriors.

vojenta (voh-ZHEN-tah): leader of an Eskandelic harem.

About the Author

Melissa McShane is the author of the novels of Tremontane, including SERVANT OF THE CROWN and RIDER OF THE CROWN, as well as EMISSARY and THE SMOKE-SCENTED GIRL. After a nomadic childhood, she settled in Utah with her husband, four children, and three very needy cats. She wrote reviews and critical essays for many years before turning to fiction, which is much more fun than anyone ought to be allowed to have. She is currently working on the third Tremontane novel, AGENT OF THE CROWN. You can visit her at her website **www.melissamcshanewrites.com** for more information on other books and upcoming releases.

CPSIA information can be obtained
at www.ICGtesting.com
Printed in the USA
LVOW01s0244170516
488595LV00025B/459/P

9 780692 534632